PRAISE FOR *THE ORACLE OF IX CHEL*

Another beautiful book from Rosita Arvigo. I was transported to the time of the ancient Maya. I love her vivid descriptions and characters, which come alive on the page.

Tracey Ullman

The Oracle of Ix Chel is a tour de force of narrative, history, and insight into a culture and cosmology. Set in the Mayan city of Chichen during pre-Columbian times, it tells the story of a gifted woman committed to her lineage and its sacred path. Rosita Arvigo's intimate knowledge of ancient Mayan practices infuses every page. As soon as I finished, I was ready for the next installment.

Hope Edelman
Author of *Motherless Daughters and The Possibility of Everything*

From the first paragraph, it grabbed my attention and held it. I didn't want to put it down. A wonderfully captivating book, filled with alive, complex characters.

Rosemary Gladstar
Author, *Planting the Future: Saving Our Medicinal Herbs*

I was drawn into the world of Jade Skirt like a hummingbird attracted to the nectar of a luscious, red hibiscus blossom. Reading the book was like walking in the shoes of the Oracle of Ix Chel, and it stirred a deep longing within me to know the ways of the Goddess. Rosita Arvigo expertly weaves a tale of life in a post-Toltec Mayan landscape—part fiction, part deep intuitive knowing from Rosita, but mostly a refreshing 'her'-story that brings alive these particular peoples during their time. Both immensely entertaining and deeply inspiring, *The Oracle of Ix Chel* will leave readers waiting impatiently for Book 2.

Pam Montgomery
Author, *Plant Spirit Healing: A Guide to Working with Plant Spirits, and Partner Earth: A Spiritual Ecology*

A wonderfully engaging journey through magic, myth and time. Through this beautiful tale, in her very special voice, Rosita Arvigo brings us to a place that once was. Arvigo's remarkable descriptions of rainforest plants and shamanic ritual adds a beautiful richness to the page-turning plot. Her fascinating story is written from the heart and will delight the reader as well as convey wisdom of the ancients.

Michael J. Balick, Ph.D.
Ethnobotanist, The New York Botanical Garden

THE ISLAND OF
WOMEN

Rosita Arvigo

Story Bridge Books
Tucson, Arizona 2016

Story Bridge Books
Tucson, Arizona, USA
www.storybridgebooks.com

To healers and midwives who, for thousands of years,
have held the hands and wiped the tears of the poor and sick.
Thank you for holding the torch.

Acknowledgments

Fifteen years have elapsed since I began writing this two-part historical novel about the fictional Jade Skirt, Maya midwife and oracle of 8th-century Yucatan, Mexico. Her efforts to save the life of her granddaughter, Nine Macaw, who is destined to be the queen of ancient Cuzamil Island, sanctuary of the goddess Ix Chel, has been a magnificent obsession for me. Jade Skirt's story, her time and the details of her daily life are imagined, but also loosely based on the strands of recorded Maya history that survive, the meanings of which still frustrate modern scholars and writers. This is a work of historical fiction. To write an historical novel about an ancient civilization so little understood or revealed in our modern explorations is an undertaking fraught with highs and lows. Separating myth from fact was a great challenge, and I know that I took liberties when I allowed my imagination to run rampant. Because I have juxtaposed historical facts and eras, this is not a reliable source for the study of Maya history, but I hope it will be a satisfying tale that sparks readers' fascination with ancient Maya culture.

Along the way many people have assisted my efforts: thanks to Laura Markowitz, my excellent editor, for adding shine and polish to every sentence; to my first readers for their valuable feedback: Greg Shropshire, Kayla Becker, Hilary Lewin, Donna Zubrod and midwife Amy Colo—all practitioners of Maya Abdominal Therapy; and to my sister-in-law, Dr. Claudia Pitts. Thanks to Alifie Rojas of San Miguel de Allende, Guanajuato, Mexico for her cover art and line drawings and for the map of ancient Cuzamil, which is also a product of imagination.

I am grateful to the employees of the Newberry Public Library in Chicago; Portland State University Library; Universidad Anonima de Mexico; the library staff of Merida, Yucatán; the Cozumel Island Museum; and the English Library in San Miguel de Allende in Guanajuato, Mexico.

Thanks to Maya scholars Linda Schele, Michael Coe, Lynn Foster, David Friedel, Jeremy Sabloff, Robert Sharer, Ralph Roys, France V. Scholes, Patricia McAnany, Sylvanus Morley, Nancy Hamblin, Victoria Schlesinger, David Carrasco, Father Bernardino de Sahagun, Diego de Lopez Cogolludo, Clavijero, Karl Taube, Robert Redfield and Charles Gallenkamp.

Special thanks to Shankari Patel of the University of California, Riverside for sharing with me her dissertation on Cozumel Island as an ancient pilgrimage center. Thanks to the modern women scholars who helped me to understand the various roles of ancient Maya women and children: Inga Clendenin, Andrea Stone, Traci Arden and Rosemary Joyce; and thanks to Anabel Ford, archaeologist of Belize, who helped with the Introduction to the first book of this series, *The Oracle of Ix Chel*.

Thanks to my mentors, Don Elijio Panti and Hortence Robinson, who are both National Treasures of Belize. For more than thirteen years they each helped me to understand their traditional healing systems. Thanks to the kind people and healers of Tlacotepec and Salitre, Guerrero, Mexico who took me into their homes as a guest and taught me the art of cooking over a hearth fire and making tortillas in a thatched hut far away from modern conveniences. Thanks to my dear friends during those days in Guerrero: Mary Brousseau, Jimmy Davis and Claude Allen Whitt.

Thanks to my son, James Arvigo, for his assistance with the computer, and my husband, Greg Shropshire, for so much loving support and patience during this process. Thanks to Lucy Fleming of Chaa Creek Cottages, my neighbor and best friend, for her support during long evening walks in Belize. Thanks to Katie Valk for her friendship and to Michael Balick of The New York Botanical Garden for opening up the wonders of ethnobotany to me. Thanks to Hope Edelman, Eva Hunter and Alma Villanueva for their help during the early stages of writing. I must also acknowledge the trees and plants of Central America, who have been companions and teachers to me since 1976, when I first stepped foot in their rainforest home.

Rosita Arvigo, DN
Cayo District, Belize
2016

Map of Cuzamil

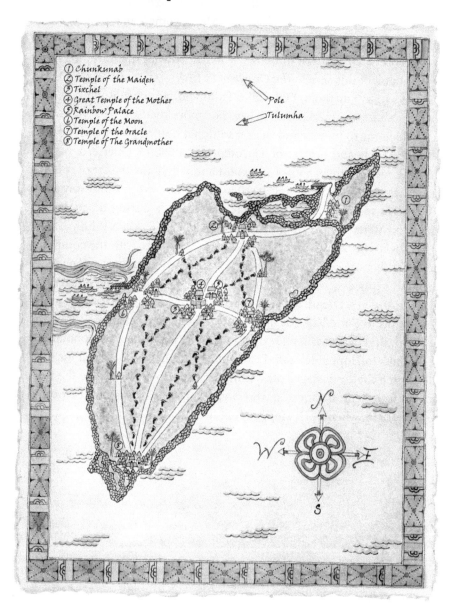

1. Chunkunab
2. Temple of the Maiden
3. Tixchel
4. Great Temple of the Mother
5. Rainbow Palace
6. Temple of the Moon
7. Temple of the Oracle
8. Temple of The Grandmother

Pole

Tulumha

Table of Contents

Cast of Characters

Jade Skirt's Family

Jade Skirt – Oracle and High Priestess of the Goddess Ix Chel

Jaguar Shield – Jade Skirt's brother-in-law and beloved

Heart of Water – Jade Skirt's elder sister; Queen of Cuzamil

Water Lily – Jade Skirt's daughter

Nine Macaw – Water Lily's daughter and heir to the Rainbow Throne of Cuzamil

Jaguar Paw – Water Lily's son; Nine Macaw's twin

Iguana Wind – Jade Skirt's slave

Spear Thrower – Jade Skirt's son

Precious Tree – Spear Thrower's wife

Tree Orchid – adopted granddaughter

World Bridge – Jade Skirt's aunt

Red Earth – Water Lily's eldest daughter (deceased)

Blood Gatherer – Jade Skirt's brother

Moon Eagle – Jade Skirt's husband (deceased)

Cosmic Turtle – Jade Skirt's grandmother; founder of the Rainbow Throne (deceased)

Nine Wind – Jade Skirt's mother; Oracle of Ix Chel (deceased)

On the Journey to Cuzamil

Blue Stone – Slave girl

Five Rain – Hearth Mistress of the inn in Coba

Long Strider – Trader from the Tzib clan

White Quetzal – Queen of Palenque

Turquoise Sky – First Princess of Coba

Fire Bird – High Priestess of the Temple of the Maiden in Pole

Pus Master – High Priest of the War God in Na Balam

Cosmic Shell – High Priestess of the Goddess's Temple of Motherhood in Pole

Seven Tapir – Bolon headman

Women of Cuzamil

Evening Star – Priestess of Ix Chel

Night Wind – Leader of Cuzamil's defensive forces; lover of Queen Heart of Water

Blue Monkey – Priestess of Ix Chel and nemesis of Jade Skirt

Eighteen Rabbit – Daughter of Blue Monkey

Snake Tooth – High Priestess of the Great Temple of the Mother

Blood Woman – High Priestess of the House of Healing

Antler Skull – Priestess and former mentor of Jade Skirt

Moon Bird – Priestess and gifted scrier

Precious Moon Beam – Hearth Mistress of the Rainbow Palace

Green Feather – Bird Oracle of the Temple of the Mother

"The writer's pen is a microphone held up to the mouths of ancestors and even stones of long ago."
— Alice Walker

1

The Wind God sends a gentle breeze through the courtyard of the *polna*, where I share a makeshift bed on the hard ground beside my granddaughter, Nine Macaw. Normally, I find the predawn stillness a peaceful time to pray to my Goddess, Ix Chel, the Great Mother. This morning I struggle to feel joy in the new day dawning. I inhale deeply and try to feel soothed by the aromas of damp earth and allspice blossoms that waft over us. For a moment it works, and I recall pleasant mornings waking in the early morning in the jungle beside my grandmother when I was a girl and she was training me to be a healer. But those comforting thoughts shred like the morning mist when I look around at the piles of snoring bodies. Only a handful are pilgrims bound for the Island sanctuary for women. Women journey from all over the Known World to that holy place to have their babies, find healing, make prayers and dedicate themselves to the service of our Creator, Ix Chel. I recognize them by the blue mantles that pilgrims wear. Nine Macaw and I should be wearing the blue, because we are also bound for Cuzamil, but we travel as refugees. First we fled our home in Chichen because the heart takers wanted to sacrifice Nine Macaw to the Rain God. A few days later we barely escaped from the violent uprising in Na Balam. All night, I have listened to these restless sleepers whimper and moan—likely dreaming of their lost homes and dead loved ones, and the blood-hungry heart takers of the New Order who turned peaceful Na Balam into a place of chaos and death.

The first weak beams of sun slant across the sky. I feel tired in my bones. I was awake most of the night, prisoner of my mind's twisting pathways.

It is a shame that sleep cannot be commanded. With a small groan I sit up and rub my aching lower back. Nine Macaw still sleeps. I tuck my mantle gently around her. After the harrowing events of the past few days, she needs rest. This girl, my precious flower—only twelve *tuns*—has an important destiny as the future ruler of Cuzamil. She is heir to the Rainbow Throne and will serve the Goddess Ix Chel as Queen of the Holy Island and also healer and Oracle when my sister, Heart of Water, steps down as ruler. But for the moment, while sleep holds her, she can forget that she is far from her home, a place to which she can never return. She can forget that she is hunted by the heart takers, who plot to kill her so they can steal the throne and control Cuzamil's riches. *Om bey*, my poor granddaughter has a heavy burden to bear! Her destiny, which was proclaimed at her birth by the Calendar Priests, was a source of joy and excitement until a moon past. Now it hangs over her head like a death sentence. But Ix Chel, Protector of Women, guides us. I trust in Her to keep us safe. I have only to bring Nine Macaw safely to Her Island and then my sister, Queen Heart of Water, will protect us and start training the girl in statecraft. I will train Nine Macaw in healing and divination.

My head is foggy and my mouth feels dry. Insomnia is a curse of the third age. There are medicines for it, but I have none with me. A sleepless night would matter little if I were still the Oracle at the Temple of the Goddess Ix Chel in Chichen, but here in Coba—still six days' walk to Pole-by-the-Sea, where the royal barge will take us across the waters to the Island of Women—I need all my energy and wits about me. I close my eyes and breathe deeply. Then I center myself within my *chu'lel* and focus on nourishing the life force flowing through me.

"Goddess," I pray silently, "guide us. Protect us. Illuminate this road with Your divine light. Send us the strength we will need in the coming days."

A shiver of Presence runs down my arms and tickles the back of my neck.

Daughter, trust in Me. All will be well.

Gratitude and peace wash over me. Ix Chel, Creator of All, watches over us. I feel awe at Her closeness. Truly, I am blessed to be Her servant!

Was it only four days ago—it feels like a *tun*!—that She helped me defeat my brother, Blood Gatherer? He is Chichen's High Priest serving the Rain God, Chac. He is also the leader of the New Order in Chichen. The New Order is a foreign way of worshipping the gods through human sacrifice. The Putun heart takers brought this practice to Chichen, and they are spreading it across the Known World. Their way of worship is death, while the Goddess teaches us to revere the life that She created. Needless to say, the New Order does not respect Ix Chel or Her servants. Blood Gatherer declared that Nine Macaw must be sacrificed to Chac, knowing full well that she is destined to serve the Gentle Goddess as ruler of Cuzamil.

Before the rains begin the heart takers sacrifice young, virgin girls. It is perverse! They tell parents their lucky daughters will become goddesses. As High Priestess and Oracle of Chichen's Temple of the Goddess, I stood up to my brother and the New Order and refused to give them Nine Macaw. Arrested and brought before Chichen's seven rulers to account for my defiance, I declared that the Goddess Ix Chel confirmed to me in oracular visions and dreams that the gods do not require human sacrifices. I reminded them that the practice of human sacrifice arrived with Putun foreigners, who came to Chichen after their cities burned and they were forced to make their homes in distant lands. I pointed out that the rains fell reliably for countless seasons when we in Chichen sacrificed only turkeys, corn and other gifts to Chac. But the New Order breeds fear in the people. Their priests cast doubts and scare the people into believing that the feckless Rain God will punish our city with drought if we don't sacrifice humans.

How did the heart takers gain such fearsome power? At first, the Putun only sacrificed captured soldiers to their War God. The people of Chichen gradually became used to the spectacle and, I am sad to say, they began to enjoy it—especially the sumptuous feasts that followed. Then it was slaves who died the Flowery Death. And then the New Order demanded the virgin daughters of our citizens as sacrifices for the Gods. Even those who dislike the heart takers' way of worship are too intimidated now to defy the powerful New Order. Even Chichen's seven rulers are too afraid to speak against the practice of human sacrifice.

I was the first to say no to the heart takers, and that made me dangerous. Fear is the source of their power, and I refused to be intimidated. The punishment for my defiance was harsh: exile for me and my family, including my only daughter, Water Lily, and her three children—Red Earth, Nine Macaw and her twin brother, Jaguar Paw—along with Water Lily's adopted daughter, Tree Orchid (whom I refused to give as sacrifice to Chac in Nine Macaw's place). Exile is the most severe punishment our rulers can impose. We lost everything that makes one a person. We are the unborn, the unknown, the scorned. They say even our ancestors do not know us, which means that our souls may not rest in the afterlife. Never again will we join in the dancing and singing with the Cocom clan, my husband's people. I am no longer Oracle, chief midwife and High Priestess of Chichen's Temple of Ix Chel. To friends, neighbors, strangers and relatives alike we are dog shit.

It all happened so quickly, and the shock was simply too much for my eldest granddaughter, Red Earth. She was only 15 *tuns,* preparing to marry in a few months. But when we became exiles her intended husband and his family rejected her. Filled with despair, she took her own life. She is with the Goddess Ix Tab now, where those who choose their day to die spend eternity. My heart is still broken. I feel guilty for leaving her alone. She needed me, but when Nine Macaw and Tree Orchid were kidnapped by Blood Gatherer, I had to save them so I left her alone. I will always regret that I underestimated her shame and grief and abandoned her when she needed me.

With the help of my beloved brother-in-law Jaguar Shield, who chose exile to be with me, the rest of us were able to escape. Well, almost all of us. Water Lily was arrested for public drunkenness before she could join us. The penalty is public stoning. I don't know what's become of her. I do not even know if she lives. Worry is a constant knot in my gut. My daughter and I were not on good terms. I was critical of her drinking habit and her neglect of home and children. Her husband left her in disgrace, yet Water Lily kept on reaching for the gourd. But no matter how disappointed I have been in her behavior, she is my child and I would do anything to save her if I could.

We fled Chichen to save Nine Macaw's life. But Blood Gatherer knew we were racing to reach the Goddess's sanctuary in Cuzamil. Although we avoided the *sacbe* and traveled through the jungle in secret, that treacherous traitor set a trap for us in Na Balam. He captured us when we sought shelter from my lineage, the Chel, who live in Na Balam. I did not know that Na Balam's ruler had lately married a Putun queen and now supports the New Order. My brother was given leave to command the people of Na Balam to present their virgin daughters so he could see if my Nine Macaw hid among them. When she wasn't found, he demanded the sacrifice of many of those girls. The people rose up in protest and Na Balam burned! We entered the city in the midst of the uprising.

After Blood Gatherer found us, he finally revealed his true intention to kill Nine Macaw and claim the Rainbow Throne for himself and his Putun allies. It sickens me that he would violate the Zone of Peace established by Ix Chel in Cuzamil and Pole and invade the women-only sanctuary of Her Island. Long has he nursed a grudge against me and our sister because, as a man, he is not allowed to dwell on Cuzamil or be considered for succession to the Rainbow Throne, which was founded by our grandmother. When he told me how he would crush Cuzamil and gloated over his victory over me—Ix Chel's Oracle—I had a chilling realization. He and his Putun allies do not merely lust for power or the lucrative trade routes and goods that come from the Island of Women; they want to gain dominion over Cuzamil so they can supplant the gentle worship of Ix Chel with bloody human sacrifices to their gods. They want to vanquish the heart and soul of Her Island and wipe out worship of the Goddess throughout the Known World!

Cuzamil is the only place where any woman, no matter what her birth, can be assured of sanctuary, safety, healing and hope. After husbands are gone and children are grown women often journey to Cuzamil to dedicate their remaining days to serving Ix Chel on Her sacred Island. Orphans, abused women, barren women and those who wish to serve the Great Mother make their way to Cuzamil to live in peace and harmony in the Zone of Peace. Women in need of healing or experienced midwives or medicines receive treatments on Cuzamil for free. There are no men on Cuzamil except in the isolated northern settlement of Chunkunab, which is cut off from the rest of the island by impassable swamps. There is no war on the Island. Even Pole, the gateway to Cuzamil where pilgrims embark on the sea voyage to the Island, is under the protection of the Goddess's Zone of Peace. Cuzamil is a beacon of light to all women, a gem in the middle of the turquoise sea. Yet Blood Gatherer would help the Putun destroy it so they can rule us all through fear and violence.

But the plotters were foiled by a single bird! In Na Balam, when it seemed as if all was lost, the Great Mother sent Tree Orchid's brave parrot, Kiki, to free us from the clutches of our enemies. I grin to myself remembering how that feisty bird flew into the room where we were held captive and attacked the ruler! In the chaos we slipped away with our rescuers. Blood Gatherer was badly wounded.

Jaguar Shield, my champion, parted from us the night we escaped from Na Balam. He journeys back to Chichen now to find Water Lily. It broke my heart to leave Tree Orchid behind with my aunt in Na Balam, but she needs time to recover as best she can from a crippling wound to her leg.

Jaguar Paw, my grandson, stayed to look after her. When Jaguar Shield returns with Water Lily he will bring them all to Pole-by-the-Sea and we will send to Cuzamil for the royal barge to bring us to Cuzamil. That day cannot come soon enough!

Now Nine Macaw and I, and my loyal slave, Iguana Wind, are traveling with all speed to Cuzamil, trying to blend in with the refugees and pilgrims in case the Putun are still looking for Nine Macaw. That is why we slept here in the courtyard instead of in the *polna's* more luxurious accommodations for nobility. Until we reach Pole-by-the-Sea, we cannot relax our vigilance. Also, I am not sure what kind of reception we will find among other nobles if it is discovered that we are exiles. Some have shown themselves to be allies, rejecting our exile as nothing but a political move to discredit me. But others spit on us.

I stretch and massage my sore feet. Nine Macaw doesn't stir. Sleep is the best tonic for her right now. In a very short span of time the poor girl has been condemned to death, kidnapped, exiled, started her first moon cycle, lost her sister to suicide, narrowly escaped another capture and then left her best friend and brother behind. She will need to be strong until we reach Pole. We will find protection there from my son, Spear Thrower, who is the Magistrate of Pole. Although I have had no message in many moons from my sister, I know she eagerly awaits the arrival of her heir and she will send the royal barge to Pole to ferry us across the waters to Cuzamil. Nine Macaw must be trained before Heart of Water steps down, and I know my sister is physically and mentally exhausted from her duties as Queen and Oracle of Cuzamil. She has served for many *tuns*, and it is past time when she should retire. If only my Water Lily had been born with the Chel gifts, she would be the next ruler, but it was Nine Macaw who has the auspicious calendar day and has inherited all the Chel gifts in abundance. She will make a fine ruler of the Island of Women.

Thinking about Cuzamil and its five temples, healing houses, mystery schools, birthing houses, gardens, shrines and sacred springs fills me with longing to be there. How I have missed the moonrise over the water, when She graces us with Her light! I miss the sounds of the swallows gathering, and I miss praying in the Great Temple of the Mother, which rises up in the center of the Island like the comforting lap of our Creator. After my grandmother, Cosmic Turtle, founded the Rainbow Throne and became ruler of the sacred Island, my mother, Nine Wind, served as High Priestess and

Oracle of the Goddess. We Chel women are gifted with true dreaming and healing powers by the Goddess. My grandmother trained Heart of Water in statecraft and my mother trained me to follow in her path as Oracle and High Priestess. I served in Chichen's Temple of the Goddess Ix Chel after marrying my husband, Moon Eagle of the Cocom clan. Heart of Water has no child and favors women over men, so it was decided when Water Lily was born that she or her daughter would inherit the Rainbow Throne if they were blessed by Ix Chel with the gifts of prophecy and healing. Sadly, my daughter inherited none of the Chel gifts, and neither did her first-born daughter, Red Earth. But the calendar signs were auspicious at Nine Macaw's birth. She has an affinity for healing, and recently her oracular gifts are manifesting, Ix Chel be praised!

An infant wakes somewhere in the courtyard and lets out a hungry wail. People grumble and someone shouts for the mother to quiet the child, which only disturbs more sleepers. Father Sun is above the horizon now, so the *chachalaca* birds fly down to feed on red fruits in the palm trees above us, squawking noisily. Their screeches rouse other birds and soon we are treated to an ear-splitting chorus of morning song.

Iguana Wind, asleep at our feet to protect us through the night, sits up and frowns to see what the disturbance is all about. I motion for him to lie back down and sleep more if he can. He is still healing from a snake bite that nearly took him from us a few days ago. My husband, Moon Eagle, captured Iguana Wind in battle and generously offered his prisoner the choice of ten *tuns* of slavery or a warrior's noble death. Iguana Wind chose slavery and has been a trusted member of our family for the last eight *tuns*. When we reach Pole-by-the-Sea I will release him from his bond so he can rejoin his family. Men cannot live on Cuzamil, so I have no need of a male slave. And he has earned the right to return to his life as a free man. I have come to love him like a son.

Ever since Moon Eagle died the Flowery Death I have longed to go home to Cuzamil, but I was waiting for Nine Macaw to start her first moon cycle so I could take her with me. I admit that there was something else that kept me in Chichen—or rather, some*one* else. Since my husband was captured in battle and sacrificed to the War God by our enemies, his brother, Jaguar Shield, has been my advisor, closest friend, protector and secret lover. As widowed in-laws, it is forbidden for us to be together, but we are drawn to each other nevertheless. We had one night together, one night of stolen embraces. The memory of it has been replayed in my mind nearly every night since!

After we escaped from Na Balam, and before he departed for Chichen, Jaguar Shield pulled me into the shadows and lifted my chin so I could look into his dear face, etched with ceremonial scars. My heart skipped a beat. He makes me feel like a girl, all weak in the knees. But I also love him for his loyalty, strength and conviction. He chose to go into exile with us because he knows the New Order is wrong, because he reveres the Goddess, and because he loves me.

"Brother, guard your life well," I told him. And because he always makes me feel naughty, I added, "My jade forest awaits you."

A wide smile flashed across his face. "Hmm. More delightful than a royal banquet. I will remember that promise when we meet again in a few days."

But the last look we gave each other was tinged with sadness. We both know how impossible our situation is. Not only are we not allowed to be together, but there is the fact that men are not allowed on Cuzamil, and Cuzamil is where I must be to train my granddaughter and serve my Goddess.

That conversation took place two days ago. Since then, Nine Macaw, Iguana Wind and I have been making slow, exhausted progress walking from inn to inn on the *sacbe* to Pole. We look over our shoulders constantly for enemies in pursuit. The great white road carries chaos now from city to city. I nearly dropped my bag when I heard a pilgrim tell another: "That High Priestess of Ix Chel from Chichen, the Lady Jade Skirt, started a rebellion against the New Order that may ignite all the provinces." A refugee walking near them turned and spit at the sound of my name and said, "She is an exile now. She doesn't exist."

Om bey! I wanted the people to stand up to the New Order, but I did not imagine it would be so violent. I try to console myself with the thought that at least the homeless women and their children can take refuge on Cuzamil. If the Putun have their way, our safe haven will end and be turned into the stronghold of the War God.

Nine Macaw stirs beside me. Those beautiful green eyes I love so much blink sleepily. Her young face looks thin and weary.

"Na, where are we?"

"At the inn in Coba, my jade. You see, we are one day closer to the sea and the safety of the Great Mother's sanctuary in Cuzamil."

"Na, I had a dream." She gives me a serious look. My sister and I also are dreamers. Nine Macaw has just begun having true dreams, a sign that she is strong in the Chel gifts given to our women by the Goddess. The gifts of prophecy manifest with our first moon cycles. Nine Macaw started hers only a few nights ago.

"Tell me, my feather."

"Before we slept last night I saw the Hearth Keeper beating a little slave girl, but the girl wasn't doing anything wrong, Na! The Hearth Keeper was being cruel. That girl was in my dream. She traveled with us to Cuzamil. I saw her wrapped in a blue mantle, standing on the steps of a white temple and holding a white rabbit."

Nine Macaw eagerly scans the courtyard, searching for the girl in her dreams. I feel proud of her, and also troubled. The novices on Cuzamil wear the blue, and the Great Temple of the Mother, in the center of the Island, is bone white. The Goddess's companion is the white rabbit. The signs of this dream are clear as rainwater. I feel in my bones that this is a true dream, yet there is reluctance in my heart. How can I take responsibility for another child on this dangerous journey?

Find the child. She must go with you to Cuzamil.

The Goddess's Presence is a gentle whisper in my mind. Gratitude fills me that She chooses to speak directly to me. I close my eyes and thank Her silently for Her wisdom. Then I open my eyes and see Nine Macaw watching me curiously.

"Shall I go and find her?" she asks, already halfway to her feet.

"It is best we stay together," I say lightly.

Fear flashes on her face, but then she takes a deep breath and looks determined. She gives me a nod. Nine Macaw has matured since we started this journey to Cuzamil. A few days ago she would have begged and cajoled and perhaps even sulked. Now, she well understands that we must be cautious. The burdens of her destiny are heavy.

Iguana Wind approaches with a gourd of water so we may drink and wash. With a healer's eye, I note that he is not limping as severely as he was yesterday.

"Mother, bright morning to you." He turns to Nine Macaw and smiles at her. "Little one, I hope you slept well."

We talk quietly for a few minutes until my stomach growls so loudly Nine Macaw laughs at me. The aroma of tamales makes my mouth water.

I can't remember the last good meal I've had. I know I've eaten in the past few days, but food has tasted like straw in my mouth since Na Balam. For some reason, this morning I have a good appetite. The three of us make our way to the hearth room and stand in line to receive our meal. My grandmother established the *polnas* on the *sacbes* that lead to Pole to ease the way of pilgrims to Her sacred Island. She knew that many of the women seeking healing and sanctuary would be sick, pregnant, grieving and poor. She began the tradition of dedicating a portion of the great wealth from the Island to stock and staff these welcoming way stations. Here, any traveler can find a free meal and safe place to sleep, as well as medicine and healers. Each *polna* is overseen by a Hearth Mistress. The staff is already hard at work preparing food for the growing crowd as morning begins in earnest.

We take our turkey tamales outside, sit on a stone bench and begin eating. Perhaps because I am so hungry it seems that the portion is smaller than usual, and I notice the tamale lacks the flavor of chilies.

I'm just licking the last of the meal from my fingers when a skinny, bright-eyed slave girl approaches and offers us water. Nine Macaw shoots me an urgent look. So this is the girl, then.

"Come, child, take a seat," I say patting the stone bench. "What is your name?"

"I am called Blue Stone," she answers with downcast eyes, reluctantly sitting beside me. Her hair, black as obsidian, is cut above her ears in a careless way. Other than a red *spondylus* shell strung over her female parts, she is naked. This means she has not started her moon cycles, nor has she had a coming-of-age ceremony. Her breasts are little curved buds, so it will be soon. Her thin legs are marked with red welts from a recent beating.

"And your lineage?" I ask gently.

Nervous fingers drum on the gourd. "Grandmother, I don't know."

"How is it that you are a slave?" I ask. "No one in the Known World is born a slave. What happened to your family?" I am sorry to ask her questions that clearly make her sad, but I must know.

"They say I was sold as a baby during a long drought because my mother and father could not feed the children they already had."

"And where did they live?"

"They tell me that my family is from Piste." She looks up at me, suddenly curious and hopeful. "Do you know where that is, Grandmother?"

"Yes, I do. It's five days' walk from Chichen. But tell me, how did you come to work here at the *polna*?"

She hunches her narrow shoulders and looks down again. "I've been sold seven times, Grandmother."

Like an old bone necklace passed from one to another, I think to myself, feeling sorry for the girl. But she gives a shrug as if this is nothing unusual.

"I have been here not long. Since the cedar trees were in bloom. Hmm, maybe five full moons now."

"And how do they treat you here?" I ask gently.

She looks wary. "I do as they tell me and when they beat me I don't cry, most of the time. When the men get drunk, I know to hide until the morning."

"How many *tuns* have you?" asks Nine Macaw, imitating my gentle tone.

"I don't know," she shrugs again. Then she flashes a quick, friendly smile at Nine Macaw and says, "I've been alive as long as I've known me!" Her black eyes twinkle.

What a delightful, beautiful child! I tune in to Blue Stone with my Oracle's inner Knowing and see standing beside her a benevolent spirit surrounded by a powerful ring of light. He smiles at me, one hand on Blue Stone's head. In spite of her sad situation, Blue Stone's *chu'lel* is as clear and strong as a wild river current. I see no dark green of greed or murky brown of subterfuge. Right now, unwashed and nearly naked, she looks like a little turtle in the mud, but she is a gem. My intuition is never wrong about girls.

"Please stay here, Blue Stone, with my granddaughter and our slave while I return this water gourd to the Hearth Keeper and have a few words with her."

Eyes wide, she starts to rise. "No! You mustn't, Grandmother! Please, I will take that for you. It is my job."

"I would like you to leave it to me," I say gently, but firmly.

"The Mistress of the Hearth will beat me."

"Trust me," I say with a smile. Nine Macaw catches the other girl's hand in her own and speaks to her quietly. I can see their friendship quickly spark. When I see that the girl will obey, I motion to Iguana Wind.

"Son, keep an eye on the girls while I run an errand." He nods reassuringly and crouches down protectively beside them.

It is easy to find the Hearth Keeper in the half-walled hearth room despite the buzz of activity of workers and travelers. The mistress is a buxom woman with muscular arms crossed over her chest. She surveys everyone and everything with hard, hawkish eyes. I return the gourd to one of the many washing troughs and help myself to a cup of allspice-and-honey tea from a large clay jar. Then I claim a seat on the end of a bench at the Noble women's table and continue my observation as I sip the soothing brew. It's obvious she is the queen bee in this hive. The Hearth Mistress delivers orders and reprimands. Nothing escapes her notice. She is taller than most women, and so buck-toothed that the flesh of her lips can't cover her teeth. Her high, white-paper headdress makes her seem like a giant among the other women. Her plain white mantle reaches just below her knees, indicating her social class. She is not a Noble. That is useful for what I am about to do. I finish my tea and approach the forbidding woman.

Right hand to my left shoulder, I stand confidently in front of her. "Sister, I would speak with you."

Scowling, she turns to face me, but her expression changes quickly when she sees my flattened forehead and realizes that in spite of my unwashed, plain clothing, I am a Noble. She flashes a false, toothy smile.

"Of course, Sister. Is something the matter?"

"I wish to inquire about the slave called Blue Stone. Is she yours?"

She scowls. "Yes. Why do you ask? Has she been disobedient? I will punish her!"

"Let us speak outside," I say, my dislike for this woman growing. I turn and walk outside without checking to see if she is following. I know she must, for I am a Noble and she is not.

Once we are standing away from the crowds she looks at me with suspicion. "You'll have to be quick," she snaps. "I work for a living, as you can see."

We stand under a guava tree swarming with yellow songbirds. The morning is quickly getting hot. I draw a deep breath and borrow some of the brightness of their morning joy.

"What is your name?" I ask.

"Five Rain," she responds curtly, eyebrows furrowed.

"What can you tell me about the slave girl?" I ask her.

She shrugs and draws down her lips. "Not much to tell. I bought her a few moons ago from an herbalist who plies the southern rivers. He was anxious to sell her because she will soon start her cycles. He didn't want to bother with her coming-of-age ceremony. Why do you care?" she asks with annoyance. What an unpleasant woman.

"I have taken an interest in her. I may want to buy her from you."

Her fingers twitch as if she is rubbing together two stones. Her *chu'lel* ripples with green rings of greed. Good. I know what she wants, and I will pay. But it is always better to bargain so I don't seem too eager.

"She seems weak and small for her age," I continue. "Not very attractive, either."

"Oh, but she is good with the travelers and knows the uses of many herbs. This can be very useful knowledge." She considers me shrewdly. "After I spent so much time training and feeding her, I won't let her go cheaply."

"Hmm. She may not be the slave I need, then. I seek a suitable companion for my granddaughter on our journey to Cuzamil."

"Blue Stone is an obedient child. She will do fine for you. You can pay me a small fee and take her with you and then send her back to me after you get to Cuzamil. That will be cheaper for you and I won't lose my valuable slave."

Five Rain sees my irritation and knows she has me in a corner. It is clear I want to buy the girl. I drop all pretenses. I don't have time to waste.

"Blue Stone's services will be needed when we get to Cuzamil. The priestesses can use her skills with herbs." Five Rain's eyes narrow as she thinks about her slave in this new light. "The Goddess would be grateful to you," I add lamely.

Her squared chin juts toward me. "What will you pay?"

"Three jade beads," I say quickly. This is surely more than twice what she paid for the girl.

"Let me see them," she answers, glancing over her shoulder protectively.

I reach inside a slit in my mantle where I keep the bag of precious stones. I find the jade beads by their shape. My fist tightens around three of the smallest. I show them to Five Rain. Her eyebrows lift. Hot *chu'lel* of greed flows out of her. I take a step to the side and let it blow past me.

"It's very hard to train a slave," she says, her eyes never leaving my palm with the stones. "And these days they are in such high demand for sacrifice. I will have to travel to find her replacement. That costs."

I resent her toying with me. I know that my sister pays those expenses, but there's no time to draw this negotiation out, and I'm not very good at it anyway.

"Sister, three stones of jade and ten cacao seeds. No more. My last offer."

"Four jade and twenty cacao seeds" she counters.

"Three jade and five-plus-ten cacao seeds."

"Sold!" She looks triumphant. "And good riddance! She thinks she is better than everyone around here."

Perhaps she is, I think to myself as I count out the payment.

Five Rain studies me curiously as I hand over the stones and seeds. "If you plan to take the child to Cuzamil, then you must know someone there?"

"I know Queen Heart of Water."

Her expression transforms to one of fury. "Then answer me this: What is the queen thinking these days!?"

"What do you mean?"

"Hmmph!" She stamps her foot. "What do I mean? Supplies! Food! Workers! Chocolate! Chilies! That's what I mean! We have not had any supplies delivered here for two moons. The men hunt, the children gather wild food and berries, but it will not feed this multitude. We are prepared for pilgrims, not refugees flooding in here like bees from Na Balam because of some troubles there with their ruler and his foreign queen. How will we feed them? Our gardens are stripped bare. There will be no crops to harvest for at least another moon. Right now, we need corn, beans, pumpkins, fruits and avocados. Tomatoes! Do you know how long it's been since I've seen a tomato or an onion? My baskets and sacks are all empty. Empty!"

This is troubling news, indeed. It is unlike my sister to neglect her obligation to the public inns. Her slaves carry supplies on their backs and always inquire about the needs of every *polna* and report back to Heart of Water personally. Our grandmother vowed to feed and house all pilgrims to Cuzamil. Cuzamil is wealthy beyond imagination, with great patches of rich soil and countless fresh-water wells fed by a deep, underground river, so the harvests are always plentiful. Our control of the salt and honey trades has been in place for generations. There are nine travelers' inns between Chichen and Pole-by-the-Sea, one for each of the nine days it takes to walk between the two centers. For Heart of Water to supply even five-times-twenty inns would be like taking a feather off a bird or a hair off a dog. So what is going on?

"When did you last get supplies?" I ask Five Rain, who glowers at me as if I, personally, am responsible for her hardships.

She rolls her eyebrows and stamps that big foot again. "Ten-plus-five days!" she shouts into my face. "With a horde of people like this, I will be out of food tomorrow! What will I do!?"

This woman is like a giant child throwing a tantrum.

"You will hunt deer, peccary and birds," I say sternly, losing patience with her. "You will send the children into the jungle to gather wild fruits, herbs and bird chilies."

"Easy enough for you to tell me what to do," she grumbles.

How impertinent of her to speak to me like this to a Noble, much less a priestess of the Goddess! But then I remember that I have not told her who I am.

"You mind your tongue," I say less harshly than I might. I realize she's been overwhelmed.

"Our business is concluded!" Five Rain pushes out her lips and stalks off to shout at an idling worker.

What is going on in Cuzamil? I glance around the milling crowd to see if someone returning from Cuzamil might be able to give me news. I notice a trader sitting on a bench on the far side of the hearth room. One can always tell traders by their bright red cloaks and feather-topped wooden staffs that, by law, they are required to carry. As they wander from center to center selling and buying, traders are a rich source of news, which is one of their trade items. Acting as royal spies, they carry more than gossip. Information bought by the highest bidder has won many a battle. From itinerant traders one can learn the fate of family members in distant lands, hear the latest court intrigues and keep up with the current prices of any commodity in the realm. I head over to him, moving past refugee families huddled miserably together. Babies cry, toddlers whine and the mothers and grandmothers try to comfort them.

This trader notes who comes in and out of the hearth room as he sips his tea. His long topknot, tied high with strips of deer leather, sprouts from the crown of his head. Under his red cloak he wears only a plain white loincloth. His shoulder tattoos of ocean waves and canoes announce his profession as a sea-going trader. I cast my eyes to the earth and turn slightly to the side.

"Brother, may we speak?"

He stands up, towering over me. Hand to his heart, head bowed, he gestures to a wooden bench outside where we will have more privacy. I follow him out and smell rich oils and spices on his skin and in his hair. Currents of confidence and ability stream from him. I find myself liking him. We settle ourselves on the mahogany log, which has been polished smooth by generations of travelers. In the tree behind us, a flock of parakeets feeds noisily on acacia pods. Families clutching their bundles shuffle past us in search of a meal in the hearth room.

"Greetings, Noble Sister. How may I assist?"

I surprise myself by blurting out: "I am Jade Skirt Chel Cocom. I am—I was—the Oracle of Chichen until a few days ago."

"I know who you are," he says, giving me a frankly curious look. "You're the talk of the roads and towns everywhere. They say you alone may bring down the rule of the New Order."

"I doubt that," I reply humbly, brushing the idea away as though it were a fly. "If they are brought down, it will be because the people have had enough of their cruelty and abominable practices. But I would have news of the Island of Women, where my sister rules. Do you know her?"

"Oh, yes, we have met many times. Heart of Water is a tough negotiator. All trades must be in her favor." He says this with grudging respect.

"Have you seen her lately?" I ask tentatively. I don't want to give away too much to this man, who is a gossip by profession.

"I have not seen her for almost a *tun*, but she is much discussed by traders. We do not love her greatly these days."

"Why not?" I am surprised. Heart of Water has always had a good reputation with traders.

"Traditionally, the Island of Women claims one-fifth of all trade, but this last moon she announced that she will take double the usual share. If we don't pay, she will ban us from doing business on the Island."

I am shocked. Why would Cuzamil need more wealth?

"This news of Heart of Water's greed—if it's true—is deeply disturbing," I say, frowning.

"She is unchallenged by other rulers of the Known World, at least for now," the trader continues, "But there is talk." He lowers his voice to a whisper and waits for another group to pass. "The people of Pole-by-the-Sea know that your granddaughter, Nine Macaw, is ready to take up her destiny. We are waiting for her to come of age and take the throne. We traders want a new queen on the Island, someone who will offer us the fair dealings we once had with the Rainbow Throne. We want the Island to prosper as well because politics and profits aside, our mothers, sisters, wives and daughters revere the sacredness of Ix Chel's Island where the Goddess dwells. We want it preserved for our daughters and granddaughters, but we fear that Heart of Water's new greed will make her a target."

My heart is pounding. I hear the threat under what he is saying. The Rainbow Throne could fall if we are not careful to treat fairly with the people.

"I thank you for your honesty, Brother. May I know your name?"

"They call me Long Strider, but my *coco kaba* is Smoking Frog. I was born on the day of Eight Lizard; thus, I was destined for the road. My lineage is Tzib, also of Chichen, but I have not lived there in many *tuns*. I travel, as you know."

"Where do you rest your head?" I ask curiously. What must it be like to have the freedom of men to travel as they wish and ply their trade on the road and in every city? I find I am a tiny bit envious.

He adjusts his topknot with one hand and turns his hook-nose profile to me. "Nowhere in particular, but in Pole-by-the-Sea more than most other places, I suppose. I prefer the Great Water's cooling breezes to the dry, hot winds inland." My envy evaporates as I realize that he has no home or hearth of his own. His road now seems like a lonely one to me, but he shrugs as if it is no great matter. "I need to be where the business is, in the thick of it all. That means close to Cuzamil. Living at the sea, we are the first to know the goods and prices that come up from the south and down from the north. All prices are set on the Women's Island, as you must know."

"No wife?" I ask.

"No wife," he says lightly. "I never stay in one place long enough. I am at home on the road. I love the gossip and the inns."

"Have you no regrets?"

"There are times, yes," he answers honestly and warmly as though we are old friends. Traders have this ability to make friends. If they did not their roaming lives would be intolerably lonely. "My Tzib lineage has held contracts with your Chel lineage for generations. When my cousin married a Chel boy we were given control of macaw feathers from the south. Those red-and-blue feathers, so prized by kings and queens, are our livelihood and guarantee our position in the Traders' House, so it is to my benefit to see the Rainbow Throne remain secure."

I am glad to hear that I am related to this man through bonds of marriage.

He shakes his head and purses his thin lips. "This is a bad time for Heart of Water to become unpopular with the traders. There is talk of war."

"War?" I gasp. "Who dares to speak of war in Ix Chel's Zone of Peace?"

"Sister, I have heard the southern Putun boast that taking the Island of Women would be as easy as taking corn from a baby. They are gaining supporters across the land, you know."

"Outrageous! The Great Mother forbids the spilling of blood there!"

He shrugs. "Lady, the Putun care nothing for the gentle Goddess or the Zone of Peace. They have their War God, and they have their soldiers. They have been busy the last few *tuns* capturing sea ports along the southern coast and establishing new ones far to the north. Your sister has not been able to stop them. They are determined and greedy, which is a dangerous combination." He pauses, choosing his words carefully. "Your sister has made enemies. Times are changing. The Putun are swine, but they offer better profits than your sister ever has."

I can't believe my sister is turning a blind eye to the danger. Perhaps she is amassing more wealth so she can hire an army to protect the Island? Whatever her reasons, she should explain it to the traders so they don't resent her.

"This is madness," I mutter to myself.

"Some are saying that Heart of Water has gone mad."

I feel a chill down my spine. Memories of disturbing dreams about my sister over the last few nights come back to haunt me. In the dreams she stands on the shore of Cuzamil as Nine Macaw and I approach in the royal canoe, but instead of greeting us with joyful welcome she scowls with an expression of pure hatred in her eyes. Or is it madness? I take a deep breath to steady myself.

"It's an ugly story," he continues. "Gossip from the Island says that the Oracle's formula has driven her mad. Women close to her say she has lost her senses and neglects her duties. Administration of Island affairs has broken down. She even neglects to send her people out to resupply the *polnas*."

I feel nauseous with anxiety. "One more question, Brother. Do you have any news of a noblewoman named Water Lily of the Cocom courtyard in Chichen?"

My stomach does its lurching act again. I want to know, but dread to hear.

He leans forward to face me. "Sister, I was there," he says tenderly. "It was two or three days ago, I saw your daughter." I clutch my mantle tightly around me to still my trembling hands. "Three priests dragged her by the hair into the public plaza. She screamed and cried and begged to be released. A great crowd witnessed her shame. They hurled stones. They shouted, 'Faithless drunk! Your ancestors do not know you.'"

"Does she live?" I ask, trembling.

"After the stoning, soldiers dumped her in a ditch outside the city. No one was permitted to help her, as she was declared an exile." He turns away and sighs. "That is all I know. I'm sorry for your troubles, Sister Chel." I grasp the jade beads around my neck. They were cut from the same piece of jade as the ones on the necklace Water Lily wears. I pray to Ix Chel to send me a sign, and for a moment I feel the stones vibrate in my hands. I squeeze tighter and close my eyes, but I can't feel my daughter. Is the vibration a sign that she lives? Or is that just a mother's hope?

"There is news of your brother, the High Priest Blood Gatherer," Long Strider says when I open my eyes again. He glances around to make sure none are eavesdropping and lowers his voice. "Two days past, he lay bleeding in Chac's temple at Na Balam. It is said his head injuries are severe and he might not recover. He was speaking to all who attended him about his hatred for you and Heart of Water. He swears revenge against you both." Long Strider pauses to swat at a bothersome fly and then asks curiously, "How did that one come to hate his own sisters? It is unnatural."

I hesitate for a moment and then decide to tell him. It will be good for me to say it aloud, and I don't mind if he spreads the story—which he most certainly will.

"Ever since we were children on Cuzamil, he was jealous of me and my sister. As granddaughters of the queen, we were constantly being trained to wield power—Heart of Water was to be ruler and I was to become Oracle. There was no role for our brother. Our father was Magistrate of Pole. We saw him infrequently. When we did meet he was warm and attentive to me and my sister, but indifferent toward his son. Like all boys born on Cuzamil, Blood Gatherer was sent away at eleven *tuns* to live with our father. Blood Gatherer was mocked for not knowing the ways of men and the other boys were jealous of our brother's royal lineage. They laughed at his asthmatic wheezing and teased him brutally."

Long Strider nods, able to imagine the humiliation my brother suffered. "I heard a story about that many *tuns* ago. Your brother was not well-liked before he went to Chac's temple to become an acolyte."

I sigh. "I remember the day his jealousy turned to hatred. Heart of Water and I were returning from the mainland to Cuzamil and our father and brother accompanied us on the sea voyage. A sudden storm rose up during the crossing and the paddlers lost control. The canoe tipped and we tumbled into the raging sea. As high as a mountain, the water swelled over our heads and the rain beat down. It was one of the most terrifying moments of my life! Our father grabbed me and my sister and dragged us over to the canoe so we could cling to the side. Blood Gatherer was being carried away by the waves and we could hear him screaming. Our father might have saved him, but he was knocked unconscious by debris in the water. We never found his body. It was one of the paddlers who saved my brother. After that, Blood Gatherer became truly bitter toward me and my sister, and our grandmother and mother. He left Cuzamil to train with the priests of Chac and had little to do with any of us."

"Hmm," he says with professional interest, filing away this piece of gossip about Cuzamil's ruling family. "So the brother blamed his sisters for being more precious to the father. Hmm."

What possessed me to say so much about our private family matters? Suddenly anxious to change the subject, I ask him, "What do the traders say about this recent uprising in Na Balam?"

He shakes his head ominously. "This is only the beginning. There will be many more deaths, and more fires and destruction in other cities now. This is an overdue rebellion you have started, Lady, and none can tell where it will lead. It was long-ago written that these troubling events will occur in our time, when comes the *katun* of Mountain Movement."

I quote the scrolls, "'What Is has already Been and will Be again. As move the Sky Wanderers, so go the affairs of the earth.'"

"Things cannot possibly stagnate under that influence," he says, nodding. "A purge is coming. Even when it is good for us, it is always painful. The calendar prophecies tell us that the *katun* of Mountain Movement brings changes countered by powerful resistance. Dark forces will activate to prevent change." He looks pointedly at all the refugees in the courtyard. "Human sacrifice is a way to control people with fear. As their power and wealth crumble, the priests will not fold their hands and do nothing. Your brother plots with your enemies. Your sister is compromised. You and Nine Macaw are exiles. Your daughter's fate is unknown. Sister, I pity you. This is a desperate situation."

"Save your pity for others more deserving," I snap. I thought I had already faced the worse that can happen—exile and shame, Red Earth's suicide, Water Lily's public stoning, Iguana Wind's snake bite, Tree Orchid's injury, my brother's betrayal. But no, there is more to come. I vow to make offerings at every shrine to the god who carries this unlucky *katun* of twenty *tuns* on his back.

"I need to know whether the traders will stand with me and Nine Macaw to preserve the Rainbow Throne if it comes to war."

He takes time to consider. "That depends. You know how it works. Cuzamil's ruler will have to promise control of trade routes to some, and to others offer favors and special appointments in the administration in order to secure allies. I can speak for my own lineage: our trade in feathers is vital to our prestige and marriage contracts. If we lose that niche we are finished. So the Rainbow Throne can count on us to defend its cause on the Island if its ruler guarantees that our trade with Cuzamil will continue to be profitable."

Loyalty has a price. As High Priestess, my involvement in politics has been limited, and I am honest enough about myself to know that I have never been well-suited for that sort of intrigue. Heart of Water was always adept at making deals and negotiating. She even seems to enjoy it.

"You are likely to be the one we negotiate with until Nine Macaw comes of age," the trader says, which brings me up short. This eventuality never occurred to me. I have been so naïve! But of course he is right. If my sister truly has gone mad then it will fall to me to rule as Nine Macaw's regent until she reaches the age of reason, twenty *tuns*.

Om bey! This conversation fills me with dismay. Once I get to Cuzamil I will be swimming in the dangerous waters of politics, whispers and double-dealings. How will I know who to trust? I never wanted to sit on the Rainbow Throne. Women in our ruling lineage take pride in being cooperative, not competitive.

I am sure I have revealed the distress I am feeling to this trader, and suddenly I am uncomfortable with how much I have told him about my affairs and the affairs of our family. He is a stranger and now I know he wants something from me—or he will, one day soon. I must be more careful of who I trust and make no promises that will come back to trouble me later if and when I must be acting regent.

"There is another matter," Long Strider says. "Your slave, Iguana Wind— he is from Tulumha?" I nod, amazed that this man knows all the details of our lives. "I heard that his son died less than a *tun* past from the bloody flux. His wife and two daughters left their lineage home to live at Cuzamil in the village of widows."

More terrible news! I put my head in my hands and sigh. Iguana Wind will be devastated. When he first became our slave Moon Eagle sent a messenger to his wife to let her know he lived and would be free in ten *tuns*. Why has she gone to the village of widows? Did the message not reach her? How terrible it would be if she had believed all this time that Iguana Wind was dead!

"Sister, I am sorry to bear such hard news as these things about which we have spoken," the trader says with surprising gentleness. "But for all of our sakes, you must be wary. Blood Gatherer is allied with a Putun priest known as Pus Master. Before the uprising at Na Balam, during a council meeting, the priest shouted that it was his spiritual duty to see Nine Macaw go to paradise as Chac's bride. He said Chac has told him that he desires this girl and only she will be acceptable to him. If there is a drought or crop failure, Pus Master will lay the blame on you. Blood Gatherer is powerful, but Pus Master is the mastermind of political intrigue and when he speaks the people believe whatever he tells them. Putun priests have their own soldiers. The priests themselves carry daggers as tools of their trade. Underestimate them at your peril! Their goal is control of all sea trade in the Known World and making the people obedient to them in the name of their War God. They see you and your sister as mere pebbles in their way. You and the child you travel with are as vulnerable as newborn rabbits in the forest. The *nacom* Jaguar Shield is not with you; your slave is injured; you have no soldiers to protect you."

My spine fizzes. "How do you know all this?"

He gives a hearty laugh. "Information is my livelihood, dear Lady, and I am good at what I do."

"What do I owe you for the information, Long Strider?"

"Lady Jade Skirt, I would gladly offer you a trade," he says boldly.

"A trade? What do I have that you want?"

"When Nine Macaw is on the throne, you will be her regent?"

I answer cautiously. I can guess where this is going. "If Heart of Water no longer rules, and if Nine Macaw has not reached the age of reason, then yes, I will be her regent."

"Well, then I ask only that you remember that we are kin. As such, it would be beneficial if you appointed one of our Tzib woman to be your close advisor, and another Tzib woman to be close advisor to Princess Nine Macaw."

This talk makes me very uncomfortable. What would Heart of Water think if she knew I was planning to sit on her throne and promising an alliance of the Rainbow Throne with the Tzib?

"If this comes to pass, and I hope it will not, then I must rely on the advisors my sister has trusted during her reign," I say firmly. "But I promise I will remember our kinship."

Adjusting his bright-red cloak, he shrugs as if knowing that was the best he could get in the bargain. He stands and puts his right hand to his heart.

"Remember my name: Long Strider. Remember my lineage: Tzib. You may need us one day. We Tzib need you and Nine Macaw to stay alive and restore order on the Island. Our bundle of fortune is knotted with yours. I hope to do business with you again, Lady Jade Skirt. Soon."

He heads back into the hearth room leaving me alone on the bench. I notice that he did not treat me as an exile. That is heartening. But everything he said sits heavy on my heart. Then I remind myself that there is another way to look at it: as my mother always used to say, it is far better to bear the weight of the lamp of truth than to stumble blindly in the dark.

Nine Macaw and the little slave girl, Blue Stone, walk on either side of me as we make our way from the inn to Coba's marketplace to purchase blue mantles so we can better blend in as pilgrims on the *sacbe*. Also, Blue Stone will need sandals. The soles of her feet are thick as leather from a lifetime of going barefooted, but it will be many days of walking to Pole and I want her to be comfortable. Iguana Wind waits with our belongings at the *polna*. He was crushed to hear the terrible news about the death of his only son, and to learn that his wife believes she is a widow. I convinced him that we will reach Cuzamil as fast as any messenger we might send today. I persuaded him to take some time alone to grieve and make prayers at the shrine to Ix Chel on behalf of his boy. Blue Stone assured him that she could guide us through the market.

I catch the younger girl casting nervous glances behind us. She expects Five Rain to chase her down and drag her back to the *polna*, even though I explained to her that the Hearth Mistress has sold her to me and that I plan to free her when we get to Cuzamil. I can practically hear her thinking that my words are simply too good to be true. I'm hoping when I give her new sandals and a mantle it will convince her that I am speaking the truth. I would like to erase those lines of fear from her young face.

Coba's marketplace is even larger than the one in Chichen. Standing at the entrance, I can see no end to the stalls and mats piled with wares from around the Known World. The din of hawkers, bleating animals and excited conversations overwhelms us. We pause, hand in hand, to acclimate before we plunge into the crowd. Pineapple season has begun in earnest so men and women bent at the waist rush past us hauling hemp sacks and nets full of the spiny fruits. A sweet aroma of fruit and sweat fills my nostrils. The ever-present sweepers scour the marble pavement, cleaning up discarded pineapple rinds and tamale shells. I have a yen for chocolate this morning. A short distance inside the market we purchase three cups brewed with honey and take a few moments to sip them while sitting on a low bench in front of the chocolate seller's stand. The three of us gawk at the crowd that rushes past like a churning river.

With five lakes, Coba is rich in aquatic fowl, dried algae and fish. We head for the mantle sellers' stalls and a pungently fishy aroma assaults us as we cut through a section of the market dedicated to goods made of lake reeds. There are a seemingly endless variety of household and cargo baskets, floor mats, smoking pipes and even clothing for the poor made from the fibrous reeds. Blue Stone leads us through an alleyway where fortune tellers promise answers to life's mysteries with the toss of a handful of yellow corn kernels and black beans. A line of Na Balam refugees has already formed. The poor souls hope for good news about their uncertain futures.

"Na, Blue Stone says there is a seed-cake vendor near the sandal maker," Nine Macaw says, squeezing my hand and looking at me hopefully. "Can we buy some for the journey? Please, Na?"

Blue Stone's presence has brightened Nine Macaw's mood. The little slave girl's eagerness to please fills the void left by Tree Orchid, who was my granddaughter's constant companion for all of her life. It was hard to leave Tree Orchid behind in Na Balam, but she was in no shape to travel. She needs rest and medicine. I am afraid she will never walk easily again. An obsidian blade severed a tendon in her leg when we were captured. I pray to Ix Chel that she will heal quickly and join us soon. I have had dream visions of Tree Orchid in Cuzamil, and I know she will play an important part in helping Nine Macaw fulfill her destiny.

"Please, Na?" Nine Macaw begs as the seed-cake vendors come into view. My bag of stones and cacao seeds is still quite full. We can afford the seed cakes, but not the time it will take to make the purchase. The line is too long. We must leave Coba before the sun is much higher so we can arrive at the next public inn before Father Sun drops into the horizon, and we already took too much time lingering over our chocolates.

I shake my head. "We are on a mission," I tell the girls.

"It is not far," Blue Stone says confidently, guiding us toward the western corner of the busy marketplace. We weave around slaves carrying sacks of goods and shoppers with their bundles.

"*Om bey*! Watch where you are going!" A woman shouts with annoyance as avocados and pineapples spill from a large basket. The noisy crowd pauses to see what is happening. Suddenly, there is concerned murmuring.

"Her infant arrives right here in the street!" a man shouts. "Someone get help! Find a midwife!"

I hurry over, pulling the girls along. I wish I had my healer's bag, but it is back at the inn with Iguana Wind.

"I am a midwife! Step aside. Step aside. Let me see." The crowd parts for us. The urgency of our need to get to Cuzamil is forgotten in this moment. The most important thing now is to be the Goddess's hands and deliver this new life safely.

I crouch beside the woman. "All will be well, little one," I murmur soothingly. "All will be well. The Goddess will help us." Her eyes roll back in her head as a spasm wracks her womb.

This is unfortunate. She is already in the late stages of labor. I estimate that she is full term. She lies in a pool of her own blood and the water from her womb. Next to her is the spilled basket of fruit. How could she have possibly managed to keep up with her duties during labor? And who would order her to carry such a burden in her condition? I position her on her back with knees up. When she winces I realize that she must have fallen under the weight of the heavy fruit and landed hard on the stones of the *sacbe*. Did she land on her belly? I touch her abdomen gently and she cries out with a strangled sound, like a wounded animal.

With no word from me, women in the crowd push the men away and form a protective circle around us. Concerned faces peer down at us. I am accustomed to emergency deliveries, but this is the first time I have had to deliver a precious feather in the muddy street, surrounded by a gaping crowd.

"Lady!" Blue Stone quickly hands me the wide piece of woven cloth that fell with the basket. I fold it three times and place the wad under the woman's hips to raise her up a bit. The mother's face contorts with agony. When the contraction passes she looks at me pitifully. She should have been allowed to stay home in these last days of her pregnancy. Her mantle is unwashed, her sandals are worn through and she looks and smells as though she has not been allowed to bathe. I am appalled that anyone would treat another human being this way. I'm thinking these things while my hands move automatically to check the baby's position. Nine Macaw moves into position to support her back and cradle the poor woman's head in her lap so she can keep the mother from hurting herself as she writhes in pain.

"Try not to push the little one out yet," I tell the mother soothingly, but it's too late. I see a bluish foot dangling from between the mother's legs. Firmly, I push the little foot back inside the womb. I must convince the baby to stay in the womb for a few minutes more while I turn it around.

"Let us all pray hard, Sisters," Nine Macaw says in her clear, young voice. "Let us ask Ix Chel to help my grandmother save the mother and her precious feather."

My heart swells with pride. Nine Macaw is a born healer and a born leader.

The women begin to sing a lilting, beautiful song well-known to all mothers:

> Come, precious feather
> Meet your Father, Sun
> Meet your Mother, Moon
> Join us in this world
> Goddess Ix Chel, Guardian of Birth
> Bless the hands of Your midwife
> And bless the mother in her time of need
> Bless the child who waits to be welcomed
> Into Your rainbow light
> Ix Chel, Mother of all,
> We thank You for Your gifts
> Please deliver this precious jade to us now.

Their singing brings me to a state of inner calm. I place my hands over the pregnant belly and close my eyes. I have spent most of my life in service as a midwife in Ix Chel's temple. I know what to do. I sharpen my inner vision and focus within on feeling the position of the cord. There! Not around the neck. Good.

Slowly breathing with the mother, I carefully massage her belly and coax the infant to turn. I was taught to have a clear image in my head of the outcome, so I focus entirely on the infant turning in the right position and birthing with no complications until I feel the right outcome is clearly set into the field of intention around us. I lift the mother's feet and legs and find Blue Stone is already waiting to support the legs so I can pound as hard as I can on the bottom of her heels. The mother's body jerks. Her belly churns.

"Cough, Daughter. Cough hard!"

She coughs once, twice, three times. Good. Now I massage her taught abdomen, this time more deeply. The poor woman groans with pain. The girls and I help her to rise and squat over the bundle of cloths. I give my granddaughter a look and she leans over the slave and presses down hard on the top of her uterus. Even I am surprised at how quickly the baby pops out, head first, flailing and crying. It's a girl. I hold her in a mantle donated by someone in the crowd, keeping her near the mother because the cord is not ready to be cut. Supported by Nine Macaw, the mother lets out a primitive, guttural sound. The placenta quickly spills out.

I don't know how she managed it, but Blue Stone has somehow procured a large gourd of water and a shawl. I wash and swaddle the infant, carefully wiping her little red, pinched face. Then I put the placenta on the baby's belly and gently hand the newborn to her mother. The exhausted woman looks deeply into my eyes with an expression of relief and loving gratitude. An almost inhuman sound pushes forth from her mouth. That is when I realize she is a mute.

"To whom does this slave belong?" I ask the crowd of onlookers. None answer, but I see a few glancing nervously at the palace.

"I know her," Blue Stone whispers in my ear. "She is the slave of the youngest princess. They live there." She points to a house atop one of the low hills surrounding the central plaza.

I start to rehearse the words I will say to this irresponsible young princess. She will get an earful about her lack of care for this poor slave.

Two naked male slaves from the royal household burst through the crowd.

"You again! Nothing but trouble!" one of the men scolds the new mother. "How long must the princess wait for her fruit? You will be punished for this! There is always trouble with you!" His brown male member bobs back and forth above the woman's head. She cringes and grasps her newborn infant in her dusty arms.

"Get up! Now! Get up!" commands the second slave. "And pick up those avocados!"

"Enough!" I bellow, making the slaves jump. I stab my finger in their direction. "You will pick up those fruits and then you will go to your mistress and tell her to send a litter to carry this woman and her infant home. This slave is in my care. I will not release her until I am sure she and the child will be looked after properly."

There are loud murmurs of approval from the crowd. They have just witnessed a miracle, and anyone can see how misused this slave has been.

"You heard the Lady Midwife," a noblewoman commands. "Go to your mistress and do as she says!" Intimidated, the men back away and then run for the palace.

Nine Macaw and Blue Stone sit down on either side of the slave woman. She puts the baby to her breast. The other women close the circle tighter.

Someone hands me a narrow strip of cotton, which I use to bind the slave's abdomen. I wrap the ends around her groin to catch the bleeding. I feel for the pulse at her wrist. It beats steadily, and I sigh with relief. I hold her wrist and close my eyes. In a whisper I recite the birth prayers for mother and infant. I know the slave cannot hear my words, but I sense the moment she feels the Great Mother enter her ring of *chu'lel*. I see the raw, red of terror and despair turn golden with peace and contentment. Just then, the child begins to suckle.

Nine Macaw lays a slender hand on my shoulder and joins me in the prayers while the other women hum a low chant to Ix Chel, who is also Goddess of Fertility. Blue Stone's eyes are wide and her head is cocked to one side as she listens intently to the words Nine Macaw and I say:

"Mother of All Creation, You who are the Knower, the Sower. Here you have sent us one of Your own, a precious necklace, a precious flower come into our world. Born into the land of mystery and rain, she is a creature of the earth who will find her sustenance from Your corn and Your water and from Father Sun. You, Creator of All that exists, hold these two in Your bosom and protect them throughout their days."

The two slaves return at a jog carrying a sturdy litter made of tree branches and palm leaves. They are accompanied by an official of the royal palace. Scowling, but obedient, they carefully lift the mother and infant onto the cot.

"You!" I point to one of them. "Be sure that someone cuts that cord properly once it stops pulsing." I narrow my eyes and look at him sharply. "I will hold *you* responsible if it is not done correctly!"

The slave gulps and nods, casting his eyes to the ground. He barks at his fellow slave to be careful, and they gently lift the litter and carry the new mother away, aware of the crowd watching them critically.

The royal officer stays behind. When they are gone, he sidles up to me.

"Noble Lady, are you Jade Skirt Chel Cocom?" he asks in a low voice. The one-armed man is attired in puma skin and a feather jacket. I'm grateful for his discretion. I don't need the whole marketplace to know Nine Macaw and I are here in Coba.

"I am, yes," I answer quietly.

"Lady Turquoise Sky, my mistress, who is First Princess of Coba, requests your presence in the palace. She awaits you in the royal apartments, if you will kindly accompany me now."

"Is this the same mistress who owns that poor woman who just gave birth?" I ask, glaring at him. "If so, then I will gladly meet her just to give her a piece of my mind."

"No, Lady. The Princess Turquoise Sky is cousin to the mistress of that slave."

I stifle my groan of irritation. We have a journey to make and I had hoped to get on the road before the sun was much higher in the sky. I do not want to be held up at the whim of an idle noble who is curious about me. But it would be rude, and perhaps dangerous, to refuse so I graciously nod my head. The official nods back with relief, the brown turkey feathers in his topknot bobbing back and forth.

Blue Stone sprints back to the *polna* to tell Iguana Wind what has happened and to convey my instructions to bring our belongings to the palace. Nine Macaw and I follow the official through the busy marketplace and zigzag through a maze of towering temples. The royal district, lined on four sides by high-stepped pyramids painted in deep reds and yellows, is magnificent in the morning light. All around us I see colorful, high-feathered headdresses, elaborately painted faces and nobles wearing the finest garments, sandals, necklaces and earrings. In Chichen they say Coba is a place of wealth, prestige, idleness and arrogance. It was settled only a generation ago by the Kamchen royal lineage of Tulumha. But it prospers because it is a bustling outpost at the crossroads of sixteen *sacbes* that meet in the central plaza. Already aware of the rapacious Putun gobbling up land and trade everywhere, the king established his rule by constructing the longest, widest *sacbe* in the Known World. It runs from Chichen all the way to the Eastern Sea. Surrounded by five blue lakes, Coba's ingenious irrigation canals water verdant fields of corn, beans and pumpkins. Their pineapples are the sweetest of any province. Known as the "Land of No Sweat," Coba has abundant fish, snails, water fowl, wild turkeys, reeds for weaving and tobacco pipes and wild foods, as well as a dense forest of valuable trees and medicines. Great flocks of pink flamingos strut on the shores of the lakes like troupes of elegant soldiers.

Tugging on my dress, Nine Macaw asks nervously, "Why does the princess want to see us?"

"I have no idea, my heart," I answer quietly. "Whatever happens, let us not be separated in the palace. It may not be safe." I see my granddaughter nod gravely. I am sorry to remind her of the danger we are in. To distract her, I say, "You did very well back there with the birth!"

Nine Macaw brightens. "And did you see how Blue Stone knew what to do?" I love my granddaughter's generous spirit.

"Yes. You were a good team in a serious emergency."

"I wonder what name they will give the baby. He looks like Bobo, our monkey!" She chatters happily about possible names as we follow the man to the palace. "Born in the street? Market Monkey?" she says with a giggle.

The palace official halts in front of a long, stone building and dips his head, placing his right hand over his left shoulder.

"Lady, I humbly thank you for your cooperation. I must leave you here. There are no men allowed in this area of the palace. An attendant of the princess awaits you inside."

"I would be grateful if you would inform my slave when he arrives, and see to it that he has a place to rest," I say. "Also, please send my slave girl to me when she arrives."

"I will see to it personally."

The palace is a long series of stone rooms set on a low hill. Stone serpents line both sides of its nine doorways. Greeted at the gaping maw of the main entrance by a noblewoman of the third age, we follow her into cool shadows. In this stone building the pampered royal family is protected from the oppressive heat of these wet lowlands. A maiden walks toward us, hands outstretched. I am aware of how bedraggled and unwashed we are, but she only smiles, touches her hand to her heart, bows her head and motions for us to follow her to the end of a long, narrow hallway. My delight grows when I see she is leading us to the *nulha*! Thanks be to Ix Chel! A steam bath at last!

Footsteps pound behind us and an out-of-breath Blue Stone catches up to us. She flashes me a quick smile and a nod. The message has been delivered to Iguana Wind. The attendant gives her a curious look, then politely ushers us into the antechamber of the baths.

"First Princess Turquoise Sky, and her honored guest, the Queen of Palenque, eagerly await your presence," explains the young attendant. "They offer you time to freshen up first, if you desire?"

I assure her that yes, we desire. I am literally itching to get clean after so long on the road. Ah, the simple pleasures of life! In this moment I am not an exile, not a woman chased and hunted like a rabbit. I am a Noble visiting the royal family. It feels wonderful.

"Princess Turquoise Sky hopes you will accept her gifts of new mantles for each of you," the attendant is saying, "and hair ribbons and new sandals."

"That is very generous of the princess," I say. The girls exchange delighted smiles.

We pass through a perfectly round door bearing the symbol of Ix Chel, the Moon Goddess. All steam baths are dedicated to Her. A superb stone carving of the Great Mother in Her three phases as Maiden, Mother and Grandmother crowns the doorway of the *nulha*. We are met by another young woman, who hands us each a sea sponge and a gourd of soap made from from *guanacaste* tree pods.

"You may undress here. Leave your dirty garments in this basket. I will wash them for you and return everything later today."

Demurely, Blue Stone removes the red *spondylus* shell tied around her hips and places it in the basket.

"It's my first time," she exclaims, looking nervous. Nine Macaw takes her hand reassuringly.

"Then may the Goddess Ix Chel grant you many more days in the *nulha*," answers the attendant. I appreciate her kindness to the little girl and give her an approving look.

The steam room is large and filled with a dense fog of aromatic steam. I take a deep, grateful breath, exhaling with a happy sigh. Women of the first, second and third ages are seated on benches against three walls. Like me, they all have pressed foreheads—a symbol of nobility. Some are buxom, with rolls of fat; others are thin as reeds, with nippled bumps for breasts. We lean against dripping white stones and all our chest tattoos make a patchwork of flowers, snakes and animal heads. Two slack-breasted grandmothers lie on the stone floor while attendants deftly scrub them with rough sponges until they are lobster-red all over. Another attendant holds a handful of wild basil branches ready to lightly beat each bather from head to toe.

Hiding her face against Nine Macaw's shoulder, Blue Stone clings to us nervously.

"It's alright. They won't hurt you," whispers Nine Macaw reassuringly. "It feels good to be clean!" As a child of nobility, Nine Macaw has been to countless steam baths.

We three take a seat in a vacant corner. An attendant throws a gourd of water against a solid stone wall that makes up one side of the steam bath. It sizzles and a cloud of steam puffs up. We make good use of our sponge and soap and take off the grime of the road. Nine Macaw and Blue Stone take turns scrubbing each other's backs, and then they scrub mine. It feels indescribably good to be clean!

Then I am content to lean back against the stone and close my eyes and listen to the murmurs of the women. I catch the thread of a story told by a stocky woman of the second age with intelligent, piercing eyes. Piled high atop her flattened forehead, braids and blue ribbons announce her recent pilgrimage to Cuzamil.

"So then," she continues, "I was instructed by the gentle Goddess Ix Chel, the Blameless, to seek healing at Her temple on Cuzamil." A broad smile reveals jade-encrusted teeth. "She appeared to me in a dream with Her snake to tell me the midwives of Cuzamil would heal my womb, which has wept blood for many months." Her chest is devoid of the usual tattoos, which means that she is childless—perhaps barren.

Splash! Another gourd of water hits the wall. A blast of comforting, cleansing steam envelops us. The woman continues: "I was cured by Her midwives, just as the Goddess promised. I stayed for three-times-twenty days and twice I slept in Her sacred dream chamber. Twice She came to me." This woman's voice is full of gratitude and love. "In the second dream, Her snake crawled over me. I felt cold, scaly skin gliding over my naked flesh." Both hands crawl over her legs and torso, demonstrating. "Then, it licked me all over from head to toe." She continues darting out her tongue at the girls. Nine Macaw and Blue Stone gasp and hug each other, but they are excited by the story.

"What does Ix Chel look like, Mother," asks Nine Macaw, wide eyed. "Is she lovely?"

"Oh, yes! Lovely and kind and gentle. Tall. Very tall. She wears a blue mantle."

I smile, thrilled to hear a familiar story and to know that in spite of political intrigue, threats of war and uprising, the Goddess of Healing and Fertility still appears to Her supplicants in dreams. This is what I am fighting for: to preserve our healing sanctuary where women seek and receive Divine assistance from our gentle Goddess; a sanctuary where women at all stages of life can find healing, shelter and peace in the community of women. I feel proud of my Island home. Whatever I have to face once we cross the sea, I am more eager than ever to stand on Her sacred ground and to live again in a place that rejects the cruelty and barbarism of human sacrifice. I feel a wave of gratitude to my courageous grandmother, Cosmic Turtle, founder of the Rainbow Throne, who had the wisdom to send away all the men from the Island of Women with the exception of a small community of traders on the far north side of the Island. They are separated from the women's sanctuary by impassable swamps infested with snakes and covered with thorns.

The woman has finished her story and we are all content to share a companionable silence. A few minutes later, Nine Macaw leans over and whispers, "Na, do you see it?"

Within the clouds of steam a wide, pulsing ring of pink light hovers over us. My heart opens wide with love.

"Is it the Goddess?" she asks shyly.

"It is Her Presence and Her love, always watching over us in this sacred place."

Nine Macaw squeezes my hand with joy. I feel her *chu'lel* brimming with it and I thank Ix Chel for sending us this much-needed respite to replenish our energy.

The bath attendant taps me on the arm and I lay down gently on the hot stone floor. Another pours a large gourd of soapy water over me while, vigorously, she scrubs me with the fibrous insides of a gourd. She scrubs until I am pink as a newborn. Another appears to wash my hair with the *guanacaste* soap. Nine Macaw and Blue Stone are also being scrubbed, and they can't stop giggling. They are like slippery wet fish, and the young attendant laughs with them and grabs their ankles, flipping each girl over to scrub once more.

Then we are doused with several gourds of cool water. Delightful! I am so relaxed I could fall asleep right here. Finally, we are sprinkled with water in which vanilla pods have been soaked. Then we are rubbed dry with clean cotton cloths and helped into new, fresh-smelling clothes. I adjust Blue Stone's mantle—something she has never worn before. Her hand brushes over the material again and again, the wonder in her eyes a sight that tugs at my heart.

"It looks very fine on you," I tell her. She grins at me shyly.

A young girl of Nine Macaw's age appears to braid our hair. Blue Stone looks away as our hair is brushed and braided. When we're done, Nine Macaw puts her arm around the younger girl's shoulders.

"Your hair will grow and one day soon you will have braids, too. Just think how nice it will be to braid each other's hair!"

The little girl throws her arms around Nine Macaw and gives her a hug.

"I have brought gifts from the Lady White Quetzal, who is Queen of Palenque and the honored guest of our princess," the attendant tells us, unwrapping a fine cloth. Within are two necklaces of precious, pale-green jade. The girls are speechless with wonder. Nine Macaw waits for me to select one and then she eagerly reaches for the other. She hesitates and looks at Blue Stone. The slave girl shyly puts her hands behind her back.

"I think you should wear it!" Nine Macaw says generously.

"But I am not—I am a slave! It is not proper!"

"You won't be a slave much longer. Let us share it! You wear it first and I will wear it tomorrow. Please?"

Nine Macaw is a precious jade, indeed!

Blue Stone looks at me and I nod. She lights up with a smile. Nine Macaw helps her slip it over her head. Blue Stone beams at us, her eyes filled with grateful tears.

"I think this day must be a dream!"

Nine Macaw giggles. "I wish you had dreamed us some seed cakes!"

The attendant leads us through a tree-lined courtyard into a sunlit room of cushioned benches and gauze draperies. I feel some trepidation about meeting the princess and this queen who gifted us costly necklaces, but at least I am bathed and wearing fine, clean clothes. A lake-scented breeze billows the curtains. Through the windows, I glimpse two of the five lakes sparkling like gems in the morning sunlight.

Surrounded by attendants, two young women lounge on a stone bench, which rests on the bent backs of four gods carved in stone. Jade and amber jewelry cover their arms and ankles. The older one is pregnant, and she reclines on a jaguar pelt, rubbing her belly.

"Ah, at last! Lady Jade Skirt, here you are!" says the younger one. "Do you know who I am?" she asks, nose in the air.

I place a hand over my heart and bow my head. The girls do the same, but because they are so much younger they also touch the ground with one hand.

"I assume I have the honor of meeting the First Princess Turquoise Sky," I answer, unruffled by her poor manners.

"Just so!" she answers. "We love Oracles and I am not accustomed to waiting! You should have come to us as soon as you arrived in Coba. I'm disappointed that you chose to stay in the *polna*. There is so much riffraff about these days."

"Thank you, Princess, but it was late and we had much to attend to when we arrived. I trust you do not feel slighted as it was not my intention. Thank you for your hospitality, the bath, and clean clothes."

In the fashion of her lineage, Turquoise Sky's black braids form two great coils that hide her ears. Her face is painted heavily with the expensive purple dye made from the rare mollusk that lives only along the shores of Cuzamil. White rings around her eyes make her look rather more like a badger than a woman. I do not find her lovely in countenance or manners.

"Come to greet me, good healer. Let me see the infamous Oracle and midwife up close."

"Yes," says the pregnant woman, patting her jaguar pelt. "Come here and sit with us. I am Lady White Quetzal, Queen of Palenque. I am in need of your services, as you can see." She pats her belly bulge. "Children, you may both sit over there," she says pointing a long finger at the opposite wall where three attendants wait.

Their indolence and idleness make me feel judgmental. I can't help it. They are so pampered, protected from strife. I'm sure they have never worked a hard day in their privileged lives.

"Lady White Quetzal, we thank you for the gift of these precious beads," I say politely.

"You will stay with us, of course," says Turquoise Sky.

"Yes, here in the palace," says White Quetzal. "That way, you won't get away from us again. This precious feather in my womb must be attended. I had quite a fright on the *sacbe*. My porters stumbled in the melee outside of Na Balam. The imbeciles dropped me! You need to be sure that all is well. I am relying on you to assist me. I carry not just any child, but a future king."

"Lady White Quetzal, I am on an urgent mission to the sacred Island and we must leave Coba today. But I know there are competent midwives here. Many who trained on Cuzamil were sent here to serve." I pause and try to choose my words carefully. "Much as I would like to serve you, not even a queen and a future king must keep me from performing my duty to the Goddess."

White Quetzal narrows her eyes to stare at me. I stare back. She raises her chin. I raise my chin. Silence. Then she laughs out loud.

"*Om bey*! Jade Skirt, you are a clever fox." She nods to Nine Macaw and Blue Stone. "Girls, observe how your Noble Grandmother faces down a tyrant. Well done! You must have that same courage one day."

"I do not see you as a tyrant, Lady," I protest lightly. "You are an expectant mother. Your concern for your precious flower is completely understandable."

"Well, thank you for that, but this is a good lesson for your future Queen of Cuzamil. Oh, yes, I know all about your mission and Nine Macaw. We know you were exiled." She waves her hand as if it matters not at all. "We don't pay attention to what those rulers in Chichen say."

"Yes, and thanks to you, now everyone in the Known World will know the leaders of Chichen have been corrupted by the Putun," says Turquoise Sky, spitting out the last word. White Quetzal nods her agreement. I relax a fraction. They are allies. "Come, Nine Macaw, sit next to me," White Quetzal says more kindly this time, patting a space beside her on the bench. "This other one, the little slave. What's her name?" she points her flat nose at Blue Stone.

"She is Blue Stone. "Mindful of the poor treatment of the pregnant slave woman in the marketplace who belongs to a member of this royal household, I feel immediately protective. "She will be freed as soon as we reach the sacred Island."

"Those jade beads suit her," says Lady White Quetzal, "but it won't due for a slave to look more noble than a princess!" She casually removes an even finer and longer jade necklace from around her own neck and drapes it over Nine Macaw's head. "There! You must have this one."

Nine Macaw tries to protest, but White Quetzal shakes her head imperiously. "I insist, so you must not argue!" Nine Macaw looks pleased and embarrassed, but she admires her new necklace with obvious delight.

"Come, Jade Skirt," says Turquoise Sky patting a puma pelt. "You sit right here next to me. I would absorb some of your *chu'lel* for myself."

Just like them, I think. They would take your very essence. Turquoise Sky moves over to make room for me.

"Dear little feather," White Quetzal says to Nine Macaw, "I will give you your first lesson in statecraft. You must learn to be arrogant. It is a queen's prerogative. It is not attractive on commoners or lesser nobles, but we must present this commanding air of assumptions—even those that seem unreasonable—to hold our power in place. If our subjects think we are kind, they will take advantage because they see kindness as a weakness. Terrible isn't it? But now you know so you will do what is necessary."

Nine Macaw glances at me with a wince as if to say, "Na, can this be true?" I have tried to instill a sense of humility and compassion in her.

"She will be Queen, that is true," I say, "but she will also be a healer and Oracle. Rulers of the Rainbow Throne serve the Goddess and therefore must rule with compassion, not arrogance. In the world of men, arrogance may be a sign of strength, but on the Island of Women our strength comes from wisdom, kindness and most of all our sacred connection to the Great Mother."

"With respect, Lady Jade Skirt, you are wrong," counters White Quetzal. "You are royalty, of course, as granddaughter and now sister of the Queen of Cuzamil, but you have lived your life in service to the Goddess as a High Priestess and Oracle, and not as a princess promised to the throne, as Nine Macaw will soon be."

"My royal sister speaks true," Turquoise Sky chimes in. "A High Priestess and healer must be kind, but a queen cannot be kind! Her first duty is to the affairs of the state—the realm that she rules. A queen must be ruthless. She has to look out for the welfare of thousands. Our responsibility requires us to have a commanding nature. A queen must be unafraid to offend and must be ready to rule with a hand as hard as obsidian."

"We of royal lineage are one with the gods," explains Lady White Quetzal. "They speak to us and through us. Our rites and ceremonies bring the gods' guidance and favor to our people, to our battles, our captives. We queens let blood from our tongues so the gods will bring us sacred dreams, fertile wombs and visions that help us to rule wisely. We are they. They are we."

"Yes," agrees Turquoise Sky, "we cannot be perceived as mortal, you know. The scepter of our high office is a sacred thing. Every ruler's *kawil* is inhabited by a god or a goddess."

I realize with a start that the Rainbow Throne can count only three generations from my Chel grandmother, who founded it. But these queens come from lineages that have ruled for countless generations. I know that White Quetzal's ancestor, Raised-Up Sky, took the throne as king more than ten-times-twenty *tuns* ago. And her grandmother fought like a warrior to preserve the throne for her lineage. She, too, ruled with a heavy hand, but was considered to have been a good queen. Turquoise Sky has never actually ruled her realm, but her father, her husband and uncles are all of royal blood from Tulumha, and she has been raised on the lessons of ruling nobility.

"Jade Skirt, I would have a private moment with you," says Lady White Quetzal. Her words are commanding, but her tone is one of a noble speaking to an equal.

"You two stay here," says Turquoise Sky cheerily. "I will take the girls to the courtyard to visit our aviary." She slaps one arm with her hand, a sign that the attendants must leave the room.

Most royal women raise rare birds for their elegant feathers. The birds are kept in magnificent courtyards filled with fountains where the birds nest, but never leave because of a hemp-woven net that covers the entire yard. I can hear the gurgling fountain and the birds chirping nearby.

Once they have gone, I sit beside White Quetzal and, seeing her up close, I realize she is quite young. I wait patiently for her revelation, but the Queen of Palenque is nervous, as if she's not sure how to say this thing that is eating at her heart.

"Lady Midwife," she whispers, although we are alone, "I had some bleeding since the fall outside of Na Balam. I fear I almost lost the child! I need you to be with me every day—every single day—to ensure that I deliver this baby on the Island of Cuzamil on the feast day of 1 Zip. During my blood-letting visions the Goddess revealed that I carry a male child who must be born then."

"It is very auspicious to be born on Creation Day," I agree.

"It is more than that," the Queen of Palenque says with undisguised urgency. "I have a special problem, you see. I am of the royal lineage, of course." Up goes the nose. "But my husband is only a high noble. In Palenque, ascension to the throne can come only through the male line. But a prince born on Her Creation Day, 1 Zip, on the sacred Island itself, can rule by Divine right."

"Lady, if your vision is a true one, the Goddess will arrange it so that you deliver the child on the right day. Have faith in Ix Chel."

"Of course I do!" she says, exasperated. "It's just that, if anything goes wrong and the birth is delayed or comes too soon then this precious feather will lose his Divine right to rule! I require your services. On the eve of 1 Zip, you must give me a potion so that my son will come into the world the moment before dawn on Creation Day. We will be on Cuzamil, of course, and under your expert care the future king of Palenque will be born with Divine right to rule. This is what the Goddess showed me, and it must come to pass!"

"I see," I respond, choosing my next words carefully. "You know, surely, that every child's day of birth is a destiny ordained by the Calendar Gods."

"Do not instruct me, Jade Skirt," she snaps irritably.

"You are asking me to mettle with your child's destiny," I say.

She glares at me and then casts a guilty glance around the room in case anyone might overhear. Manipulating the calendar date of a future ruler is a conspiracy—probably a state crime. She plays a dangerous game, and I resent her drawing me into her political machinations.

"You know what a treacherous path this is for us both," I say in a low voice. "Why should I help you?"

"Because Ix Chel wills it!" she hisses urgently. "You must believe me, I would not scheme this way if it was not the Goddess's plan for Palenque!"

"How do you know Her will?"

"She came to me in visions during the marriage blood-letting rites with my husband. She showed me that when he and I came together we would be living symbols of the sacred act of Creation by First Mother and First Father, and that our son—the product of this blessed union—will be Her representative on earth. He must rule Palenque when he is of age. But for this to come to pass, he must be born on the holy Island of Cuzamil when 1 Zip dawns. No one will ever dare to challenge his Divine right to rule, no matter what his father's linage is, if he is born at that most auspicious moment."

Midwives must be above all politics. I don't want to get involved, but what if this truly is Ix Chel's plan? I sink my awareness deep in my spirit and call to the Goddess for guidance, but no clear answer comes to me. I sigh deeply. What should I do?

White Quetzal watches me anxiously, and I see not a queen, but a scared woman desperate to secure a good future for her child. Still, that is not reason enough to meddle in the affairs of the Calendar Gods or commit a state crime. I am about to tell her so when she grasps my arms and gives me a beseeching look.

"In strictest confidence, Jade Skirt, I tell you these things," she whispers. "The future of Palenque is in your hands. Please!" The proud queen is not used to begging, and her sincerity begins to sway me.

"If I do decide to help you with this plan, what do you offer in exchange?"

A look of relief passes over her face. Negotiation is familiar ground for her. She releases my arm and straightens her mantle, giving herself time to regain her dignity.

"Times are dangerous now. Thieves abound on the roads, yet you travel alone to Cuzamil with two girls and one male slave," she says shrewdly. "Princess Nine Macaw's life has a price on it. Since Na Balam fell there is unrest throughout the provinces. I offer you safe passage to Pole, protected by my soldiers, in exchange for your service to me and my precious feather. One hand washes the other, right?"

I want to refuse her. I already have enough complications; I don't need to be stuck attending to this spoiled queen on top of everything. But there is no doubt that White Quetzal believes this is Ix Chel's will, and she is right that Nine Macaw and I are too vulnerable on the *sacbe* with only Iguana Wind to protect us.

"Let it be so." I tell her, resigned.

Goddess, please let this be Your will, I pray silently.

Lady White Quetzal sags with relief, her hands cradling her abdomen. I reach over and feel her belly. "Now tell me, Lady, what did you experience after the fall on the *sacbe*?"

"Ah, just so; it is good that you ask. I bled slightly for a day and only today has it ceased. And, my back, how it hurts!"

"You must be worried. Let us take a look."

She lies back so that I can examine her. Just as I thought, the fall has caused her womb to drop low. At this stage of her pregnancy, the weight of the infant's body could force the cervix to open before the proper time. We are less than one moon away from 1 Zip, feast day of the Great Mother. It will be no great feat to delay her birth until then, but to assure that the baby will be born on exactly that day is another matter. The waning moon will not be favorable for a birth.

My hands automatically feel the child and start to massage the womb. She groans with pleasure as I gradually lift her womb to release the pressure. She needs to wear a belly band to strengthen the ligaments that hold her ripe uterus against the downward strain. Even if she had not fallen on the *sacbe*, the jostling motion as she rode on the palanquin would have been a problem.

"You have a belly-band?"

"Yes, of course."

"Then you must send for it. I will bind you and check it daily."

"Yes, Sister! This is why you must stay here in the royal chambers and travel with us. You cannot leave me! I will be forever indebted to you." She is nearly moved to tears with gratitude. "I give my royal word that I will return this favor one day. Your Nine Macaw will need all the allies she can muster in the coming *tuns*, and when we are successful—when my precious jade is born on 1 Zip—I will be her staunchest ally. I will do what is necessary to preserve Ix Chel's sacred Island sanctuary for the Chel lineage. You have my pledge."

I sigh. She is right that Nine Macaw will need allies. She continues:

"My people need a leader to rule over our lands to the south. If it is not my son, then it will be my uncle. He is a cruel man, and I know he will be a heartless despot. I shudder to think what will become of the people of Palenque. I prayed to the Goddess and she sent me an answer."

"And your son and his dynasty—will it also stand against the heart takers?"

Her head nearly flips off her shoulders as she whips around to make sure no one is eavesdropping. Such is the fear those bloodthirsty priests inspire in the people—even a queen.

"That is another matter altogether, Jade Skirt. I cannot promise to force an end to the sacrifices in my lands, but I swear to you and the Goddess that I will help you keep them out of Cuzamil."

One must always weigh all words with queens. A slip of the tongue can be fatal. But in this moment I speak plainly: "What can you do to help Cuzamil?"

"There are forces afoot that you know nothing about, even though you are an Oracle," she says haughtily. Is she bluffing?

"I know that my brother was badly wounded in Na Balam."

Sitting up, she shakes her head. "Jade Skirt, your brother is dead. My spies reported that the blow to his head crushed his skull. No manner of healing, prayer or ritual could save him. He has gone to the waters."

Dead! I take a sharp breath in and let it out with relief. Blood Gatherer is gone! I will walk lighter and sleep better knowing he has crossed the nine great rivers of the Underworld. A short time ago I might have mourned the brother I once loved, long ago when he was a little boy and sucked his thumb and clung to my mantle. But after everything he has done all I feel in this moment is relief that he is dead.

"May the gods forgive him," I say grimly.

She pats my hand as if to offer comfort. Little does she know that her news fills me with relief. But if what Long Strider told me is true, then we are still not safe—even with Blood Gatherer dead.

"Lady Queen, do you know of one they call Pus Master, a Putun priest?"

"I know all about him. He is High Priest of the War God's temple in Na Balam. The Putun are vultures feeding on our world as it crumbles. Pus Master is busy rebuilding and organizing Na Balam to his liking. War, sacrifices, beheadings and de-fleshing will be commonplace there now."

This is shocking news. I never could have imagined that in the homeland of the Chel, who worship the gentle Goddess, the War God would rule. As if reading my mind, White Quetzal says, "Truly, it is an affront to Her. And you must have heard that Pus Master demands that Nine Macaw be given to Chac. He said there is no other maiden in all the Known World like her and he said that Chac told him he must have her. No one else will do. But his real purpose is to kill the heir to Cuzamil's throne."

"And you believe you can keep us safe and deliver us to Cuzamil?"

"Just so," she responds evenly. "While I do not rule here, a queen's word is powerful everywhere. I will say that I saw in a vision that Nine Macaw must live to rule Cuzamil. Other queens and priestesses will support us, I know."

As an Oracle, I cringe at her words. Lying about a vision is anathema to me. It makes me wonder if she has lied to me about the vision she had about her son. Perhaps she is simply a mother ambitious for the success of her dynasty. Politics leaves a bad taste in my mouth.

"You must stay as still as possible until the bleeding stops. I will be here with you to ensure that your womb holds the infant king until the day Ix Chel has appointed for his birth. Whether that is 1 Zip or not, I cannot guarantee. But you must cooperate with all my instructions. Agreed?"

"Yes!" she says, breaking into a radiant smile. "I will do whatever you say, Noble Lady! I trust you completely. Truly, the hand of the Goddess is in this meeting."

I hope she is right.

I wake in a soft, clean bed in Turquoise Sky's palace. I allow myself to enjoy the rare feeling of laziness.

"Na! Is it morning?" Nine Macaw puts her sleepy head on my shoulder. She speaks quietly. Blue Stone is still deep asleep on the floor, wrapped in her mantle.

"I dreamed again," my granddaughter says, snuggling close. "There were five pink butterflies and one pure white. They landed on the shores of the sacred Island and then a great rainbow appeared. It was so beautiful! What does it mean, Na?"

"The rainbow is Her most potent symbol of success and promise," I tell her. "When we dream of rainbows it is a sign that we must prepare for trouble, but also trust in a successful outcome. Butterflies are the souls of warriors, and there are five temples on Cuzamil. Four are made from a rare pink stone, while the Great Temple of the Mother, in the center of the holy Island, is made of shining white stone. Often, our visions and dreams are unclear, but this dream gives me a feeling of hope!"

Nine Macaw smiles. "Me, too!"

It has been two days since we became guests of Princess Turquoise Sky. I am anxious to get to the Island, but White Quetzal needed this time to allow her womb to rest and recover from the fall. Nine Macaw, Iguana Wind and I have also been resting and recovering from the hardships we have endured since leaving Chichen, and Blue Stone has been accustoming herself to her new station in life as companion to Nine Macaw. I keep reassuring her that I will make her manumission official when we arrive in Cuzamil. I also told her of Nine Macaw's dream showing her as a priestess of Ix Chel on the sacred Island. The girl's eyes went wide with wonder.

"Would that please you?" I asked.

Blue Stone bowed her head and put her right hand to her heart. "I will serve Her with all my heart, Lady! There is nothing I want more than to dedicate my life to Ix Chel, guardian of the plants I love so much!"

When she lifted her gaze to meet mine there were tears of joy in her dark eyes. This child delights me more with each passing day.

Iguana Wind grieves deeply for the son he barely knew, and he can hardly contain his impatience to be reunited with his wife and daughters. These days of waiting have been torture for him, but the snake-bite wound he suffered before we reached Na Balam has mostly healed. He walks with barely a limp now. As for me, I had two good nights of sleep in a row and visited the steam baths once more, which has done much to restore me. But I am ready to be on the road.

We will leave today. I was relieved that White Quetzal followed all my instructions without question. So far, I have no complaint with her. In fact, I am starting to enjoy the Queen of Palenque—some of the time. I am genuinely grateful that she has taken a strong liking to Nine Macaw and instructs my precious jade in the ways of the great web of trade agreements among the provinces. Although she has only twenty *tuns*, the queen is knowledgeable and generous with royal advice.

While Nine Macaw was occupied with White Quetzal yesterday morning, Blue Stone and I went outside the palace to find Iguana Wind. We sorted through my medicines to see what needed to be replenished. Iguana Wind, who was an army herbalist before he was captured by my Moon Eagle, quizzed the child on the different roots and leaves and their preparations. We were both impressed by Blue Stone's advanced understanding of medicinal plants.

"My last master was a trader in herbs," she told us, rubbing her hands over her new mantle and smiling with pleasure.

"Was he a good master?" Iguana Wind asked quietly.

"When I made mistakes he beat me across the hands, knees and feet and then left me alone without food for three days," Blue Stone answered matter-of-factly, no self-pity in her voice. Iguana Wind and I exchanged a look. The Goddess surely favors this child, keeping her still innocent of spirit after such brutal treatment.

"Lady, you need more wild plum bark. I know a place in the forest not far from here where it grows," said Blue Stone.

"And do you know how it must be gathered?" I quizzed her.

"Oh, yes!" She recited prettily: "It is to be taken from the south-facing side of the tree. The waxing moon is just right now."

"And what are the uses of this medicine?" Iguana Wind raised an eyebrow as though skeptical, but I could tell he was charmed.

"It's the same bark Lady Jade Skirt gave to the queen to stop her womb from bleeding. And my master used it for bloody flux, too. I think it is very good for washing sores."

"You are correct!" I hugged Blue Stone and she shyly hugged me back. "Take Iguana Wind with you and bring us back two double handfuls." I gave her a small, deerskin bag. "When you return let us prepare it together and make another tonic for Lady White Quetzal."

She sparkled with energy. Catching Iguana Wind's hand in her small one, she tugged him toward the doorway. I saw the worry lines ease from his face and heard him laugh. Blue Stone is good medicine for all of us.

Now we are preparing to travel again. As we drink our chocolate, there is a flurry of activity around us. Servants, slaves and attendants carry sacks of food, clothing and other supplies to the front of the palace, where soldiers and male servants wait to load everything for the journey. My heart lifts. Finally, we can get on the road! Iguana Wind paces restlessly in front of the palace.

"Patience, Son," I greet him.

He gives me an apologetic look and sits down to sharpen his obsidian blade, which already has a razor-sharp edge.

Before the morning grows too bright we are packed and ready for our journey. The Queen of Palenque perches regally in her chair atop a wooden platform carried by six naked slaves. A priest-attendant walks ahead of her palanquin to sweep the path and burn incense for the royal procession.

It turns out that Nine Macaw and I are also meant to ride on covered palanquins. I try to protest that it is not necessary, but both princesses give me stern looks and remind me that I am accompanying the future queen of Cuzamil.

"Jade Skirt, you should know it is beneath a noble's dignity to walk!" Turquoise Sky scolds affectionately. Before I climb into the chair I bow deeply and thank her for her hospitality and generosity.

"We will visit you when you sit on the Rainbow Throne," she tells Nine Macaw. "You will need our advice!"

I sigh inwardly, but place my hand over my heart and bow my head again. I remind myself that she means well.

On cushions and pelts atop our less-than-comfortable perches, we bounce above the other travelers on the *sacbe*. Iguana Wind walks in front with Blue Stone, the two talking like old friends about herbs and medicines. The novelty of being carried wears off quickly for Nine Macaw. She looks longingly at her new friend, who is stopping to pick flowers.

Progress is frustratingly slow because the Lady White Quetzal insists we stop at every stone shrine to Ix Chel and offer amaranth cakes and grains of *copal* incense. As pilgrims journeying to Cuzamil, this is the proper way to travel, but I must tamp down my impatience and try not to rush the pregnant queen through any of the rituals. By the third shrine, I find my heart has changed and I am moved by the devotions of the other pilgrims. I have not been thinking of Nine Macaw's and my journey to Cuzamil as a pilgrimage, but of course it is. When our palanquin is set down beside a large stone shrine and the queen begins her rituals, I give Nine Macaw and Blue Stone permission to gather wild flowers to offer at this peaceful place. Iguana Wind accompanies them. I sink to the ground before a stone image of Her in the guise of Mother. I close my eyes and feel Her presence. I commune with Her and feel my strength and gratitude renewed.

We journey at this slow pace for three days, sleeping each night at inns along the way. The *polnas* are noticeably short of supplies. The bean soup has been thin, flavorless and lacking salt. The *chaya* tamales taste of the mealy corn that comes from the bottom of the bin, and the hot sauce is made from little wild bird peppers, which is considered starvation food. The other pilgrims notice and grumble about it. More than once I hear my sister's name invoked with disgruntled tones. We experience little hardship because the Queen of Palenque's attendants supplement our meals with delicacies from her private stores. But I am dismayed by the disappointment among the pilgrims.

We are two days from Pole-by-the-Sea when we reach the little town of Chaktun. Lady White Quetzal commands the best rooms available. Her servants, who have been carrying her all day, leap into action to unpack her belongings and arrange for her bath. I want nothing more than to go off by myself and find a quiet place under the trees to merge my *chu'lel* with the plants of the jungle and feel their peace and calm. But I hesitate to leave the pregnant queen. The journey is refreshing the princess spiritually, but riding in the palanquin takes a toll on her lower back. The skin around her eyes and mouth is pale. I help her lie down on cushions to release the tension on her back. Then I motion for Nine Macaw to bring my medicine bag. Rummaging around, I find a small pouch of bright-red *chacah* bark, which is a good blood tonic for pregnancy.

As the girls brew the tea—both know what to do without being told—I massage White Quetzal's back and feet. She moans with relief. After she drinks the tea, I feel her pulse.

"Lady, as I have said, walking will be good for you for short stretches of time. You must move the blood more vigorously through your veins to nourish the child within."

She immediately calls for her attendant to help her rise. Holding onto the woman's strong arm, she goes for a stroll around the *polna*, trailed by a contingent of her ever-present guards. Nine Macaw and Blue Stone hunker down on a sleeping mat to play a game with stones. Iguana Wind helps a servant repair one of the carrying bins. For a blessed moment, no one needs anything from me and I am free to wander around on my own. As part of the queen's entourage we have received curious looks from the other travelers, but none seem to have recognized me or Nine Macaw. I realize I no longer constantly look over my shoulder for Pus Master. I am not regretting my agreement to journey to Cuzamil with White Quetzal.

This inn is not as large or as crowded as the one in Coba. It is a thatched building with a hardened dirt floor and half-walls that open to the outside. The Hearth Mistress here has placed reed baskets with flowering vines around the beams, creating a very pleasant atmosphere. I am impressed with the *polna*'s cleanliness and inviting ambience. The hearth room is furnished with long wooden tables that shine from regular scrubbing. Dry herbs hang over the hearth and the walls are lined with neat rows of shelves where pilgrims can borrow a clay bowl and gourd at mealtimes. It is a room large enough to seat three-times-twenty and still have plenty of room for brooms, water jugs and hanging baskets. But looking into the baskets I see that where dried fruits and fish should be stored there is only dust.

After our simple evening meal, we lie down for the night, but for me sleep is like an absent lover. I spend hours tossing and turning. Again, the twisted pathways of my mind rule me. Where is Jaguar Shield? Has he found my daughter? Are Tree Orchid and my grandson, Jaguar Paw, safe? Have they left Na Balam yet? Surely at the turtle's pace we have been traveling they should be able to catch up to us by now! What will I find once we get to Cuzamil? What is Heart of Water's state of mind? What is going on that makes her neglect her duties?

Just as I doze off, morning arrives with a light drizzle of rain. A throng of women and children dressed in pilgrims' blue-and-white mantles are packing up and leaving to get an early start on the *sacbe*. We eat our breakfast with Queen White Quetzal, whose attendants provide additional seed cakes and balls of dried blue corn.

"Lady, today I must walk," I announce as the palanquins appear. I have no patience for another day of bumping up and down. My mood is sour enough as it is. Lady White Quetzal gives me a disapproving look.

"I commune with my Goddess while I walk," I say, and she immediately accepts my explanation and orders her guards not to approach me. I know she hoped for my company so she would have someone to talk to, but I am weary of her haughtiness and constant, empty chatter.

"Nine Macaw must also walk for the rest of the day," I say firmly.

The queen sighs, but gives a nod. Nine Macaw shoots me a grateful look and eagerly runs off to join Blue Stone and Iguana Wind. As we walk along they hunt for ripe *nanci* fruit in the trees that grow alongside the *sacbe*. I can tell that we are nearing the ocean because the vegetation is changing and the soil is softer and sandier. Along the way, villagers cry out their singsong verses to tempt hungry travelers with slices of pineapples and roasted *guanacaste* seeds. For a time we walk on a length of road that is built over a swamp. I marvel at the engineering that accomplished this feat of raising a road to the height of a man.

Walking on the smooth, stone *sacbe* in the fine sandals gifted by Turquoise Sky is very pleasant. We are surrounded by guards and servants, and my bags are carried by the Lady's slaves. I feel practically carefree. Unfortunately, now that I am left to my own thoughts, all the uncertainties that worried me in the night spring back to mind. I wish I knew what was happening with the rest of my scattered, exiled family. I wish I knew what Nine Macaw and I will face when we get to Cuzamil. Is my sister being poisoned? Has one of her attendants betrayed her?

The girls walk ahead of me, laughing and pointing to birds, monkeys and flowers. They are happy to be alive on this bright morning cooled by the early rains. It fills my heart with joy to watch them. They are nearly the same height, but Blue Stone is thin as a reed. From the back, her shoulder bones stick out and her little arms are thin as twigs. Iguana Wind has been encouraging her to eat, but she is shy about eating in front of us. I guess that she doesn't want to seem greedy. Slaves who eat too much are often sold. She still doesn't quite believe that I will free her when we get to Cuzamil.

When we stop for fresh water at a shaded *cenote to rest* I hear Nine Macaw tell the younger girl, "It is not fitting for a queen to climb trees!" She imitates White Quetzal's haughty tone. "Picking fruit is the work of servants and slaves!"

Blue Stone looks devastated. She cringes and ducks her head as if expecting a blow.

I pull my granddaughter aside and have a few stern words with her.

"Child, being a good queen means not just being strong and proud, but being gentle and gracious. I know Lady White Quetzal is teaching you the manners she has learned as a ruler, but Cuzamil is not Palenque. The queen who sits on the Rainbow Throne must be known for kindness and generosity to all, no matter their station in life. Do you know why?"

Eyes down, Nine Macaw shakes her head.

"It is because you will rule in the name of Ix Chel, the Gentle Goddess, Protector of all. You will be queen, but you will also be a leader among the healers. Are the words you spoke to Blue Stone words of healing and kindness?"

Nine Macaw looks ashamed. "I understand, Na. I will apologize."

I smile at her. "Good girl."

Blue Stone has made herself scarce. Nine Macaw darts through the queen's entourage calling her name. For a few minutes, I enjoy quietly sitting by myself on the edge of the *cenote*, my tired, hot feet dangling in the cool water. Other travelers and pilgrims are also enjoying the shady rest spot. The pregnant queen dozes on cushions in her gauze-covered palanquin and has no need of my company. My mind drifts and I think about Jaguar Shield. How happy I will be to see him again! I list the probable reasons why he has not yet overtaken us on the road. Perhaps Water Lily is injured and cannot travel swiftly. Or Tree Orchid is not strong enough to leave Na Balam.

"Mother, have you seen Nine Macaw and Blue Stone?" Iguana Wind is out of breath. In his arms are ripe avocados. "I stepped off the road to gather avocados for the girls. Blue Stone loves them. On my way back I thought I heard Nine Macaw calling out for you."

I look around frantically, but there is no sign of them.

"Girls!" I call, panic in my voice. "Girls! Come here now!"

Lady White Quetzal hears my shout and barks an order to her soldiers and servants, who fan out and methodically move through the dense forest around us. The other pilgrims looks at us curiously and I cringe. As if they can feel our tension, a flock of dark birds take sudden flight. Their high-pitched squeals rattle my nerves even more.

Iguana Wind and I hurry to the edge of the dark forest and call Blue Stone's name. I don't want to call Nine Macaw's for fear an enemy will recognize her name and know we are here.

How could I have been so foolish, so lost in my own thoughts? Of course Pus Master knows where we are headed. Everyone in Coba saw us leave in the entourage of the queen of Palenque. I have been lulled into complacency and now Nine Macaw is missing. I shiver with dread.

"Calm yourself," the queen is beside me, her hand on my back, her tone one of genuine concern. "Perhaps they only wandered too far and got lost. Have faith. Your cause is Her cause. She will protect the child."

Her words remind me I am not just a worried grandmother, but a priestess of Ix Chel. Before I can ask my Goddess for Her help Iguana Wind shouts: "Over here!"

We rush over to find him examining tracks in the dirt. They lead into the thicket of vines and trees.

I start to march in that direction, but he grips my arm. "Mother, you must stay here. It may not be safe."

Iguana Wind races into the dense jungle accompanied by four burly slaves—the ones who carry the queen's palanquin.

"Over here! Come! Be quick!" we hear them call to one another.

My heart is in my throat and I am ready to race away to join them. Two stern-faced soldiers stop me. "Noble Lady, please—you must wait here."

White Quetzal grips my hand. "Sister, it will be well," she says, gripping my hand.

I pray she is right. Ix Chel, protect my precious feathers! I grip my *pi*, the medicine bag I wear around my neck. I gather strength from it and try to calm myself.

A limb crashes to the ground. Faintly, I hear shouts and curses and the sounds of struggle. Someone yells. Was that a cry of pain?

"I must go to them! I am a healer!"

"Not yet." White Quetzal holds me firmly in place. "This is work for soldiers, not healers."

It feels like an eternity passes. I am about to lose the contents of my stomach from anxiety. Finally, out of the sun-dappled jungle, Iguana Wind staggers toward me. In his arms he carries Nine Macaw. Behind him one of the queen's slaves carries Blue Stone.

"Goddess, thank You!" I moan with relief. "Thank You for delivering my precious feathers back to me!"

I run to meet them. Iguana Wind is bleeding fast from a nasty slash across his right arm. The girls are bruised and battered and sobbing in their rescuers' arms. Their mantles are torn and dirty. One of Blue Stone's sandals is gone. The child has a look of utter terror on her smudged face and I see a welt the shape of a handprint rising on her cheek.

"My precious jades, tell me what happened!"

Nine Macaw collapses in my arms and we hold each other tightly. Blue Stone clings to Iguana Wind.

"We were just looking for fruit," Nine Macaw says in a trembling voice. "We climbed a tree to pick sour cherries. I went first. I heard a shout and there was a man grabbing Blue Stone by the leg! He yanked her out of the tree and she screamed at me to climb higher, so I did."

"There were two of them," says Blue Stone, still in shock. Iguana Wind lifts a gourd to her mouth and she obediently drinks water. Wiping her mouth, she leans back against him and clasps her knees. "Na, I didn't know what to do! I had to protect the princess, but it all happened so fast. I didn't... I couldn't..." She starts to sob.

"You are both safe, and that is the most important thing," says Iguana Wind. He and I exchange a look. Only by the hand of Ix Chel are these girls with us now and not in the hands of Pus Master.

"Blue Stone, you did save me!" says Nine Macaw. "I did as you said and climbed as high as I could go. I heard you fighting them, and I wanted to help. I saw a rotten branch and tried to kick it loose so it would fall on the men."

"That was very quick thinking," Lady White Quetzal says approvingly. She and her soldiers are standing in a circle around us. Word of the near-abduction has spread among the travelers and the commotion is drawing a curious crowd. The Palenque *nacom* shoos them away.

"But I couldn't kick it hard enough and they were hurting Blue Stone! So I jumped on the branch three times until it cracked, and then I fell with it."

We all gasp. What a terribly brave thing to do!

"The branch and Nine Macaw landed right on the shoulders of the man who was holding me!" Blue Stone says, her eyes lighting up a bit. "He fell on top of me and I couldn't breathe, but he was slippery with grease so I was able to wiggle out."

"I was scared, so I prayed to the Great Mother to protect me," Nine Macaw says, picking up the story. "The branch fell away and hit the man and then I came down on top of him and rolled to the side. The second man lunged at me. He was furious! He held me on the ground and started to tie my feet. I grabbed a sharp stone and hit him on the head as hard as I could!" She waves her arm, demonstrating how she did it. "Blue Stone kicked him in the knee and pulled me up and then we ran! He chased us, and we shouted and shouted and then Iguana Wind came!"

White Quetzal puts a gentle hand on Nine Macaw's head. "Well done, little Sister. You and your slave are safe. That is what matters most. Now you will witness the execution of your would-be kidnappers."

"Regrettably, they ran like deer through the jungle and disappeared, Noble Lady," her *nacom* reports. The eagle tattoo on his face indicates that he holds the highest military rank possible to achieve, and the many scars on his arms and legs are proof that he has survived many battles. But he still cringes at his queen's disapproving glare. "From the girls' description we know they are Putun," he continues quickly. "Their spies use an old trick, greasing themselves with peccary fat so that none can hold onto them. But we have nets. I assure you, my men will catch them."

White Quetzal gives him a pointed look and he immediately barks out an order. Four fierce soldiers step forward.

"Do not return without those two slippery eels," White Quetzal tells them. "A fine reward for you if you find them; severe consequences if you do not."

The four sprint into the jungle and the rest of the soldiers fan out in a defensive formation around the *cenote*. "Sister, let us stay off the *sacbe* for now," White Quetzal says to me quietly, eyeing the gossipy crowd. "We are still a long day's walk from the safety of Pole-by-the-Sea. Here we can stay in the temporary shelter."

Along the route to Cuzamil, between the inns, are small stations set up near roadside shrines. These are places where travelers may rest. The shelter here is a stone platform beside the *cenote*. It has a basic, open-air hearth and a tidy pile of kitchen utensils, water gourds and clay pots for travelers' use. Nearby, a pile of stones indicates a *chultun*—an underground store of dried food. I hope Heart of Water's slaves have been here recently to replenish the stock.

It is not for me to command the queen on this journey. She and I both know that we will do as she desires, but I appreciate her effort to couch her command in polite terms.

"That is a wise idea, Lady. The girls are exhausted from their ordeal and you must rest, too, for the sake of the baby. I would like to make an offering at this shrine to give the Goddess my thanks before we move on."

"Just so!" she perks up. "I will come with you." I sigh to myself. "But we must remain here until my guards return with the prisoners. How dare they attack someone in my entourage! It is an insult to my lineage and my dynasty! Before I kill them we will get the truth out of them."

While the energized queen directs her servants to set up a pavilion to her specifications, a slave brings my medicine bag. Nine Macaw is only limping a little. Goddess, thank You for preserving my precious jade! I shudder to think of Nine Macaw falling from that tree! But I am concerned about Blue Stone. Her pulse is thin and uneven and her eyes are out of focus. It could be a concussion on top of shock. I brew a tea of cedar bark and urge the little girl to drink it. Iguana Wind is the one who soothes her. Even though he insists it's just a scratch, Iguana Wind's arm wound needs attention. We both know the dangers of knife wound going septic—even a scratch. We also both know the Putun routinely poison their blades. I check his pulse and pupils and look for redness where the blade split open the forearm skin. I see no evidence of poison at this point. Blue Stone watches with professional interest as Nine Macaw and I bind the wound with a freshly crushed poultice of *axcanan* leaves, which are powerful healing agents.

"Son, thank you," I say as I gently tie off the cloth bandage. My voice is husky with tears.

"Mother, I only wish I had kept a closer eye on them. It's my fault—"

"No, it's all my fault!" cries Blue Stone. "If only I had not gone for cherries."

"But it was I who sang in the tree," says Nine Macaw. "It's my fault that those men heard us and—"

"This is no one's fault but the filthy Putun's!" I tell them all sternly. "And this is the fault of my brother, Blood Gatherer! This is the fault of the greed of men! This is the fault of the War God. None of you are to blame, do you hear me?" I look each one in the eye until I see a nod of acknowledgment. "Good. But now we must not let our guard down even for a moment. Not until we are safe in Cuzamil."

White Quetzal's attendants have prepared the open-air pavilion for us with cushions and animal skins. Perfumed gauze curtains give us privacy. The slave women rush about preparing our evening meal of corn cakes stuffed with beans and chili along with dried fruits and berries from the *chultun*. I guide the girls to a quiet corner and they lie down. Holding their wrists, I murmur prayers to soothe fright, sending my calming *chu'lel* into their racing, bouncing pulses. Finally, they relax.

The queen assigns two women to attend us for our baths in the *cenote*, with four guards standing close by. The soldiers glare at the nosy pilgrims, who back off and leave us in peace. Then the guards turn their backs to us and watch for approaching danger.

Once again clean and dressed in fresh mantles, we fill our bellies and life looks a lot brighter. The girls are recovering. They still cling to me, but I see color coming back into their faces. Blue Stone's pulse is strong and even and her headache is gone. She holds a poultice of *axcanan* to her cheek to reduce the swelling. I turn my attention to Nine Macaw, then rifle through my bag and find the last of my salve. I slather it on her cuts and darkening bruises.

Blue Stone and Iguana Wind talk quietly and watch the forest edge for the return of the soldiers with the Putun prisoners.

"Na," Nine Macaw whispers, sidling up beside me. There is a serious expression on her face that I have never seen before.

"What is it, precious one?"

"Na, there are other girls of the Chel line with the Goddess's gifts, are there not?"

I nod. "You have cousins who serve the Goddess. What is this about?"

"Na, I think—it is better if I join Red Earth."

I am confused for a moment. Her older sister hung herself by a rope so she could join Ix Tab in the paradise for suicides.

"That way, the heart takers would never have me, and our family would be safe," she continues. "I could see Red Earth again and keep her company in Ix Tab's paradise. Na. I would do it to protect our family. I have thought it through and it is the only way to be sure Cuzamil will be safe!"

I am too shocked to speak. Nine Macaw lays her head on my shoulder.

"Na, I know you love me, but I would not put the people I love in danger anymore. There is nowhere in the Known World where the Putun won't hunt for me, is there? Even if we go to Cuzamil they will bring the war to the sacred Island of Women and more people will be hurt. If I die first their plans are ruined. They will have no cause to attack us. My family will be safe."

"No!" I finally find my voice. "No! Nine Macaw, you have it all wrong, child! You must promise me that you will never—"

Triumphant shouts from the perimeter guards announce the arrival of White Quetzal's men dragging the Putun kidnappers behind them. The *nacom* runs up to congratulate them and make sure the prisoners have been well-secured before they approach the Queen of Palenque. I give my precious jade a long, sad look and tell her we will continue this conversation later. She nods solemnly. *Om bey!* How could such a terrible idea come into her head?

The *nacom* shoves the prisoners to their knees and then drags them forward by a rope secured to wooden rings around their necks. The Queen of Palenque sits on her cushion-covered chair with her feet up to support her lower back. She lazily licks the last of her dinner from her fingers before deigning to look at the small, grease-covered men cowering before her. They are two scrawny, half-starved commoners—evident by the bald circle at the crown of their heads. They reek of animal fat gone rancid. One of them has a puckered socket where his left eye used to be. Were it not for the seriousness of the situation they would look a comical pair because one is very tall and the other very short. The *nacom* grinds their faces into the dirt while White Quetzal watches impassively. The prisoners choke and cough. The *nacom* nods to two of his men, who come forward and whack the captives' ankles with heavy clubs. I cringe to hear the sharp crack of bones breaking and shrieks of pain. Two more soldiers step forward and efficiently go to work breaking wrists and fingers.

Much as I detest these would-be kidnappers, I have no stomach for violence. White Quetzal is in charge here and it is not my place to tell her how to conduct these affairs, but I subtly avert my eyes. The girls can't take it. They hide their faces in their hands.

"Enough!" the queen says. "Find out everything they know."

The guards drag them away for interrogation. The sudden silence is a relief.

"Tea!" White Quetzal commands, and her servants run to fill her gourd. I am just coaxing the girls to drink some soothing tea when the *nacom* returns. His legs are splattered with blood.

"They have both gone to the waters," he reports, his nostrils flaring so that the jade piercing juts out even more.

Lady White Quetzal sends her retinue and the disappointed onlookers away and motions me closer. The girls, still clinging to me, try to follow, but White Quetzal shakes her head once. Iguana Wind puts a protective arm around each of them and ushers them to the other side of the pavilion.

"What did you learn?" she demands of her captain when I settle beside her.

"Noble Lady, they served the one called Pus Master, the High Priest of Na Balam. Their orders were to bring Princess Nine Macaw back to Na Balam before we reached Pole-by-the-Sea. Pus Master planned to sacrifice the girl to his War God on the day of Ix Chel's festival." He turns and spits, as if even having to utter those words has poisoned his lips. "It was meant to have been an insult to the Great Mother Ix Chel, who favors the Chel women of the Rainbow Throne. Pus Master planned to make a public display of the War God's dominance over the Goddess of Life by beheading the princess, peeling off her skin, dressing himself in it and then dancing atop the Temple of the War God."

I feel sick. I know what would have happened next. The priests would have carved up my granddaughter and distributed her body parts to the other high priests and Putun warriors. They would have made a grand show of eating the heir to the Rainbow Throne to prove to the people that the War God was victorious against the Great Mother. I am trembling with rage, fear and sorrow. What savages are these Putun! How can our people—how can any people—allow these atrocities to continue?

"Filthy demons!" White Quetzal pounds her fist into her hand. "That Pus Master has a twisted mind. He declares war on Ix Chel? Who is he to defy the Goddess who gave him life?! Heart takers are an abomination! They must be cast out of our lands!" She fixes me with an imperious look and points a long, ringed finger at my nose. "You are not to let the princess out of our sight until we reach Cuzamil! Not even for an instant! This dispute Pus Master has with you is bigger than I realized. With Chichen under their influence and now Na Balam fallen to the Putun, we must not give the War God a victory over Cuzamil—not at any cost! Otherwise, it will not be long before Palenque and our neighbors fall to these foreign interlopers. We must stop them before they consolidate their power!"

I vehemently agreed with everything White Quetzal is saying, yet as I listen to her I feel strange, as if I am floating above these concerns. What is happening to me? All the strength seeps from my limbs. I feel dizzy, yet I rise and try to walk.

"Jade Skirt! What is the matter?" The queen is still riled up and her tone is more annoyed than concerned.

"I must go to the shrine now and pray," I say, feeling strangely calm, yet also alarmed at this sensation. "I need to understand better what She wants of us."

"Yes, Oracle," White Quetzal says, nodding her approval. "I wish you would. We need Her protection and guidance now more than ever. I still smell a stink on the wind. More Putun will surely make an attempt to grab Nine Macaw. When Pus Master learns that his spies have failed he will send an army after us. What will we do, with only twelve soldiers and twenty slaves to protect us?"

She would say more, but I am starting to slip away. I am aware of tingling in my hands and feet, my heart pounding. As if in a tunnel, I hear Her call my name, and then Nine Macaw and Iguana Wind are speaking to me urgently. Have I fainted? No. I recognize this state. This is how I feel before She speaks through me as her Oracle. But how is this possible when I have not been prepared with the ritual baths or taken the necessary enemas and herbal preparations?

The need is great.

Her voice inside me is my own voice, yet it is also Hers.

Use me as you need. I serve You, Lady Mother.

Hear Me now, Children, and heed My words.

The voice coming from me is not my own. It is the voice of the Goddess, as indescribable as the voice of water, wind and thunder. The part of me that maintains awareness of Jade Skirt is aware of the others gasping in surprise.

You do well to defy the heart takers, but you cannot defeat them if you become like them.

My body rises to its feet without my will. The others back away respectfully. Rainbow light fills my eyes and the part of me that is still me receives this miracle with amazement. To see through the eyes of the Goddess—it is beyond description! I See everyone's pulsing *chu'lel* like iridescent bubbles floating in the air. This gaze falls on White Quetzal. The queen's eyes are round with wonder.

Remember. All life is precious to Me. I created each one of you, even the heart takers. I am the Mother of All. To serve Me is to revere the life force I have placed in each of you!

I See the young queen surrounded by a warm glow, but there is a small blotch of darkness spreading in her womb like a blooming bruise. My healer hands remember that this is where she landed when she fell, but before I can worry about what it means for the child the Goddess lays a finger—my finger, I note with calm detachment—on White Quetzal's abdomen. A ray of light pierces the womb. The queen gives a small gasp of surprise and the stain is gone. Through Ix Chel's eyes I can See the baby. He is perfectly formed and positioned to come into the world safely. I experience the Knowing of Ix Chel. This child will one day become a just ruler devoted to honoring Her and Her creation. I See him as a man, tall and proud. On his forehead is a birthmark in the shape of Her serpent. Blessed indeed is this future king of Palenque! That mark will assure the success of his dynasty.

The Great Mother turns Her gaze to the *nacom*, whose eyes reveal his fear and awe. She sees through to his soul. There is a frayed brown rope wrapped around his throat, chest and hands strangling him with inner conflict and self-doubt.

Better it is to win their hearts to Our cause than to still their hearts with sharp blades.

He lowers his eyes in shame. Then She speaks a word I cannot understand, although it is said with my voice. Rainbow light flashes for an instant and burns away the brown ring. The *nacom* gasps with surprise. Now I See his *chu'lel* emanates a sea blue. Strength and loyalty pulse from his heart to his hands. He stands taller and bows to Her. She lets me See that he understands that his heart must guide him and not his desire for the powerful feelings he experiences when he carries out violent acts in duty to his queen.

Even the Gods and Goddesses suffer. It is the nature of existence.

She speaks now to Iguana Wind.

But I made you to be strong. Love is worthy of you even though it brings all to grief one day.

I am dismayed to See a sickly yellow thread moving through my dear Iguana Wind's body as if woven into his very fiber. With Her understanding I realize it is the accumulation of *tuns* of longing for his true family. And now there is a fresh blot of grief for his dead son, which covers his heart.

Please, Mother, please help this beloved son of mine!

Ix Chel purses my lips and three times She blows Divine breath into Iguana Wind's *chu'lel*. The first breath loosens the yellow strands. The second causes them to drift apart like smoke. The third whistles with the sound of springtime calling to the plants to rise from their sleep. Iguana Wind's life force surges up in lush greens as rich and deep as the jungle. I See Iguana Wind as She Sees him: goodness and kindness pump through every part of him like sap in the great *ceiba* tree.

I never abandon any of My children. I am always with you.

This She says to Blue Stone. This abandoned child is surrounded by a blue light as clear and strong as the sky. Even so, black clouds darken her bright spirit and Ix Chel shows me that this is the pain the little girl carries from a lifetime without love, caring or kindness. The Great Mother gazes into the child's eyes with the expression a new mother has when she meets her precious feather for the first time. Blue Stone drinks it in like a dry field when the rains finally come. The Goddess lays my/Her hand on Blue Stone's forehead and a pulse of pure, white love fills the child and burns away the darkness. The Goddess allows me to See one more thing: a glowing mark in the shape of Her serpent on Blue Stone's forehead. She lets me See that one day Blue Stone and White Quetzal's son will be linked in a significant way through this mark of the Goddess. The Gods and Goddesses lay their plans across countless generations.

Finally, She turns to Nine Macaw. Through Ix Chel's sight I See my granddaughter as a tall sapling with first leaves just starting to unfurl. Nine Macaw's opalescent aura is shot through with rainbows. She is unimaginably beautiful! The Goddess lets me feel Her pleasure with this precious heir, who carries all the gifts with which Ix Chel has blessed our lineage.

Nine Macaw, you have I chosen to guard and protect My sacred Island. You have I chosen to shelter all women and to inspire and instruct them to become compassionate and wise healers.

Nine Macaw bows her head. Through the Goddess's vision I See her struggle with her doubts and guilt.

My child, you doubt yourself, but all things happen for a reason, even if you cannot understand it. Trust in Me, and trust in yourself.

Our Goddess holds my/Her hands above Nine Macaw's head and throws back my/Her head. My/her hands gather rainbow light that falls from the sky and rises from the earth. I feel like I am standing in a stream of bliss! Ix Chel, blessed Mother, weaves the rainbows into Nine Macaw's *chu'lel*. Nine Macaw stands before us glowing and pulsing. With Her vision I See the maiden become a living rainbow!

I offer you the Divine right of rule on the Rainbow Throne. You will preserve My sanctuary for generations to come. To serve Me well you must study and learn and grow wise. I will bless your hands so that they may heal. I will speak through you so that wisdom falls from your lips. If you accept Me and trust in Me, I will be with you always. Nine Macaw, if you choose this path. You will ever be My most precious jade.

My/Her hands hold Nine Macaw's face and through Her vision I see rainbows swirling in the girl's eyes. When finally the Mother of Life draws my/Her hands from Nine Macaw's smooth cheeks I hear gasps from the others as She allows them to See the mark of the rabbit on the girl's left cheek and the mark of the serpent on the right. The glowing tattoos, drawn in pure light, fade to the others' sight, but I can still See them through Her vision.

Then Ix Chel speaks a last, private word to me:

Daughter, rest your fears for now, but not your vigilance. Tie up your turkeys first; then trust in Me.

Ix Chel's Presence sings a farewell through my *chu'lel* like the sweetest honey, and then She is gone. Iguana Wind catches me as I start to fall and he gently lowers me to the ground. The others are still staring in wonder at Nine Macaw. She stands before us, her sight turned inward, gazing still at what the Goddess has shown her. Then she sighs and looks up at us. Before she can speak, White Quetzal grasps her *nacom's* arm and holds him as she struggles to her knees. Ceremoniously, she touches her forehead to the ground in front of Nine Macaw. The others follow suit, prostrating themselves before the chosen one of the Goddess Ix Chel, Mother of the World. Only I catch the look of horror on my granddaughter's face. Being chosen by the Goddess is a great destiny, indeed, but it is not an easy path. I give her a sympathetic look. Nine Macaw nods, but for the first time ever I cannot read the meaning in her expression. I do not know what is in her heart. It leaves me with a light feeling of foreboding, but I remember the Goddess's advice. I will focus on what can be done and trust in Her to guide our steps.

4
● ● ● ●

As Father Sun settles in the west, we finally arrive at Pole-by-the-Sea. I am so relieved to see my beloved ocean and smell the salty air of home that I must wipe away a tear or two. Cuzamil is just a tiny dot I can barely make out on the horizon, way past the white-capped waves. So close! I cannot believe we are almost there!

With the festival of Ix Chel approaching there are crowds of pilgrims waiting for the barges to make the night crossing to the Island of Women. The women come from all parts of the Known World, and I know each feels as relieved and excited as I do to be this close to the sanctuary sacred to Ix Chel. Pole is the gateway to Cuzamil and even at this late hour the market stalls are busy selling salt, honey, weavings and other wares made by the industrious women on Cuzamil. The air is redolent with *copal* from the countless shrines to the Goddess that are placed every twenty paces along the shore. Thankfully, White Quetzal does not feel the need to stop and make offerings and prayers at each one. I insisted that she walk for a part of the day. The belly band is working, but too much sitting and jostling is not good for her. Thankfully, she readily agrees to follow any advice I give her, but the walking tired her out. Our journey was delayed as she stopped often to get on and get off her palanquin.

After our extraordinary visit from Ix Chel yesterday evening we all gradually returned to ourselves. Nine Macaw drew into herself. She seems older to me—still the same sweet girl, yet something has changed. That is to be expected, I tell myself, after such a blessed experience as she had with the Great Mother. I do not ask her to speak of her experience with me. Well do

I remember the first time Ix Chel used me as Her vessel when I became Her Oracle. Even my mother, who had long been Her Oracle, accorded me the respect of privacy. From that day forward she treated me as a beloved equal. I must do the same now for Nine Macaw. She is on the path the Goddess has ordained for her and it is not my place to intrude on their intimacy.

Blue Stone has only just stopped gaping at Nine Macaw in adoring wonder. It happened after Nine Macaw swallowed water the wrong way and ended up spitting it out of her nose, which caused both girls to collapse in giggles. I am glad Blue Stone remembers that Nine Macaw is still just a girl. I hope she will be a true friend to my granddaughter. When Nine Macaw is Queen of Cuzamil she will have plenty of devotees and priestesses jockeying for favor and power, but few true friends, I fear.

Pole is a seaside center dedicated entirely to Ix Chel and the needs of Cuzamil's pilgrims. Seeing the diverse clothing, body paint and hairstyles makes me nostalgic. Our father lived here and I have many pleasant childhood memories of visiting him. Heart of Water, Blood Gatherer and I loved to guess where the different pilgrims came from. When we had the chance, we asked them for stories of their journeys through jungles, over mountains and even across wide rivers. Ix Chel's most sacred festival, which celebrates the day the Great Mother and First Father came together to create the world, is less than half a moon away, on 1 Zip. It is the most popular time of the calendar for pilgrims to visit because it is considered the most auspicious day of the *tun*. Cuzamil celebrates with five joyous days of dancing and festivities at all five temples on the sacred Island. The celebrations start at sunrise and continue until late each night. The excitement here in Pole is contagious and my heart lifts with anticipation. It is my favorite festival of the *tun*!

People make way for our entourage. Nine Macaw and I are both riding in our palanquins. The *nacom* insisted that it would be easier to protect us in these crowds. It makes me nervous to see so many staring curiously at us, but soon I am distracted by the happy chaos of Pole. There are a group of women of the third age patiently herding a group of children into the *polna* for orphans. They will be ferried to the sacred Island, where they will be cared for by our childless women. Beside that building is a larger *polna* for maidens seeking entry to the most famous mystery schools, our *calmecacs*, to train as midwives, healers, weavers and priestesses. Scrying with crystals and water is one of the specialties of Cuzamil-trained priestesses.

Many of the women who come to Cuzamil to learn will eventually leave the Island and serve Her in Temples and *polnas* all over the Known World.

We pass by the *polna* dedicated to pregnant women awaiting passage to the Island, and I know it will be filled to the brim for the next few days as expectant mothers flock to the Island. Like the Queen of Palenque, every woman hopes that her child will be born on the Island on the Goddess's sacred feast day of 1 Zip, because those fortunate children will live doubly blessed lives. The *polna* is staffed with midwives, because often the babies don't wait until their mothers reach the Island. Thankfully, White Quetzal's servants ran ahead and arranged rooms for us at the *polna* for nobles, which will be a more peaceful place for us to rest.

We pass the *polna* for widows who will be making a one-way trip to Cuzamil. They will spend their last days in the company of other women, well-cared-for and peaceful. These elders are tended by abandoned and abused women who find sanctuary and productive work on the Island of Women and who in turn are cared for by the ruler of the Rainbow Throne. Heart of Water spends much time encouraging and honoring these women, for whom the sanctuary of Cuzamil means the difference between life and death. Their wisdom and life experiences are prized on the sacred Island.

Finally, we arrive at the inn for nobles. I am delighted to climb down from the palanquin. This *polna* has a famous steam bath. I am looking forward to visiting it. But first White Quetzal sends her royal messenger to the canoes to carry a message across the sea to Heart of Water this very evening to tell her we have arrived in Pole and await the royal barge.

"You see, Jade Skirt, I kept my end of the bargain," White Quetzal says to me smugly as the hearth mistress hurriedly brings us gourds of tea sweetened with allspice and honey. "We have made it to Pole safely. But do not relax your vigilance! The Putun scum have spies everywhere!"

I bow to her and thank her for her care of us on this journey.

"Just so," she says. "Now it is up to you to hold up your end of the bargain!" She rubs her pregnant belly and gives me a meaningful look.

I hope I can keep my promise. Even knowing the Goddess has blessed the child in her womb, I still don't know Ix Chel's plans. Perhaps she does not want him to be born on 1 Zip. Only She and the Calendar Gods can say when this precious feather will be born. Unlike me, White Quetzal seems to be unconcerned that she is interfering with the Gods of Fate and the Bearers of Days.

The *nulha* is every bit as wonderful as I remembered. We go to sleep on soft beds of sweet herbs.

In the morning, Nine Macaw and Blue Stone wake before dawn and beg me to take them to the beach. Nine Macaw was born on Cuzamil, but she has no memory of it or of the ocean crossing. Blue Stone has never seen the sea and peppers Iguana Wind with questions about it, too excited to listen to his answers. I am easy to convince. I have been missing the sea for many long *tuns*.

"Lady, I insist that you take four soldiers with you. We must assume the Putun have spies in Pole," says White Quetzal.

I readily agree. Iguana Wind asks my permission to go make inquires about his wife and daughters at her distant relatives' compound. Of course, I tell him yes. When he is finished he can join us at my son's house. Anyone can tell him where Spear Thrower, Magistrate of Pole, lives.

After our breakfast of dog tamales delivered to our rooms by the Hearth Mistress herself (a tiny woman from the Coc lineage with a pleasant disposition), the impatient girls rush me and our guards down to the shore.

Nine Macaw stops in her tracks, overwhelmed by the vast horizon.

"So much water gathered in one place! And listen to it—the water growls and roars!"

Blue Stone giggles, but I know what my granddaughter means. The sea has its own voice. The girls and I splash in the shallow surf. Even the Palenque soldiers smile at our antics.

"Na!" shouts Nine Macaw. "It's just like *cenote* water. I thought it would feel different."

Blue Stone scoops water in her palm and bends down to drink.

"Better not!" I warn her. "It's salty! You can't drink this water."

Nevertheless, she has to lick it with her tongue. "Pah!" She spits it out with great force. "*Om bey!* Yuck!" She laughs and jumps back, nearly crashing Into a naked toddler playing in the waves with his older sister.

We walk along the beach splashing in the water. The girls stoop down to admire shells and sea-polished stones. We pass canoe paddlers—these are always men of the Bolon lineage, who proudly serve the Rainbow Throne in this capacity. They stand in the lapping waters engaging in their usual morning debate about the day's weather and winds. The sea crossing can only be attempted when the currents are calm. It is their responsibility to determine from day to day if it is safe to paddle women and children through the unpredictable currents that surround Cuzamil. Only the Bolon men know how to navigate safely to the Island. It is a closely guarded secret. Those who do not know the routes and temperaments of Cuzamil's ocean find themselves tossed back on the shore of Pole again and again. It is a very effective way for the Goddess to protect Her sanctuary. The Bolon paddlers are engaged in a heated discussion. The headman, who wears nine blue feathers in his topknot, points repeatedly to the north where wisps of clouds can be seen, and shakes his head ominously.

We walk on and I breathe in the perfect sea air and suddenly all I want to do is sit on this warm sand and enjoy this moment. While the girls frolic in the water, I squat down beside a group of women of the second age.

"Blessings of the day," I say amiably.

Curious eyes turn toward me. "Blessings of the day, Noble Lady." They look curiously at the soldiers guarding my back, but I look away and they go back to their conversations and watching their little charges playing in the waves. They talk about where they are from and where they are staying. Some are nobles like me, with flattened foreheads, jade-inlaid teeth and jade jewelry. The commoners wear simple jewelry made of fish and bird bones. Since we are all pilgrims, we dress the same regardless of social status—plain blue mantles with white trim around the neck and hem. Two younger women from the south, both heavy with child, have shaven heads and red-painted hands and feet. Bellies bulge under purple-ringed nipples. And there are three women from the far south who wear coils of braids twisted in high towers and bright-red faces with paint made from the seeds of the *annatto* tree. We watch the naked children frolic in the turquoise waves and shout encouragement as they build sand temples with courtyards and little houses edged with sea shells.

"Sisters, did any of you get dinner last night at your *polnas*?" one woman asks.

"I did not," scowls one of the southern women. "They ran out of food! What is going on? I never before heard of any shortages at the pilgrims' inns."

"I hear all is not well with Queen Heart of Water."

"That is what everyone has been saying all along the *sacbe*. We heard complaints about food shortages and not enough help to cook and clean for the pilgrims. It's a scandal!"

I'm glad when Blue Stone and Nine Macaw run over to get me. I leave the group and take the girls' hands. Trailed by the soldiers, we stroll along the beach and are pushed along by a strong ocean breeze.

Suddenly, I hear a familiar, faint sound of a conch shell blowing. It makes my heart soar. From atop the highest tower on the Temple of the Moon, which sits on the west side of the sacred Island, the conches blow twice daily—morning and evening. There are four shells, each oriented toward one of the four directions and each sounding a different note. As the morning wind passes through the shells, the intensity of the tone tells the wind's strength and reveals its direction. The sound the paddlers fear blows from the east. Huracan, God of Winds, blows from that direction. I recognize today's conch song. The wind blows from the north. A cheer goes up from the pilgrims and paddlers waiting on the beach. Despite a few ominous clouds on the horizon, we can expect a benevolent wind. The Bolon men jog to the beach to lift their canoes and carry them into the shallow surf. Paddlers and passengers start to load bundles quickly. They want to start their journeys quickly to take advantage of this auspicious weather.

"Na! Look!" Blue Stone points to a group of nine blue-robed priestesses from Cuzamil standing in a half-circle. Their crowns of rainbow-colored ribbons remind me of my sister, my mother and my grandmother. Priestesses come every morning, I explain to the girls, to bless each boat and each pilgrim as she boards the canoe. They operate within a thick cloud of *copal* smoke. The smell drifts over to us on a breeze and I enjoy a deep breath of the sweet fragrance.

"Sometimes the paddlers will set out when conditions are deemed favorable, only to find the fickle sea has changed its mind and wants to send them off course," I say. "They ask for Ix Chel's protection on the journey."

"Ix Chel, Queen of the Sea, protect Your pilgrims and bring them to safety," the priestesses intone. "Huracan, God of Winds, hold back Your force until the feet of these pilgrims touch firm ground."

"You say I might be one of them someday?" Blue Stone asks me shyly, her eyes never leaving the priestesses.

"Yes, if you prove worthy, humble and obedient. Ix Chel has a plan for you, little one."

"I will be Queen!" Nine Macaw says proudly, glancing at me for approval. I frown a little. Although what she says is true, boasting is not a trait the future queen should indulge. Nine Macaw sees my disapproval and looks away, stung.

"How many people can that boat carry?" Blue Stone asks.

The boats are two strides wide and eight strides long. "Every boat can carry twenty women and children," I explain, "with room for twelve paddlers and a headman to call the strokes." Palm-thatched canopies above the wooden benches protect the passengers from Father Sun's burning rays.

The lapping sound of the waves against the canoes mixes with the priestess's prayers and the excited shouts of children. It awakens so many sweet memories in me.

It will be a full dawn-to-dusk day of paddling to reach the Island of Cuzamil, even with favorable winds and cooperative currents. At day's end, the rowers will take their rest in their own *polna* on the west side of the Island, the landing place for pilgrims' boats in Cuzamil. This is the only place men are allowed to stay on the Island, save for Chunkunab, the small traders' settlement in the isolated north side of Cuzamil, where mosquitoes are as big as a hand. During their brief stays on the Island, the Bolon men may not go further than twenty strides into the interior of the Island. The Bolon are fiercely honorable. None would ever even think of breaking Her law. After a good meal and comfortable night's rest, they ferry back pilgrims making the return journey to Pole.

I search the horizon for the royal barge, but of course it is too soon to expect to see it. Our message only went across to the Island on last night's boat. It will take some time to relay it to the interior of the Island, where Heart of Water resides in the Rainbow Palace. Then a message must be sent back to the paddlers and only then will the canoe make its way across the sea to fetch us. I am impatient for it to get here, but I don't expect it until tomorrow evening at the soonest.

In spite of my eagerness to get to the Island of Women, I have such a sinking feeling about my sister. Is she well? What awaits us across the waters? I hold my *pi*, the medicine bag I wear always around my neck, and send a strong current of *chu'lel* across the water.

"Heart of Water, precious Sister, I will be with you soon!" I say in my heart.

"Na! Look at the clown with the monkeys!"

Blue Stone points to a wooden boardwalk where a clown performs handstands and somersaults with six well-trained monkeys. Past the clown is a group of girls a few *tuns* older than Nine Macaw and Blue Stone. Dressed in colorful mantles and crowns of marigold flowers, they dance in a circle, spinning and leaping with startling grace. Nine Macaw is captivated.

"Can we go see?" my granddaughter begs, not even able to tear her eyes away to look at me and ask properly. She is so caught up in the dancing she has forgotten to breathe. I hesitate, worried for our safety in the crowd, but two of the soldiers stick so close to us we could stumble over their feet. Today they wear plain white loincloths and turkey feathers in their topknots rather than the bold colors and feathers of soldiers of their queen, so as not to draw attention to their presence. The older one gives me a slight shake of the head. I agree that we are not safe here. We are so close to reaching safety. But Nine Macaw is trembling with her need to see the dancers up close.

"You must both hold my hands and promise not to let go," I say sternly. "And we will not stay long." Behind me, I hear a deep sigh of frustration from the soldier.

"Thank you, Na!" Nine Macaw flashes me a brilliant smile and then tugs us over to the dancers. My granddaughter wiggles her way to the front of the crowd, eagerly towing me and Blue Stone along. The guards struggle to stay with us.

A young boy beats a well-polished gourd drum in a fast rhythm and suddenly the dancers whirl into the middle. They twist and leap with breathtaking ease, turning in the air as if they are feathers blown in the wind. They are extraordinarily good. Although I don't recognize the dance, I recognize the woman of the third age who watches the dancers with a proprietary eye. She is a relative of my son's wife's mother. The family is famous for their dancing schools. These must be her students.

When the dance ends Nine Macaw begs us to wait and see if they will perhaps perform another.

"Don't you want to visit the vendors?" I ask, amused by her enthusiasm.

She glances at the line of merchants doing a brisk morning business selling turkey stew and tamales, and statues and amulets of the Goddess that were made and blessed by priestesses from Cuzamil's five temples.

"I would rather see the dancers," says my granddaughter wistfully. But a moment later the dancers march off with their teacher. Nine Macaw stares after them, disappointment on her face.

"I see someone eating amaranth-and-honey cakes!" Blue Stone reports. Nine Macaw perks up a little.

"*Cox!*" I say with a smile. "Let's go get some!"

We munch on cakes molded into images of the moon rabbit, licking the sticky honey from our fingers. Nine Macaw looks regretfully at her last bite and then pops it into her mouth and sighs.

"Maybe one more," I say, just for the pleasure of seeing her light up with happiness. She chooses one molded into the shape of a *cuzam*—a swallow.

"In honor of Tree Orchid," she says solemnly, and then bites the head off and giggles. "She would not approve of me eating one of her friends!" Tree Orchid has a special affinity for birds.

We stroll back to the *polna*, stopping only once. The girls are enchanted by the netted butterflies pilgrims purchase and release to carry their prayers to the Goddess. I give them a few minutes to enjoy the spectacle and then hurry us back to the inn.

I sent a message to my son last night, and his slave is waiting for us. I keep him waiting for another minute to check on White Quetzal. She is happy to be spending the day in bed resting and feasting on delicacies her attendants bring her. I assure her that amaranth-and-honey cakes will be quite nutritious for the babe. I promise to return by mid-morning.

"Don't be long," she grumbles. "I have no one to talk to here! And I want us on that royal barge as soon as it arrives. My attendants have already packed our things. We can leave at a moment's notice." She gives me a significant look to remind me that 1 Zip is just days away.

White Quetzal's *nacom* adds two more guards to our escort and the seven of us follow the slave to the nobles' district, where the Yacab lineage lives. The courtyard is bustling with women, children, dogs and turkeys. The Yacab men have already headed out to the corn fields to supervise the slaves.

My son, Spear Thrower, is Magistrate of Pole. He is my sister's administrator on the mainland, representing Cuzamil's trade interests. The Rainbow Throne is popular in Pole because its wealth and prestige depend on trade with the Island and the constant influx of pilgrims. Spear Thrower receives enormous tribute for his service to the Island. An astute trader, he turned his tribute and his wife's expert weaving skill into even more wealth. My son's home, which was built in the middle of the courtyard, belongs to his wife's lineage, the Yacab. His is the largest stone house. It is built in the honored position closest to the well. I have not seen Spear Thrower since Water Lily and I brought Nine Macaw and her twin, Jaguar Paw, home from Cuzamil when they were only two-times-twenty days old. I regret that my duties in Chichen allowed me no time to get to know his four children and wife, Precious Tree.

I see her on the patio, kneeling in front of a back-strap loom weaving a bright red garment. She smiles broadly when she sees us, arms extended in welcome. Gracefully, she rises and places her right hand on the earth and then on her heart.

"Mother!" she exclaims with genuine gladness. "You're here at last! We were so worried." She looks curiously at our guards, who fan out strategically around the house. Yacab neighbors also stare at them, and at us. A few point to Nine Macaw, but they keep a respectful distance. Precious Tree ushers us in. "We heard the news, and now here you are safe! Come in, come in!"

Right hand to my heart, I greet her. "Thank you, Daughter. You know Nine Macaw, Water Lily's daughter? And this is Blue Stone, who joined our family only a few days ago."

"Welcome, children. Come meet your cousins. Are you hungry?"

We step out of the bright morning heat into the cool shade of my son's stone home.

When Precious Tree married my son, Water Lily and I helped her plaster the walls of her new house with red and blue dyes inside and out. Memories of happier days fill me—the days before Water Lily became a drunk, when my grandchildren were babies, when Moon Eagle was alive and we lived as respected nobles in Chichen.

An atmosphere of warmth and serenity suffuses Precious Tree's well-kept hearth room. I sense good fortune is with my son and his family. Precious Tree is a strikingly beautiful daughter of a wealthy Yacab noblewoman and a famed warrior noble. Like me and my lineage, she is *almehenob*—one who can claim noble ancestry from both mother and father. She is short and square-framed. Her round, ruddy face is not just beautiful, but also kind, and she moves with the grace of a young deer. She wears a white-gauze mantle over a blue, embroidered dress. Heavily perfumed with vanilla, she has twined her two long braids with fresh flowers and wrapped them around her flattened forehead, managing a look both fashionable and practical. As a young girl, my daughter-in-law trained in the school of sacred dance on Cuzamil. Now she is director of the women's dance in Pole.

This is an honored position that was also held by her mother when my grandmother was queen of Cuzamil.

We pass a doorway and I see her vegetable garden bursting with squash, beans and herbs. A lush garden is one of the benefits of living close to the compound's well.

"Na! Look!" Nine Macaw points with delight to the tree-lined back patio where my son's wife raises birds, dogs, rabbits, iguana, parrots and even two pet deer. Precious Tree nods her permission and the girls tentatively reach their hands out to pet the soft deer. They giggle when the gentle animals blow into their palms.

Precious Tree laughs along with them and gives the deer an affectionate pat. "Two Deer Pech and his sister are happy to meet you."

I remember she has always had a peculiar habit of giving her animals lineage names. "Tonight, we will roast White Belly Tzib, the dog," she announces.

My son's six-room home is bustling with servants, slaves and children who are peeking curiously out of the back rooms, waiting for their mother to invite them to come meet their grandmother and cousins. My inner vision sees clouds of pink and pale blue floating through the air signifying harmony and tranquility.

"Noble Mother!" exclaims Precious Tree as I take the offered cushioned seat. "How worried we've been about you and the rest of the family. You are the talk of all the *sacbe* in the Known World."

"So I am told," is all I can say. "Come, here, Daughter. Sit close to me." Sudden homesickness overcomes me. I miss Water Lily, Red Earth and Jaguar Paw. I miss Turtle Star, my temple attendant at Chichen. I miss the ordered life of my own home and hearth. I rest my head on Precious Tree's shoulder. She pats me tenderly on the back and waits.

Finally, I say, "Let me see your precious feathers."

She calls out, "Children, come! Greet your Noble Grandmother and your cousin!"

Four beautiful children approach, hands over their hearts with heads bowed respectfully. Two very young boys and two girls about Nine Macaw's age each touch the ground before me, then kneel at my feet for their blessing. I place a hand over their heads and say the short grandmother's prayer to Ix Chel. When they raise their faces to me I see four pairs of gold-green eyes that match my Nine Macaw's. I smile at them fondly and then the children noisily crowd around Nine Macaw and Blue Stone and pepper them with questions about the journey.

"Mother is making costumes for the dance on Ix Chel's feast day," the oldest girl says. "Come see them! We have blue feathers!"

At the mention of dance, Nine Macaw's eyes light up. She and Blue Stone run off with the children. With the soldiers outside, the enclosed Yacab courtyard feels safe. I can let them out of my sight for a little while.

"Where is the rest of the family?" Precious Tree asks carefully, smiling to show her jade-filled, sharply etched teeth. She wears no body paint or face paint, but jade and amber jewelry adorn her arms, ankles and neck. Her ear spools of rare pink crystal are unusually elegant.

Just as I am about to tell her, Spear Thrower rushes in.

"Mother! Finally! You have arrived safely!"

My handsome, self-assured son scoops me up in his arms and lifts me right off the bench. He twirls me around like a rag doll as I laugh and protest, and then he holds me close to his heart.

"Noble Mother, how I have missed you! And how I have worried about you! And now here you are at last, Ix Chel be praised."

It is as though my deceased husband stands before me as a young man again. The resemblance between Spear Thrower and Moon Eagle is eerie. I am overcome with emotion at the sight of him. My son now has twenty-plus-fifteen *tuns*, exactly twenty *tuns* younger than I, which is very auspicious for mother and son. He still has that puckered scar on one cheek, the result of an infected ceremonial scarring I warned him not to get in the marketplace at Chichen. On the other cheek is an expertly etched raised circle of dots. A thick, tattooed line on his sloped forehead runs to the bridge of a hooked nose, where dangles the amber ring given to him as a wedding gift by Moon Eagle. As vain as his father and uncle, Spear Thrower's fashionable hairstyle of stepped levels lines a handsome, sincere face. My heart lurches a little with missing my husband, who would be so proud of his son. He, too, has the same greenish-gold eyes as Nine Macaw.

Hearing his voice, his green-eyed children run to greet him. He sweeps all four of them into his arms at once and there is much laughter and shouting as he pretends to be a jaguar making a feast of them. Nine Macaw gapes at her tall uncle, who looks so much like her.

"Nine Macaw! What a beauty you have become. Look at you!"

He lifts her up off the ground and gathers her in a warm embrace. Then he greets Blue Stone with a graciousness that makes her duck her head shyly. Even though she wears clothing now, it is obvious to anyone from her cropped hair and tattoo that she is a slave.

"Children, play outside while I speak with your grandmother."

Precious Tree offers us cups of vanilla-flavored chocolate while Spear Thrower and I talk. He has heard most of the events of the past days from his reliable informants. He knows that we left Tree Orchid and Jaguar Paw in Na Balam and that Red Earth went to the heaven of suicides. He has also heard accounts of Water Lily's public stoning. That last piece of news puts a grim mood on us both. He and his sister were once close.

"Mother, where is my uncle Jaguar Shield? I heard he accompanied you."

I explain the mission my brother-in-law is on, to find Water Lily and bring her to Cuzamil, stopping in Na Balam to pick up the two children as well. I end by admitting, "I am worried. He should have overtaken us on the road by now. We traveled slowly and had many delays."

"Hmm," he says, "You've been very brave, mother. I admire the courage you show against these heart takers. You heard, I suppose, that my uncle Blood Gatherer went to the waters?"

"Yes. The Queen of Palenque gave me the news. May the gods forgive him and may the white dog be there to help him cross the rivers of the underworld. He caused much destruction and I have not yet forgiven him, but I wish his tortured soul to be at rest and cause no more harm."

"He became very powerful. Many feared him."

"Power should not be bought with fear! I worry for our people, Son. How can they be so blind? They are too easily misled."

He shakes his head, "Mother, it was always so and always will be thus. Fear is an easy tool for controlling the masses. The priests of the New Order gain more power each day. Even here, in the homeland of the Great Mother, they tell people that She is no longer relevant; that this *katun* of Mountain Movement has wrought great changes and the gods are hungry as never before and will not be sated with mere butterflies and turkeys."

I move close to the window to reassure myself that Nine Macaw is safe. She is admiring the dance costumes of Spear Thrower's two girls. Even from here I can see longing in her eyes.

"Mother, tell me how I can be of service. Let me help."

I sigh. "Son, there is so much that needs fixing, but it would ease my mind if you would settle the future of your nephew, Jaguar Shield. Because of our exile from Chichen he has lost his lineage. I worry about what will become of him. Nine Macaw and Tree Orchid have a future on Cuzamil, but he cannot join us there. Will you look after him?"

"Of course, Mother! He was in training to be a military doctor like father, yes?"

"Yes, but Jaguar Paw shows no gifts and no inclinations to soldiering or healing. He is an artist. His gift is apparent, as you will see from the wood carvings he makes."

"Hmm, yes. That is a fine trade for a nobleman. There is a gifted sculptor, cousin to my wife, who does all of the fishermen's shrines to Ix Chel. He would be happy to accept the brother of Princess Nine Macaw into his trade. I can easily arrange it. Jaguar Paw will have a good life here, Mother, I promise you. He will be another son to me and Precious Tree, and he can dedicate his life to carving images of the Great Mother. Aunt Heart of Water pays well for those shrines."

The mention of my sister's name sends a chill up my spine. Precious Tree notices. She holds my hand in her warm, soft one.

"Ah. That is another matter," I say carefully. "What news have you had from Heart of Water? I have heard only disturbing gossip."

Spear Thrower rubs his head, troubled. "I have not seen her in a long while. She used to come to Pole every few new moons to discuss trade, or I would meet her at the paddlers' inn on the sacred Island so we could discuss her business and what was needed. But for the past three moons, my aunt has not left the palace or answered my messages. She has not communicated with me—her own magistrate!—in all that time."

"My cousin whose husband's sister is an attendant in the palace says Queen Heart of Water has gone mad," Precious Tree confides. "No one except her closest attendants have seen or spoken to her in the past twenty-plus-two days. Food is taken to her rooms and empty bowls are left outside, but she will not receive visitors, messengers or even the High Priestesses. She has not attended to any of her duties at the Great Temple of the Mother."

"What do the healers say?" I ask, alarmed.

"She will not allow healers to examine her," my son says with frustration. "That is why there is talk of madness."

He hesitates. I can tell there is more.

"Just tell her, Husband!" Precious Tree pauses in her work sewing feathers onto a headdress for a dance costume for the upcoming 1 Zip festival and shakes a finger at him.

"My sources say that Heart of Water speaks ill of Nine Macaw and that she has decided to choose another to train as her heir to the Rainbow Throne."

"Another?" I ask, shocked. "Who!?"

"We have not been able to find out. All we know is that there are rumors that Heart of Water denies the legitimacy of Nine Macaw's Chel gifts and therefore her right to the throne."

Stunned, I can find no words. My sister is the queen of Cuzamil. She may do as she pleases, but I thought the matter of Nine Macaw's ascension was decided when the twins were born. Every sign pointed to a great destiny for the girl.

Om bey! The Goddess tried to prepare us for this when She showed us Nine Macaw's rainbow light. There is no doubt in my mind that Nine Macaw is the Great Mother's choice—She revealed it to Nine Macaw! Would I—could I—start a war over the succession? Why would my sister do this? Until this moment, I didn't really believe the rumors of madness could be true, but now it seems the most likely explanation.

Spear Thrower interrupts my dark ruminations. "Let us not wait for the royal barge, Mother. We can make the journey in my canoe. We will leave at first light tomorrow if the wind blows right. Surely, the Goddess favors our cause and will guide us. We must know what is in Heart of Water's mind before the rumors cause divisions among the people and create openings for our enemies to exploit."

In the Yacab courtyard I hear the beat of a rhythm on the *tikul* and someone calls out the dance steps. Glancing through the window, I see my precious jade and her cousins giggling and twirling around one another. She looks like the carefree girl she was before our exile and shame. What perils awaits her next? Cuzamil was supposed to be our sanctuary.

Om bey! If White Quetzal could hear my thoughts she would scold me! After all She has revealed to me and done for us, there should be no doubts in my heart that Ix Chel guides our steps. Where is my faith in Her?

It is yourself you doubt, not Me.

Creator of All, you know my heart. Help me find the courage to do what needs to be done!

"Mother? Are you well?" Spear Thrower looks concerned.

"It will be as you say, Son. We leave as soon as your boat is ready. I only wish your uncle Jaguar Shield and sister Water Lily and the children were here. I should not have left them. I feel in my bones that something is not right."

"These are uncertain times," says Precious Tree, taking my hands in her warm, strong ones. "Just remember, you are beloved by the Great Mother, and your own wisdom and strength are formidable."

Her kind words move me to tears. "Daughter, I made many mistakes. Water Lily is a drunk whose husband left her. My granddaughter is a suicide! My family are all exiles."

"Let your heart not be troubled," Spear Thrower says soothingly. "It is a heavy burden you have carried on your shoulders all these *tuns*. Father would agree with me that you did the best anyone could have done. My sister and niece made their own choices. You are not to blame."

That is generous of him to say, but we both know Moon Eagle was the better parent to Water Lily. She adored her father and he understood her as I never could. No doubt losing him to the Flowery Death of the heart takers affected her greatly, too. We never spoke of our grief with each other. Now, I regret that.

"I will send a scout to search for Uncle Jaguar Shield on the *sacbe*," Spear Thrower offers. "Perhaps they are close."

The thought of seeing my beloved again fills me with longing, but I set that aside, and also I set aside my doubts, fears and guilt—at least for the moment. There is work to do, and time is short.

"Before I leave, there is one more duty I must perform. Iguana Wind, your father's war captive, has served us well these past eight *tuns*. He is like another son to me. It is time to set him free. Will you help me gather what is needed for the ritual?"

"I know the trader who sells items for the ritual to free slaves," says Precious Tree. "I will send our servants to the market. He has the sandals, mantles, feathers and headdresses, and he even makes his own perfume. His brother is the one who tattoos the freed slaves, so it can all be arranged quite easily."

I thank her gratefully. Iguana Wind will have the best possible ceremony. I plan on giving him a sack of precious stones and seeds so he can start his new life with dignity.

It occurs to me that we should also perform the ritual for Blue Stone. Precious Tree ticks off the items we will need for the girl's ritual and her head servant jogs off to purchase what is needed.

"While we wait, let us share our first meal together in these many *tuns*," says Precious Tree. "The servants have prepared a wonderful feast for your arrival."

She calls the children. Nine Macaw and Blue Stone tumble into the hearth room with the others, flushed with excitement from dancing and playing with the animals. I have never heard Nine Macaw giggle so much. Water Lily's home was always strained with tension because of her drinking. Nine Macaw has not had a happy childhood, I realize with a pang. Her parents separated; her mother a drunk; her sister resentful of her destiny. Her grandmother—well, I doted on her, but did I ever see her as a girl with her own hopes and dreams, or did I only see the future heir to the Rainbow Throne? The thought makes me uneasy. As if she can read my heart, Nine Macaw looks up and I see a flash of guilt on her face as she straightens her mantle and sits up more regally. She is aware of herself as not just a girl, but as a princess with an important destiny. No one should envy Nine Macaw. The lives of queens are complicated, dangerous, burdened with cares and, too often, very lonely.

After a delicious meal of delicately spiced and roasted deer meat with amaranth tamales, Iguana Wind arrives. He lingers outside the hearth room, but I beckon him in.

"Son, come in. Meet your brother and his family."

Spear Thrower greets him like a family member, hand to his heart, head bowed. Iguana Wind is overwhelmed by this warm welcome from Pole's Magistrate. He copies the gestures and also touches the ground at Spear Thrower's feet to show respect. Then Spear Thrower gives him a hearty embrace.

"Brother," says Spear Thrower, "tell us what news you had about your wife and daughters!"

"I know that they are well!" Iguana Wind smiles happily. "A Bolon paddler is married to my wife's sister and he took them to Cuzamil himself nearly a *tun* ago."

"That is wonderful news," I say. "Let us give you more good news. Today, let us make you a free man once again."

He looks stunned and then relief and longing flash across his countenance. I embrace him and then Spear Thrower embraces him again. Precious Tree urges him to sit and join us for the meal. He glances at me and I nod reassuringly. He will have to get used to the customs and privileges of freedom soon enough.

The servants return with new sandals and loincloth, a fine cape, feathers for Iguana Wind's top knot and a woven shoulder bag. When he became Moon Eagle's captive his clothes were stripped from him. Today, he will once again dress as a free man. The servants also purchased a fine bolt of cotton cloth as a gift to his wife, so that he will be able to meet her with the dignity that he deserves. His countenance and demeanor are already different. He holds himself like a free man. How I admire him! I will miss him very much.

Precious Tree and I prepare for the ritual while Iguana Wind and Spear Thrower engage in deep conversation and smoke reed pipes. I send a messenger to the *polna* to inform Lady White Quetzal that we are safe and will be staying with my son's family this evening. If she needs me, she can send a messenger and I will come. I imagine she will be annoyed that I am not hurrying back to attend her, but this family reunion is too precious to cut short, and she will be just fine on her own for a night, surrounded by her capable retinue.

"It is time," I tell Iguana Wind with a smile. "Are you ready?"

He beams at me. "I am ready, Mother!"

"Let us all go together as a family," says Spear Thrower. How I love his generous heart. "Precious Tree, tell the children to come quickly."

In only a few moments, our happy group is marching to the sea cove. I lead the parade with a smiling Iguana Wind at my side, his head held high. Behind us on the cobblestone street are Spear Thrower and Precious Tree and their four children. Alert to possible trouble in crowded Pole, my son and his wife keep Nine Macaw between them, and Blue Stone scampers behind. Ever-present and vigilant, the queen's soldiers march on either side of our party. Another brings up the rear and another stays close to me at the front. Three household servants carry the clothing and other items for the ritual. Spear Thrower's two young sons beat a lively drum in time to our steps. Nine Macaw suddenly dances in front of us as she walks. We all laugh with delight.

"Look what a talented dancer we have in the family!" Precious Tree declares. "If she was not destined to be the next ruler of Cuzamil, she would surely become a celebrated dancer!" Nine Macaw blushes with pleasure.

People turn and watch us with curious gazes. Some catch our excitement and smile as we pass by. I feel pride brimming in my heart. This moment of joy with my family is the best medicine for the grief I have been carrying for a long time.

A delightful, honey-scented afternoon breeze blows our way. Lined up on the shore are a handful of canoes recently arrived from the sacred Island. Men unload large clay honey pots. Others work together to heft blocks of salt wrapped in wide, green leaves. Honey and salt are the Island's two most profitable trade items. I refuse to let my thoughts be pulled back to the problems awaiting us on Cuzamil. This moment is for Iguana Wind and Blue Stone.

Precious Tree directs us to a *cenote* a short walk from the market square and central plaza. The afternoon light slants into the half-moon-shaped cavern, which is ringed by small statues of Ix Chel in her guises of Maiden, Mother and Grandmother. Each beautifully rendered stone carving faces the sparkling blue water. Small gourds in front of each statue overflow with offerings. The others gather to one side and Iguana Wind and I approach the carving of Ix Chel the Mother.

"Mother of All," I pray, "please accept our offerings of thanks."

Iguana Wind kneels down and carefully places a turkey feather and a beautiful pink shell in the gourd. I add an amaranth cake. Then we rise and turn toward the sun. I raise my hands.

"Father Sun, we thank You for shining light on this long-awaited day!"

Precious Tree hands me a clay incense burner already lit with a chunk of glowing ember from the hearth. Her oldest daughter drops several grains of white *copal* resin into the clay burner and a moment later we are enveloped in cloud of heady incense. I nod to Iguana Wind. With trembling hands, he removes the loincloth worn by slaves and lets down his long black hair, which falls to his shoulders. We are both crying with joy, and for me also there is sadness because soon we will be parted. Precious Tree hands me a gourd, a sea sponge and *guanacaste* soap pods. Iguana Wind and I wade into the knee-high water together. He kneels before me, head bowed, hand to his heart. Gourd by gourd, whispering ancient prayers, I pour the sacred, cleansing water over him. Then I wash his dear body. The purple snakebite scar on his leg will be with him for the rest of his life. I linger over it a few moments to say an extra prayer. Behind us, my youngest grandson beats the *tikul* while Spear Thrower leads the family in a song written by one of our poets for this ceremony.

When Iguana Wind rises, I take his hands in mine.

"Son, you have served well and I declare your term of slavery completed. May the pain of separation be washed from your *chu'lel*. May your family meet you and greet you with open arms. May the Goddess Ix Chel favor you with many blessings from Her bounty of corn, beans and pumpkins. May your life as a free man from this day forward be a benefit to all who know you. As I release you from your bonds to Moon Eagle and his family from this moment forward, know that you have earned our love and respect. We honor you, Noble Son."

"Thank you, Noble Mother!" he cries, embracing me and weeping. I feel deeply honored by his love and his trust.

With a bolt of newly woven white cotton, Spear Thrower dries Iguana Wind's body so vigorously that all the children giggle. I shoot a glance over to Blue Stone, who looks on with wide eyes. Iguana Wind twists his wet hair into a high top knot and secures it with nine white egret feathers, which I hand him one by one. He stands before me tall and proud as any noble. I anoint him with vanilla-and-*copal*-scented oil. He holds out his work-worn hands to receive the white loincloth from Spear Thrower, and methodically wraps it around his waist and groin, grinning the whole time. A long strip falls from his waist to his knees. I hand him an elegant skirt of embroidered feathers to drape over the loincloth. Precious Tree places new sandals at his feet with a smile, and as he slips his feet in and swirls the bright blue cape around his shoulders he lets out a great shout of triumph. We all cheer loudly and rush to congratulate Iguana Wind, patting him on the back, rubbing noses and laughing. Nine Macaw squeezes into the melee to cling to his arm and rest her head on his shoulder. I wish Moon Eagle was here to celebrate with us.

"My Son," I say loudly to get everyone's attention, "before we go to get your tattoo removed so that no man can ever again claim you as a slave, we have one more task to perform. Blue Stone, let me bathe you in the waters of your freedom today."

She gapes at me, her hand over her mouth, too shocked to speak. I see fear in her eyes, but I understand that what she fears is not freedom, but waking up to find that the thing she longs for more than anything else was just a dream.

"It is no dream," I promise gently. "Come, granddaughter. Shall we do this today?"

Nine Macaw takes her hand and draws her forward, murmuring encouragement. The girls stand before the shrine of Ix Chel the Maiden. Precious Tree hands the little slave a beautiful blue gem to place in the gourd. It is a fitting offering from Blue Stone. With trembling hand she places it in the cup and whispers a prayer to the Goddess. Is it only I who sees the sign of Her serpent flare on the girl's forehead? I place a long, red macaw feather beside the blue gem. Blue Stone looks stunned and shakes her head as if this can't be happening. A macaw feather is one of the most prized and expensive feathers. It is worn by royalty.

"You are worth more to us than any feather, little treasure," I assure her with a smile.

Precious Tree hands me a gourd, a new sea sponge and *guanacaste* soap pods. Nine Macaw helps the girl undress and the three of us walk into the knee-high waters together. Blue Stone kneels before me, head bowed, hand to her heart. Gourd by gourd, I pour the sacred, cleansing waters over her, but it is Nine Macaw who carefully washes her while the *tikul* is played and the others sing the joyful ceremonial songs.

When she rises from the water, Blue Stone looks radiant. Nine Macaw and I dry her tenderly with newly woven cotton and then dress her in new clothes.

"But the clothes you gave me already—" she starts to protest. I shush her.

"These clothes belong to you as a free person now. You have earned them. Wear them with pride."

Nine Macaw combs back Blue Stone's short hair and threads pink shell earrings through the holes in the younger girl's ears. She places the jade necklace from Princess Turquoise Sky around the girl's neck. It is the first time Blue Stone has worn it since the day Nine Macaw gave it to her, and she can't stop touching the precious jade stones. Nine Macaw and I anoint our dear Blue Stone with the vanilla-and-*copal*-scented oil. Next, we put soft, deerskin sandals decorated with fine beadwork on the girl's leather-hard feet. Blue Stone wiggles her toes and giggles. I take her hands in mine and I smile down at her.

"Precious Daughter Blue Stone, you are part of our family now. I free you from your bonds of slavery from this moment forward. I formally adopt you into our family. From now on, you are sister to Nine Macaw and Jaguar Paw and Tree Orchid. You are my dear granddaughter!"

"And a beloved niece to us!" Spear Thrower adds.

"And our new cousin!" the children chime in. Everyone is laughing and hugging a stunned Blue Stone. Last to congratulate her is Iguana Wind. He kneels in front of her and embraces her for a long time, both of them crying. Only he really knows what she has had to endure to reach this day.

"Blue Stone, little Sister, if ever you need a friend or big brother, you can call on me," he says, holding her at arm's length so she can look into his eyes and see that he is sincere in this pledge. She is too overcome to speak, but she nods and then flings herself into his arms to sob some more.

"Let there be no doubt that you both have served with loyalty and courage," I say gently. "Let us go now to complete the tattoos, my children."

"I know the man who will do your tattoos. He did all of mine," says Spear Thrower, proudly showing off the expertly drawn geometric tattoos that decorate both his shoulders, his chest and knuckles. The scroll-and-scepter designs that identify him as Magistrate are, indeed, beautifully rendered. The tattoo for a freed captive slave looks like a broken rope wrapped around the right upper arm. With that on his body, Iguana will be known to all as a war captive who served a noble and has been bathed and freed for life. It is a mark of honor that all respect. Blue Stone carries a mark of a slave sold in childhood, which is a circle within a circle on her left bicep. It will be transformed with feathers around the outside circle—a symbol of freedom.

The tattoo artist uses stingray spines and pots of colored dyes. Sitting cross-legged on a straw mat, he works quickly and does a beautiful job for both. Nine Macaw holds a wincing Blue Stone's hand the whole time, distracting her with happy chatter.

The walk back to the Yacab compound at dusk is more subdued. I feel happy inside. The ceremonies were exactly as I had wished for Iguana Wind and Blue Stone. For all the days of difficulties we have faced, this day fills my heart with light.

When we return home, Blue Stone and Nine Macaw sit inside with the Yacab daughters and servants and help embroider dance mantles for the coming festival of 1 Zip. I catch Blue Stone admiring her sandals and running her hands over the soft threads of her new cotton mantle. What a memorable day for us all! When I see her tentatively touch her tattoo, I catch myself before I call Iguana Wind to bring my medicine bag. He is no longer my slave! It is Nine Macaw who helps me prepare a wash for the tattoos to prevent infection, which is all too common. She takes a handful of *pixoy* leaves and steeps them in a gourd over the hearth. When the decoction cools it's ready and she gently washes Blue Stone's cheek. How gruesome the crusty blood and dyes look on the first days of a tattoo.

I bathe Iguana Wind's arm and then we sit companionably under a guava tree on the back patio.

"Mother, you have honored me today," Iguana Wind says, catching my hand in his. "I am grateful and will never forget your kindness to me. It has been an honor to serve your family."

"I am grateful for all your loyalty and kindness to me and Moon Eagle and our family," I say truthfully. "Before we part, I have one last gift for you." I hand him the sack of stones and cacao seeds I brought from Chichen. There is enough wealth in it for him to take his family back home to Tulumha, build a new house and make a new life. He has become an expert herbalist under my tutelage and will be able to make a good living selling cures and medicinal plants.

"Mother! This is—"

He is speechless with gratitude and I pat his hand comfortingly.

Later, sleep eludes me. I sit outside and watch the Sky Wanderers make their stately way across the sky. I wonder if we, too, are set on an inevitable course by the Gods and Goddesses.

Ix Chel, Great Mother, Your path is my path. Please protect my loved ones who are scattered from me—my sister, my beloved, my grandchildren, my daughter.

Before Father Sun peeks over the eastern horizon Spear Thrower gently shakes me awake.

"What's happened?!" I bolt up from my pallet with alarm, for why else would my son wake me at this hour unless something is wrong?

"Nothing bad, Mother. Uncle Jaguar Shield has just arrived! Come, come!"

My heart leaps with joy. At last! I adjust my mantle and follow my son into the hearth room. Three weary travelers are seated on wooden stools, sipping chocolate and hungrily devouring leftover tamales from last night's meal. Before they see me I take a moment to drink in the sight of my loved ones, about whom I have worried and fretted for days. Jaguar Paw seems less like a boy and more like a young man since we parted, and little Tree Orchid looks too thin. She wearily slumps over, nearly asleep as she eats. Her ankle is bandaged. I wince in sympathy remembering the knife slashing her tendon the night we were captured in Na Balam. Jaguar Shield— how calm and handsome his angular face looks, even lined with fatigue as it is now. I stare at him and feel warmth and gladness.

Jaguar Shield must feel my gaze because he glances up and then leaps to his feet with delight. His wide smile gleams with the jade inlays in his teeth. In two steps he catches me up in his arms and we embrace with perhaps more enthusiasm than is proper for a brother-in-law and sister-in-law, but in this moment I don't care. I inhale his scent, redolent with the vanilla tobacco he favors. I have longed for this reunion since we parted in Na Balam. I wish I could lay my head against his chest and feel his heartbeat against my cheek, but we are mindful of our audience and release each other after a moment. Jaguar Shield touches the earth with his right hand.

"Noble Sister. Goddess be praised! You are well?"

"At this moment, Brother, I could not be better. I give thanks to Ix Chel for your safe arrival." I touch my hand to my heart.

I don't ask about Water Lily yet, although my heart sinks that my daughter is not with them. Reflexively, my hand goes to the jade beads around my neck, the twin of which—made from the same piece of jade—is worn by Water Lily. I gave it to her before she wed. Such was the power in the stones that when I touch my necklace I can usually feel for a moment how my daughter is feeling. But ever since we left Na Balam I have felt no connection to Water Lily through the stones, and this, more than anything, makes me fear that my daughter has gone to the waters.

But I can hear no bad news until I greet my grandchildren. Tree Orchid struggles to stand, leaning heavily on her cane, which I notice has a cunning carving of a toucan on the knob. I recognize the fine work of my grandson. I save her the effort of walking to me, rushing to her and gathering her up in an embrace.

"Child! I am so glad to see you! We will change your bandages in a moment and I will check your wound. You are very strong and brave to have made the long journey! I am so proud of you."

She grins up at me, some of the old sparkle still in her eyes. I hear a familiar sound outside and recognize the call of her loyal parrot, Kiki, no doubt hiding in the avocado tree. Another familiar voice scolds from the guava tree. It is Tree Orchid's monkey, Bobo! I should not be surprised that they followed her the entire way from Chichen to Pole. Kinship with animals, and especially birds, is one of the gifts with which Ix Chel has blessed my adopted granddaughter.

"Grandson!" I say, and Jaguar Paw stands before me, right hand over his heart. He grins and then touches the ground by my feet.

"Grandmother. My heart gladdens at the sight of you."

"I am so proud of you," I say when he rises, grasping both his hands in mine. "You did a man's duty since we left Chichen. Your father and grandfather would be very proud of you, too."

"I am proud of you, Nephew," says Spear Thrower, and Jaguar Paw gives him a shy smile. My son hands me a cup of chocolate and a servant brings another wooden stool for me.

"Mother," says Spear Thrower, "uncle has much to tell us, I am sure."

I motion to Jaguar Paw to sit beside me. I want my grandson close. Before he takes a seat he helps Tree Orchid move her stool close to my other side. I give a nod of approval at his thoughtfulness. It is such a relief to have them here, safe with me. My heart brims with gratitude.

"Goddess, we thank You for this reunion," I pray fervently, resting a hand on each child's head. "Ix Chel who protects us, Mother of us all, thank You for giving us all the strength to survive this journey!"

There is a moment of quiet after my prayer, each of us communing with the Goddess. Jaguar Shield breaks the silence with a sigh.

"I am only sorry that not all of us could be here," he says. I know I must brace myself now for the bad news. Water Lily. What has happened to her? I grip my grandson's arm.

"Sister, only a day after we parted in Na Balam I was hurrying back to Chichen on the *sacbe* when a runner caught up to me to tell me that your aunt, World Bridge, was dead."

I take in a sharp breath. This was not the news I expected. As a maiden, I spent many *tuns* in Na Balam with my mother's sister, World Bridge, when she helped to train me as a healer and midwife. She was a fun-loving woman who always saw the best in everyone. When we left her in Na Balam, her husband had just been killed by Blood Gatherer's priests, but World Bridge seemed in good health. What happened to her?

"Your aunt died a natural death. She went to the waters peacefully in the night," Jaguar Shield says gently. "Perhaps it was the grief of a broken heart over the death of her husband, but she passed in her sleep. As soon as the messenger reached me I turned back to Na Balam to make sure the children were not in danger. I arranged for the children to move into a house of healers. Your Chel cousins and Jaguar Paw took care of Tree Orchid."

Tree Orchid stares at the ground, no emotion on her face. I sense from her pulsing *chu'lel* that she has been lonely and afraid.

"My dear, I am so glad you are healing," I tell her, reaching for her hand. "Even if you never walk easily again, you must never fear. Ix Chel has a plan and purpose for you."

"Bird Oracle?" she whispers.

"That's right, little one. Remember how She sent Kiki to save us? The Goddess protects us all, and you will serve Her when we get to Cuzamil."

Tree Orchid sighs with relief. She is not a slave, but her status as an adopted child of Water Lily's makes her feel always vulnerable. If we were living in Chichen her condition would be a dire matter, because who would marry a crippled orphan? But with her gift for communicating with birds, she has a bright future on Cuzamil.

"Your grandson conducted himself like a true nobleman," my brother-in-law continues. I feel Jaguar Paw sit up straighter. "In fact, I consider him a man now, even though he has not yet had his coming-of age-ceremony." He claps his hand on the boy's shoulder. "That will be a mere formality." Spear Thrower also claps him on the shoulder and my grandson tries not to show emotion, but I can see pride in his eyes.

"I expected no less of him," I say. Now my impatience is building. "Brother, please tell me: what of Water Lily?"

"It was a matter of days before I could leave Na Balam for Chichen to search for Water Lily," Jaguar Shield explains. "We helped World Bridge's sons bathe her and bury her under the hearth room. When the rituals were complete I left again for Chichen. It took me three days to complete the journey. When I arrived, my status as an exile made it difficult to get information." He frowns at the unpleasant memory. "Eventually, I learned the story from listening to gossip in the marketplace."

He glances at the children. I see from his bleak expression that Jaguar Paw has already heard the news about his mother.

"The priests of Chac dragged Water Lily by the hair into the central plaza," Jaguar Shield reports grimly. "Chichen's magistrate read aloud the charges of public drunkenness. But it seems her real crime was being the mother of the girl who would not go to Chac's well. The crowd was furious and pelted her with stones until she was left for dead. Slaves tossed her body into a ditch past the corn fields, where she was left to be food for the vultures."

I am aghast at this news. Water Lily, my child, stoned to death, left in a ditch, buzzards pecking at her flesh. Blood Gatherer's hatred and bitter heart did this to my child! Visions of Water Lily as an infant and an adorable, obedient little girl flash through my mind. Her happiness on her wedding day. Our joyful trip to Cuzamil to birth her twins. Can she really be gone? I touch the jade beads around my neck and feel nothing of our connection.

Tree Orchid starts to weep silently beside me. Spear Thrower lays a consoling hand on her shoulder. His face is contorted with rage and grief.

Jaguar Shield continues. "I went to seek out her body—or her bones—to give them a proper burial. They were not there. I searched everywhere. I concluded that she must have been taken. But dead or alive, I did not know. I risked approaching the soldiers who went with us to Na Balam and they found out for me that Putun soldiers snuck into Chichen and carried her body away."

"Surely it would not be fit for any of the heart-taker rituals," Spear Thrower says, aghast.

Suddenly we hear a rustle from the room where the young girls are sleeping. Nine Macaw comes in rubbing her eyes to see why we are awake. When she sees Tree Orchid and Jaguar Paw she gives a happy shriek and runs to Tree Orchid first, who struggles to rise. Jaguar Paw is at her side and together the three of them hug. Jaguar Paw adores his twin.

Nine Macaw remembers to give her uncle a proper greeting. She bends on one knee to touch the earth with one hand before Jaguar Shield. "Uncle, Goddess be praised that you are with us and have brought my brother and cousin. It is all I could have hoped for. My mother? How is she? Where is she? Is she here, too?"

She can see the grief on our faces, but I don't want her hearing this story. Not yet.

"No, child," I answer before anyone else can. "Your mother has not been found as yet, but we will not lose our faith that Ix Chel watches over her and that one day our family will be whole again."

She turns her face away, one hand over her mouth to stifle her cries. *Om bey*, how could I have forgotten about Red Earth? Our family will never truly be whole again. I wish I could take back my words.

The other children comfort her and then they are comforting one another. I wish I could join them, but I feel apart and perhaps even unwelcome. I realize it is guilt that I feel. Their mother is missing, their sister is dead. Do they blame me? Do I blame me?

"Na!" Nine Macaw is looking at me with a troubled expression. "I just remembered! I had a dream right before I woke. It was terrible."

More dreams. Just as I thought: Ix Chel has turned Her attention to Nine Macaw. I have seen that this is the way of the gods. When we are young they are forthcoming, attentive with guidance in dreams and visions, but as we mature their intervention is less and less. This is what my mother told me and how it was for me until these dire times, when the Goddess began speaking directly to me more often.

Precious Tree sits Nine Macaw on a stool and wraps her hands around a gourd of chocolate. The girl takes a sip and collects herself.

"Na, I know that we must not go to Cuzamil today. I saw the sea waves churn into high mountains though the morning conch sounded a favorable wind from the north. We were drowning! It was awful!"

Listen to her. She speaks for Me.

I feel a frisson of awe. Ix Chel stands beside me in Her aspect of Mother. She gives me a look of love and then the vision fades.

"Na? Was that—"

Nine Macaw shared my vision! We smile at each other, tears in our eyes at the great blessings the Mother bestows on us. Nine Macaw closes her eyes and makes a silent prayer of thanks and my heart fills with joy at her reverence and respect. How quickly my granddaughter's life is changing. My sister and I both had powerful dream visions by the time we were ten-plus-three *tuns*, but our aunt, mother and grandmother had to be consulted to interpret our visions until we were old enough to understand. Nine Macaw's visions from Ix Chel are so clear and direct, despite her youth. Perilous times have brought us a seer with wondrous powers.

"You speak a true dream," I say. "We will heed Her warning."

Nine Macaw looks deeply relieved and slumps against me. She holds her brother and adopted sister's hands tightly.

Spear Thrower calls his messenger into the hearth room. "Inform the Bolon paddlers that Princess Nine Macaw has had a vision from the Goddess Ix Chel that it is too dangerous to cross the waters to Cuzamil today, no matter what direction the conch blows from the sacred Island."

The slave touches the earth and then rushes out to deliver the message.

"Good then, it's settled," says Precious Tree brightly, coming into the hearth room. She embraces Nine Macaw, Jaguar Paw and Tree Orchid and declares. "You must wait here until the signs are favorable. Let us enjoy this rare time to be together. I am no oracle or seer, but I sense that once you arrive on the holy Island, there will be many trials and dangers. Mother, this is a perfect time to have the coming-of-age ceremonies for Nine Macaw, Blue Stone, Jaguar Paw and Tree Orchid. Don't you agree?"

The children clap their hands with excitement.

"Bless you, Daughter! What a fine idea!" I say, although my heart is so heavy with this news of Water Lily that I don't feel capable of celebrating. But she is right. The ceremonies should take place before we are separated from Jaguar Paw.

There is so much to do. My mind is weaving like a spider, trying to catch all the threads. I close my eyes, trying to think. White Quetzal will be impatient. I must attend her. And now that he is here, Jaguar Paw must be settled into an apprenticeship with a master carver. And we must see how Tree Orchid's wounds are healing. I may need to prepare a poultice for the wound, and that can take some time. And even though Cuzamil calls to me, and my anxiety over the rumors surrounding Heart of Water sit heavy in my heart, I am not ready to be parted from my beloved Jaguar Shield. Selfishly, I want time alone with him. There can be no gainsaying the Goddess, so at least the decision has been already made for me and I don't need to feel guilty about postponing our departure.

Spear Thrower makes arrangements to take Jaguar Shield and Jaguar Paw to the steam baths. "After, we can visit the royal sculptor to ask about an apprenticeship for you," he tells my grandson. "Would you like that?"

"More than anything, Uncle!" Jaguar Paw's smile is a treasure to see. I will memorize it so I can remember it in the days to come.

I am being maudlin. Of course I will see my grandson again. I can make the journey from Cuzamil to Pole any time I want. It's this news about Water Lily. Such a shock. I still can't believe it. Never see her again? That seems impossible and when I search deeply within I do not feel that her soul has traveled to the Underworld.

"What is this?" Precious Tree is saying to Jaguar Paw. "You are a sculptor?"

"Show them your carvings, Nephew. Don't be shy about your talent," says Jaguar Shield.

Jaguar Paw passes around several small carvings in wood and one in stone. They are expertly rendered creatures of the forest. The crouching jaguar he started making when we first went into exile is magnificent. It looks alive.

"He did this, too," chimes in Tree Orchid, holding up her cane for all to admire.

"Extraordinary," says Spear Thrower. "Show me your tools."

Jaguar Shield has only an obsidian blade for wood and a crude chisel for stone.

"My friend, the royal sculptor, will be very lucky to have you as his apprentice," says Spear Thrower.

As the sun lights up the hearth room, I am suddenly aware that, for the first time in days, I can take a full, deep breath. It is dizzying. I didn't realize how much fear and anxiety I was holding in my body while I was separated from these three. Something Lady White Quetzal said to me a few days ago comes back to me. Why should I worry when I know the Goddess is with me always? It is all in Her hands. Even Water Lily's fate. I have fretted for so long. I would like to enjoy this moment without worrying about the next. Here in this hearth room are nearly all of the people in the world whom I care about, sipping chocolate and planning for a happy future. What good did all that worry do? Did it change one single thing? In my heart I know with certainty that Ix Chel guides us and protects us. I know that our cause is Her cause and our cares are Her cares.

I step outside to greet the rising sun and make a quiet prayer to release the last cords of fear that are wound around my heart.

"Goddess, I regret that I ever doubted You, for You are Creator and Protector, Wise Mother to us all. I pray that You protect your daughters, Heart of Water and Water Lily."

To seal the prayer, I visualize both of them sitting in the Goddess's lap, caressed by Her and bathed in Her rainbow light.

The current of tension flows out of me. I bow my head to the ground nine times in thanks. Feeling the earth centers me and fills my *chu'lel* with peace.

When I rise, Nine Macaw is standing in front of me with a look on her face that says she understands. I am struck by how mature she is now. She is no longer a child, and not yet a full woman. In that in-between place there is already great wisdom and knowing.

"Mother," Precious Tree sticks her head outside, "are you in need? Is all well?"

"Yes, Daughter, all is well. Truly well."

"Good, because I have a heavy load of planning to do for the ceremonies. Leave it to me to decide on food, clothing, sandals, tattoos, body paint, and of course the guest list. Perhaps you can speak with the priestess?"

"We will all help!" Nine Macaw says eagerly. It is clear she adores her aunt, and that the feeling is mutual. I give them a grateful smile. In Precious Tree's capable hands all will go perfectly.

A servant brings me a gourd of fresh guava juice and I rest on the back patio. Surrounded by tall, brown reeds, it is a quiet place to sit. I send Jaguar Shield a silent thought to come join me here, but I hear Spear Thrower calling him:

"*C'ox*, Uncle! The steam bath awaits!"

Ah, well. We will have to find a moment for each other later. A cooling sea breeze smelling of salt water and flowers sweetens the morning air. How pleasant it would be to spend my third age resting here on this patio in this happy home, watching my beautiful grandchildren flourish. I sigh. That domestic contentment is not my destiny.

I eat a tamale and then tell the soldiers that I must return to the *polna* to speak with their queen. I hope White Quetzal will enjoy an invitation to the coming-of-age ceremonies today. It will at least distract her from her impatience with me and soften the news about delaying the voyage to Cuzamil. We have some days yet until 1 Zip, but I know she is fretting.

I walk slowly back to the *polna*, trailed by the soldiers. My body is tired from the interrupted night's sleep, but really it is my heart that makes me feel slow and sick. In spite of my resolve not to worry, thoughts of Water Lily return. My child stoned to death. Was it the Cocom neighbors who threw the first stones? People can be terribly cruel, and the heart takers encourage bloodlust and anger.

Despite the early hour, the pregnant queen is already harrying her servants to pack for the crossing today. White Quetzal shouts orders and supervises the refolding of baby garments as she reclines on her cushions.

"Jade Skirt! Good you are finally here. We leave in a matter of moments. I was up before dawn. The conch from the north just blew, so the sea is calm. I must take at least six servants with me, since only the Goddess knows what my needs will be once the prince is born."

I interrupt. "Lady, I have news. You may not like it."

She carefully lowers herself onto a stone bench. Her womb is now shaped like a perfect full moon. "I don't like the look on your face. What is it? Tell me."

"Nine Macaw has seen in a dream that this is not a favorable day to make the crossing to Cuzamil. Ix Chel showed her that the morning conch will sound a benevolent wind, but that it will suddenly shift in the afternoon and become a dangerous storm."

Her face falls with disappointment. She sighs and motions for the servants to leave us. Always alert for eavesdroppers in her retinue, she whispers, "1 Zip approaches in a few days! Are you sure about this?"

"The Goddess spoke to me Herself and told me to heed Nine Macaw's vision," I answer truthfully. "We have no choice but to wait and have faith in Ix Chel."

Whit Quetzal nods her agreement. "Of course, this is all Her plan. I just wish to be there already."

"Of course," I murmur, reminding myself that this is her first child. For all her imperious manners, White Quetzal is still quite young. She needs reassurances from her midwife. "Have no fear," I tell her. "You show no signs of early labor. The last time I examined you, all was well and the future king has not yet descended into the serpent canal. There is time."

"Perhaps you should examine me again?" she asks. I note the slight uncertainty in her voice. She has no mother with her, no sisters. I take her hand.

"Of course, Noble Sister. Let me examine you now and set your mind at ease."

As I perform the examination, I ask her about her appetite and bowel movements and I feel her pulses. When I look at her *chu'lel* I see a strong blue light of health. I tell her this and she visibly relaxes.

"Goddess be praised," she says, looking suddenly weary. "Nine Macaw may have saved our lives and the Palenque dynasty. I am grateful to her. Many have perished on that sea voyage because of a sudden rise of ill winds. Did She tell your granddaughter when it will be safe for us to depart?"

"I cannot be certain, but I think we will leave in two days' time. We can use these days in Pole well. You must sleep as much as possible. When the baby comes there will be little sleep for you. And walk back and forth every three hours to keep your blood circulating. Breathe deeply of the sea air and eat fish daily. Tomorrow, we will have coming-of-age ceremonies for my grandchildren. Please, you must come as our most honored guest."

"Of course I will be there," she says, perking up as I knew she would. She is lonely and bored here. "You!" she shouts to a servant. "Stop preparations. We will stay here for another few days. Tell the Hearth Mistress!"

I make her an herbal brew to ease her backache and show her servants how to prepare it, leaving enough herbs so the queen can have more when she needs it. I instruct one of her attendants on the proper way to massage the queen's lower back with some of my rattlesnake salve.

"Use this time to make your prayers so that your son can hear your heart and Her heart in communion," I suggest to White Quetzal. She brightens at this suggestion. Her devotion to the Goddess cheers me. "I am going to the temple of Ix Chel, the Maiden, to seek a priestess of Cuzamil to conduct the coming-of-age ceremonies," I tell her. "I will make an offering to the Goddess on behalf of you and your precious feather. I promise to return each day to check on you, and you can send for me any time if you have a concern."

She touches her hand to her heart and thanks me most sweetly.

The guards escort me to the seaside Temple of Ix Chel the Maiden. It is small and elegant. I remember from my time learning here that it is situated in such a manner that both the rising and setting moon appear for a few moments atop the roof of the temple before sliding down to the middle of the eastern and western doors. This sends magnificent beams of light onto the altar within. As young girls, my sister and I spent many days in this temple when we visited our father or when our mother had business to conduct in Pole. I do not know who is presently in charge, but I am confident that she will be eager to assist with a ceremony for the future queen of Cuzamil.

The sun warms my back as I climb the nine stone steps of Her temple, which is dedicated to maidens, weaving, moon cycles, fertility and knowledge. Each of the nine steps is decorated at the rise with carvings and paintings of spiders, snakes, rabbits and rainbows—symbols and glyphs of the Goddess. A stone serpent slithers down the steps to rest its enormous head on the sandy ground. One of the guards goes to find the head priestess while I enjoy a moment of quiet. I inhale the familiar, sweet aroma of white *copal* incense and my heart lifts. Honoring my promise to White Quetzal, I offer another handful of *copal* grains from my shoulder bag and say a prayer to the Great Mother for the queen and her son.

A dozen acolytes dressed in blue and wearing rainbow ribbons in their hair busily sweep the stone floor, arrange fresh flowers in vases and carry buckets of clean water to the rooms in the back. My attention is drawn to the lovely courtyard bursting with fruit trees and song birds. I recall there is a particularly fine stone fountain carved into the shape of Ix Chel at Her loom. I can hear it gurgling—a light counterpoint to the high bird song.

"Honored Oracle Jade Skirt!" a priestess hurries over, a smile of welcome on her face. "Our High Priestess is on her way to greet you."

I can't remember her name, but her familiar countenance bears the lines of the third age. She touches her heart and her head and I do the same. Curious, bright-faced maidens edge closer, eager to see who the noble visitor is, but they are too well-trained to speak. At the clap of someone's hands the young women briskly get back to work.

"Greetings, Noble Lady," says a strikingly beautiful priestess. A perfectly round face frames enormous charcoal eyes. Her slender frame is covered by a blue mantle under a white gauze cloak and a wealth of jade and amber jewelry. "You are very welcome here, Oracle," she says with a smile.

"It is a pleasure to be received so warmly in Her temple school," I say, returning the smile. "I once was a student here. Forgive me, but I do not know you."

She places an elegant hand to her brow and heart, then touches the ground before me. Her forehead is beautifully flattened to a steep angle few are able to achieve.

"Mother, my name is Seventeen Deer Nine Rabbit, my *coco kaba* is Fire Bird. My lineage is Canul. Please come. We can talk in my chambers and have refreshments."

She leads me down a long hallway of gleaming white stone. I feel a sharp pang of longing for the temple in Chichen and my dear apprentice, Turtle Star. I sigh. I wonder how she is faring as the new Oracle and Head Priestess. By necessity I had to leave rather abruptly and Turtle Star had no time to gather supporters among the other priestesses before I left her.

Along one side of the courtyard are instruction rooms for the young women who attend the School of Firm Hearts and Wise Minds. Classes have just started. I hear a priestess speaking about how to uphold the mores of society. I feel nostalgic as the students recite: "Honor your parents in all things at all times. Obey the sumptuary laws that say commoners may not dress as Nobles do. Do these things and you will help your elders to preserve the order of the state In heaven and on earth."

Nine Macaw should be training in a temple such as this. I have taught her what I could, but now it is time for her formal training to begin.

I peek into other rooms as we pass by and see girls working at back-strap looms, bending over divinatory crystals and studying maps of the stars. A heady aroma of herbs and spices wafts out of the herbal studies classroom. At the end of the corridor, Fire Bird pushes aside a curtain and invites me into her private quarters. Much like my rooms in the Temple of Ix Chel in Chichen, the accommodations are not elaborate, but they are adequate and comfortable. We sit side by side on a blue-painted stone bench under a round window. I had a similar window in my room. It is right for the high priestess to sleep in the light of Her full moon. I could imagine myself back in Her temple in Chichen if not for the view outside this window. There are no brown hills of Chichen, but a sparkling, azure sea. My eyes well up with emotion. I long to be home in Cuzamil. I long to hold Water Lily in my arms again, and Red Earth. *Om bey!*

Fire Bird holds my hand tenderly. "Mother, is all well with you? We have heard of your recent troubles in Chichen. I think you are very brave. Here in Pole, there have been many discussions among the priestesses of Ix Chel. We are in agreement that any one of us would have done the same as you even it meant the loss of all that is dear. We honor you, Jade Skirt."

"Your words gladden my heart and lift my spirit, Sister. These are dark times, and I have recently had troubling news. But Ix Chel lights our way."

"How can we assist you?" she asks in such a sincere tone that I want to hug her.

"Princess Nine Macaw, the heir to the Rainbow Throne, has had her first moon cycle. I am arranging her coming-of-age ceremony for tomorrow, for we are in a hurry to get to Cuzamil. Three others will join her: her twin brother, a freed slave whom I have adopted, and an orphaned cousin who is an adopted sister to Nine Macaw and her brother. I seek a priestess to conduct their ceremony, but first I must be sure she knows that my grandchildren were declared exiles."

"I will do it myself. It will be an honor!"

"Sister, are you sure? It could create problems for those from Chichen."

"Pah!" says Fire Bird dismissively. "None of us recognizes your exile. To all of us who serve Ix Chel you are a shining example of faith in the Great Mother. We walk in your footsteps and defy the heart takers! Here, we recognize only the Rainbow Throne and the Goddess who blesses us."

I feel deeply relieved. I had hoped for such support, and it is wonderful to hear her generous, loving words.

We make arrangements and sip chocolate brought by a shy acolyte. I am loathe to leave this place, which feels like a second home to me, but Precious Tree must be anxious to confer with me about the ceremonies. I am about to rise when Fire Bird leans forward and whispers, "Lady Jade Skirt, may I speak plainly about a difficult matter?"

"Of course," I say.

"Your sister is not well. Things are amiss and awry on the sacred Island. For more than three moons there have been no meetings allowed with the Queen—not for any of the instructors or priestesses of Pole and Cuzamil. Always she would meet with us at the new moon. Now It is rumored that she locks herself in her rooms inside the Rainbow Palace. They say Queen Heart of Water has lost her mind. For the past three moons she has not conducted an oracular session. Never has that happened before, as you know."

This is worse than I imagined. "Is it known which attendants prepare the divinatory enemas?" I ask.

"At the start of the dry season the Queen replaced all of her closest advisors and maidens and allowed only a group of Cob priestesses to attend her. It was all very unsettling, but none would challenge our Queen. Since then, her administration has been neglecting its duties. We are worried about her, Lady. So you can imagine that we are all doubly relieved you are here."

She gives me a significant look. I sense that like the trader Long Strider, who spoke with me in Coba, Fire Bird expects that I will fix this—that I will somehow take my sister's place as regent until Nine Macaw is of age. But how can I even think of removing my sister from the Rainbow Throne?

"Thank you for your honesty," I say, feeling dread in the pit of my stomach. "Your faith and loyalty to the Goddess and the Rainbow Throne do you great credit, Fire Bird. This visit has given me heart."

I make no promises and nothing more is said except a few pleasantries and then our farewells, but we both know what is at stake. Now I know I have the support of the Temple of the Maiden and Her priestesses.

I'm so distracted by the conversation that as I leave the temple grounds I nearly trip over an old man. He is seated cross-legged on a ragged cloth. I make my apologies and notice that his wrinkles are astonishing. Empty earlobes dangle down to his chin, tattered from a lifetime of blood-letting, but his eyes are sharp and clear. He grins, showing his nearly toothless mouth.

"Dark!" He shakes his head with a dire, yet almost playful look, daring me to ask him what he means. When I just stare he says, "Very dark forces surround you, Noble Lady."

So he is a public soothsayer, a *h'men*. They often do divinations and make prayers on behalf of customers in front of temples. I would pass by, but in spite of myself I look at his *chu'lel* and it glows a luminous white, which is very rare. I give him a closer look. He wears his long, white hair as a commoner, carelessly piled atop his head and matted into thick strands. He is clothed only in a plain hemp loincloth. His unshod feet are wide with splayed toes, indicating that he has gone barefooted for most of his life. Despite being in a hurry, and aware of the soldier escorts waiting for me, I sit down. It almost feels like a wave has tugged me to shore. I wonder if he uses sorcery, but I feel no threat; only curiosity. He meets my assessing gaze and his *chu'lel* merges with mine in a pleasant rush. This unlikely intimacy surprises me. I'm amazed I allow it. But I sense no danger or threat from the old man. I wonder if I am having a waking dream or if this is a vision from a helpful spirit.

"Lady Jade Skirt, hard times abound in this time of Mountain Movement."

It is possible he knew my name from hearing it spoken in the temple. On the other hand, legitimate soothsayers know such things without being told.

"Worse for you," he continues, "forces of darkness haunt you and thwart your efforts. Let us ask the *sastun* for advice."

From a reed bag he removes a small clay jar with a starburst pattern baked into one side. He places a flat stone between us and tips the clay jar into his leathery palm. Out falls a *sastun*, the sacred divinatory crystal of *h'mens*. I also use the *sastun* in my role as Oracle and midwife of Ix Chel, and like mine his crystal is perfectly round and clear. Three times he blows on the *sastun* before returning it to the jar. *Clink, clink, clink.* He twirls the *sastun* in circles inside the tiny clay pot again.

"*Sastun, sastun* with your great power show me what surrounds Jade Skirt, Jade Skirt. Is it good? Is it evil? Is it jealousy? Is she in danger? *Sastun, sastun* with your great power answer my plea. Jade Skirt, Jade Skirt."

He spills the crystal into my waiting hand. I know what to do so he only makes a slight upward motion with his hand. I close it in a fist and shake it next to my breast several times. The old *h'men* scratches his belly for a moment and then reaches over and opens my hand to read the augury of the sacred divining stone. I try not to do my own interpretation because one cannot read the *sastun* augury for oneself. This we learn when we are apprentices in the ways of the Goddess.

The ancient one mumbles prayers to himself and moves my hand around to look at all sides of the streaks and bubbles in the crystal. He shakes his head and frowns, then moves my hand so he can study the crystal from a different angle. He sighs.

"What is it, Brother. Tell me, please," I say, trying to rein in this feeling of foreboding.

"Many strands. They plot against you. Intrigue and sabotage surround you. You have come far and suffered to protect what you love and to do what your heart tells you is right. Some have fallen who opposed you and others have risen in their places. Beware of sorcery. There is one near and dear to you who betrays you even now. Only the brave and blessed could withstand your path, Noble Lady. Ix Chel's love lights your way, and Her will protects you, but beware of a virtue so intense that it turns to oppression." He sighs and then looks at me with sympathy. "That is all."

I bow my head for a moment, forcing back my feelings of fear and turmoil and make a devout prayer to the Great Mother for Her protection and wisdom as I face this future fraught with dangers.

"A dedicated life of spiritual seeking is a constant discovery of what strength lies within," I hear the old man say.

When I open my eyes the *h'men* has vanished.

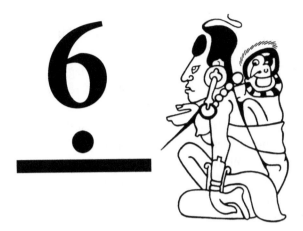

I return to the Yacab compound to find Precious Tree organizing the ceremonies like a seasoned *nacom*. Everyone is occupied with a task for tomorrow's event. I see her eyeing the guards and wondering if they can be put to use, but I give a slight shake of the head. We cannot forget how close the Putun came to capturing Nine Macaw. Until we get safely to Cuzamil they must remain vigilant. The four soldiers guard the front and back of my son's house, hands ready on spears and obsidian-studded clubs.

Tomorrow, four young people will pass through the gates of childhood into maturity. Nine Macaw and her cousins are trying to teach Blue Stone the coming-of-age dance for maidens. Nine Macaw looks radiant. She glances often at her aunt, shyly hoping for a word of praise, which she receives often.

While dancing is not possible for Tree Orchid, the crippled girl sits on a stone bench and accompanies the dancers on a small *tikul* and taps her good foot. I remember Tree Orchid dancing like a bright butterfly just a moon past and my heart hurts for her. But she looks happy enough sitting in the shade, participating as she can. Her parrot, Kiki, sits on her shoulder. Blue Stone is clumsy, but enthusiastic, as Nine Macaw reviews with her the basic steps. She has never danced before, but her trust in Nine Macaw is unwavering. Bobo, the monkey, cavorts overhead on a guava branch mimicking the girls.

My granddaughter was born to dance. Her lithe body bends and twists with joy. Precious Tree steps in to correct a step and calls to her two older daughters, who have already had their ceremonies, to practice with the girls. Precious Tree comes over to praise Tree Orchid as well.

"It is like your hands are dancing the steps!" she says, and Tree Orchid's face lights up. I am so grateful for Precious Tree's kind nature. My son is a lucky man.

I ask after the others and she tells me that Jaguar Paw has gone with Iguana Wind and my son to a private place to receive instruction in his part of the ceremony.

"Uncle Jaguar Shield has gone to the hairdresser's stall in the market. He said to tell you he will return for the noonday meal." I feel a pang of disappointment. When will we have a moment together, in private?

I report to Precious Tree that the high priestess of the maiden's temple will perform the ceremony. She claps her hands in delight. The servants are preparing tomorrow's feast and slaves are out shopping for the supplies we will need. There is no time to weave four new garments, so the servants have been instructed to purchase the mantles.

"Well done, Daughter."

"There is more news," she says. "Spear Thrower spoke with the royal sculptor who has accepted Jaguar Paw as his apprentice. He can start the day after the ceremony."

What a relief! Everything is working out better than I hoped, at least for the children. Water Lily, you should be here with us for the coming-of-age ceremony of your children. My poor daughter.

Precious Tree declares the dancers ready to perform and sets them to new tasks. Tree Orchid is left behind with the less enviable task of spinning cotton thread while the other girls are sent to gather fruits for the feast tomorrow. Nine Macaw is followed closely by one of White Quetzal's soldiers. Two servant women of the third age work at Precious Tree's hearth grinding corn and tending the fires.

I take a seat next to Tree Orchid, child of my husband's lineage. Her mother died during the girl's birth and her father quickly followed with his suicide to join his wife in Ix Tab's paradise, leaving the child an orphan.

"My feather, how are you?" I hardly need to ask, for just sitting next to her I feel grief emanating from her *chu'lel*.

She shakes her dear little head and struggles to hold back tears. Her bottom lip quivers. The spindle whirl stills in her hands. I pull her close to me. Her head falls onto my chest and she releases wracking sobs. I join her, both of us crying for all we have lost. Water Lily was the only mother Tree Orchid knew. Red Earth was her sister.

"I know, my feather, I know."

Tree Orchid also cries for her lost future. She dreamed of dancing for the temple. Lameness is yet another blow to this poor girl, who is without lineage. I know she will be a powerful Bird Oracle, but right now she grieves the losses of the life she cannot have.

"You know, the most important part of coming of age isn't dancing, or wearing a fine, new mantle. It's accepting the path the Goddess sets before us, and embracing it with as much grace and courage as we can muster," I tell her.

"I don't have any courage," she whispers. "If I did, I would have joined Red Earth and my parents in Ix Tab's paradise. That is the only place I truly belong."

It hurts me like a stab in the heart to hear this pronouncement, but I let her get it all out.

"I am a burden. No one wanted me before, without a lineage, and now no one will want me because I can't walk right. What use am I? I watch the others run and dance and I feel bitter, Na. I don't want to wish them misfortune, but I do! I want them to know how it feels to have no hope. Not really," she adds, miserably. "But sometimes. You see, that is why I should just die."

"Tree Orchid, Granddaughter of my heart, my precious jade, we all love you, and the injury to your foot changes nothing. It isn't true that no one wants you. We do. Tomorrow you will have your coming-of-age ceremony with the others."

"You may as well send me to sacrifice or sell me now that I am useless," she says bitterly. "Nine Macaw is to be a queen. Blue Stone is her new best friend. Jaguar Paw will have a trade. The cousins here are all so perfect and beautiful. What use am I?"

"Tree Orchid," I say holding her even closer. "You are a Chel woman now, and Chel women do not surrender to misfortune. You have a gift, my love. Just ask Kiki and Bobo and all the other friends you have in the forest. There is a great future for you on Cuzamil. You will be the greatest Bird Oracle the Island has ever known." She looks up at me, her teary eyes hopeful, yet also wary. "Child," I say in a low voice, "I tell you now a secret we tell only those who are one of us: all oracles and healers must suffer hardships. It is the way of the goddesses and gods to teach us courage and compassion. We cannot change that. You must accept it and embrace it as part of your journey. You will discover strength in you that you didn't know was there. This I know, because the Goddess has shown me."

"She has?" she sniffles, wiping her eyes with the back of her hand.

"Yes, my feather. She has. Now no more of these tears. Let us pray to Ix Chel and tell Her you are ready for the great future She has in store for you."

Tree Orchid looks at me and in her eyes I see the spirit of the wise woman she will one day become. "Na, thank you. You are always so kind to me. I am the most fortunate orphan in the Known World." She gives me the sweetest hug.

Just then Kiki swoops down and lands on her shoulder, yellow head bobbing. "Don't cry! Don't cry!" he screeches, making us both laugh.

"What is this?" Jaguar Shield is standing in front of us, his eyebrows raised with mock scolding. "There is no time for joking around when your ceremony is tomorrow. Your aunt's apprentice needs your skills with the costume making."

Tree Orchid grins at us both and heads inside. We watch her bravely make her way into the house. The lower half of her wounded leg flops back and forth, but she leans on her fine cane and moves along doggedly.

Jaguar Shield sits down next to me. His new hairdo is stacked high and bound up in a wooden carving in the likeness of an eagle's head. Two great tufts of graying black hair sprout from both sides of his head. He wears a new blue loincloth and a puma-skin apron over it, and a red, cotton cape and beaded sandals. I love his vanity. I admire him while he looks straight ahead and enjoys my eyes on him. The steam bath left him smelling of soap and jasmine oil. Without turning his head he murmurs, "I have waited long enough. My heart seeks yours. My body aches for yours. I have it all arranged."

"Let us go to the market to buy gifts for the ceremony tomorrow," I say aloud for the sake of those who may overhear. Desire pounds in my veins.

We rise at the very same moment, the excitement between us palpable. But one of Lady White Quetzal's guards hurries over to accompany me. Jaguar Shield gives him a nod, one military man to another.

"I will be guarded by my brother-in-law," I tell the young man. "You may join your comrades and guard Princess Nine Macaw."

"We can split up and protect you both," he says.

"If you come with us to the market you may as well announce to everyone that the Lady Jade Skirt is there," Jaguar Shield growls. "The Putun spies will already know the Palenque guard her. Stay here and protect the girl and we will slip into the market and slip out quickly with no Putun the wiser."

The guard hesitates, but in the face of Jaguar Shield's confident gaze he backs down and nods. We watch him jog away and then Jaguar Shield leads me in the opposite direction. He guides me to the *sacbe* and we head toward the market area. A strong wind blows in our faces. Wasn't the sky blue a moment ago? The others on the road glance nervously at the black storm clouds roiling and massing overhead and break into a jog. The air is charged. My beloved suddenly grasps my hand and pulls me off the road and into the trees. In giddy silence we backtrack on a tiny foot path through the overgrown jungle. I can't imagine where he is taking me, and then we have arrived at a lonely thatch-and-stick hut. Behind the abandoned house is a thick stand of seaside palms, which bow and bend in the gusting wind.

There is no door curtain, but the place is shelter enough from the rain that is starting to fall. My love leads me through the humble hearth room to a small back room facing the jungle. No one lives here, but someone has recently swept the floor. Jaguar Shield smiles and offers his hand and I feel like a girl again. Only he can make me feel this magic. He turns me around and I see the surprise he has prepared: a low pole-and-thatch bed strewn with yellow flowers!

"This time there will be no biting ants!" I say and we laugh at the memory of our lovemaking in the jungle the first and only time we came together.

He twirls his red cloak off his shoulders and spreads it over the mattress of dried palm leaves. With deliberate slowness, he loosens my braids and twirls my hair in his hands. The wooden eagle headdress lifts off easily. The two tufts of his hair that stick out from the side of his head would be comical if this were not such an intimate moment between two hungry lovers. He lifts my dress over my head then removes his loincloth. His tattered member rises up hard and throbbing. His breath is hot against my face and when he whispers in my ear, my whole body melts.

"Are stolen embraces the sweetest?" he asks.

"Stolen or given, I care not. I must have you!"

One hand on my shoulder, he plays with my nipple. My knees grow weak with desire. My hands explore his muscular frame. I can feel him hard and long against me. I pull him down to the bed. We find each other and meet our long-held passion head on, shamelessly, wildly exploring every orifice the Goddess has given us for pleasure. At last, he enters my jade forest and lets out a loud groan of pure pleasure. We are folded into each other and the rest of the world falls away. The bed shakes and creaks. We laugh out loud, luxuriating in the privacy we have never before had with each other. Again and again, my hips rise to meet his. He knows the needs of my body and deftly with one hand lifts my buttocks to find the head of my jade forest to complete the perfect union until our love juices finally flow together in a wracking current that shakes me from head to toe. The moment of climax the Goddess has gifted to lovers lasts a very long time. Pulsing from head to curling toes, I have a fleeting thought that it may be the last time in my life I will feel such exquisite sexual pleasure. If it is, then so be it. Never will I forget this moment.

After, we stare into each other's eyes for a long time. He moves strands of hair away from my face and drinks me in with his obsidian eyes. I tell him his eyes are a pool of night.

"Your eyes are dark as coals, but glowing," he whispers. "Jade Skirt, you are the most radiant woman I have ever known. I would follow you every-where just to watch you. You nourish my soul."

My hand traces the lines of his scarred face, then down his shoulders to the tattoos on his muscled chest. "You are the greatest love of my life," I tell him honestly.

"And you are the only woman who has given me such passion. What we have is precious and rare. Our stars are crossed, Jade Skirt, but our hearts are not."

Passion rises again. I want to feel him holding me. I stand and he lifts me up as if I weigh no more than a quetzal feather. Legs wrapped around his waist, I straddle him as he pushes my hips back and forth onto his eager member. Outside, the storm predicted by Nine Macaw's dream continues to gain strength. The wind howls. Jungle creatures scurry to hide. Limbs crash to the ground and the little thatch hut creaks.

"Even the gods feel our passion," he whispers in my ear, sending more shivers of pleasure through my body.

We lie in each other's arms after, and I allow myself to imagine how sweet it would be to lie here with my lover every night, cook for him, turn this humble thatch hut into our home. Of course, it can never be. But it is a pleasant dream and I savor it a bit longer.

By the time we dress, it is storming furiously. Tree branches crack and fall and rain blows in through the cracks in the walls, churning the dirt floor into mud.

"It is best that we return to your son's house. There will be no market in this storm," he says. "I will leave first and whistle if no one is nearby."

We meet no one as we retrace our steps back to the deserted *sacbe*. I grasp his hand and give him one last embrace before we run for home. We are completely soaked by the time we return to Spear Thrower's house. Precious Tree fusses over me and orders the servants to bring me a dry mantle. Jaguar Shield disappears to check on Spear Thrower. It is a good thing, because being in the same room would surely give us away to any who know us. I dry off and help Precious Tree string together flower garlands of yellow marigolds. As she chatters pleasantly I make small noises to let her know I am listening. But really I am remembering every details of my delicious afternoon with Jaguar Shield.

The storm finally abates. We are drinking allspice-and-honey tea when we hear a commotion in the courtyard.

"Let us see the Princess!" someone yells. The soldiers run to the front of the house and hold their weapons up.

"Stay back!" one says.

What is going on? I see traders, pilgrims, pregnant women, a woman nursing a baby, and even a few Bolon paddlers. The Yacab neighbors are pouring out of their houses to see what's happening. There is a crowd of more than two-times-twenty people outside the house!

"We must see the Princess!" another shouts.

The Palenque guards form ranks in front of the door and brandish their spears.

"What do you want here?" one demands.

"The prophecy of the Princess saved us!" says one of the paddlers. "We want to know what else she has seen!"

"The Princess saved many lives today with her dream," declares another. "We want her blessing!"

"We want to ask her to say prayers for us!" shouts a pilgrim. "We want her to give us the Goddess's blessing for our safe journey!"

"Please ask her to bless my womb!" says a pale woman who looks ready to give birth at any moment.

"And ask her when the storm will stop and when it will be safe to make the journey to Cuzamil," a paddler shouts.

Nine Macaw and her cousins are listening by the window. I catch her eye.

"Stay inside with your aunt and cousins while I speak to everyone."

"Are they angry with me?" She sounds scared, poor child.

"They are not angry. They are desperate and scared," I say. "I'll explain later."

I gather my *chu'lel* and then hold up my hand commandingly. I have addressed countless crowds at festivals and rituals. I know how to speak with the authority of the Goddess's representative.

"The Goddess blessed us today with Her vision of the storm. Let us give thanks to Ix Chel, the Great Protector." I hear people murmur their thanks to the Goddess.

"The Princess Nine Macaw is only a child," I continue sternly. "You have no right to come here making demands of her. She has yet to have her coming-of-age ceremony. She is not yet ready to shoulder the tasks of a priestess or queen! Thank the Goddess that She sent us this warning today, but leave the child be and go back to your homes."

A few start to protest and I hold up my hand. "Come, now, she is still a girl. The Goddess does not mean for her to be burdened with all your requests just yet. Be thankful for her true vision and know that in a few *tuns* you will have her as your Queen and Oracle. But, for now, you must respect the peace of this home and disperse."

"Let us see the girl!" someone yells.

A long-haired priestess of the second age makes her way to the front. Her red robe marks her as one who serves in the Temple of Sacred Sexual Union. She raises her hand and the crowd quiets.

"The Noble Lady speaks true," she says in a husky voice. "Listen to her. Did we not just receive a strong sign that the heir to the Rainbow Throne is blessed with the gifts of the queens of Cuzamil? She has a sacred destiny to rule on the Island. But she is not the queen yet. So if you need blessings or healing, go to the temples. The priestesses who serve the Great Mother will help you. And take those infants and expectant mothers out of this bad weather!"

Still the crowd will not leave. One of the traders shakes his fist at me and shouts, "Things are not right on Cuzamil. What do you say, Noble Lady? There have been no prophecies now for three moon cycles! We are left adrift, yet you tell us to go home. We need assurance that things will be as orderly and secure as they were before on Cuzamil."

The crowd begins to murmur their discontentment and I am starting to worry that our few guards will not be sufficient to hold them back if they decide to take out their frustrations with Heart of Water on us.

Jaguar Shield and Spear Thrower shove through the crowd and join me at the front. Spear Thrower strikes the ground with his carved Magistrate's staff. That gets their attention.

"Good people of Pole. Blessed pilgrims. You must return to your homes and the *polna*. We understand your frustration, but we should be celebrating that the Great Mother has not forgotten us. She sends visions to the heir to the Rainbow Throne to let us know we are under Her protection! I promise you the affairs of Cuzamil will be settled to your satisfaction. Go now. Leave us to manage our family affairs."

Spear Thrower's presence fills the people with confidence. The priestess bows to us prettily and then leads a group of pregnant women and mothers with infants back to their *polna*. The rest of the crowd disperses. We are left alone at last. Inside, the household is in a dither.

Blue Stone sidles up to me and whispers, "*Na*, Nine Macaw is in the girls' room. She is upset!"

Precious Tree and I find Nine Macaw curled up in the arms of her oldest cousin.

"What is this, child?" Precious Tree asks. "The crowd outside is gone now. You are safe here with your family."

"Safe?" Nine Macaw says angrily. "I will never be safe! Why do I have to be a princess? I never asked for a sacred destiny! Why do I have to go to Cuzamil? I want to stay here with my cousins. I want to be a dancer like you!"

I am speechless. Has she forgotten so soon the vision Ix Chel gave her—the rainbow light? Precious Tree squeezes my hand and murmurs, "It is the age, Mother. Emotions take them. It will pass." To Nine Macaw she says steadily, "We understand that you are upset right now. When you have your coming-of-age ceremony, everything will look better to you."

"No it won't!" she screams. I can hardly believe my ears. Our children do not speak to their elders like this. I am about to say so when Precious Tree squeezes my hand again.

"Perhaps you are not ready for your ceremony," she says agreeably. "This is not the behavior of an adult."

Nine Macaw's eyes widen and she sits up. "I apologize, Aunt, for the way I spoke." She touches her hand to her head. "But please, please let me stay here with you! Let me learn the dances! I want to stay with you and my cousins. That is all I want! I feel so happy here with you."

Precious Tree's oldest daughter says, "Mother, Grandmother, let her stay here with us at least until 1 Zip has passed so that she can dance with us! She speaks of nothing else. It seems so unfair to force her to be a queen if she does not feel it in her heart."

"We will consider what you say," Precious Tree says, her face closed. I am about to speak, but she tugs my hand and pulls me out of the room.

"Come, Mother," she whispers. "We must give her time."

"She can't be serious!" I explode when we are out of Nine Macaw's range of hearing. "She has a destiny! She is chosen by the Goddess herself! Ix Chel blesses her with powerful visions. How can she turn her back on it!? I won't allow it!"

"First of all," says Spear Thrower soothingly, casting a knowing look at his wife, "we cannot expect a future queen to be easily controlled—not even by her own family. This is to be expected for someone with her calendar day. Her destiny is to rule, and she has started with us."

"Do you not remember Water Lily at this age?" Precious Tree asks me. I pause for a moment. Yes, I do remember my daughter having unreasonable fits of temper. I hear the wisdom in what Precious Tree is saying to me. I count back and realize that Nine Macaw should start her monthly course soon. I tell myself this mood of Nine Macaw's will pass and she will be as she was—compliant and willing. But a shadow falls over me. Isn't this what the soothsayer predicted—that someone close to me would betray me? But it is unthinkable that it would be Nine Macaw. Everything I have done, every sacrifice, has been for her!

Nine Macaw refuses to take the evening meal with us so Precious Tree brings food to the girls' room and we leave her to sulk. When I lie down to sleep at night, memories of my delicious afternoon of lovemaking are overshadowed by Nine Macaw's angry face and my self-doubt. She wants to give up the Rainbow Throne and her heritage to be a dancer! Where did I go wrong this time?

The day of the coming-of-age ceremony dawns with a low howl from the southern conch on Cuzamil, signaling an unfavorable wind for the journey. The servants have been up before dawn preparing the house. I admire the palm branches tied to doorways and posts. The entrance is framed in a palm-leaf arch woven with Ix Chel's sacred marigold flowers.

The children are still sleeping. I tiptoe into the girls' room and wake Nine Macaw silently. She sees my face and scowls, but she doesn't dare to turn her back on me. Good. At least there is that.

"Outside," I whisper, "so we don't wake the others."

We sit on a bench in the early gray light and she folds her arms and will not look at me. I sigh.

"Child, I know you never asked for this destiny, but the Goddess has called you. Have you already forgotten the vision She gave you only a few days ago?"

Nine Macaw looks up, her wide-eyed face bright with emotion, but her mouth is set in a firm line and she does not speak.

I try again. "There is nothing I would like more than to see you happy, and I know you love to dance, but do you not also love healing, and plants, and Her sacred rituals?"

A flash of doubt crosses her face. Still no words. I press on.

"If we were not pursued by the Putun, I could leave you here to train at the Temple of Maidens. It is a fine place. My sister and I trained there, and the head priestess, Fire Bird, is a good woman. You could train and dance. But it is too dangerous to leave you on the mainland. Only on Cuzamil will you be safe."

Now she is openly scowling at me. I offer my last enticement. "You know there is dancing on Cuzamil. Why could you not dance on 1 Zip at Her festival on the Island?"

Nine Macaw looks at the ground and scuffs her bare foot in the dirt. I sigh.

"I am not your enemy, precious one," I say. "Let us enjoy your coming-of-age ceremony and speak more of this tomorrow."

She gets up and flees inside.

I recount the one-sided conversation to Jaguar Shield and Spear Thrower.

"I believe Nine Macaw could be kept safe here," Jaguar Shield says, surprising me. "We can hire soldiers to guard her while we go to Cuzamil to investigate the situation. It might be safer than bringing her there. We don't know what we will find."

"That is a temporary solution," I say heatedly. "What if Nine Macaw truly wants to walk away from her destiny?"

"Mother," says Precious Tree, joining our conference, "you know that passions cannot be ordered to surface and sink like fishing lines. Leave her here for now. In time, she may choose to take her place on the Island, and if that happens then she will go willingly because it will be her choice. If you insist she go to Cuzamil now she will resent you. Can she truly rule if it is not in her heart?"

"But her training must begin!" I sputter. They do not understand. Nine Macaw must develop her inner life now; otherwise, the Divine rapture will not develop channels to flow into her. The time to open to these mysteries is right now, just as she starts her moon cycles, which is when a young woman is like a basket the Goddess can fill with Her Presence. It has always been this way with our lineage.

I groan. So much has been risked; so much lost for her sake. Lives have been sacrificed to assure her reign. Heart of Water has been waiting. I have been waiting.

"Is it wise to allow a child to conduct our lineage affairs?" I say angrily.

"The circumstances are extreme," Spear Thrower says diplomatically. "She has been through more than most adults must face in a lifetime—exile, tragedy, suicide, kidnapping, danger at every turn, losing sister and mother. We should be proud of her, really. She has the power to stand up for herself against her lineage, her calendar days and her all-knowing grandmother."

My son's words are wise, yet they sting me. Am I overbearing? My hand moves to the jade necklace Moon Eagle made me. Whenever I feel insecure, the feel of the smooth stones soothes me.

"For now," says Jaguar Shield gently, "let her be. We do not have to make any decision today, and in her state of mind it will only make Nine Macaw more stubborn."

There is a bitter taste in my mouth, but there is nothing I can do but wait for her to come to her senses. Precious Tree takes the girls to the *nulha* to prepare for the ceremony, but I don't go with them. I know my presence is not welcome by Nine Macaw, and the others are confused by our conflict. I want to cry, but I feel reluctant to show Nine Macaw how much power she has to hurt me. She is, after all, the child; I am the adult.

I have my bath after they return. Sweet Blue Stone comes to me, shyly asking if I will comb her hair. Her hair has not yet grown past her ears. She is really here to make sure I am well. I hug her and we talk about what it means to be an adult. She and Tree Orchid have not yet started their moon cycles, but they are the right age for the ceremony so they are allowed by convention to participate in the ritual. I describe to her what we will do when her moon cycles finally do come, because she has had no mother or grandmother to tell her these things, and then we speak about what her life will be like on Cuzamil.

"Na, I am eager to go to the Island. The same is true for Tree Orchid. It is only Nine Macaw who wants to stay in Pole."

I know what courage this takes her to say, devoted as she is to Nine Macaw.

"Nine Macaw is not the only one who has a great destiny waiting for her on Cuzamil," I tell the young girl. "We each have a path to walk. We each face choices along the way. We must make the wisest decisions we can."

"And ask the Goddess for guidance," adds Blue Stone.

"Great Mother, please protect this precious feather and guide her feet on the path of wisdom and joy," I pray aloud. Blue Stone bows her head devoutly. "Goddess of Women and Girls, please bless my grandchild Blue Stone on this most auspicious day of her coming of age ceremony and shower her with Your blessings." A tingle of Presence brushes across my heart. Blue Stone's head shoots up and she looks at me with wonder.

"Was that Her?" she whispers. I nod, pleased beyond words that this child has found us, and we have found her.

• • •

The day is busy with preparations, but mostly I stay out of the way. Precious Tree leaves me to my thoughts. It has been a long time since I had time to myself, and I spend it on the sheltered patio watching the sky. Tantalizing smells from the hearth room make my stomach rumble. Throughout the day, Blue Stone and Precious Tree bring me samples to taste and cups of basil-and-marigold tea sweetened with honey. I wish for Jaguar Shield's company, but he is busy preparing Jaguar Paw for the ritual. The coming-of-age ceremony ensures that children are known to their ancestors and may enter a profession or marry when the time is right. If Moon Eagle was still alive he would initiate Jaguar Paw into the rites for men, as his father did for Spear Thrower. My husband was a good man. I am sorry he is not here to witness his grandchildren moving into adulthood. I never felt with him the passion I feel for Jaguar Shield, but we loved each other well and I miss his kindness and his courage. Many of the things I love about Jaguar Shield are the same things I loved in Moon Eagle, but Jaguar Shield and I have a connection that is blood calling to blood; lust calling to lust. We were careful never to acknowledge it while our spouses were alive, but once we were both widowed we stopped holding back.

Thinking of Jaguar Shield, a smile plays at my lips. What a man! How can he make me feel strong and wild, and at the same time safe and protected? I don't let myself think about the goodbye we will have to say very soon. Today is not the day to think about farewells.

Throughout the day I hear the beat of the *tikul* and laughter from the girls' room. The time of preparing for the beginning of their moon cycles is when girls are initiated into womanhood. The coming-of-age ceremony revolves around the dances. Precious Tree is far more useful to them than I would be.

I am making excuses to stay out of Nine Macaw's way. I want her to enjoy her coming-of-age ritual, and my presence will only make her tense and unhappy.

By the middle of the afternoon the courtyard is filling with Precious Tree's Yacab relatives, Spear Thrower's friends and even my father's relatives. They bring gifts for the children and baskets of fruits and tamales and gourds of fresh juices for the celebration feast. The thought of greeting them all and answering their many questions—where is Water Lily, what really happened in Na Balam and all the rest—makes me tired. Dressed in my embroidered blue robe and rainbow ribbons of a High Priestess of Ix Chel, I cultivate an air of aloofness and thus am I able to avoid their idle chatter.

The one person I do greet warmly is the Lady White Quetzal. She arrives with great pomp carried on her palanquin and flanked by soldiers and attendants carrying gifts of finely beaded sandals and embroidered mantles for the children. She personally hands Precious Tree a deerskin sack filled with precious stones as a gift to the family. I settle her on a special bench I have had prepared for the comfort of a very pregnant queen, and she favors me with a haughty nod. Guests line the courtyard, leaving an aisle for the children, who will be welcomed in when the area is prepared for them.

At the appointed time, four priestesses solemnly process single-file into the courtyard chanting a song of praise to Ix Chel. The crowd quiets. Fire

Bird walks in last. I admire the bright blue feathers in her stacked braids, which are bound up in the headband worn by all Cuzamil priestesses. The design on it represents the Wasp star. The priestesses arrange themselves according to the four directions. Dressed in colors representing the directions, the one in red stands in the east, the one in yellow to the south, black to the west and white to the north. Then Fire Bird, in blue representing the fifth direction—the center—creates the ritual space by laying a braided hemp rope in a large circle. Precious Tree, in a dazzling costume of yellow feathers, dances elegantly into the center of the roped-off area and holds aloft a newly made palm broom. She dips it in a clay bowl of rainwater in which *copal* grains have soaked overnight. As she sweeps the space, Spear Thrower dances into the ring. My son looks impressive in a bold costume of red feathers. His feet pound the earth as he scatters aromatic leaves of allspice and *chacah*. Together, they dance in perfect rhythm to the four corners, bowing to the priestesses who hold each direction. The priestesses sing a song of praise and welcome to Ix Chel and Itzámna, First Consort. When Spear Thrower and Precious Tree finish their rounds and step to the side they bow to each of the directions and then to Fire Bird as she stands at the outside edge of the ritual circle.

I can feel this priestess's *chu'lel* reach out and embrace the crowd. It is a bright pink, emanating peace to all of us. I am overcome by the power and grace of Fire Bird, and my *chu'lel* opens wide and meets hers. It is as if I am walking with her when she circles the rope barrier nine times. She carries a clay incense burner that emits billowing puffs of *copal* smoke through the mouth and ears of a god's face to dispel evil forces. The priestesses sing nine times the prayer to Ix Chel to bless this coming-of-age ceremony. Shaking an *aspergillum* made of rattlesnake tails, Fire Bird completes her circuit and repeats it on the inner area of the ceremonial ground. The prayers vibrate in my body and my *chu'lel* expands to hold the sacred space with Fire Bird's *chu'lel*.

"Let the initiates enter!" she calls out from the center of the circle.

Now come the children. Led by Jaguar Paw, the four emerge from the doorway and parade single-file through the doorway of the house and into the circle. I notice that my grandson moves slowly so that Tree Orchid can easily keep the pace. Smiling guests toss petals of marigold blossoms on them as they pass. Nine Macaw, walking behind her brother, holds her head high with the natural grace of a dancer and looks straight ahead. Blue

Stone's eyes are as wide as saucers. Tree Orchid catches my eye and gives the smallest nod.

Atop each of their heads is the traditional white, square cloth worn for this ceremony. They look beautiful in their new, white mantles and red-tassled sandals. Jaguar Paw wears a white loincloth with an embroidered apron down the front. Already he carries himself with the dignity and grace of a man. With a sharp pang, I wish with all my heart that Water Lily was here to see her children enter into their adulthood.

The children form a circle around Fire Bird. An attendant brings a bowl of rain water carefully collected from rock hollows in the forest. It was good that it rained yesterday! In the bowl also float flower petals and cacao. Fire Bird dips a bouquet of marigolds in the bowl and slaps each child on the head, chest, and stomach with the bouquet. She repeats this on each joint and in between every toe and finger. Nine Macaw is last to be thus washed. Her face is serious and unsmiling, while Blue Stone and Tree Orchid can barely keep from giggling. I remember the tickling sensation between the toes during my coming-of-age ceremony when my grandmother anointed me with the marigolds.

At last, Fire Bird removes the white cloths from their heads and presents each young person with a bundle of nine feathers and a small statue of Ix Chel carved in cedar wood. An assistant offers a puff from the reed pipe and a sip from the clay jar of fermented plums. Each child inhales the sacred tobacco and tastes the plum beer.

"Today is the first day of your adulthood," speaks Fire Bird in a voice that carries well through the crowd. "You now take your place in the world. Each of you has been formed and shaped by the Creator Parents for a unique role. You are the stems, the offshoots; you are descendants of your forebears. What will be your contribution to make a better society? Be always respectful and kind. Do not walk aimlessly. Do not dishonor yourselves or those who preceded you—the ancestors. Assist the aged, widowed and orphaned. Honor the Thirteen Gods of Heaven and the Nine Gods of the Underworld. Never destroy a *ceiba* tree, where our First Mother and First Father reside. Plant *nopales* so that you may always have food. Let the dawn not find you idle. Let your days be full of purpose and your nights repose. Plant when the moon is right and harvest your corn, your beans and pumpkins with gratitude. Do not over indulge in drink or smoke. Tell no lies. Never cheat and never steal from another lest you be not known by your ancestors. Bring offerings to the temple. Care for your parents in their old age. And most important of all, find and cultivate your Inner Treasure, which is union with spirit." The children touch their hands to their heads and hearts and then touch the earth in front of Fire Bird.

Tree Orchid picks up her *tikul* and begins to play. Nine Macaw and Blue Stone dance the steps of the Maiden's dance. Nine Macaw whirls and leaps flawlessly, her face filled with joy and pride. Blue Stone, to her credit, does a fine job, and I smile at Tree Orchid, who catches my eye and smiles back. When the Maiden dance is ended, Jaguar Shield takes up the drum and Jaguar Paw dances the Jaguar dance wearing mittens made from jaguar skins. He looks very fierce and dignified.

Now I step into the circle and throw my head back and cry: "Ix Chel, Great Mother; Itzámna, First Father, I call to you to witness this ceremony for these four worthy children whom You created and nurtured and brought to this day." My spirit grows larger than my body and I can See as if from above the spirits of all gathered here. "I recommend my four precious feathers to you: Jaguar Paw, Nine Macaw, Tree Orchid and Blue Stone."

The children kneel before me and I put my hand to my heart and one by one give them my blessing. When it is Nine Macaw's turn she faces my gaze, but it is as if she is a stranger and I falter a little over the words.

I step back out of the circle and a priestess from the Temple of Ix Chel the Grandmother enters with her two young scribes to read the calendar destinies of the initiates. They spread a reed mat and all sit cross-legged across from the four young people. The priestess opens a long, painted book and moves her wooden stylus down its pages line by line. Coming of age is considered a person's second birth, so the nine portents of the gods of this day, month, *katun*, moon and planets must be considered for each of the young people. These calculations will guide their paths for the rest of their lives. The crowd waits in respectful silence while the priestess mumbles and the scribe records her words. They will be read later, in private, by the young people and our family.

After the calendars are read and recorded, my grandchildren offer the priestess bouquets of flowers and touch their heads to the ground in front of her. Then the drummers play a lively beat and the new adults leap to their feet. The ceremony is over. Now the celebration begins!.

Guests are served according to age, from eldest to youngest. I stuff myself with honey roasted deer and dog, boiled lobster and crab served with yams. I still manage to find room to eat avocados, corn tamales and a generous dollop from a great tub of hot sauce. Precious Tree has done a remarkable job putting this feast together on such short notice and I tell her so. She looks very pleased by my praise. I thank my son as well. He has paid for all of this.

After the eating, nine maidens, nine mothers and nine grandmothers arrive to perform the ritual coming-of-age ceremonial dance, accompanied by four musicians. The dancers bob and weave in and out of three circles until the long wreaths of marigold flowers they carry build a spider's web. This is what Nine Macaw wishes to do, I think, shaking my head at this twist in the fabric of Ix Chel's plan. My stubborn granddaughter would rather dance at the ceremonies of strangers than serve the Goddess as Queen of Cuzamil!

Many pots of fermented corn beer are consumed. Lady White Quetzal drinks sparingly, but I make sure she eats heartily of the deer and lobster. She enjoys herself and praises Precious Tree's home and costume. She retires before the moon rises high in the sky, on my advice.

"Tomorrow we leave for Cuzamil if the conchs are favorable," I assure her. "I believe they will be."

She pats my hand and nods. "Ix Chel guides us, Sister. Everything works out as She wishes." Neither of us mentions the conspicuously absent royal barge.

For the rest of us feasting, drinking and dancing last until the moon sets in the West. Four priestesses from the Temple of the Grandmother stand by to help the drunks get home and make sure there are no illicit romances. One of the Bolon boys is too interested in Nine Macaw for my liking, but Precious Tree seems unconcerned. Nevertheless, I keep a close eye on her, even though my granddaughter throws me annoyed looks.

A drunken Jaguar Paw is carried to bed by Jaguar Shield. Iguana Wind, who has been off on his own these last days, but of course returned for the ceremony, brings me a last gourd of beer and we reminisce about the days when the children were young. We recount their antics and laugh.

I don't remember curling up on my palette to sleep, but I must have because sometime just before dawn Tree Orchid's parrot, Kiki, flaps into my room and wakes me. Just as I am about to grumble at him I hear a commotion outside. At this hour, that can't be good. With a feeling of foreboding I wrap my mantle around my shoulders against the damp sea air and make my way outside. It sounds like an army is marching on the *sacbe.*

Spear Thrower and Jaguar Shield and two of the Palenque guards join me in the courtyard. Without a word, we hurry to the edge of the *sacbe* and crouch behind a sprawling *ceiba* tree.

"Let us see what comes before it sees us," Jaguar Shield whispers hoarsely.

We don't have to wait long. The noise grows louder and I realize it is not just the sound of feet slapping the *sacbe*. It's also the drone of voices chanting. Soon I can make out the words. It is the War God's cry. The Putun are marching into Pole!

Spear Thrower leaves us at a run to rouse Pole's guard. Jaguar Shield tries to tug me away from the approaching danger, but I resist. I must witness this. I know in my bones that there is something I must see.

It looks like a royal parade. Black-robed priests appear first, chanting their monotonous drone while their acolytes burn rubber incense in their wake. The acrid smoke mingles with the reek of dried blood from the unwashed priests, making me gag. Next comes an honor guard dressed in quetzal-feather jackets. They hold aloft spears tied with strips of cloth, the colors of which I can't make out in the dim light. Then comes a line of drummers beating time on their hideous drums made from the skins of human sacrifices. The sound wounds my ears. Then come two palanquins carried side by side. One is curtained so that none can see who rides on the backs of the six slaves. The second bears a single man who sprawls arrogantly like a king in his basket. Behind the palanquin march two files of guards numbering ten-plus-twenty. Their spears are sharp and their bodies painted in ochre designs dedicated to the War God. Tears roll down my face. The presence of these demon soldiers is an abomination. Pole is part of the sacred Zone of Peace ordained by the Goddess and yet here are the followers of the War God violating it openly—arrogantly!

Yacab neighbors are beginning to gather on the edges of the *sacbe* to see who comes, and I see looks of outrage on their faces. They mutter, "How dare the Putun march into Pole, stronghold of the Goddess and Her temples?"

Jaguar Shield seizes my hand and I realize I've been holding my breath. We creep along under the cover of trees so we can shadow the procession.

Spear Thrower managed to summon the night guard of Pole. My son stands bravely with the ten soldiers. Spears bristling, they block the *sacbe*. *I am relieved to see more armed men of Pole* racing over.

"Pole will defend itself!" my beloved whispers to me. "This is not Na Balam, where the ruler was a puppet of the Putun. Your son is a brave man and a good leader, and the people of Pole revere the Goddess. They will defend what is Hers!"

The priest in the palanquin waves his hand lazily and the procession stops. The chanters and drummers fall silent. He makes another gesture and his soldiers lower their spears. The sun breaks over the horizon and in the first weak light of day I can make out his expression. He grins like a hungry panther, showing his blackened, jade-filled teeth and the same jaw-bone tattoo that my brother, Blood Gatherer, wore to mark him as a High Priest.

"What is this?" he says mockingly. "I thought Pole-by-the-Sea was a Zone of Peace!"

My son holds up his *kawil*, the ceremonial Magistrate's scepter topped with a carving of the double-headed snake.

"You violate that peace by bringing soldiers here. You will tell me your name and your business."

The priest laughs and leans back in his seat as if this is a mere inconvenience. "I am Pus Master, High Priest of the War God in Na Balam." I gasp. My enemy stands not a stone's throw away! Great Mother!

"As for our business," he continues in a mocking voice, "we are pilgrims, of course. We bring one who would go to the sacred Island where all women are welcome."

"Who travels with you?" Spear Thrower challenges, pointing his ceremonial staff at the covered palanquin. "Show us!"

"Very well," the loathsome Pus Master smirks. "You may all bow to the heir to the Rainbow Throne, the Princess Water Lily Cocom Chel."

Om bey! Water Lily is alive! My first feeling is a rush of relief. Then I register what Pus Master has said and I am appalled. Water Lily is in league with the Putun!? It can't be true!

Pus Master pulls the gauze curtain aside and I cry out in grief. My child! Her face—what did they do to her? In place of her left eye is a sunken, blue pit. A mass of purple and yellow bruises cover her face. Raw patches of scalp show where her hair was pulled out by the roots. Her jaw and nose are broken. Spittle runs down her chin because she can't close her mouth properly. Her face shows no expression. Does she even comprehend what has happened to her? She looks drugged. My hands go automatically to the jade beads around my neck, but then I see that she no longer wears hers. Instead, she wears a necklace made from ears and teeth of human sacrifices.

Jaguar Shield's strong arm around my shoulders is the only thing keeping me from collapsing to the ground in shock. I pull myself together. This is no time to go weak in the knees. That repulsive man has my daughter! I must go to her!

Pus Master takes advantage of the shock on Spear Thrower's face. He waves his hand. Slaves close the curtain and raise the palanquin. In a jangle of spears and footsteps, they simply walk past the dumbfounded Magistrate and Pole's guard and head for the area of the beach where the canoes are pulled up on the shore.

Jaguar Shield anticipates me before I even realize what I am about to do. His arm ropes around my neck and his hand firmly covers my mouth so that

I cannot call to my daughter. I struggle against him with all my strength, but he holds me until I weaken and then I collapse in his arms and sob.

"Mother!" Spear Thrower runs up to us. "Uncle! Hurry back and take Nine Macaw to safety!"

Of course—what am I thinking? Nine Macaw has never been in more danger than she is now! But where is there safety for the hunted girl with a royal destiny she rejects? For a fleeting moment I wonder if it would not be better for her to turn away from Cuzamil and live life as a simple dancer, as she so dearly wishes.

"Goddess," I pray, "send us a sign. Guide me now!"

But no voice comes to me. Disappointed, I take a deep breath and steel myself.

"Take her and the other girls to Fire Bird," I tell Spear Thrower and Iguana Wind. "They will be safest there, under the Goddess's protection."

"And my sister?" Spear Thrower demands of me in a harsh tone. He looks ready to charge Pus Master's small army single-handedly.

"Thank the Goddess she lives! But you must find a way to speak to Water Lily alone," I tell him. "She…she may not think kindly of me after all that has happened since we left her behind in Chichen. But you two were once close. Take Jaguar Paw with you." Perhaps seeing her son will help her remember her duty to her family lineage.

"Pus Master is just a man," Spear Thrower growls with frustration and tightens his fist angrily. "I am not afraid of him."

"Yes, Nephew, but the problem is that not everyone in Pole is unafraid of the High Priest of the War God," Jaguar Shield says calmly. "Many have come to fear the power of the heart takers. Even here in Pole, it is whispered in the market and the hairdressers' stalls that the Goddess is no longer strong enough to defeat the War God. With recent gossip about Heart of Water's madness people have doubts. They are fickle. Their loyalties too easily shift. Be careful." He glances at me and we're both remembering the destruction of Na Balam.

The wind carries the sound of the conch shells from Cuzamil. The southern blast comes three times, signaling a day of favorable tides.

"I will speak with the headman of the Bolon courtyard," Spear Thrower says. "I am still Magistrate here, and I say no one may take Pus Master or Water Lily across the sea. The Bolon will stand with us—I know it. Their livelihood and their honor depend on it. They are sworn to Ix Chel and

Her sacred Island of Women. None of them could ever lie with their wives again if they allow the Goddess's sanctuary to be taken by the War God."

A soldier runs up to me wearing the colors of Lady White Quetzal.

"Noble Lady!" he says, catching his breath while he touches his forehead and bows. "The Queen requires your presence immediately. She says to tell you there is blood."

Om bey! What else can go wrong!? I send him at a run to Spear Thrower's house to fetch my medicine bag.

"And ask the girl Blue Stone to attend me," I say. I may need assistance, and I know the pregnant queen trusts her.

"We must get to Cuzamil today," I declare. "There is no time to lose. We must clear up the question of ascension and thwart Pus Master's plans to install Water Lily on the Rainbow Throne." *Om bey!* I feel overwhelmed. What is Heart of Water's true state of mind? I am so anxious about my sister, and my daughter, and my granddaughter!

I suddenly miss my grandmother. "One worry at a time, one step at a time," she would tell me in her calm, husky voice.

"Jaguar Shield!" I grip his arm. "Ask Precious Tree to pack my bags for the journey, but you must carry my Ancestral Stone to me. Keep it safe for me." He nods reassuringly.

In Chichen, my Ancestral Stone was kept in a sacred place, but since my exile I have carried it with me in a shoulder bag worn close to my heart. It is my most precious possession. It holds the spirit energy of my Chel ancestors. When it is my time to die, a part of my spirit energy will flow into the stone and become a wise and nourishing presence for my descendants. The Ancestral Stone keeps our past, present and future connected. Heart of Water, who by rights should have kept it since she is the eldest, tucked it in my hands after our mother died.

"As Queen of Cuzamil I hold the three treasures of the Island in trust," she told me. She meant the legendary crystal skull, rainbow bowl and obsidian eye, which are the most sacred objects of Ix Chel's followers. "Jade Skirt, dear sister, you take our Ancestral Stone and keep it safe. Let the wisdom and light of our ancestors comfort you through the stone when you are far from Cuzamil." For these many *tun* it has done that. Just to hold it in my hands fills me with strength and resolve and enhances my Chel gifts.

I rush to the *polna*. The queen's servants are waiting for me in the doorway, wringing their hands in fear. I give them tasks—boil water, bring clean cloths, send Blue Stone to me as soon as she arrives.

White Quetzal lies on a stone bench, her legs propped up. Her pale color worries me. I take her wrist and feel her pulses. She is agitated, but the pulse is strong and mostly regular. That is good.

"Jade Skirt! Finally! I needed you and you were not here!"

I am happy to hear strength in her voice.

"I am here now. Tell me about the bleeding," I say in a calm and professional voice as I slip into a familiar role.

"A few spots only," she admits, "but I was afraid. It has stopped now."

Her female attendant shows me the cloth with the three spots of blood. I check the womb and the baby is still well-positioned. The queen confirms that there have been no contractions.

"We will make you a tea and you must eat and drink now even if you don't want to, because today we make the crossing to Cuzamil and you must be strong," I tell her.

The queen looks at me arrogantly. "Of course I will be strong!" But I see relief in her eyes, and trust.

I fuss over the pot while I brew her a simple herb tea. I debate whether to tell her about Pus Master. I don't want to cause her more stress.

"Sister," she says, sipping her tea and looking at me curiously, "my soldiers told me the High Priest of the War God is here, so if you think to spare me the bad news, don't bother."

Ah, well, no bird travels faster than gossip. I tell her what we saw. Saying it aloud makes it even more real, and I have to keep myself from crying again. The queen is shocked when I describe how Water Lily looked.

"I am not sure what Pus Master is planning, but we must reach Cuzamil before them!" I say. "The Magistrate prepares his boat for us."

"I think this may be the last day I can make such a voyage," she admits. "This little prince wants to come out!"

I hold my hands on her belly and send a quiet prayer to the spirit of the child to soothe him and encourage him to enjoy a few more days of comfort before he meets us outside the womb.

"Na?" Blue Stone is panting from running hard. "I have your bag. What do you need?"

It is such a relief to see my little helper. I set her to work brewing the wild plum and *pixoy*-bark tea for the queen. When the tea cools Blue Stone helps the pregnant woman sit up and drink it. Then she coaxes White Quetzal to eat the tamale and some fruit.

"Na, the others have gone to the *calmecac*, to Lady Fire Bird," Blue Stone tells me privately. Her little face is serious. "We heard the Putun are here in Pole! Even Nine Macaw understood and she did not complain about going. But Na, I want to stay with you."

My heart warms to hear this. "I go to Cuzamil today, and it is uncertain what will happen there. It is safer for you to go to *calmecac* with the others."

"But I want to help you! I can look after the Noble Lady during the voyage."

She gives me such a pleading look. I hesitate, but only for a moment. Who is to say Pole will be any safer than Cuzamil? It will be a relief to have her help with the demanding White Quetzal.

"Alright," I say, and her face lights up with a shy smile of pleasure. She hesitates and I see she has more to say.

"What is it, Blue Stone?"

"I have not known Nine Macaw long," she says carefully, "but we all witnessed the Great Mother bless her with Her rainbow light. So how can she…how can she turn her back on the Goddess?"

I sigh. "Nine Macaw has lost much in the last moon. We sometimes wish we could return to simpler times, but the wise know this can never be. Nine Macaw must discover this for herself. Someday, I hope, she will accept her destiny and her responsibility as a Chel woman."

Blue Stone nods thoughtfully. "Nine Macaw expects me and Tree Orchid to stay with her in Pole, but Tree Orchid and I want to go to Cuzamil. Na, Tree Orchid begged me to speak of this to you. She says you will understand. The *cuzam* are calling her. She had a dream last night, but she would not tell us more except that the swallows call her name again and again and she must go today, and that we must leave before the sun reaches the midpoint of the sky. The birds say a late storm comes from the south."

Goddess, thank you! You awakened Tree Orchid's gifts just when we needed them. My heart lifts with gratitude that Ix Chel's hand is guiding and protecting us. With a former slave girl, a crippled girl and a pregnant queen by my side, how can Pus Master possibly defeat me? My laughter surprises everyone in the room. I wave my hand and brush a tear from my eyes.

"Something amuses you?" the queen asks.

"Only that this day brings the unexpected at every turn," I say, "but somehow I feel it must all work out because it is all in Her hands!"

"Blessed Mother!" Lady White Quetzal prays aloud, "Thank You for Your faithful servant Jade Skirt, whose wisdom and gifts will deliver us all safely to Your holy sanctuary on this day!"

"Creator of All," Blue Stone says in a quieter voice, "we are ready to do whatever we must in service to You. And please protect the Noble Queen's precious feather and let this son of Palenque draw his first breath on Your sacred Island, on the day of Your most holy festival of 1 Zip!"

"Sister, I like this girl," the queen says imperiously. "She must stay with me until the child is born." Blue Stone and I exchange a private smile.

A servant appears to tell me Iguana Wind awaits me outside. I leave Blue Stone to help the queen.

"Mother, I like this not at all," Iguana Wind says when I insist he take me to *polna* Pus Master has taken over with his attendants, priests and soldiers.

"Pus Master cannot harm me with so many of Pole's soldiers surrounding the *polna*," I say with more confidence than I feel.

"And I will be with you," he says, grimly tapping his obsidian blade against his thigh. "But this is too big a risk!"

"I must see my daughter," I say simply. "And that vile man should tremble before me! Have you not heard that a mother's wrath is more fearsome than a warrior's spear?"

A crowd of the curious make a ring around the *polna*. Someone recognizes me and shouts, "Is the Goddess going to protect us?" Someone else cries, "Show us the heir to the Rainbow Throne!"

Iguana Wind makes a path for us into the hearth room. Spear Thrower and Jaguar Shield and twenty or so men are facing off against that many Putun soldiers. On a bench against the wall, seemingly unconcerned about the seething tension, the vile Pus Master lounges. A snarl comes from a *coatimundi* perched on his shoulder. The animal raises its ringed tail and bares its long, sharp teeth. The priest strokes it absentmindedly with blood-encrusted fingers.

He glances at me and spits at my feet. "Who brings filth into the hearth room?"

My enemy is a short, slight man. Either he is enjoying himself immensely or he always has a tight grin on his face. Pus Master's gaze bores through me like a snake mesmerizing its prey before it strikes.

"I am here for my daughter!"

"Someone tell this monkey turd of an exile that the Princess Water Lily does not wish to see her."

One of the War God's priests steps forward and speaks to the air above my head. "Princess Water Lily does not wish to see you, monkey turd."

"I insist," I say through clenched teeth.

Pus Master laughs and says conversationally to his priest. "Have you heard that the famous Oracle Jade Skirt, of whom we have heard so much, is just a piece of exile garbage now?"

Spear Thrower, Iguana Wind and Jaguar Paw have their knives out, but Pus Master ignores them. He rises and paces across the room, hands laced behind his back, relishing this moment. He knows the men of Pole will not break the Zone of Peace by attacking first.

"Release my daughter!" I yell in my voice of authority as Oracle and High Priestess. Some of the Putun priests flinch, but then the *coatimundi* hisses and strains against his tether as if to lunge at me. I jump back, startled. The heart taker laughs at me.

"Ix Chel has no more power to help Her servants than a rabbit can call down the rain!" he says mockingly. He intentionally brushes by me and I jump back like a rabbit, which makes him and his soldiers and priests laugh derisively. "I am disappointed. I thought you would be more impressive. Like the one you serve, you are weak and pitiful."

The men of Pole mutter angrily and grip their studded clubs, and the Putun sneer and goad them, but they know Ix Chel forbids them to make the first move and break Her Zone of Peace. Their muscled frames twitch with readiness to pounce if the Putun strike first.

"I will see my daughter," I say forcefully, throwing my *chu'lel* wide to command him.

"Will you?" Pus Master asks, and he's standing so close his stench makes me gag. I reflexively pull my spirit back to keep it from being tainted by the brown miasma that surrounds him. "Are you sure she wants to see you?" he taunts. "No, you're not sure at all. Because of you, her precious feather suicided. Because of you, her other children are exiles. Because of you, she has no home. Because you left her she was stoned and half-blinded and nearly killed. All of this could have been avoided if you had not defied the priests and kept Chac's chosen bride from Him!"

"You cannot keep me from my daughter!" I say boldly. Privately, I wish his words did not sting me so.

"*Om bey!* Why doesn't your Goddess save her?" he asks with feigned concern. "Why didn't Ix Chel show Her chosen Oracle how the priests of the War God saved the Princess Water Lily after her own mother and beloved Goddess left her to die?"

"That is enough, you vermin!" Spear Thrower yells. His men take a step forward, and the Putun men take a step forward.

Pus Master looks delighted. He shoves his face in Spear Thrower's face. The wretched animal darts down his arm and hisses at my son.

"Did your all-powerful Ix Chel save Water Lily? No! I did, and so she is loyal now to the War God. She knows which way the winds blow. The time of the gentle Goddess is over. The War God will rule the Known World, as is His right! And none shall stand in our way, especially not you pitiful lot." He spits contemptuously on the floor in front of Spear Thrower and then turns his angry glare to me.

"You rejected your own daughter," he shouts at me, stabbing a finger at my face. I move my hands in front of my heart in the defensive posture taught by the secret Red Hand Society to ward off evil energy. It works and he backs away, but continues shouting: "She knows you passed her over for Nine Macaw and left her to die! Princess Water Lily Chel Cocom is the rightful heir to Cuzamil and I intend to see that she gets what belongs to her!"

"By what authority do you meddle in the affairs of the Chel lineage?" I challenge, pushing him back two more steps with a subtle flick of my fingers.

"By the authority of Ix Chel, Herself!" He fights my will with his own sorcery, blowing his noxious breath in my direction. "Water Lily is a Chel woman of the Rainbow Throne lineage, great-granddaughter to Cosmic Turtle, first ruler of Cuzamil. She is the rightful heir."

"And you expect some reward from Water Lily when she rules," Spear Thrower says darkly. "No true queen of Cuzamil will be a puppet of the Putun. You Putun have cast your greedy eyes on the most revered treasures of all the provinces of Tzimentan. To hold the East would be a great strategic victory for you and the Island's great wealth would finance your endless wars for sacrificial victims. If you have your way, your priests will tear down Ix Chel's temples and erect temples to the War God!"

The men of Pole are growling now, spears aimed at the hearts of the Putun men. Pus Master only laughs. "What interesting ideas you have, Magistrate! Hmm…There is merit to much you say. Perhaps, as you say, there will be some small reward due the Putun when Queen Water Lily is settled in the Rainbow Palace."

Our men are a breath away from shattering the peace when Jaguar Paw steps forward. My grandson crosses his arms in a manly way and faces Pus Master. "I insist on seeing my mother. It is my right and duty. None will stand in my way!" How brave he is!

Pus Master only grins wider and says, "Of course she will see her own children. But where is your sister? She dearly wants to see Nine Macaw."

"That's enough!" Spear Thrower steps between us. "We will hear from Water Lily's own mouth if she cares to speak with us. You will not stop her son from asking her." Pus Master gives a shrug as if it is a small matter. Then he gives a nod and his priests and soldiers stand aside. With great dignity, Jaguar Paw walks between their ranks and into the sleeping-room area of the *polna*. We wait in tense silence.

When my grandson returns, he glances at me, but speaks privately to Spear Thrower, who shakes his head in disgust. *Om bey!* I can't believe my child will not see me!

"We will give her time to rest," I say while my heart shatters. I cannot bear to see the grin on that evil man's face another moment. I leave the *polna* in a wake of scornful laughter from Pus Master and his priests.

Water Lily, how could you!

Iguana Wind takes my arm and hurries me away from the crowd. Spear Thrower, Jaguar Shield and my grandson are right behind us. We gather in a secluded spot under a stand of palms. Jaguar Paw reports that his mother was veiled from his sight, but he knew it was her from her voice.

"She told me, 'I have no family any more. Leave me!' and when I begged her to speak to you, Na, she refused." He looks dismayed. I put my arm around him and even though he is a man now he allows it.

"We must hope Water Lily comes into her right mind again," I say. "But for now we cannot help her. We must focus our energy on getting to Cuzamil with all haste." I tell them about Tree Orchid's dream and warning of a storm later today.

Before the men race away to finish loading the boat, Jaguar Shield hands me my shoulder bag. I feel the comforting weight of the Ancestral Stone and with a sigh of relief loop it over my shoulder. Ancestors, lend me your wisdom now! There is one more thing I must do before we leave.

With two of the Palenque guard in tow, I hurry to the Temple of the Maiden. When we arrive, I'm taken aback by the crowd in the courtyard. What is this? I see four-times-twenty or more acolytes of Ix Chel garbed in various colored mantles to distinguish their temple roles. My guards clear a path for me, but we are stopped by an officious high priestess wearing the jade-encrusted headband of her office. She plants herself in front of me.

"Sister Jade Skirt," she announces in a voice that commands the attention of the crowd. "I am Cosmic Shell Mai Tzib, High Priestess of the Goddess's Temple of Motherhood here in Pole. We have waited for the Princess Nine Macaw to take up her place in Cuzamil as heir. Today, we heard that her ascension is being challenged by your own daughter. Is this true? Do the Putun intend to take your daughter to the sacred Island of our Goddess to claim the Rainbow Throne?"

"That is their intention, yes," I answer. A thought twitches in the back of my head. Long Strider, the trader I met days ago on the *sacbe*, mentioned that the Tzib priestesses could be counted on as allies. I hope this is true of Cosmic Shell. I raise my voice so that I speak to this crowd with the authority of the Oracle of Ix Chel.

"My faith is in the Great Mother," I say. "I am in council with my family. Our Goddess guides us now to protect the Rainbow Throne, just as She always has."

For a moment everyone is silent, but then the questions start up. I ignore the clamor and lean over to speak quietly to Cosmic Shell.

"Your kinsman Long Strider tells me the Rainbow Throne can count on the Tzib women as allies. I hope this is true?"

She straightens and looks me in the eye for a long moment. Her gaze sears through me and I realize she can read my *chu'lel*. Then Cosmic Shell gracefully touches her forehead and then the ground in front of me, honoring me as she would a queen. The voices grow silent. One by one the others kneel down to me. Inside, I am filled with distaste, but I imitate White Quetzal and nod regally, then try not to look like I am hurrying away as I climb the steps to the Temple of the Maiden.

Twenty soldiers of Pole guard the doors. They let me through and Fire Bird hurries over and grasps my hands and then leads me down a familiar hallway and gestures to a doorway. I enter alone.

"Nine Macaw Chel Cocom," I say gently to my granddaughter, who sits stony-faced on a bench, her arms crossed. Sad as the moment is, I rejoice to see her in the acolyte's white-and-blue mantle. Tracks of tears streak her cheeks and her eyes are puffy from crying. "I have come to say goodbye."

She looks at me with surprise. I smile gently and continue:

"I leave now for Cuzamil. You have asked to stay here, and so you shall. Our enemies are in Pole, and they will kill you if they can, so you will have guards around you day and night. There is nothing I can do about that." She gulps and then nods a little. I sigh and sit down beside her. She stares at her hands. More fat tears roll down her face.

"You are a woman now, and I will not force you into a destiny you don't want. The Great Mother gives Her blessings as She sees fit, but it is up to us to decide what we will do with them. I have lived my whole life in service to Her, often sacrificing my own desires to do Her will. My mother, my grandmother and my sister also accepted the burdens and gifts of the Goddess wholeheartedly. If you cannot do the same then you should not sit on the Rainbow Throne." She looks up at me, her expression unreadable. I say simply, "We will find a way without you. But I will miss you, Granddaughter. Whatever happens, whatever you decide, you will always be my precious feather."

She chokes back a sob. It would be easier for her if I was angry, but when I look in my heart I realize I'm not. Every word I speak to her is truth. I do not say these things to try to manipulate her. I realize with some bitter-sweetness that this is the first conversation I have had with Nine Macaw as one woman to another.

"I would give you my blessing now, the blessing of a grandmother to a grandchild. Would you allow that?" She gives a little nod.

I face her and open my Sight to her *chu'lel* and see a raging storm of anger, despair, doubt and fear. I let it all wash past me. I lay my hands on her head and whisper a prayer to the Goddess to keep her safe.

"If you wish to dance, then dance beautifully and with all your heart," I add.

When I leave I hear her sobbing quietly. I don't look back.

The first test is the hardest, Daughter.

Great Mother, hearing Your voice brings me the deepest comfort. Please protect my dear Nine Macaw. She would have made a wonderful Queen, but none can make her take up a destiny she does not want—not even You.

• • •

The sea is calm and flat. Terns and seagulls ride the wind calling out to one another. Lady White Quetzal, abdomen firmly bound in strips of cloth, is already seated in the canoe. Blue Stone and Tree Orchid flank her. She sits up as straight as she can, and her imperious look tells me that she is determined to be fine. She has insisted on bringing far too many bundles and women servants, but since these sea-going canoes are made to hold twenty passengers and we are not that many, there is plenty of room. Jaguar Shield, Jaguar Paw, Iguana Wind and Spear Thrower are last to board. To prevent sunburn, the Bolon paddlers rub their skin with armadillo salve infused with *chacah* bark and *axcanan* leaves and then slather it on the backs of their companions. They pass the gourd over to us and we do the same. Although we women will stay under the thatched roof during the journey to shelter from the sea winds and strong sun, the extra protection does no harm.

Paddlers of the Bolon lineage wear their long black hair pulled tightly up to the crown of their heads and secured in place with strips of deer leather. Black and red feathers around the topknot signify their *tuns* of service. They wear only white, unadorned loincloths and shell jewelry on their necks, earlobes, wrists and ankles. The clinking sound of the shells takes me back to the many, many times I have crossed this sea when I lived on the Island before I married Moon Eagle. The paddlers' tattoos are designs of waves, fish, stingrays and paddles. Theirs is a dangerous profession and the work of paddling is grueling. Young men only do it for nine *tuns*—it is considered bad luck to do it for longer. Like the others here at Pole, they are all paid by my sister, Heart of Water, and she rewards the Bolon with great riches. They, in turn, are supremely loyal to her and the Rainbow Throne. It is a good arrangement for all.

"Noble Lady, I am Seven Tapir," says the headman, placing his hand on his forehead and heart. "We will carry you safely to the Island, Goddess willing." He smiles confidently, his white teeth contrasting sharply with his darkly tattooed face.

A swallow darts up to Tree Orchid and lands on her shoulder. The girl strokes its gray feathers and makes a light clicking noise. The *cuzam* responds with a series of chirps and then flies off. Showing off, Kiki bobs and dances on her other shoulder.

"What does the little bird tell you?" White Quetzal asks, looking at Tree Orchid with new respect.

"A storm comes," she says grimly, "later today."

The Bolon paddlers cast one another looks. The sky is blue and cloudless, but well they know how quickly the mood of the sea can change.

"From which direction?" Seven Tapir asks politely.

Tree Orchid points to the west and the man nods, as if confirming his own suspicions. "There are many storms at sea," he says calmly. "We will be ready for it. The winds are favorable this morning. But thank you, little Bird Oracle!"

Tree Orchid blushes shyly. Then Seven Tapir nods again at me. Everyone in the canoe places a hand over his or her heart while I join the other nine priestesses who stand in a circle in the lapping waves to say the prayer of crossing to Cuzamil.

"Great Mother, You who are the Heart of Water, Queen of the Sea and Heaven, grant us safe passage over Your sacred body. May we travel peacefully, calmly in the lap, in the bosom, in the embrace of our Father the Sun and our Brother the Wind. Ix Chel, show us Your mercy and compassion."

I drop a few grains of *copal* into the waters of the sea. Then Jaguar Shield lifts me into the boat and the headman wastes no time getting underway. He shouts a word and the paddlers pull together and expertly position us in the current. We glide away with Pole at my back and Cuzamil before me—a faint smudge on the eastern horizon. At last, I am on the final leg of this exile's journey home. My heart is heavy, though. I can't shake the feeling that Nine Macaw should be sitting here beside me. I wish for Water Lily and Red Earth to be sitting beside me, too.

A few minutes into the voyage I see a sight that lifts my spirits. A long, blue-painted canoe shoots toward us from Cuzamil. Finally, Heart of Water has sent the royal barge! Spear Thrower waves and shouts, and the rowers draw the two boats together.

"We had given up on you!" my son calls cheerfully. "As you can see, we are bringing my Noble Mother to the Island ourselves."

The Bolon man in charge of the royal barge looks uncomfortably at his crew mates. "Magistrate, we follow Heart of Water's direct orders," he says awkwardly. "We were not sent to bring the Lady Jade Skirt. We were sent to bring the Princess Water Lily to Cuzamil."

Treachery! I can't believe Heart of Water chooses Water Lily to be her heir! She knows my daughter, a gourd-tipper, lacks the Chel gifts and does not have a favorable calendar day. All the rumors about Heart of Water's state of mind made me uneasy, but up until this moment I still nurtured hope that it was all a misunderstanding—that Heart of Water would explain herself when I arrived in Cuzamil. Now I see that was only my own comforting fantasy.

Long Strider warned me to prepare for a power struggle. The old *h'men* I met on the temple steps warned me that someone dear to me would betray me, but never did I believe it could be Heart of Water. I honor my sister, but I will do whatever the Goddess requires to preserve Her sacred Island.

Pus Master waits like a panther on the shores of Pole, ready to pounce on Cuzamil. The Island of Women has its own female soldiers who are well-trained and constantly ready to defend the Island. But will they see me as the enemy if I defy Heart of Water's plan to name Water Lily as heir? *Om bey!* If Nine Macaw had come I would be proud to be bringing the rightful heir to Cuzamil. Her Goddess-given gifts would shine like a beacon and all would see that she is Ix Chel's chosen one. Without her it will be hard to convince the priestesses and soldiers to contradict their queen.

Jaguar Shield moves over to sit beside me. Feeling his thigh press against mine brings me comfort, but I also ache with the goodbye we must say to each other when we reach the shore. The memory of our afternoon of lovemaking rushes through me and I feel his *chu'lel* respond. A moment later we both sigh. With the sound of the paddlers and the constant song of the wind, at least we have some privacy to speak our hearts.

"My love," I murmur, "when you return to Pole you must tell my son to send patrols to search for Putun boats. They no doubt plan to invade Cuzamil whether or not they succeed in installing Water Lily as the new queen."

"Jade Skirt, my jewel, it is already done. His men scout the shores at this very moment. They will torch the boats when they find them. But Pus Master is tricky. The boats might come from Putun ports further south. They can easily be disguised as trader vessels when they embark at the trader's port in the north of the Island, at Chunkunab. You must stay vigilant at all times, precious heart, even while we trust in Ix Chel, who guides all of us who love and serve Her."

Why do I need reminders from others to trust Her when the Goddess speaks to me directly? "It is your nature to worry," he says, as if reading my mind. "I am sure She knows you trust in Her. But She also knows you like to tie up your turkeys first, is it not so?" he asks playfully, a boyish grin on his beautifully scarred face. Even in the midst of the greatest crisis in my life, I cannot help but admire his sharp profile, his regal nose and flattened forehead.

"And what of us?" I look down at my hands. If I gaze at his face right now everyone on the boat will know my feelings.

"I will wait for you in Pole," he says simply. "While you serve the Goddess on Her Island, will you not sometimes come across to visit your son, to look after Nine Macaw and seek the wisdom of the priestesses in Pole?" I smile at him. "Ah! So we will have our stolen time together, my dove."

My heart lifts a little. He presses his leg against mine more firmly and I close my eyes and let my *chu'lel* merge with his. The rock and sway of the boat is gentle as a mother's arms. I am so tired, and it is a relief to feel his spirit united with mine. My head sinks to his shoulder and his arm comes around me. One of White Quetzal's servants sings a lilting lullaby that we all know from childhood.

Next thing I know I am waking up with my head still cradled against Jaguar Shield's shoulder. I sit up and he passes me a gourd of water. I feel a leap of joy when I see how close the Island is now. We still have a ways to go, but I can make out the shoreline and the faint outline of the famous stone tower of the Temple of the Moon.

The Bolon paddlers pull their oars vigorously to the rhythm of a small drum. Their muscular backs keep the canoe from drifting out of the current that bears us to Her sanctuary. We cross paths with a pod of frolicking dolphins, which delights us all. White Quetzal dozes under the thatched roof along with Tree Orchid—her bandaged foot propped up on a bag—and several of the queen's attendants. Awake and wide-eyed, Blue Stone gives me a big smile. She scoots forward and hands me a pouch filled with dried fruits and another of guavas. Jaguar Shield and I each take some and then he moves to the back to share them with Spear Thrower, Iguana Wind and Jaguar Paw. I turn to see how they are doing and that's when I see a blue dot behind us. It's the royal barge racing back to Cuzamil. Do they bring Water Lily?

I let out a shout and point to the canoe. Suddenly, a gust of wind picks up and shoves us out of the current. It nearly topples the great canoe. Seven Tapir gives a shout. The drumbeat quickens, and the paddlers pull hard, and again, and once more. Now we're back in the current and we're flying over the water as if the Goddess's own hand pushes us! The paddlers shout with excitement and cast me looks of awe as though I am responsible for moving us back into the current.

"Thank you, Mother of All Creation," I pray. "You hold us in the palm of Your hand."

A disappointed shout from Spear Thrower and I turn to see that the same wind is also hurrying the royal barge to Cuzamil. The bigger canoe starts to gain on us, but a new wind suddenly blows across the waves and churns up ferocious waves. The sky darkens with thick clouds. I just barely catch a glimpse of Water Lily when we lose sight of the royal canoe behind a white-capped wave. Then the thatch roof over our heads shreds like paper and blows away. The queen's women shriek as fat, cold raindrops pelt down on us mercilessly. We're all grabbing our seats and the sides of the boat as the waves toss us back and forth, up and down. I hear a scream from White Quetzal, who starts to tip over the side. I lunge across and throw my arms around her to keep her from being hurled Into the sea.

"Steady now, Sister," I shout over the sound of the wind. I can feel her trembling, whether from fear or the chill of the drenching rain and waves I can't tell. I must help her to calm down or the fright could bring on an early labor.

Above the din of the storm I cry: "Ix Chel, Great Mother, Creator of All, Goddess of the Sea, protect this mother and her precious feather. Ix Chel, Guardian of the Womb, deliver this mother and her baby to safety. We trust in You."

As the waves continue to toss our boat from side to side, Blue Stone and I manage to cushion the queen between us. We must hold onto her because she has wrapped her arms around her belly protectively and she cannot be convinced to let go and grab the bench, crazed as she is with fear.

"Close your eyes, Daughter," I tell her. "We are close to Cuzamil. The Goddess will not forsake us now. Be strong!"

"Help!" Tree Orchid screams. Jaguar Shield leaps up and grab her just in time as the canoe flies up the side of a mountain of water. Now we are all screaming as the boat slams down in the valley between the waves. A breath later we're up again, and then back down, and again and again. All of us save the Bolon paddlers are losing the contents of our stomachs.

"Goddess! Have mercy!" Lady White Quetzal shouts at the wind, but another wave as high as a mountain takes us up and slams us back down. Have we come this far only to die just before we reach Cuzamil? Is this why we left Nine Macaw in Pole—to spare her life? I pray Jaguar Shield has a tight grip on Tree Orchid. I hope Spear Thrower and Iguana Wind are holding onto Jaguar Paw. The queen's attendants have managed to link arms and are keeping one another from going over the side.

"Mother of the Sea, calm Your forces!" screams the queen.

Her servants decide to lie down in the bottom of the canoe, which is sloshing with sea water and vomit.

"Get up! Get up!" shouts Jaguar Shield over the roar of the storm. "You are slipping around there like a fish." He rips off his loincloth, cuts it in two with his knife and claws his way forward to tie the queen down to her seat. With the other half he straps me to the seat. He shouts to Spear Thrower, who crawls back with a length of hemp rope. Despite the rollicking motion and pelting rain they manage to secure the girls and the rest of us to our benches. I push away every thought of the day my father died in just such a storm and remember that we three children were saved by the paddlers.

The rain lets up for a moment and I dare to hope that we have passed through the worst of it, but then stinging balls of hail bombard us.

"Help me!" White Quetzal begs, truly desperate. She clutches my arm. "I can't take any more! You are the Oracle! Do something!"

"Divine Mother of Life, our trust is in You." I shout to the wind, the words giving me strength. "Ix Chel, defend us from the anger of the sea! Ik, God of Winds, cease your fury!"

As if they hear me, the winds die down a little, and then a little more. A minute later, the rain is just a drizzle. The choppy waters still toss us about, but less roughly. The paddlers give shouts of relief and praise the Goddess for Her mercy. They look at me as if I am Ix Chel, Herself.

"That wasn't so bad!" Seven Tapir says with a hearty laugh.

At that moment, the storm clouds break and the fog lifts. The Island is before us, a lush, green teardrop in the azure sea. We all exclaim in wonder. The storm brought us right to Cuzamil's shore! We are close enough to see the carvings on the white towers of the Temple of the Moon! The sacred Island has five great temples: this one in the west, and to the east the Temple of the Oracle. To the north is the Temple of the Maiden and to the south, the Temple of the Grandmother. In the center of the Island, the heart of Cuzamil, is the Great Temple of the Mother, and beside it sits the Rainbow Palace, built by my grandmother, Cosmic Turtle. I send my thoughts there. Does Heart of Water feel how close I am? I focus my inner Knowing, but I cannot feel her.

There is no sign of the royal barge, which is a relief, yet my Water Lily was on that boat. I feel so conflicted. I pray the Goddess will keep her safe, but she cannot be allowed to take over the Rainbow Throne. She will hand it right to the Putun. If the barge was lost in the storm... No! I mustn't think it. As usual, when it comes to Water Lily, I wonder if I am a bad mother. How could she have been duped into this conspiracy with Pus Master against her own lineage, her own daughter and her mother? Perhaps she is outside her senses.

Bruised, battered and drenched, we all managed to make it through the storm alive. I untie my bonds and check White Quetzal. She is pale with exhaustion, but not bleeding or having contractions. I reach for her wrists and murmur nine prayers into the pulses. I feel her relax and she sighs with relief and finds her voice once again.

"You should have listened to the little Bird Oracle before we left Pole, Jade Skirt! What were you thinking?"

"We will be there soon," I say to her. "It won't be long now. Faith, dear heart."

"Well, I should hope—oh!"

We all look up and gasp as an enormous rainbow appears, stretching from Pole to the center of Cuzamil.

"Praise be to Ix Chel!" everyone on the canoe cheers.

There are more gasps of awe when the rainbow doubles. We touch our hands to our hearts in reverence at this stunning sign of Her benevolence.

"A blessing!" Lady White Quetzal says, deeply moved. "She welcomes us with the clearest possible sign!" She crosses her hands over her pregnant belly and murmurs a prayer of thanks.

It still takes some time to paddle around to the beach where we can disembark, and the waiting is hard. We are all wet and cold, and the water in the canoe smells unpleasantly of vomit. The queen's attendants do their best to make their mistress comfortable, but there really isn't anything anyone can do and she snaps at them to sit down and leave her alone. Blue Stone is shivering. Tree Orchid is grimacing in pain. The bandage on her foot is soaking wet. The salt is good for the wound, I assure her, but I know it must be uncomfortable and could become infected. I draw both girls in for a hug. I tell them how brave they are and how proud I am of them both. How fragile is life, and how precious these beloved maidens are to me. Goddess, thank You for delivering us safely!

As we draw close to the beach, the Bolon men sing the song of arrival, their harmonies twisting together with remarkable beauty. They sing their gratitude to the Mother, Goddess of the sea and patroness of paddlers and fishermen. Their song and the slapping of the paddles awakens happy memories of childhood. I used to love it our grandmother allowed me and Heart of Water to greet the pilgrims.

Great Mother, Queen of the Sea.
You battled the Storm God.
You battled the Rain God.
You battled the Wind God.
You saved us so we may live another day.

"Men!" shouts Jaguar Shield to the paddlers. "Goddess be praised! We owe our lives to you. I will never forget how you managed this canoe in the worst weather conditions."

The men look at one another. A few of them laugh. "*Nacom,* this is far from the worst storm we have been through. It was bad for a moment or two, but the Goddess was at our side."

The waves are now calm. It seems impossible that this same sea, which is flat as an obsidian blade, nearly overturned us moments ago.

Several paddlers jump out of the canoe and drag it up to the sandy beach so we can disembark. Other canoes are lined up waiting to embark on the dusk-to-dawn passage back to Pole if the seas and the wind conches allow. Returning pilgrims wait by the boats no longer dressed in blue, but wearing the usual garb of their homes. I see joyful new mothers with infants at the breast; pubescent girls glowing from their coming-of-age ceremonies on the Island; and women of the second age who came for rest, healing and prayers and who look calm and refreshed. All the women are laughing and pointing at the rainbows and exclaiming.

Barely able to contain her excitement, Blue Stone and Tree Orchid look around in all directions as if they expect Ix Chel Herself to appear. "Cuzamil is the very center of the earth, the navel of creation, the divine womb of the Mother from which all the world was created," I tell them.

"It is the furthest point of the East where Father Sun and Mother Moon rise," White Quetzal chimes in. "It has always been the brightest star in the Known World."

I nod. "And it is the perfect combination of Divine feminine and masculine *chu'lel*. That is why this Island is sacred to Ix Chel."

I am the first to disembark. As I set my feet on the earth of Cuzamil the bumps rise on my skin as I feel Her gentle power and Presence. The bustle of the acolytes and pilgrims fades and I am one with the pulsing heartbeat that rises up from the ground. It travels through my eager feet and Her tender welcome suffuses me with a feeling of homecoming. Beyond words, deeply still in my spirit, I breathe in deeply and drink in the beauty of the double rainbow.

The beautiful moment is cut short by a moan from White Quetzal.

"Sisters!" I shout to the acolytes, "Bring a chair to carry the Queen of Palenque! Hurry!" They race off to find a palanquin and I take the queen's hand in both of mine.

"We made it," I tell her. "You were wonderful! They will tell the story of your courage for generations to come."

"Jade Skirt," White Quetzal moans. "The babe is complaining! He wants to come, but it is not time!"

"He wants you to know he is strong and healthy," I say reassuringly. "We have arrived on the sacred Island." Then in a whisper, I say, "He need only wait a few days more for 1 Zip to dawn, and then he can join us in the world."

"But how will I hold him in if he insists on coming out?"

I say with mock severity. "Are you not the Queen of Palenque?! You will command this pup to stay put until you give him leave to be born!" She bursts out laughing, and her attendants and the girls join in. How good it is to be standing on the shore of Cuzamil laughing!

The men secure the boat and unload the baskets while the acolytes offer gourds of fresh water and welcome each of us. The chair bearers arrive and five of us support White Quetzal as she clambers out of the boat and into the conveyance.

"What a terrible storm we just had!" exclaims a round, blue-robed priestess. She bustles over to us and the acolytes greet her with respect. She wears the same style of jade-decorated headband as the Tzib priestess Cosmic Shell, but I would have known her anyway as a woman from the steamy southern jungles of the Land of the Turkey and the Deer by her high cheekbones and wide mouth. For a moment she gazes up at the fading rainbows and her countenance is serene. A woman of the second age, she is exactly my height. A butterfly nose ring made of pink shell indicates her high status among the Island priestesses. Butterflies, the returned souls of warriors, have always been revered on the Island.

"Just look at this destruction," she sighs, waving one hand in the direction of the jungle where leaves and limbs and palm fronds litter the ground. "The Island is a terrible mess for your arrival. It will be days before we can clean up all the debris. But Her rainbow is very auspicious indeed!" Her eyes fall on me and widen in recognition. "*Om bey*! Noble Lady Jade Skirt Chel Cocom!" Flustered for a moment, she forgets she is standing in the lapping waves and makes as if to touch the ground.

"Who greets me?"

"I am Evening Star Mai Itza," she answers warmly, touching her forehead then her heart. "Finally, you have come! We have been waiting for you and the young princess. Praise be to Ix Chel that you are here! Where is she?" She looks eagerly at Blue Stone, who is busy supporting White Quetzal, and at Tree Orchid, who is being helped out of the canoe by Jaguar Paw and tries to limp a few steps before stumbling.

"There is much to tell, Evening Star. Help get the Queen of Palenque settled and then I will explain everything. I have many questions for you as well."

"Of course, Lady. Forgive me. That is the Queen of Palenque, you say?" She greets the queen with a respectful bow and assures her that the best accommodations have been prepared and that the attending midwife will visit her after the queen has bathed. Nose in the air again, White Quetzal nods regally despite her obvious exhaustion.

Evening Star calls out rapid instructions and another group of acolytes runs down to the boat carrying a second basket-chair.

"After you bathe, you must rest and drink as much water as you can," I tell White Quetzal. "Try to eat a little meat and fruit before sleeping. Blue Stone and Tree Orchid will stay with you."

She gives me a look of despair as if to say, "How can you leave me like this?" But Blue Stone steps up and murmurs in her ear. White Quetzal clutches her arm and nods.

When the pregnant queen and Tree Orchid are settled, the strong young women lift the chairs as if they weigh nothing and carefully lead the way across the beach toward the grove of thirteen sacred *ceiba* trees. Blue Stone jogs to keep up, her head swiveling this way and that to take in all the exciting new sights. Tree Orchid grins happily from her perch. Kiki flies above her and a flock of *cuzam* call down a noisy greeting as the group heads to the *kulha*, the sacred spring of Cuzamil.

It is a tradition that before pilgrims embark on the five-day, round-the-Island procession to leave offerings and make prayers at each of the five great temples on Cuzamil, each pilgrim is washed by the acolytes and spiritually cleansed by Her sacred waters, *copal* smoke and prayers.

"You are only the second canoe to make the crossing today," Evening Star tells me. A chattering clutch of earlier arrivals is just leaving the sacred spring. A young temple maiden dressed in the white mantle of an assistant escorts the happy group from the baths to the interior of the Island, where they will be housed in a *polna*.

"Did the royal canoe return?" I ask casually, a lump in my throat.

"No!" She shoots me a curious look. "No, the canoe was sent, but we have not seen it return. We thought you and the princess would be on it."

"Mother, the baskets are unloaded," Spear Thrower says, coming up from the boats. Evening Star gapes at Spear Thrower for a moment and then bows her head and places her right hand above her ample chest. "Noble Magistrate, welcome again to the land of your birth."

"Thank you, Sister."

"You come in a time of trouble," she murmurs quietly. "News from Pole is troubling. Many of my Sisters would welcome accurate information from the Magistrate."

"Yes, we must talk," answers Spear Thrower. "But first, should my Noble Mother be housed in quiet quarters this evening, or in the palace with her Royal Sister?"

"Quiet quarters would be most restful," Evening Star says carefully.

"Thank you, Sister. That is very considerate," I tell her. We exchange a look of mutual understanding.

"Please, Noble Lady and Noble Magistrate, first you must bathe and change your wet clothing." Evening Star's take-charge attitude is just what we need right now.

"We will do as you say," I reply graciously. "But my son Iguana Wind must send a message to his wife and daughter without delay."

She calls a white-clad acolyte to consult with Iguana Wind. The girl sprints away and Iguana Wind looks after her with hope in his eyes. Jaguar Shield joins us, still naked, and introductions are made. Then the Bolon men escort our men to their area to bathe and Evening Star takes me to the women's baths. I can't wait to rid myself of the stomach-turning stench of the voyage.

As Father Sun sets in the West in a fiery ball of color, Evening Star and I remove our clothes and settle into one of the many deep, blue pools in a private area reserved for priestesses who return to the Island. For we who are priestesses of the Great Mother, the spring is a joyful reunion of our *chu'lel* with Her, the source of life. It is one of the sacred mysteries into which we are initiated during our consecration to the Goddess. Evening Star and I murmur the prayer together, while overhead a noisy family of howler monkeys watches us, their hairy black bodies clambering up and down the tree limbs. Purple orchid petals blown by the storm float in the sparkling pools. Through the trees I can see the now-calm sea turning crimson from the reflection of Father Sun.

Evening Star's young assistant washes us both with a soft sea sponge soaked in *guanacaste* pod soap. In a larger pool below ours I see the girls, the queen and her attendants enjoying their baths. I am impressed that Blue Stone is attentive both to the needs of White Quetzal and Tree Orchid. Like a true healer, she shows compassion for those in need and has an innate willingness to help.

For now, at this moment, all is well. It makes me recall the priestess who trained me so many *tuns* ago. She always liked to remind us, "There is only this moment. Nothing else is real no matter how dire the circumstances may seem."

I breathe deeply and shift into communion with Ix Chel. In the rush and violence of our journey as exiles, I have neglected my spiritual practice of seeking the quiet, calm presence of Ix Chel within. I close my eyes and feel Her. She is in the sun-warmed water, the azure sea, the gurgling spring and dancing branches of the *ceiba* trees. Her watchful presence from within and without renews my strength and calm. In this moment, I have no favors to ask of Her, no burdens to unload, no probing questions. I am content to be here.

With deft, practiced hands, Evening Star combs my hair and then braids in rainbow ribbons. I feel like a child again when she tugs too vigorously at my scalp. When I don the white undergarment and blue mantle of the Island priestesses, it feels as if I've finally and truly come home. No longer am I a pilgrim, an exile, a disappointed grandmother. I am Jade Skirt Chel Cocom, High Priestess and Oracle of the Goddess Ix Chel, a princess and daughter of Her sacred Island of Women.

I am grateful for Evening Star's companionable silence as we walk through the jungle on a well-traveled path. Ahead of me, her plump frame moves gracefully. Through the *ceiba* trees, I can see the glowing hearth fires of the women and children who stay near the beach in a *polna* to be ready to make the dawn crossing. I marvel at the power of this holy place to take in and nurture so many of us throughout our lifetimes. All those lives, all those heartaches and sorrows shed here; all the joys, blessings and boons taken back to their homes. Faint sounds of the evening chant to the Great Mother mixed with infant wails reach my ears and touch my heart.

Evening Star and I climb a narrow path that winds up a rise to a patio-encircled thatch hut used for meetings between male visitors and Heart of Water's administrators. The single oval room has a small, expertly fashioned hearth of white limestone where a warm, inviting fire crackles. Bathed and wearing fresh capes and loincloths, the men are already seated and drinking hot cups of *cacaltun* tea. I love the rich aroma of the wild basil, one of the Island's most prized healing herbs. Known for its relaxing and warming qualities, the herb tea is the smell of my childhood and brings a smile to my face. A young maiden hands both me and Evening Star cups of tea and offers the clay jar of aromatic Cuzamil honey. She bows and leaves us.

I take a seat on the bench beside Jaguar Shield. Crackling warmth from the hearth fire is delicious after the cold bath. We are only steps away from the wild jungle where sea palms, unconcerned by our human troubles, wave like children at a festival. Keel-billed toucans flit clumsily back and forth, their rainbow colored beaks swishing the air as they pass. Father Sun has already begun his nightly journey as a black jaguar into the Underworld.

"So," I start, after a few sips of tea, "Sister Evening Star, we hear troubling reports about Cuzamil. What can you tell us?"

Nervously, her hands play with her necklace of crystal beads, "Lady Jade Skirt, a messenger from Chichen reached us with news of your exile and we have been waiting for your arrival ever since. As the Queen's sister, only you can set things right here on Cuzamil."

"What is the situation with my sister?" I ask impatiently. "She is neglecting her duty to the *polnas*. The traders are upset that Cuzamil now demands twice the usual share of profits. The Putun wait on the shores of Pole like jaguars ready to pounce on our Island. We sent her word days ago that we awaited the royal barge in Pole and she ignored us. What has happened here?"

Evening Star's plain face, illuminated in the firelight, looks tense and worried. She wrings her hands. "These are dark times, and we pray for Ix Chel's protection during this *katun* of Mountain Movement. Queen Heart of Water warned us seven moons ago that we must prepare for the worst." She sighs. "We had no idea it would be this bad!"

"What has happened? Tell me!" I say impatiently.

"Lady, as you know, Lady Heart of Water is nearly three-times-twenty *tuns* and has been doing the oracular duties for two-times-twenty *tuns*. She told us that although she had surpassed the span of time allotted to an Oracle, the Goddess was strengthening her so she could continue until you arrived with the princess. But three moons past, the queen collapsed after embodying the Goddess. She sent a message to you to come at once. She said her body could not withstand another dose of the powders and enema."

Why did I not hear she was so ill? Messengers are extremely reliable, yet I received no such message.

"Sending the message was her last sane act, Lady." Evening Star gives me a nervous look. "We love our Queen, but she has not been herself since then. She rants and raves and beats her attendants. She barely eats and cannot sleep. We hear her screaming in the night. The healers tried to help, but she sent them away and claimed they were trying to poison her."

It is certain, then. The Oracle's madness is on Heart of Water. Well I know the exhaustion that comes after each full moon, when the Oracle embodies the Goddess. The very fibers and sinews of the body feel frayed to wisps. Headaches, nightmares and malaise can haunt an Oracle for days after. That is why one can only embody the Goddess for a few days of each month. For twenty-plus-five days we must take special cleansing herbs and foods, spiritual baths and time for meditation and reflection. Our attendants see that these basic requirements are met. It is they who must inform the High Priestesses if they see signs of overdose or exhaustion so that the Oracle's duties can be passed to another before permanent madness sets in.

"The rituals, trade talks, scrying—all Queen Heart of Water's duties were neglected. But we knew you would come so we did as best we could and sent the royal barge to wait for you and Nine Macaw in Pole. After a moon had passed the barge returned with news that you and the princess were exiles. We hoped and prayed that our message had reached you in time and that you were on your way here. Every day, the Queen asked for you. Every day!" She shakes her head, the long jade pieces in her ears wobbling.

Om bey! Heart of Water must have thought I was ignoring her summons. No wonder she appeared so fearsome and angry in my dreams.

"I will take over my sister's healing and be the Oracle of Cuzamil until Nine Macaw is prepared," I say, not ready to think about what we will do about the succession without Nine Macaw. I want to leap off the bench and run to the palace and clear up this misunderstanding with my dear sister, but Evening Star's husky voice pulls me back.

"Your proxy has been here, fulfilling some of the duties," says Evening Star.

"Proxy?" I have no idea what she's talking about.

"The Cocom priestess who carried the first message returned to us with a reply from you that she was to serve as your proxy until you could come. So Heart of Water took her into her inner circle to serve with her two closest assistants, Cloud Tree and Sky Mirror."

What?! Who is this Cocom priestess she speaks of? Before I can ask, Evening Star continues:

"Your priestess took charge and not three days later Heart of Water dismissed Cloud Tree and Sky Mirror! She banished them from the sacred Island! It was a shock to us all. After nearly twenty *tuns* of dedicated service, they were sent to serve in the temples of Tulumha."

I am speechless. Sky Mirror was second Oracle for many *tuns*, and was a dear friend to my sister and me since childhood. She trained Cloud Tree herself, and the two are as close as family to Heart of Water.

"Why would she banish them?"

"Some evil tongues whispered that Sky Mirror was poisoning the Queen," Evening Star says.

That is absurd! Both women would give their lives for Heart of Water.

"What is the name of this proxy?" Jaguar Shield asks, frowning deeply.

"Blue Monkey Tzib Cocom. "

"What!?" I spring up, my fists clenched, "That demon is here, ruling in my name?!"

Evening Star is taken aback. "Is Blue Monkey not married to one of your husband's lineage? She brought also her daughter, Eighteen Rabbit."

I am too furious to answer. Blue Monkey! In Chichen, that traitorous woman broke clan secrecy and revealed our plans to run away with Nine Macaw. Because of her, Jaguar Shield and I were arrested. And now she is here, controlling the Rainbow Throne?! I can barely contain my rage. Of course she never delivered Heart of Water's message to me. She must have been plotting long before Nine Macaw was chosen to be sacrificed. *Om bey*, how deep did her plotting go? Was she in league with Blood Gatherer?

"I did not send Blue Monkey here!" I say when I finally get control of my anger. "I despise her! She has been my enemy since childhood days. She covets the Rainbow Throne for herself and that dull daughter of hers, Eighteen Rabbit."

Evening Star looks shocked. "She has lied about this?" Then her expression turns to one of great relief. "Oh, Lady, I am so glad to know she is not one of your trusted priestesses! We did not want to think badly of one whom you sent to us, but many of us were suspicious, especially when she announced that the crystal skull would be taken from the Island for safekeeping."

Take away the most treasured item on the sacred Island?! Twenty-times-twenty *tuns* ago, our Chel ancestor Cosmic Serpent was guided by the Goddess to find the crystal skull buried deep in a cave on Cuzamil. Equal in size to a human head, it embodies the ancestors, Ix Chel and the Nine Spirits that rule the earth. It is the symbol of the Chel's right to rule on Cuzamil. As talisman, spiritual guide and protector, the skull speaks to Ix Chel's priestesses in dream visions. When the Queen sleeps with the crystal skull next to her, she is strengthened and filled with the wisdom of the ages. In times past, Tun, as it is affectionately called, served as the Oracle, speaking Her words through its moveable jaw. One day it turned silent and thus my grandmother, Cosmic Turtle, became the Oracle in its place. It was Tun who guided my grandmother to expel all the men from the Island and declare Cuzamil a sanctuary for women. Tun directed my grandmother to found the mystery schools. To remove this priceless treasure from the Island would be the ultimate sacrilege. Legend says that anyone who tries will die. Blue Monkey has always made trouble, but she should know better. She is a priestess of Ix Chel!

Spear Throwers says reasonably, "Mother, if it is only Blue Monkey and her daughter who have falsely gained authority in your name then our task will not be difficult. Now that you have arrived, we can let the other priestesses know that you did not send her; that she lied and must be punished."

Evening Star shakes her head and sighs. "Magistrate, it will not be that easy. Blue Monkey has been coming to the Island every second moon for more than a *tun*. Each time, she brought more priestesses of the Cob lineage. We have nearly three-times-twenty of them now housed in their own *polna* in Tixchel, right beside the Rainbow Palace. Blue Monkey insisted you wanted them to have it. All of the Queen's attendants have been replaced by either Cob women or their allies from the Itzam lineage. They control Cuzamil's administration in the name of the Rainbow Throne."

"What are the names of these Cob priestesses?" I ask. If they are from Chichen, I will know them.

Evening Star names them, but none of the names are familiar to me. Jaguar Shield sits up straight.

"I know two of those names," he says. "They were Cob women who served in the Temple of Chac in Labna. They were temple assistants to the heart takers. The others must be as well."

Heart takers! On Her sacred Island! How long has Blue Monkey been in league with the heart takers? How deep does her subterfuge go? Does she serve the War God? Is she Pus Master's pawn? The Cob women surely must know we have arrived. Blue Monkey might have spies to watch the beach. While we are sitting here drinking tea, she is no doubt weaving her sticky web. May she stand at the river and never cross. May her *nopales* never flourish!

Jaguar Shield leaps to his feet. "The situation is more dangerous than we anticipated," he says. "First, we must protect Lady Jade Skirt, next heir to the throne."

My heart flutters a little at his caring glance. I still don't think of myself as in line for the Rainbow Throne, but so I am.

"Where is the princess?" Evening Star asks with concern. "Is she safe?"

I don't want to tell Evening Star the whole story, so I simply say, "Nine Macaw is in Pole's Temple of the Maiden, under the care of the priestess Fire Bird."

"We need to bring her to Cuzamil," Spear Thrower says. "Her presence on the Island will strengthen the Chel position and weaken Blue Monkey's."

"No!" I say, glancing at Evening Star. I can't speak freely in front of her, so I say. "She...is a woman now and may not want to interrupt her training in Pole."

Spear Thrower looks like he wants to argue, but only says, "Then let her brother go to her and explain the situation and hear what she will do."

Jaguar Shield sends my grandson off at a run to inform the Bolon men to prepare a canoe to return to Pole and also to send men to guard us here this night.

While we wait for reinforcements Jaguar Shield, Spear Thrower and Iguana Wind take up positions outside the hut, urgently whispering and making plans for our defense. How grateful I am to have my strong protectors with me, but Blue Monkey is a sorcerer. Soldiers will not protect them or us from her evil.

"Who knows I am here, Sister?" I ask Evening Star when we are alone. I make the subtle sign of the Red Hand society, but she does not notice, which tells me she was not trained in those higher arts.

"The acolytes heard me call you by name, Lady. We were all so eager for your arrival—I am sure word has spread." She looks dismayed. "I am sorry! I should have thought—I didn't know."

"No matter, Evening Star. But now I need you to pray to the Sheltering Mother with me. I must cast protections around us immediately."

She gives me an awed look and then bows her head to the ground and calls on the Creator's source of strength, opening her *chu'lel* to me. It is a steady flow of dark purple, strong in faith. From the top of my head, I send her a pulse of light and feel her receive it. Good. She has spiritual reception.

Now I close my eyes and grasp my *pi*. The powerful objects in my deer-skin medicine bag will help shield me from Blue Monkey. I pull in my *chu'lel*. As easy as breathing I feel my own pulse quicken and then merge with the pulse of the sacred Island. I feel the presence of night creatures in the jungle beyond these walls, and the strong hearts and resolve of my beloveds. I am with the soaring sea birds. I cast my net further out and… there! In a tree not two-times-twenty paces from us I sense a presence. Another presence creeps in from the north. Malice and violence are in their thoughts. I feel a fizz in my spine that always warns me when treachery is afoot. I pull my awareness back to the room.

"Brother!" I call quietly.

Jaguar Shield is at my side in a heartbeat and I quickly describe where the enemy lurks. He nods once. He and Spear Thrower melt into the darkness. I close my eyes to extend my awareness again and scan all around us. I sense my grandson like a beacon of light. He has nearly reached the *polna* where the men are housed. Good. I cast my attention to the south and search for the spirit bodies of Tree Orchid and Blue Stone. Their *chu'lel* is a ring of calm blue. The Queen of Palenque and her precious feather glow with a warm yellow light of contentment that eases my heart.

Just as I start to feel relieved, a shiver comes over me. I feel something malicious at the edge of my awareness. It is hard to pinpoint, as if it is being hidden by a wavy shadow. I recognize this feeling. Someone is using sorcery to hide! I try to push through the shadow, but it is like a wall that cannot be breached. I need more power. I feel Evening Star praying calmly beside me and I touch her *chu'lel* with a question. Her inner awareness extends to me. She answers my probe with a surge of her own *chu'lel*. Gratefully, I channel it into my own and then push toward the shadow. I struggle against the wall until I am nearly spent, but with a snap the shield around it is gone and I see it clearly. In shape it looks like a black scorpion, but larger than any native scorpion of the Island, and far more venomous. Blue Monkey's spies must have told her where the girls are staying. She assumed Nine Macaw is among them and sent the scorpion to kill the heir to the throne.

I pull my attention back to the room. After several focused breaths, my ordinary senses return.

"Evening Star, how long will it take to reach the *polna* where the Queen of Palenque stays?" I keep my voice even and calm, and hide the tremble in my hands.

"It is the length of many canoes, Lady."

No time! I drop back into my meditation and throw my energy out along a channel of wind until it touches the spirits of Blue Stone and Tree Orchid. I feel their fatigue and pleasant sensations of being full from a meal. Tree

Orchid's foot throbs with pain. I extend my awareness and...there! The scorpion is close. Tail in the air, its black, scaly body crawls to the edge of the deerskin door. I gather in my energy and then call out with my spirit. "Girls! Attend me!"

Blue Stone's *chu'lel* suddenly flares. Good girl! I feel Tree Orchid's confusion. Kiki flies up in the air, sensing danger and ready to protect her. Urgently, I send them an image of the scorpion outside the door and a strong feeling of doom. I hold this image and this message as long as I can, until it feels as if I am falling from a long height, spinning down into an abyss. Dizzy. Swirling.

"Sister! Jade Skirt, wake up!"

Evening Star is leaning over me, fanning my face. I open my eyes.

"I am well," I assure her, struggling to rise. "I simply overextended myself." I have never sent my spirit so far or so intensely before—or under such duress. But was my message received? Before I can ask Evening Star to send a runner to check on the girls, Jaguar Shield and Spear Thrower crash into the hut, out of breath.

"An attack!" my son says, gasping. "A small force of Putun on the beach. They killed one of the Bolon men. We killed two. Three others ran off into the jungle!"

"It is happening sooner than we expected," Jaguar Shield says, clasping my hand. "We sent men to find out where the Putun boats landed. We must strengthen our defenses!"

Evening Star is stunned. "Putun violating the Zone of Peace? They are here on the Island? This is...this is..."

"This is war," I say grimly. "Ix Chel protect us all."

That's the last thing I remember.

After such a big sending my body simply collapsed into a deep sleep to replenish itself. When I wake several hours later—barely refreshed—I wonder for a moment why I feel so agitated. Then I remember: the peace of the Goddess's Island sanctuary is shattered. Violence and bloodshed have come to Her sacred Island. Is it me or the Island folding in on herself and moaning in grief?

Ix Chel, Great Mother, will You not stop this before it gets worse?

There is no answer. Ix Chel asks for our devotion, but She also requires Her children to learn their own lessons, like any good mother must. Perhaps we have been taking the Island sanctuary for granted? Is she teaching us that we must learn to appreciate it or we will lose it? Who can ever know the mind of the Great Ones? Even I, who am Her Oracle and vessel, cannot guess why She allows the Putun to bring war to Her sacred shores.

I sit up and adjust my mantle and Blue Stone appears in the doorway with a gourd of water. I embrace her and she grips me tightly. I am so relieved she is safe!

"Where are we?" I ask. I don't recognize the simple hut, and I can hear the ocean very close by.

"This is the men's *polna*. It is the last place your enemies will look for you," Blue Stone explains. "Noble Jaguar Shield says this place is more easily defended because it is in a clearing so we can see the enemy approach. They have not seen any more Putun. He believes the men who invaded last night were probably just scouts." That's a small relief, but I know more will come.

"We heard you," the little girl says shyly. "The scorpion would have killed us, but you talked to me in my head!"

I sigh. "Thank the Goddess you heard me!" I say.

"I ran to the door and saw the scorpion and screamed. Tree Orchid smashed it with her cane. It was not hard to kill, once we could see it. I think it didn't expect to be seen. We burned it in the hearth fire. The smoke was dark red! Na," she hesitates, "how was this possible? How could you show us how to see through the shadows?"

"Child, you will learn these things soon, in your own training. Truly, the Goddess sent you to me just when I needed you. Your spirit is stronger than you know. You will have a great destiny here."

Blue Stone smiles shyly, but suddenly I feel heavy-hearted. How many times did I say those words to Nine Macaw? How certain I was her path was assured, and how wrong I have been. But Blue Stone is not Nine Macaw, I remind myself. The hardships of her life have made her strong and grateful to have a family to call her own.

I murmur soothingly to Blue Stone about her courage and she drinks it in like a thirsty plant. My bag is lying near me. I reach inside and my hand brushes against the comforting, cool weight of my Ancestral Stone. The feel of it brings me comfort and a sense of peace. I almost laugh aloud to realize that I, too, am like a thirsty plant lapping up the stone's reassurances. My ancestors' presence encourages me to be patient and trust in Ix Chel.

Blue Stone hops up and looks guilty. "I forgot! Please wait for a moment, Na!" She rushes out and comes back a moment later carrying a bowl of stew and a gourd of tea. "Lady Evening Star says I am not allowed to speak to you until you finish both," she says.

"I will eat now, but please tell Jaguar Shield I must speak with him," I say.

I comb my hair and arrange my mantle and wait. The small room feels suddenly claustrophobic. I move into the hearth room and find a throng of Bolon men milling around, sharpening obsidian knives and tying stingray spines dipped in deadly toxins to the tips of their spears. I need air. I step outside and find a bench in a secluded garden behind the *polna*.

That is where Jaguar Shield finds me. We smile wryly at each other, not daring to touch in case someone sees us together, but each of us imagining how lovely it would be. Any privacy we can steal is a precious gift. I hear the constant ocean wind playing in the palms and smell the salty brine. I feel so alive and awake when I am with Jaguar Shield.

"So it comes to this," he says, looking deep into my eyes. "A dark day for Cuzamil. Ix Chel's Zone of Peace is breached. Treachery by Blue Monkey, one of our own Cocom wives. But now that we know the names and faces of our enemies, we will prevail."

He lifts his hand to stroke my cheek, but Evening Star chooses that minute to come find me with a second gourd of tea.

"Sister Evening Star," I say to her as Jaguar Shield pulls away quickly. "Tell us: among the priestesses of the five temples, who can we trust?"

"All but the High Priestess of the Great Temple of the Mother," she replies confidently. "That one is a Cob woman named Snake Tooth. She was appointed by Blue Monkey one moon past and removed all the priestesses and replaced them with women from the Cob lineage."

I will deal with this Snake Tooth after I take care of Blue Monkey. It is cheering news that four of the five high priestesses can be counted on. I rise from the bench and feel the earth under my bare feet. The earth of Cuzamil, my home and now my responsibility. I know the path that I must walk now. The next thing I say will change everything.

"Priestess Evening Star Mai Itza, in my name as lineage holder of the Chel, call the Council for tomorrow at noon."

She looks at me with surprise and then a wave of emotions crosses her face. Only the one who sits on the Rainbow Throne has the right to call the Council, summoning the Island's High Priestesses and administrators. She gracefully sinks to the ground and touches her forehead to my feet, as one must do for a queen.

And just like that, I declare myself ruler of Cuzamil. Queen Jade Skirt. There is a sour taste in my mouth. Heart of Water, forgive me!

"The Island's warriors must be told," I continue. "Send word to Night Wind to attend me." She is Cuzamil's *nacom* and has been my sister's on-again, off-again lover for many *tuns*.

"She has been notified," Evening Star assures me.

"Where is Spear Thrower?"

"He prepares to leave on the night currents," Jaguar Shield says, quickly adding, "with your permission, Lady. He will return to Pole and bring soldiers back tomorrow."

I wonder how many men he will be able to spare with the Putun camped right in Pole. He will need a second army! Tulumha can be counted on to send many canoes loaded with soldiers and weapons, but will they come in time?

"He has my permission. Send a messenger to catch the Magistrate before he leaves," I tell Evening Star, "and instruct him to send his fastest messenger to Tulumha saying that we need assistance, and another to Palenque saying that the Queen of Cuzamil requests their aid to protect Palenque's queen and heir."

Even if they march as soon as they receive the message, Palenque soldiers will arrive too late for the start of this war, but knowing reinforcements are coming will be good for morale, and perhaps we will last long enough against the bloodthirsty Putun to make use of their spears when they get here.

"And Evening Star, send for my grandson." Evening Star bows and leaves the room.

"Well! I like you in this role, Queen Jade Skirt." Jaguar Shield whispers flirtatiously in my ear. His hot breath sends shivers through my body.

A few moments later, Jaguar Paw interrupts us, jogging into the garden out of breath. "Na! I was helping Uncle load the boat."

"Grandson, you are a man now, and I am sending you on a man's mission."

He stands straight as a soldier and nods with dignity. I have to hold myself back from smiling. Instead, I explain the situation on Cuzamil. His eyes go wide when I tell him I have temporarily declared myself ruler of Cuzamil. I lean forward and speak to him privately, as one adult to another, so he can understand the gravity of his mission. His face is thoughtful and determined when I finish. He bows to me as subject to ruler, but then flashes me an affectionate grin.

"Goddess protect you, Na!"

After he sprints off, Jaguar Shield gives me a curious look.

"He returns to Pole this night with Spear Thrower," I explain. "I have told him he must slip away and go in secret to Nine Macaw and keep her safe. If the Cob priestesses are here on Cuzamil, they could very well be hiding in Pole among the temple priestesses, waiting to harm her."

"Hmm," my brother-in-law says, giving me a measuring look. "A big assignment for one so young. What are you planning?"

I do not answer. I only smile at him.

"Hah!" he says, squeezing my hand. "You think to let the brother convince the sister to do her duty?"

"Perhaps it will turn out that way. If Nine Macaw sees that everyone she loves is dedicated to preserving the Island of Women, perhaps she will remember her duty. Perhaps not." I shrug.

A sudden movement in the brush and Jaguar Shield leaps in front of me with obsidian knife at the ready. A lithe woman holding a spear slips out of the shadows and stands before us.

"Sister Jade Skirt," she says with a slight bow, ignoring my beloved's blade at her throat. "It is good to see you."

I rise to greet Night Wind, leader of the women warriors of Cuzamil. She is responsible for keeping peace and order among the thousands of Island residents while guarding the Cuzamil's immense treasure troves and securing the northern borderlands. How much did she hear of our conversation?

Right arm to her left shoulder, she greets Jaguar Shield as one warrior to another and then embraces me. Night Wind's short, black hair is slicked back from her noble forehead and held in place by a leather headband. Tattoos of twisting snakes cover both forearms. A plain, belted, brown dress ends in a shell-edged hem just above her knees. Her demeanor is calm and commanding.

With my second sight, I see her *chu'lel* is muddled with dark yellow rings of swirling intensity. "You have much to answer for, Sister," she says, arms toned from *tuns* of military training casually wrapped around her spear. "What were you thinking sending Blue Monkey and those Cob priestesses to us?"

"*Sister*, I did not send Blue Monkey or any of the others. They used my name to gain access to Heart of Water. They are traitors and liars!."

A look of relief passes over her face, followed by an expression of fury. Three times she pounds her spear on the ground.

"They will be brought to justice for this!" she promises, a deadly look in her eye.

I invite her to sit beside me, but she prefers to pace as she talks.

"So Blue Monkey lied! This explains much. It is three full moons since I saw Heart of Water." Her face tells me she grieves. "The Queen and I quarreled. She hid it well from the priestesses, but I knew the toll her oracular duties had taken on her body, her mind and her *pixam. She went beyond* the limit of endurance. At night she ranted like a madwoman, plagued by nightmares of *tzitzimin*. She said the little demons chased her in her dreams and beat her with thorny sticks. I insisted that she stop taking the oracular herbs, but she would not hear it, even though she knew I was right! She grew angry and sent me away."

"Perhaps she was already in her madness," I say consolingly.

"We quarreled at other times over the many *tuns* we have been together, but always she would send for me within a few days, full of forgiveness," continues Night Wind. "But the next day she dismissed Cloud Tree and Sky Mirror. I went to see her to find out what she was thinking. That was when Blue Monkey barred me from entering our apartments in the name of the Queen." Night Wind's voice is hoarse with emotion. "Heart of Water and I had been arguing for a moon about those Cob women. I said they were scorpions burrowing their way into her administration and I urged her to send them away, but Heart of Water said we could trust them because they were sent by you. Since I was banished from the Rainbow Palace, Blue Monkey ordered me to report to her, but something smelled wrong. I have been giving her false military reports."

"It was good you did," I say, shaking my head at this terrible story. "Blue Monkey brings danger to all Cuzamil. We believe she conspires with the heart takers!"

Night Wind gapes at me, shocked.

"*Nacom*, we have more bad news," says Jaguar Shield. "We were attacked on the beach earlier this night."

"Putun!" Night Wind spits. "Three days ago we spotted three Putun canoes landing in Chunkunab, in the north, but they appeared to be traders. Today we caught Putun spies trying to land near the Temple of the Grandmother, in the south, and we had reports from our spies that a small boat would try to land here at the Temple of the Moon. I have called the Bolon men to arm themselves from our arsenal. They stand with us."

"The Magistrate has gone to bring soldiers from Pole and Tulumha," Jaguar Shield says. He places his hand on his heart respectfully. "It would be an honor to serve the Great Mother and the Rainbow Throne in any way you can use me, *Nacom* Night Wind."

"*Nacom*, your experience is welcome and needed," says Night Wind, returning the gesture.

"Sister," I say carefully, "I have called the Council of High Priestesses."

Night Wind's eyes narrow and her hand tightens around the hilt of her spear. Only the Queen of Cuzamil calls the Council. Night Wind is Heart of Water's first defender and the love of her life. I open my *chu'lel* to her and let her see my heart, my intentions; let her see that I have nothing to hide from her. It takes her several moments, but finally she relaxes her grip on the weapon.

"There is no other way?" she asks sadly.

"I hope it will only be temporary," I assure her. "You know me. I have never had any ambition to be queen, and that has not changed. But something must be done, and I am the one with the authority to do it."

"My spies say the princess did not come on the voyage with you. Where is Nine Macaw?"

"She is safe."

Night Wind shakes her head. "There is much you are not saying, Jade Skirt, but I trust you."

I am moved by her words and embrace her as a sister. When our hearts touch I know she is sincere and trustworthy. She returns the embrace and I feel immeasurably relieved to have her as friend and ally in this fight.

We move inside. The hearth room is packed with three-times-twenty priestesses, Cuzamil guards, acolytes and Bolon men. Night Wind whispers to a young soldier, who shakes her head emphatically and fades into the crowd. All around us the room is abuzz with anxious gossip and speculation, but it dies down when Night Wind stands on a bench so she can be seen and heard by all. I spot my beloveds huddled in a corner together. Tree Orchid and Blue Stone lean against Iguana Wind, half-asleep.

"Queen Heart of Water is not well," Night Wind begins, her voice strong and commanding. "For three moons she has been sequestered where only the Cob priestesses can see her. Today, her Noble Sister Jade Skirt returns to Cuzamil and reveals that we have been betrayed! Blue Monkey and her Cob priestesses are trying to take control of Cuzamil and overthrow the Rainbow Throne. Even worse, they are in league with the Putun heart-takers and the War God!"

The crowd gasps. There are cries of shock, dismay and outrage. Suddenly, I see the young female soldier signal to Night Wind from the back of the crowd. The *nacom* nods and the soldier suddenly twists the arm of the priestess in front of her.

"What is this?" one of the Bolon men protests.

"A Cob spy!" the young soldier shouts. Two more soldiers bind the woman's wrists and ankles as she curses and thrashes. "For two moons she has been spying for the Cob women in the Rainbow Palace."

The crowd pushes in angrily, but Night Wind calms them with a shout. "She will be dealt with," she says. The soldiers drag her out of the *polna*. "This shows us how deep the treachery runs on Cuzamil. Even our own women have turned on us. We must be vigilant. Nothing said here tonight must leave this room."

There are nods and murmurs of agreement.

"The Putun are at our shores," the *nacom* of Cuzamil continues, "but the Goddess is with us. She sent us Her wise Oracle and High Priestess, defier of the heart-takers, and sister of our Queen Heart of Water. Until Heart of Water is made well again, Jade Skirt will serve as Queen of Cuzamil."

Another gasp goes up from the crowd, but as Night Wind drops to the ground before me and twice presses her forehead to the floor, the people are impressed. A moment later, they all bow before me. Acutely uncomfortable, I keep my face impassive, imitating the haughty nobility of White Quetzal. The people need to see a confident leader.

Do not doubt yourself, Daughter. I am with you.

Like sweet honey poured through my soul, I feel buoyed by the grace of Her presence. When I speak, my voice resonates with Her love and confidence. I tell my people what we are up against and what we must do to save the Island of Women.

"Surely you and your warriors can overpower one priestess," says one of the Bolon men. "Get Blue Monkey out of there and restore the throne to Queen Heart of Water!"

"It is not as easy as it sounds," says one of Night Wind's warriors. "Two days ago, our *nacom* commanded us to make sure the Queen heard with her own ears that the Putun canoes landed in the north. When we tried to get into the Queen's apartments, twenty of us were blocked. Blue Monkey has moved two-times-twenty Cob women into the palace. They are priestesses, children, the elderly, nursing women and pregnant women. When we moved one out of the way, three more stepped in to take her place. We cannot harm women or children on Her holy sanctuary. We were forced to retreat."

The men draw in their breath and grunt their disapproval. Using women and children as a shield is a coward's tactic.

"*Nacom* Night Wind, why did you not suspect foul play when Blue Monkey and the Cob women took over the palace?" Jaguar Shield challenges her. "Why were you not suspicious when Queen Heart of Water dismissed her closest attendants, hid the Island's great treasures and was said to order the removal of the sacred crystal skull from Cuzamil? Why did you say nothing when the queen changed the trade agreements and abandoned the *polnas*? When there were no oracular session for these many moons, why did you not alert the Magistrate of Pole?"

There are mutterings of concern from men and women around the room who did not know all these things had transpired. The expression on the eagle headdress my love wears mirrors Jaguar Shield's own sharp, judging eyes. I am sorry Night Wind must be on the receiving end of his wrath, which can be overbearing, but I see what he is doing. Island affairs must seem poorly managed to those gathered here, and if they are to respect Night Wind's leadership—particularly the Bolon men—she must have an opportunity to explain herself. Not for the first time do I appreciate Jaguar Shield's subtle tactics.

Head high, Night Wind answers the charges calmly. "*Nacom*, Cuzamil has been a Zone of Peace and prosperity for three generations of Chel rule. There are no soldiers or spies in the palace because there has never been a need. I was conflicted about the Cob priestesses suddenly rising to power in the administration, but I believed Blue Monkey and the Cob women were trusted by Lady Jade Skirt." She pounds her spear into the earth. "I see now that I had too much confidence in our enduring peace. My love for the queen blinded me. I lost my military instinct. No more! My eyes are opened!"

Jaguar Shield gives her a nod of approval. He glances at me and says in a loud voice, "The best military leader can be blinded when the heart is involved."

A blue-robed junior priestess bursts into the room. "Apologies, *Nacom*!" she gasps. "A messenger from the palace was intercepted on the *sacbe*! Queen Heart of Water commands all priestesses, administrators and soldiers of Cuzamil to attend her in the central plaza at Tixchel tomorrow at noon!"

Heart of Water is calling the Council? Not likely.

"It is Blue Monkey, speaking in my sister's name," I say grimly. "But this is propitious. If we can't arrest her before then, we will plan to seize her and her co-conspirators right there in the central plaza tomorrow, with the council bearing witness."

"I say that we launch an attack on the Cob women's *polna* before dawn!" says Night Wind, pacing back and forth. I recall that she never liked to sit in one place for long. She moves with the grace of a panther. "Lock them in, tie them up and sequester them under guard. Take all their clothing and cover their mouths so they cannot cry out for help! Our women warriors will wear the Cob women's mantles and braid their hair in coils around their ears as the Cob women do," she continues with a feral grin. "Tomorrow in the great plaza, they will stand far enough away so that Blue Monkey cannot see their faces. They are easily recognized among all the other acolytes and priestesses because their robes are a different shade of blue, but the sun will be in her eyes. She will believe her supporters are there. She will not see us coming!"

There are murmurs of excitement in the room. The priestesses and acolytes smile in anticipation. The Cob women are not well-loved.

"What will we do if Queen Heart of Water speaks against Lady Jade Skirt?" one of the priestesses asks diffidently. "Rumor says she has named Princess Water Lily as her heir. Even if it is the result of the meddling of Blue Monkey, people will be loyal to the Queen's stated wishes."

There is an uncomfortable silence. Then something in my heart and mind becomes clear, and I know I must say it aloud:

"Heart of Water is our beloved Queen, but we cannot trust her judgment while she is under the influence of Blue Monkey, who has likely poisoned the sacred formulas. While there is a possible antidote to the oracular poisoning, it will take much time to work through the system and bring the mind back. And even if it is successful, my sister will never be able to serve as Oracle again. One more dose of the enema formula will kill her. Her time as Queen of Cuzamil is at an end."

There is shocked silence as the others absorb what I am saying. Heart of Water is beloved here, despite the problems of these last few moons.

"We must act in the best interest of the sacred Island," I tell them firmly. "We must not doubt ourselves. We will do everything we can to save my sister, but not at the expense of the Goddess's sanctuary for all women of the Known World. This is what we will tell the High Priestesses at the Council tomorrow. We must stand united against the outside threat from the Putun and the internal threat from Blue Monkey and the Cob lineage priestesses.

"Noble Lady," someone asks loudly, "why is the heir not here?"

I sigh inwardly and say with false serenity: "The Goddess will reveal Her plans to us all in due time."

• • •

In the flickering light from a small hearth fire, Night Wind uses her spear point to sketch a rough map of Cuzamil on the dirt floor. A strategy meeting is underway in a small room in the *polna*. Night Wind and I chose Seven Tapir and several other Bolon headmen, as well as Jaguar Shield, Iguana Wind and Evening Star to give counsel. Those in back crane their necks to see as *the nacom* makes marks to indicate the positions of the five temples, each half-a-day's walk from the next. The Great Temple of the Mother lies in the center next to the Rainbow Palace. Along the *sacbes* connecting the temples are many small villages with dwellings, schools, fields, shrines, workshops, houses of healing and *polnas*.

"There are hidden pathways through the jungle," Night Wind says. "They are a closely guarded secret known only to Cuzamil's guards. We can cross the Island twice as fast as walking on the *sacbe*. Each village has guards and healers to handle the crowds of pilgrims. We have a system for communicating with them quickly when necessary."

She taps a spot on the map. "Here in the west, where all pilgrims and paddlers arrive, is the shore most hospitable to landing boats, so we are most vulnerable to invasion here. Except for the port in the north, most of Cuzamil's coastline is surrounded by dangerous shoals, unpredictable currents and rocky shores. My soldiers patrol every beach where a canoe might make landing. Tomorrow, we will blow the conch that signals unfavorable conditions so that no pilgrim or trader boats will make the crossing. The men of Pole and the men of Tulumha know how to signal us when they are close so we will know they are allies. Any other boats that attempt to land will be attacked from the shore." She marks the area where the high tower of the Temple of Moon sits close to the shore and serves as an excellent lookout and vantage point for raining spears and fire pots on the Putun boats as they try to come ashore.

"Cuzamil is most vulnerable in the north," says Seven Tapir, tapping that area of the map with his spear. "The Putun may have secret allies among the traders in Chunkunab."

A glum silence falls over us. "The Putun cannot disguise themselves, with those skull tattoos they wear on both cheeks," says a Bolon man finally, "but we will not know which of the traders have turned on us."

"The swamp is an impenetrable defense," says Night Wind confidently. "None can cross it."

Jaguar Shield clears his throat unhappily. "In Chichen, our spies heard rumors that the Putun have found a way to make fire that burns on water. The Temple of the Maiden would be a strategic prize for the Putun if they could burn the swamp and march across."

"I will send a message to the guards in the north to watch for smoke," says Night Wind, frowning. "And I will deploy extra troops to that Temple."

"Stopping the Putun at Chunkunab before they can attack the rest of the Island is a good strategy," suggests Seven Tapir. "I have seen the Putun canoes. Each holds more than two-times-twenty men. You say you saw three Putun canoes at Chunkunab. So at least six-times-twenty Putun already occupy the north. Even if they cannot cross the swamp, they can use the port as a base of operations and send their canoes out with soldiers to invade other parts of the Island. They don't have to land the boats—just paddle close enough for the men to swim ashore. That is how I would do it," he adds, looking embarrassed at having spoken so boldly.

As they continue to discuss numbers of soldiers and troop movements I feel like a fraud. I am no queen to lead these people in a time of war. I can't wield a spear. I know nothing of supply lines and spies. I was trained to be a healer and a vessel through which Ix Chel speaks to Her beloved children. I have no skills that will protect the women and children who came here for sanctuary, who count on Cuzamil being a Zone of Peace. I close my eyes and feel the strong *chu'lel* of the Island. I cast my awareness out and Sense women giving birth, drawing their last breaths, and praying for Ix Chel's blessings and protection. They and countless infants, children and elders are about to find themselves in the middle of a war. And what can I do but wring my hands uselessly?

"We priestesses will do our part," I hear Evening Star say as I tune back into the conversation in the room. "We can send a bird with a message to organize the able-bodied women in the Temple of the Oracle to fortify the embankments and to prepare against the Putun setting fire to the thatch in the villages."

Her sensible suggestions impress me. I chide myself to think practically instead of lamenting that I am not a *nacom*. It comes to me then that my part in this war needs no grand plan. When the time comes, I will stand up to Blue Monkey, to Pus Master and to anyone who challenges the sanctity of the Island of Women and threatens the Rainbow Throne. I will be the mouthpiece of Ix Chel, as ever I have been. And while I know little about war, I do know about queens. I watched my grandmother and mother rule for ten-plus-twenty *tuns*, and I witnessed Heart of Water's skillfulness at leading the people. I am no soldier, but I know I can rule.

"*Nacom* Night Wind," I interrupt, "what number of soldiers are trained and ready under your command?"

This is a closely guarded secret, and she hesitates to say in front of so many outsiders, but I am making a point: the Rainbow dynasty and the Bolon lineage are firm allies. We must trust one another.

"My Queen, here in the west there are more than five-times-twenty for you to command," she reports. That is impressive. Cuzamil's soldiers are famous for being unobtrusive. They appear only on the rare occasions when they are needed to intervene in a conflict or assist in a natural disaster such as a hurricane or fire.

"Very prudent of Heart of Water," Jaguar Shield says approvingly. "And what about the rest of the sacred Island?"

I give Night Wind a nod of permission to answer his question. "Five-times-twenty at each of the five temples, with an additional two-times-twenty in Tixchel and ten at each of the pilgrim's *polna* on the procession route. There are another five-times-twenty to guard the Northern border. There we built a stone wall that is patrolled by sentries day and night."

"Excellent!" my beloved says to her with a tone of respect, "That should be more than enough to secure all five centers, the Western beach and the North, if the men of Pole and Tulumha can hold the coast."

"Yes, but are your soldier-maidens trained to fight?" A Bolon man asks skeptically.

Night Wind gives him a cool look. "Their training is rigorous and their skills should not be underestimated."

"That is what I have heard," says Jaguar Shield.

"What about communications?" asks Seven Tapir curiously. "I assume you have a system of signals?"

"There are smoke signals for the day and fire signals for dark. At every temple a soldier is assigned to watch, day and night. We do not use the conch for signaling to one another on the Island in case an enemy imitates our signals to confuse us. Our Bird Oracles provide swift and reliable messengers in times of great need. Unfortunately, we have a limited number of those with the Bird Oracle gift. Currently, there are five—one for each temple. Runners bring their messages to the commanders in those areas."

"What should we know about the fire signals?" Seven Tapir asks.

She explains the ingenious system of making signals by blocking the fires with a double-sized mat reinforced with wooden poles. "Fires can be lit on the top of any of the temples' towers. A soldier is always watching from one of the temples in Pole. The light is blocked with mats three times, signaling that we are under attack. The signal is then passed on to transfer signal stations around the island. The soldiers of Cuzamil will be on military alert. Two messengers from each of the five centers meet at prearranged positions to receive instructions for the troops."

"And our allies from the mainland?" I ask.

"With the fogs from the sea we can't count on fire signals, but always we can hear the conchs," explains Seven Tapir. "When we hear the conch sound five rapid tones six times in a row, we Bolon men know to paddle the magistrate's soldiers across to defend the Island from attack. They secure the Western beach and we Bolon then must swing around to the north to guard the sea routes. We are commanded to prevent all traders from embarking in the north."

"Do not sound the conch," I command. "Magistrate Spear Thrower is on his way back to Pole right now to marshal the troops. The Putun are already in Pole. Let us not alert the enemy that we expect an attack."

In the dark hours of the night, the last messenger has gone out and Night Wind declares that the plan of defense for Cuzamil is settled to her satisfaction. All eyes turn to me expectantly.

"*Nacom*," I say sadly, "light the fires!"

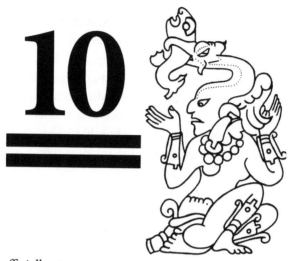

10

Cuzamil is officially at war.

Barely any time passed since the fires were lit when an out-of-breath messenger burst into the hearth room.

"*Nacom*! Queen Jade Skirt! The Putun have seized Chunkunab!"

She reports that one man hid in a tree and witnessed the terrible scene and later escaped and reported it to Night Wind's scouts.

"The Putun snuck up on the settlement of traders while they slept," reports the runner. "Their priest built a stone altar to the War God and dragged a young boy out of his hut. The boy was screaming as the Putun priests painted him blue. While the priests cut out his beating heart the Putun *nacom* told him they would honor his sacrifice. They built a fire and roasted the boy on a spit! My Queen, they devoured the child while the boy's father and the other traders watched!"

The contents of my stomach threaten to come up. Goddess, protect that poor spirit and may the white dog be there to help him cross to the other side of the river.

"Then the Putun *nacom* offered the traders twice the profits that they make from Queen Heart of Water. He said, 'Double your profits or spill your blood right here, right now. The War God will gladly welcome your *pixam* into His so you may savor the sweetness of the Flowery Death.'"

Of course the traders hastily agreed to whatever the Putun asked. They were terrified of being sacrificed and roasted like dogs.

There is shocked silence in the room. More than a few people run outside to be sick in the bushes. A powerful ocean breeze blows into the hearth sending sparks into the air. I hear an owl hoot nearby. Curse you, harbinger of death.

For the next two hours messengers run in and out of Night Wind's temporary base of operations here in the hearth room at the Bolon men's *polna*. I hear one report that the Putun spies are at large and presumed still to be on the western side of the Island. I pray they are found before daybreak.

The indefatigable Evening Star, who has appointed herself my personal attendant, brings me yet another cup of stimulating allspice tea and the news that the Queen of Palenque and the girls are sleeping peacefully in a back room. That gives me some comfort.

I start to take a sip of the tea and suddenly a cold feeling rushes through me. Letting go of the gourd and ignoring Evening Star's cry of concern as the hot liquid splashes on my mantle, I raise my hands above my heart and send my awareness out, sensing with my mind and *chu'lel*. There! A malevolent presence hovers in the back corner of the room. I feel its attention on Night Wind. How long has it been spying on us? I tune out the voices around me and track its movements. As it drifts closer to my *nacom*, I fling my right hand up in her direction and snap my fingers while whipping my *chu'lel* at the presence with full force. There is a loud cracking sound in the air above Night Wind and then a hiss like an angry serpent, followed by a rotten-egg smell. The *nacom* leaps away yelling, "Ix Chel protect us!" while Evening Star throws herself in front of me protectively.

For the next few minutes the room is in chaos as the confused crowd searches for the source of the disturbance. Evening Star fusses over me, wiping the spilled tea off my mantle. I shoo her away and stand on a bench to be heard.

"All is well!" My voice rings out confidently, although I feel shaky inside. "The danger is gone." They eye me with a new respect, no doubt remembering that I am not merely Heart of Water's sister, but I am also Oracle and High Priestess, and trained in the elite Red Hand Society.

Evening Star wisely throws two handfuls of *copal* resin into the fire. The sweet smell cleanses the room of the evil odor. Gradually, people return to what they were doing before, although many continue to glance over at me. I motion to Night Wind and Jaguar Shield to attend me, and tell them in a low voice:

"It was Blue Monkey! She was spying on us here. I don't know how much she heard, but this changes our plans. I must leave for Tixchel immediately.

Blue Monkey and her cronies must be arrested in the palace before the council meeting."

Jaguar Shield looks like he wants to argue with me, but I hold up my hand to stop him. "If we don't neutralize Blue Monkey and the Cob women before they have a chance to tell their lies to the people they could plunge Cuzamil into a civil war. If that happens we will not be able to stand against the Putun."

I feel my beloved's frustration. As a man, he may not accompany me to the palace. He can't be by my side when I face my enemy. I give him a look of understanding and he smiles faintly.

"Be on guard, all of you," I say quietly. "My husband, Moon Eagle, always said over-confidence was a dead soldier's tragic flaw. Respect the cunning of your enemy, he always said, and that is what I caution now."

Night Wind sends me with a guard of ten women warriors, and Evening Star chooses twenty-plus-ten priestesses and acolytes who are trained healers to accompany me as well. I instruct them to carry the medicines that counter the known poisons the Putun use on their blades.

Before we go I wake White Quetzal to let her know that I must leave. Tree Orchid and Blue Stone will stay behind to tend her. We both are well aware that 1 Zip is only days from now. I can only hope this war is over before then, but I can't promise her anything. Right now, I have bigger problems to worry about than the Palenque succession.

"I cannot be selfish, Queen Jade Skirt," White Quetzal says grudgingly. "The Island of Women need you. I know the Goddess is looking after me. But please remember I will need you on 1 Zip."

I put my hand on her cheek like a mother.

"We are in Her hands, so have no worries, Daughter."

Night Wind comes to hurry me and I turn to whisper a goodbye to the sleepy girls.

"Na, something else bad is going to happen tonight!" Tree Orchid tells me urgently. "The Putun are coming in canoes, right to this place! Kiki told me!"

"Who is Kiki?" Night Wind asks sharply.

"Her parrot," I say. "*Nacom*, Tree Orchid is my adopted granddaughter and she will be training as a Bird Oracle."

"We have a Bird Oracle?! Goddess be praised!" exclaims Night Wind. She gives Tree Orchid a deep bow of respect. "Your gift will save many lives this night," she says as the girl's eyes grow wide as saucers. Night Wind's aides regard the little crippled girl as if she is their most precious feather.

"With the eyes of birds we can track the Putun and cut them off!" Night Wind says with glee. Then she scolds me: "Jade Skirt, why did you not tell me right away we had a Bird Oracle?"

The expression of pride on Tree Orchid's thin face is a bright moment in this terrible night. My heart is heavy as we set a brisk pace to Tixchel. Evening Star walks beside me on the wide, white *sacbe*. In four days the moon will be full. Then we will celebrate the festival of 1 Zip, Creation Day—when First Mother and First Father created the world through sacred sexual union. Tonight, the last beams of moonlight guide our steps. In a dark sea of Sky Wanderers, my Moon Goddess holds silent witness in the western sky. I take a deep breath of night-blooming blossoms and catch glimpses of white petals of the fragrant vanilla orchids in the trees. If only I was not marching to war I would linger and savor the heady aroma. I feel the dreaming bees in their hives nestled in hollow logs along a length of the road. I smell the rich loam of the newly planted corn and bean fields.

We walk in silence, which gives me time to think about how I will face Blue Monkey and rescue Heart of Water. Only Jaguar Shield knows how my old nemesis Blue Monkey unnerves me. She has always hated me, even when we were girls, and whenever I am near her I feel hostility pulse from her *chu'lel* in overpowering waves. I have never been strong enough to shield myself fully from her toxic enmity.

With each step I feel my doubts and fears grow. This will not do. I focus my mind and remember what my mother, Nine Wind, taught me: I imagine doubt and fear draining out of my feet and into the white earth, and I draw up from the ground courage and power, tuning in to the pulsing heartbeat of Her sacred Island. After only a few steps I can feel it working. I am aware of my Ancestral Stone carried close to my heart. I feel my ancestors' strength and wisdom are with me. I squeeze my *pi* and call on the sacred contents to give me the courage of a mother jaguar.

One of the acolytes starts to sing softly. It is a sweet lullabye we all know, and I join in:

"Goddess of Light, Great Mother in the sky
Shelter us, comfort us, protect us this night."

Other voices take up the song and I revel in being home on Cuzamil and walking on the sacred ground of the blessed Island where Ix Chel dwells and Her glory abides!

Ordinarily, it would take half the night to reach Tixchel, the center of Cuzamil Island. But the soldiers lead us off the *sacbe* and onto a hidden path that winds through the dense jungle. The three maidens in the lead clear away debris and fallen branches to make travel easier for the rest of us, and the three at the rear replace the debris and branches and erase our passing so none can follow. Despite the moonlight, it is hard to see. I stumble over exposed roots and rocks. The soldiers ask us politely, but firmly, to be as silent as possible in case Putun are hiding nearby.

Although I do my best to stay calm and centered, my mind turns toward revenge. How I would enjoy seeing Blue Monkey suffer! How satisfying it would be to see Pus Master on his knees before me begging for mercy.

I sigh. Ix Chel teaches that all are Her children. Even Blue Monkey. Even Pus Master. Without peace in my heart, how can I do the Gentle Goddess's work? Moon Eagle used to tell me that a warrior must have unshakable faith in his cause and in himself. Death on the battlefield is an honor, but victory is an even greater honor. I turn my thoughts to contemplate victory. Victory is peace. Victory is a return to the quiet, ordered life on the Island serving our beloved Goddess. Victory is not the suffering of my enemies.

A woman soldier lights a pine torch when the moon sets and the trail grows too dark to navigate. Striking two flints together, she makes a spark that ignites the pine pitch quickly. The steady breeze from the sea, felt even this far inland, makes the flame dance and cast shadows at our feet.

We walk without rest, passing a sack of nuts and dried plums up and down the line to keep our energy up. In the dove-colored light before dawn, we finally reach the thatched huts and fields that lie outside Tixchel. The women in this small village sleep in blissful ignorance of the war that has come to our shores. We pass silently, not even waking the dogs. Our guides lead us back to the *sacbe* and we walk again on the smooth road, still in silence, our torches extinguished. The soldiers melt into the trees so that we appear to be nothing more than a group of acolytes and priestesses coming to the great plaza for the dawn ceremony that bids farewell to Mother Moon and welcomes Father Sun. From the Temple of the Moon in the west comes the sounding of the conch shell bidding safe journey through the Underworld to our Mother Moon. This is followed by a conch blown from the Temple of the Oracle, to the east, welcoming Father Sun back from his journey. Sun and the Moon, old quarrelling lovers, catch a glimpse of each other in the brief moment when the world is poised between night and dawn.

"Great Mother and Protector," I pray silently, "protect Your sanctuary. Father Sun, spread Your warrior shield over us today and help us to defeat our enemies."

Tixchel is the center of Cuzamil, which is the center of the world. As we near our destination the familiar landscape of fields, gardens and flower-filled shrines are kissed with pink light. A thrill goes through me when we reach the wide, central plaza that connects the Rainbow Palace and the Great Temple of the Mother. Paved in limestone blocks and crushed sea shells, it usually gleams white, but at this hour it, too, glows in rosy tones.

The others pause respectfully so I can be the first to pass through the westernmost rainbow arch. The Island has nine of these stone entryways. Pilgrims believe that those who step through Her nine arches will be honored with wisdom and blessed with fertility. I close my eyes and imagine, as my grandmother taught me, that I am stepping into the Presence of Ix Chel.

I feel my *chu'lel* drawn to the Great Temple of the Mother, the beating heart of Cuzamil. For many *tuns* it was the place I yearned for most whenever I missed my home. The Presence of Ix Chel is stronger there than anywhere else in the Known World. To pray there is to feel as if one is nestled in the lap of the Great Mother. Much as I long to visit there now, I set my feet on the path to the Rainbow Palace.

We walk past the stone platform in the plaza's center, where today's Council is supposed to meet. This is where dances and ceremonies take place. I had my coming-of-age ceremony here, and Heart of Water's coronation was held right here on the day our grandmother, Queen Cosmic Turtle, passed the throne to my sister. My sister practiced reciting the Declaration of Queenship so many times before the ceremony that I, too, memorized it. I pray it silently now as I walk past.

"Ix Chel, Mother of All, Protector of women, dedicated the sacred Island sanctuary of Cuzamil to all Her daughters everywhere.

As Queen, I welcome any woman in need, any woman with child, any woman who seeks healing or safety, and any woman who desires to serve the Gentle Goddess.

As Queen, it is my personal responsibility to comfort and shelter the pilgrim, the widow, the orphan and the rejected.

As Queen, I promise that the sick and dying, the pregnant and elderly are given healing and medicines to ease their pain. As Cuzamil gives hope to the grieving and hopeless, so do I, as Queen of Her holy realm.

Ix Chel gave us Cuzamil to be a Zone of Peace in the Known World. As Queen, I accept Her sacred charge to protect the holy Island and its shores so that none may knowingly harm another.

As Queen of Cuzamil, I worship the Great Mother as High Priestess and serve as her Oracle. I teach Her priestesses and Oracles the ways of the Goddess of All.

The Island of Women is Ix Chel's gift to all women, and from this day forward, as Ruler of the Rainbow Throne, it is my sacred duty to protect, lead and guide Her Daughters on Her beloved sanctuary."

So now this charge falls to me until we have an heir. Even though it is a role I never wanted, to serve the Goddess is an honor. My mother taught me that the more difficult the task, the greater the service rendered. I go now to do a great service to Her by getting rid of that pestilent scab, Blue Monkey!

I don't stop to admire the pink and white stones of the Rainbow Palace or the magnificent carvings of serpent and rabbit on the lintel. I climb the eighteen stone steps reciting the Declaration of Queenship to myself again for courage.

I am brought up short by four Cob women wearing black mantles and red ribbons. They wear the colors of death!

"Who are you?" I challenge them before they can challenge me.

"By order of the Queen, you are not permitted to enter here." They cross their arms and glare at us arrogantly.

Of course Blue Monkey would be expecting trouble—if not from me, then from Night Wind and her soldiers. As if thinking of those capable women causes them to manifest, a sudden, silent swarm of brown-clad warriors streams up the steps and quietly sweeps the surprised guards away with little fuss. They remember to muffle them so they cannot cry out and warn others of our arrival.

Flanked by six of our soldiers, I march through the palace and down the corridor that leads to Heart of Water's chambers. Faces peek out from behind door curtains to see who comes so early in the morning and a few voices call out in alarm, but Night Wind's troops pour like ants into each room we pass, preventing Blue Monkey's human shields from racing into the hallway to block my progress. I hear babies wail and women protest, curse and cry as they try to push past the implacable guards. Do these women know about Blue Monkey's treachery, or do they believe they are truly protecting their queen?

I burst into Heart of Water's antechamber. Warned by the noise in the hallway, ten priestesses of the Cob lineage have already linked arms to form a shield to keep me from advancing. But our warriors slide and dart under their legs and leap over their shoulders. In a heartbeat, they have the women surrounded and subdued. I appreciate how careful they are not to harm the women. Unfortunately, the Cob priestesses are not concerned about maintaining the Zone of Peace. The traitors frantically bite, kick and scratch our warriors. But it is to no avail. Our warriors deftly bind their ankles and wrists and gag them for good measure.

As soon as my way is clear, I push open the heavy wooden door and rush into Heart of Water's chamber, the very room in which I was born.

"Heart of Water!" I call. "Sister! It is Jade Skirt! I am here!"

"What is the meaning of this?!" Blue Monkey sits up in the reed bed, her daughter beside her. Hair askew, she demands, "Who disturbs the Queen?" Her scowl would set a scorpion to run!

I step forward and confront her, hands on my hips, blazing with rage. How dare she be here! How dare she speak in my name! How dare she consort with our enemies and betray our holy Island!

When she sees my face she is taken aback for a moment and I see real fear, but then her expression turns to disgust. She spits at my feet and shrieks, "Guards! What is this exile scum doing here?"

"You are under arrest for high treason to the Rainbow Throne. You will be taken to Pole where you will be tried and sentenced. Death is too good for you, you traitor!"

"No!" shouts Blue Monkey. There is an obsidian dagger in her hand and she draws back her arm to fling it at me. From my left side, Evening Star lunges at Blue Monkey with a yell and knocks her to the ground. Two soldiers quickly dive on top of Blue Monkey and grab her while she thrashes and screams curses at me. It takes two more finally to hold her still and another two to bind her wrists and ankles with hemp rope. Another two tie the hands of Eighteen Rabbit, who looks frightened and offers no resistance.

"Jade Skirt, you will never—mmmph!" Blue Monkey is finally gagged!

"Before you take out the trash," I tell the guards, "ask her what she has done with our Queen."

They pull down her gag and she tries to spit at me again, but the guard yanks her head to the side.

"Where is she, traitor?" the soldier demands.

Blue Monkey's eyes involuntarily glance toward the side of the room where an old woman lies in an alcove. With a shock I recognize Heart of Water. Most of her hair has fallen out and she is thin as a cadaver. I forget all about Blue Monkey and run to her. The color of her skin is the only thing I knew to expect—grayish-yellow, tinged with brown patches, which are signs of poisoning from massive doses of the oracular formula. Her vacant eyes do not focus. Her head turns from side to side. She looks confused and afraid. But when I try to embrace her she feebly pushes me away.

"Who are you?" she stammers. "Why are you here? What is happening?" With one boney hand she reaches out to Blue Monkey. "Help me. Help me. Don't leave me." Does she not recognize me at all? Before I can declare that I am her beloved sister she turns her head and vomits up green bile.

"Sister, it is Jade Skirt!" I say.

"My love. My love," she moans miserably. "Where is she? What have you done to her?"

"I am here, my Queen" shouts Blue Monkey as she manages to spit out her gag. "Tell these intruders to leave us! Send them away! I am the one who loves you! They are here to trick you! Don't listen to this evil woman! We do not know her!"

Before she can say more, the soldiers replace the gag. Blue Monkey glares at me with such hatred in her eyes that I am nearly blasted by a black belch of her furious *chu'lel*. Before it reaches me, I flip my hand in a tight circle and send it right back to her. She screams and kicks to get out of its path, but the warriors hold her firmly in place. When it hits, Blue Monkey's body stiffens and she lets out a strangled, inhuman groan. Something about it seems deeply wrong. Curious, I shift my focus to look at Blue Monkey through my inner awareness.

There! I see it! A grotesquely misshapen spirit of the Underworld is wrapped around her *chu'lel* like a leech. It sucks her life force away to feed its own malevolent essence. Not only is she in league with the heart takers, but she is also under the control of an evil spirit! It all makes sense. Demons are dedicated to destroying goodness and light through jealousy, cunning and deviousness. Blue Monkey was a perfect tool for them to use to infiltrate and corrupt the Gentle Goddess's Island, which they despise because it is a beacon of goodness and light in the Three Realms. I wonder how long she has been possessed. Does this explain her constant animosity toward me since first we met as girls? No wonder she always unnerved me so!

The spirit feels my attention on it and suddenly drops all pretense of hiding in human form. Blue Monkey snarls and drools. She bites at the gag and keens and laughs like a mad dog. I am appalled at what she has become, and then something truly unexpected happens: I feel compassion for her. Poor Blue Monkey is truly a tortured soul. Her hatred and jealousy of me attracted this demon to her. Even if her plan succeeded to rule the Rainbow Throne she would never have been happy or satisfied. The demon would not have allowed it.

"Ix Chel, help her," I pray. "Your daughter is suffering. She chose the wrong path, but be merciful and spare her this pain."

Heart of Water gasps with fear and suddenly collapses in my arms. I lower her to the ground and call for water, *copal* resin and my medicine bag. Gently, I take her wrist and feel her pulse, which races erratically. It could mean she was given more of the enema mixture as recently as yesterday! If that is true, Blue Monkey was surely trying to kill her!

"Question the Cob priestesses," I order Evening Star. "Find out who attended her and what she was given. And get that beast out of here"—I jerk my head toward Blue Monkey. I'm feeling considerably less charitable toward her at this moment. "And send for the High Priestess of the Healing House!"

I must gather the plants immediately to brew the oracular poisoning remedy. There are certain plants that must be used fresh and others that will not be in the healers' stores. The reason is simple: the recipe should never be needed because we Oracles are carefully monitored by trusted attendants to ensure that we will not become poisoned. My grandmother developed the antidote formula when she realized that if attendants were not preparing it correctly they could end up poisoning Ix Chel's Oracles.

"Let me through!" a woman yells imperiously. "I am High Priestess of the Great Temple of the Mother! You cannot keep me out!"

"Let her in," I tell the guard nearest to me, "but be ready with the rope." The guard grins and nods.

A tall, angular woman with a down-turned mouth rushes in and stops short when she sees Blue Monkey bound and gagged and frothing at the mouth. She makes to turn and run, but the guards grab her and bind her ankles and wrists as she sputters and protests.

"Snake Tooth Cob, you are under arrest for high treason against the Rainbow Throne," Evening Star says sternly.

"Who are you people? Why do you disturb our blessed Queen?" she demands.

I rise from the floor where I have been trying to revive my sister. I tell this priestess who I am and she visibly pales.

"I will ask you one question and you will answer it truthfully or in Ix Chel's name I will curse you," I say in as calm a voice as I can muster. "When was Queen Heart of Water last given the oracular herbs and enema?"

She gulps. "Last evening. Blue Monkey said—"

I want to throttle this woman. "Can you not see how weak she is? Did it not cross your mind that it might kill her?"

"The Goddess protects Her own," Snake Tooth says haughtily, but her eyes shift away guiltily.

"Do not speak of the Goddess again until you purify your heart and beg forgiveness from all those you have harmed," I tell her. "You defile our sacred profession!"

I gesture with my hand and the guards drag her away along with Blue Monkey and the silently weeping Eighteen Rabbit.

My sister needs healing. Have I arrived too late? *Om bey!* She is so far gone.

"Queen Jade Skirt, here is the Lady Blood Woman, High Priestess of the House of Healing."

Even I have heard of her. She is the most gifted healer on all of Cuzamil. The high noblewoman of the third age looks like she just rolled out of bed. Her mantle is askew, her gray hair spills untidily from her braids with rainbow ribbons straggling at the ends. She brushes Evening Star aside, not unkindly, and joins me on the floor beside Heart of Water. A veined hand touches the ground and then her heart in greeting. Tattoos on her hands and face mark her as being from the Central Lowlands around Palenque.

"Sister," I say, "Heart of Water is near to crossing the river." She ignores the rebuke in my words and lowers her eyes to more closely examine my sister.

"It will not take me long to find what we need to counteract the oracular poisoning," I say, "and praise Ix Chel, Her moon is in our favor. Keep her alive until I get back."

Blood Woman is barely attending to my words. Her dark eyes take in the Queen's condition and she looks incredulous. Can it be that she did not know?

"We must take our Queen directly to the steam bath," she tells Evening Star. "Prepare it immediately! She must start sweating out this poison. And bring water from the sacred spring. She must drink pitchers of it. Have we seen a sample of her urine?"

I am relieved at her take-charge attitude, and her protocol is exactly what I would do.

"Whoever has been mixing and administering the Oracle's formula has much to answer for," I say in a mild tone.

She gives me a sharp look. "That should have been Water Wizard. I trained her myself, but she was dismissed three moons ago with the Queen's other attendants. Since then, *your* Cob priestesses have been in the mixing room."

"Not mine!" I say, briefly explaining Blue Monkey's treachery.

Before she can say express her dismay we hear five blasts of the conch. My blood runs cold.

Blood Woman's eyes widen, but she stays focused on Heart of Water. She supervises her assistants as they lift the Queen onto a litter and carry her down the corridor to the *nulha*.

"Evening Star, stay with the healers. I will return soon," I say, quickly rifling through a wooden trunk to find a gathering basket. There is no time to lose.

"Lady, no one may leave the palace for any reason," one of the guards says respectfully. "The *nacom*'s orders. Putun have landed on the Western shore. Soldiers from Pole landed right behind them and they battle to keep the Putun from reaching Tixchel. We still have not caught the early scouts, and we believe more landed in secret a short time ago. Everyone on the Island is to stay inside where we can defend them."

"Yes, but—"

She gently, but firmly, stops me from pushing past her and leaving. "Night Wind commands that no one is to be on the *sacbe*, Noble Lady. We are under attack!"

"I am the acting Queen of Cuzamil!" I glare at her. "Those were my orders your *nacom* gave you, and I am making an exception for myself! If I don't collect these ingredients now, Queen Heart of Water will die. You will let me pass."

"My orders are to keep everyone inside the palace, My Lady Queen. We are at war; thus, the command of my *nacom* must overrule yours. I am sorry." She gives me a beseeching look, adding, "Forgive me, Lady, but it is my duty."

Om bey! Night Wind will hear about this! In the meantime, what am I to do?

Before I truly panic, I remember the words of my mother when she trained me in the House of Healing: If you don't have the herbs you need, use the ones you have. If you have no herbs, use prayer and water. Medicine is not just made of plants and roots and leaves. It can also be made from intentions, prayers and magic. I duck into a small room and prepare to meditate on how to make the formula so urgently needed by Heart of Water.

"No one may enter!" I hear a guard yell in the corridor. I look out into the corridor and see two guards taking up a defensive posture as twenty priestesses march toward the queen's chambers. *Om bey*! More Cob women? They are women of the second and third age dressed in varying mantles of white over blue and blue over white. They wear the same headband and shell nose ring as Evening Star, but as they near me I can see from their tattoos, braids, facial features and different-angled flattened foreheads that these are not Cob. They hail from all over the Known World.

I plant myself in front of the guards and the group halts in front of me. One of the eldest steps forward. She cradles a bundle in her arms. She nods at me and then moves the cloth aside to reveal Tun, the crystal skull! The guards and I gasp. It is the most carefully guarded treasure on our Island. There are those who live their whole lives here and never lay eyes on it. The priestess carefully covers the quartz skull and steps back.

A second elder steps forward and moves a cloth aside to reveal a flat, shiny chunk of obsidian. It is the powerful scrying tool we call the Eye. My mother used it often to witness events transpiring in distant places. I nod to the priestess and give her a wide smile. This is just what we need to know how our warriors fare.

A priestess of the second age diffidently steps forward. Her wrapped burden is large and round. Already I have guessed what she holds. She unwraps the luminescent amethyst-and-quartz-crystal bowl, which we call the Rainbow *Cenote*. It is the third of the most-precious treasures of Cuzamil. Legend has it that all rainbows of the Known World are born within this bowl.

I give these priestesses my heartfelt thanks for keeping our priceless treasures safe.

"Queen Jade Skirt," proclaims the priestess holding Tun, "six moons ago the Goddess sent Queen Heart of Water a dream and told her to send these treasures away from the palace. She knew not why, but she called me to her in secret and entrusted me with our Island's sacred scrying and divination tools. I hid them in Her temples in the east, west and south."

A very ancient priestess steps forward and takes me by the hand. Hers is soft and wrinkled with age, but I can make out the tattooed symbols of moon and rabbit.

"Last night we all sensed trouble. The Bird Oracle sent her winged servants to warn us. When we saw the signal fires lit, we collected the ancient scrying instruments and walked the secret paths to bring them to you in Cuzamil's time of need."

I look into her kind face and recognize her. Antler Skull! She was one of my own instructors in divination long, long ago. She sees the recognition in my eyes and smiles sweetly.

"Yes, Daughter. It is so good to see you!"

"Dear Mother, my heart is warmed by your smile."

"Ah," she says, touching my face with her soft, wrinkled palm, "how I loved your mother! You look so much like her."

Antler Skull makes a sign with her hand and the other priestesses do the same. It is the special signal of the members of the Red Hand Society! This is fortunate, indeed. The Red Hand Society is comprised of those most honored priestesses with the strongest gifts. I make the sign as well and we exchange knowing smiles.

I lead them to Heart of Water's chambers where Evening Star has taken charge of the priestesses in our entourage and put them to work assisting Blood Woman, treating the wounded guards, and sending messages through the palace informing the people of what has happened. Someone has also been sent to inform the Bird Oracle in the tower of the Great Temple of the Mother that Blue Monkey is under arrest so Night Wind can be told.

I head to the *nulha* to see my sister, but Evening Star stops me. "Lady, she is well-attended there. Blood Woman will call when you are needed, but there is much for you to do here."

Antler Skull's group is moving efficiently around the room gathering up a pile of jaguar pelts and arranging them in three corners. The priestesses separate into three groups, each working with a different divining and scrying tool. One group clusters around the Eye. It is usually housed in the *calmecac* where young women are trained in the mysteries, including divination and the oracular arts. I used it a few times when I was a student there, but it rarely chose to show me much.

The second group settles in a circle in a sunny corner, the magnificent crystal bowl in the center. It is normally used to collect the drips of lustral water from Her sacred cave near the Moon Temple. Just before I left Cuzamil to marry Moon Eagle, I was the young priestess who carried the Rainbow Cenote every evening at dusk to the Mother's cave, which is hidden underneath the Temple of the Great Mother. At the end of the moon cycle, when the bowl was filled to the brim, I carefully carried it up the steep, winding stone steps and set it out in the light of the full moon. I meditated and prayed beside the crystal bowl until dawn, and then carried it into the Temple and sprinkled the blessed water on the altar. Ever since then I have been very good at scrying with water.

The third group sits reverently in front of the magnificent crystal skull. Tun served as Oracle of Ix Chel before my grandmother became The Great Mother's first human oracle. It is our most important symbol of the spiritual power of the women at Ix Chel's Island sanctuary, and a powerful channel of Her power.

I have not worked with those tools for many *tuns*, but I am well-tuned to my own Ancestral Stone. I lift it carefully out of my shoulder bag. Because it holds the spirits of our Chel ancestors, including my grandmother and mother, it is strongly linked to the sacred Island. My grandmother once showed me how it could be used to enhance our connections with the other sacred treasures. Shaped from clear crystal with an opal embedded, it was used every day by my mother and grandmother, who used to meditate and pray with it in the mornings in this very room. Many times have I looked into its depths and found the answers to my questions. It feels like an old friend. I sit in the center of the room and hold it in my lap. I look up to see the oldest priestesses coming to join me. One of them lets out a gasp of surprised pleasure when she sees my Ancestral Stone. The women form a link of power with practiced ease and when I join my concentration to theirs I feel the pulsations of their collective strength and resolve. My *chu'lel* fills with light. I take a deep breath and pray aloud:

Goddess, Source of Life, Protector and Provider,
Your daughters thank You for our precious Tun, Eye and Rainbow Cenote.
Gracious Mother, we seek Your wisdom
Send us the signs we need to protect Your sanctuary.

While the others repeat the prayer, Evening Star walks among us holding a clay censer. *Copal* smoke drives the last dregs of Blue Monkey's miasma from the room. The clearing is like a delicious breath of fresh air. Sitting with these gifted priestesses in this room, I feel no subterfuge, no struggle for power, no personal ambitions. Why can't the world be like this? Why must there be so much greed and arrogance?

"Our mutual goal is peace at the least cost," says Antler Skull, as if reading my thoughts.

As our meditation begins, I am interrupted quietly by Evening Star whispering in my ear: "Noble Lady, Queen Heart of Water calls for you!"

Antler Skull gives me a reassuring nod and takes my place in front of my Ancestral Stone. I don't hesitate to leave it with her.

I race down a short flight of stairs to the palace *nulha*. I quickly strip naked and step through the moon-shaped door. I'm immediately filled with a sense of great danger. I jump back and thrust my arms out to keep Evening Star from entering.

"Who is here? Reveal yourself!" I command.

Pure evil manifests in a foul, black cloud that pulses malevolently in the stone chamber. It feels amused at my panic. Frantically, I motion for Blood Woman and her priestesses to leave the chamber. They rush past me to get out the door. I hover protectively over my sister, who is curled up on a bench and too weak to move.

"Lady, what is it?" Blood Woman calls to me.

"A demon!" I answer. But where is it? The foul presence is invisible again, but I know it is still here. I cast my inner awareness around the stone chamber, but the only presence I feel is Heart of Water. I lay my hand over her heart and tune in to her *chu'lel*, which is a faint, sickly yellow.

There! The wretched presence is pushing my sister's life force out and trying to take over! In a flash my sister's behavior makes perfect sense. Not only was she poisoned, but she is also possessed by a powerful demon! This is how Blue Monkey managed to control Heart of Water so completely. She must have summoned the spirits of the dark realm and then weakened the queen with the poison to get past her defenses. This evil magic is more dangerous than the oracular poisoning. My mother taught me that evil spirits hate the steam bath and the scent of pine bark. Most of all, they despise the *cacaltun* herb.

I bark out commands to Blood Woman and she sends her acolytes to fetch the herb.

"A demon?" she asks, bravely poking her head in the chamber. "*Om bey!* I never thought to look, but you are right. I see it! A strong one, from the color of it."

She and her acolytes come back into the *nulha*. I admire their courage. There is a sharp edge of obsidian in Blood Woman's voice as she instructs her assistants to hold Heart of Water gently, but firmly, by ankles and wrists so that the queen cannot curl up and hide from the healing steam. The pine bark snaps in the fire and in a moment we smell its tangy aroma.

"More!" I order. Another handful hisses on the coals. I close my eyes and See with my inner eye.

"The demon is arrogant, full of greed," I report. "A male spirit. One of the leaders." I take a deep breath and push deeper, nearly overwhelmed by his dark nature. "The lust for power is strong."

My poor sister struggles against the acolytes, twitching and moaning. With my Sight I can tell that she has been struggling long and hard against this spirit, who thrives on confusion and fear. She barely has strength left to fight. Her *chu'lel* is fading. As much as I want to sob, I stay detached and continue to scan my inner Knowing of this demon. I sense he is a lost soul who lived an evil life and was condemned to wander in the Middle World. He could not cross the river so he was taken by the evil spirits of the Underworld and sent to spread suffering and agony to the living. I pity him, but it is time for him to depart.

Blood Woman is ready. Wordlessly she hands me a bundle of basil—leaves and branches both. I crush them in my hands and breathe in the heady, spicy aroma while I center myself in the Earth Mother's sacred body. I feel Her power rise up through the floor and into my legs and settle in my womb. Blood Woman feels it too, and our spirits connect powerfully in the ritual. Her strong voice commands the Nine Spirits of the Underworld to come take their servant. I stand over Heart of Water and chant the prayer we learned in the *calmecac* of healing:

Great Mother, we beseech Your assistance.

We have faith in Your great power.

We call upon Your Helping Spirits to come now and remove this lost soul.

We call upon the spirit of cacaltun and the pine tree to assist us.

Escort the lost one back to the Underworld.

Lock him in the corral of wandering spirits.

Let him know that we forgive him.

Heart of Water keens and growls like a wild thing, and despite her weak limbs she thrashes so strongly that she nearly overpowers the acolytes.

"Leave her!" I cry, beating my sister mercilessly with the wild basil branches. "Goddess of Healing, Protector of the Rainbow Throne, remove this evil presence from the heart, soul and body of Heart of Water!"

Over and over I call out to Ix Chel, whose Presence fills me. She moves my arm, directs my *chu'lel*. Face down on the floor, Heart of Water quiets for a moment and then bellows out a high-pitched, ear-splitting wail. The acolytes spring back, afraid, and my sister yanks her hair out and bites her arms until they bleed. She is restrained again and I continue beating her with the sacred herb and chanting prayers. This is a very strong demon—the strongest I have ever encountered. But Ix Chel strengthens me.

"Stand firm in faith and prayer!" Blood Woman calls out to her acolytes and they raise their voices in a song of praise to Ix Chel, Protector of Women.

The demon perceptibly weakens, but then it throws a spear of piercing hatred at me and breaks my concentration for a moment.

"Fight him, Sister!" I urge Heart of Water. "*You* must be the one to banish the demon. You can do it! Shake off his grip on you! I am with you!"

Heart of Water gasps and spasms, but I feel her struggling against it. There! She is pushing against the spirit!

"Sisters, draw Her rainbow light into yourself and send it to the Queen!" Blood Woman shouts.

As the powerful healers all focus together and channel Her power there is an explosion of light. The greasy cloud of black energy that oozes around my sister's *chu'lel* momentarily releases its grip, but then it starts to reattach itself. It is too strong!

"Push, Heart of Water. Push!" I beg her.

With great effort, she bears down and screams with effort. Finally, with her last strength, she wills the demon to leave. The evil shoots out of her and ricochets off the stone walls of the *nulha* before it whooshes out the door as if it cannot depart from this field of love and faith fast enough.

Heart of Water goes limp and still and the priestesses gently release her arms and legs. I cradle her face in my hands and whisper to her how brave and strong she is. Her eyes are barely open, but it is enough for me to see that it is her soul that looks out now. Then Heart of Water curls into a ball and weeps, her heartbreaking sobs echoing in the stone chamber. I curl up behind her and rock her gently and murmur reassurances to her as I would to a frightened child.

"Precious Sister, all will be well. I am so sorry I was not here for you sooner. Great evil has been done to you, but it is over now," I whisper. Is she nodding? Does she understand? "You have been poisoned," I continue, "in body and spirit and mind. But I will make Grandmother's remedy and you will heal. I know you will. Can you understand me? Do you know who I am, dear one?"

"Jade Skirt," she manages to say, too weak for more. But it is as if she has spoken an entire folio of fig tree papers. She knows me!

The acolytes wrap her in a bolt of clean cotton and carry her gently on a litter to the antechamber, where she is moved to a low bed. I sit beside her. Her head is in my lap and her arms clutch me around the waist. She sobs quietly and I continue to pat her back and murmur to her. *Om bey*, she is thin as a skeleton. Her hip bones jut out and her elbows and knees are as large as avocados. Her hair is nearly gone and she trembles like an old woman. No punishment can ever be enough for Blue Monkey! I murmur over and over again that everything will be well now; she is safe.

Blood Woman carries the pine bark incense through the steam room and outer chambers, not trusting the task to her assistants. She smokes the doorway and all around me and my sister, in case any evil lingers. I close my eyes and pray silently that Ix Chel's Helping Spirits erase all traces of evil left behind and take away any other malevolent spirits who are present here. Blood Woman's assistant sprinkles *cacaltun* water all around us, paying extra attention to all corners of the room.

At last, Heart of Water's tears are spent. I help her sit up and drink a few sips of water. Her hands are too weak to hold the gourd. Blood Woman praises her and assures the Queen that she will be well soon, but she must keep drinking. Heart of Water sighs and tries to drink more, but she is too exhausted. We carry my sister back to her sleeping chamber. The priestesses look at her curiously, and then when they realize who it is we carry, they look shocked and dismayed.

Under Blood Woman's direction the platform bed has been moved from the middle of the room to a sheltered alcove. The old pelts used by Blue Monkey were dragged away to be burned. Evening Star has smudged the area with *copal* smoke and laid the bed with fresh pine branches and layers of quilts. I pull the covers over Heart of Water and she sinks into a natural sleep. I start to settle myself beside her, but Blood Woman shakes her head.

"You are needed elsewhere now, Queen Jade Skirt," she tells me respectfully. "I will watch over her and call you when she awakens."

I am loathe to leave her, but I have an idea. I claim my Ancestral Stone from Antler Skull and carry it to Heart of Water. Laying it on her heart, I fold her hands over it. Immediately, her breathing becomes more even and her color improves. I lay my hands on top of hers and commune with the Ancestors.

"We nearly lost her," I admit to them. "Please send her strength to recover!"

Just as I am thinking that I will defy Night Wind's guards and go gather the plants I need to make the remedy for the oracular poisoning, I feel my grandmother's spirit conveying to me wordlessly not to go yet; that this is where I will be most helpful now. She sends me reassurances that the Ancestors will keep Heart of Water alive until it is safe for me to collect the plants.

Evening Star clucks over me and wants me to rest. A part of me would love to lie down beside my sister and sleep for a *tun*, but there is still much to do. I reassure my faithful attendant that I am well, and no, I don't need more tea just yet. Then I join Antler Skull and her group around Tun. Linking my *chu'lel* to theirs, I immediately open my awareness to the crystal skull. It fills me with awe to connect to its ancient Knowing, and I feel a pulse of affection and interest from it. Then I See in my mind's eye a stain of blood red swirl up from the skull's base. My heart sinks.

I declare in a voice filled with sorrow. "The blood of innocents is shed on Her sacred Island."

I pray aloud, my voice strong and deep:

"Goddess of Creatures, Protector of Women, strengthen the arms, the hearts and the blades of our soldiers and all our allies. Shield Your innocent Daughters from harm and help us to cast out the invaders and restore Cuzamil as Your Zone of Peace."

The others murmur their support: "Let it be so, Great Mother!"

Right now, my dearest Jaguar Shield and my brave sons, Spear Thrower and Iguana Wind, may be fighting for their lives!

"Mother of Life," I add privately, "protect my loved ones."

The moment I think of them, a cold finger of dread runs up my spine like a dark certainty. Dear Goddess, no! This same eerie sensation came to me before my dear Moon Eagle died. Who will I lose next? Goddess, protect them all! I can't bear to think of it!

A cry of excitement tears me from my worry. It is the priestess who scries in the obsidian Eye.

"I can see the battle!" she says, deep in trance. "The Putun numbers are twice ours, but we hold the beach and they cannot advance. Ah, here come more canoes. The *nacom* is shouting for the soldiers and men to retreat. Wait…more canoes are coming. The men of Tulumha come to protect the Island! Goddess, help them arrive in time!"

The waiting is agony, but finally the priestess says, "The Eye is closed. I cannot see what happened!"

Our guards have edged closer to hear the report and now they race out of the room to tell their comrades and hear if there is more news from the Bird Oracle of the Great Temple of the Mother.

"Sister, what is your name?" I ask the young seer.

"I am Moon Bird Tzib Pech," she says shyly.

"The Goddess has given you a strong gift, Moon Bird, but She has Her reasons for revealing and not revealing to us Her plans. Can you look to the south now? Perhaps we will be granted a vision of that front."

"I will try, Noble Lady," she says.

She sinks back into trance and begins to hum. The other priestesses join their voices to hers to give her strength as she turns her inner eye to the south. I know she has succeeded when she ceases humming and grows perfectly still. Her eyes open and she gazes deeply into the glassy black slab.

"It goes not well in the south," she says, paling. "The Putun have taken hostages! They hold the *polna* for pregnant women, and our soldiers surround it. They dare not attack or the women will be harmed." Those Putun are evil cowards! "The Bird Oracle at the Temple of the Grandmother sends a *cuzam* messenger to the *nacom* for reinforcements. Oh! A Putun arrow struck down the swallow!" There are murmurs of dismay.

When it is clear that there is no more to report, I instruct Moon Bird to look to the east. Again she hums, and the others join her. Very quickly she has the east in her scrying tool and can tell us what she sees.

"A fire burns in the village near the Temple of the Oracle," she reports. "The Putun trampled the crops, but there is no sign of wounded or dead." I am so tense my fingernails have dug half-moons into my palms. "Ah! There is fighting in the plaza! The Putun hide in the trees, but our soldiers hold the temple! A force of soldiers is traveling from the north and should be at the Putun's backs very soon!"

There is another cheer from the women and more smiles from the guards, but we are all tense. The news is good, but the battle is not yet won.

"Look to the north," I tell our gifted seer. "Let us know if we are still under attack from the Putun who invaded the traders' settlement."

This time, it takes her longer to See. Truly she has the Goddess's gift for scrying, but it takes much out of her vital force to focus for this long.

"Sisters, there is smoke," she says with alarm. "So much smoke! It blows toward the Temple of the Maiden!"

Are the Putun burning the swamps to make them passable?

"There is shouting. I see men running. They are chased by our soldiers! The Putun are taking cover in a deserted *polna*. Our soldiers harry them. Now I see men from Tulumha and Pole, I think, by the way they dress. They are chasing the Putun. Oh, Great Mother!"

Moon Bird topples over, unconscious.

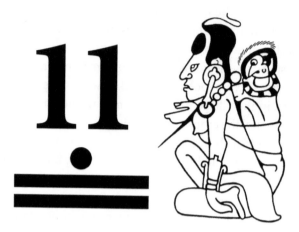

There is nothing we can do for the unconscious scrier except to lay her on a pallet and let her sleep off the exhaustion. The healers check her pulse and assure everyone that she is strong; she merely overtaxed herself.

Evening Star scolds me privately. We have all walked through the night and worked all morning. Surely it is a miracle that more of us have not succumbed to exhaustion. I accept her rebuke, since I cannot remember when last I ate and it occurs to me that I am famished. The servants flow in with baskets of *chaya* tamales and roasted rabbit. A simple meal, but it tastes more delicious than a banquet to me right now.

"The Eye has shown us much," I say grimly to Antler Skull, Blood Woman and Evening Star as we sip our teas together in an alcove with a window overlooking the deserted central plaza. "Cuzamil is at war, but with the Goddess's help and the help of our allies, it seems we are holding out against the Putun."

"But surely there is more that we can do!" Antler Skull says with frustration. "Watching events does no good. We need to help shape events!" She pounds one fist into the other for emphasis. The priestesses near us who have been eavesdropping call out in agreement.

"I believe the collective powers of Ix Chel's servants can change the course of a river, turn back the ocean tides or defeat an army without lifting a spear!" declares the redoubtable Evening Star.

"Tun did not reveal anything we did not already know," Antler Skull says bluntly, "and the Rainbow Cenote has been curiously quiet, despite the prayers and efforts of the most gifted scriers among us. It is as if they are waiting for us to do something else with them. We priestesses cannot fight with spears and clubs to save Her sacred Island, but we need to do *something;* not just whimper and hide in the palace like helpless children."

"It would be wrong for this war to be won only by spears and knives," I agree, sharing her frustration.

"I do not understand, Queen Jade Skirt," a priestess of the second age says diffidently. "Whatever brings us victory is surely sufficient, is it not?"

Then I must tell them the true extent of Blue Monkey's betrayal: not just control of the Rainbow Throne, but giving it over to Pus Master to make Cuzamil a stronghold of the War God and His heart-taker priests.

"Already they have desecrated the Island by sacrificing the son of a trader on the north shore, in the Chunkunab settlement," I say grimly. Their shocked expressions mirror what I feel in my own heart. "This is not just a battle over territory," I explain. "What is at stake are the souls and spirits of the people."

After a moment of silence Evening Star says, "Our Goddess can be as cunning and clever as the best *nacom*. She rules the sea, which our friends and foes must cross to get to Cuzamil. And the Great Mother has Her allies among the Great Ones. I imagine Her calling on Her previous lovers, the Sun, the Rain God, the Vulture God, the Morning Star, the Wasp Star God and the Death God to assist Her in this power struggle against the War God."

"But why does She allow this war to happen?" asks one of the young acolytes of Blood Woman shyly. "Why has She not already sent the Putun packing?"

"Hmm, that is a reasonable question," says my old teacher, Antler Skull. "Greed and evil will always be with us. She has never promised us Heaven on Earth, though here on Cuzamil we come close to that. Think: are we not taught that She has given each of us gifts and light to use wisely if we will? Perhaps She waits for *us* to save the Island of Women using the gifts She has blessed us with."

I need no convincing. Waiting and worrying and feeling helpless is maddening. But what can we do without spears and knives? The women talk and argue among themselves, trying to think of a way.

Antler Skull says finally. "Your grandmother once mentioned to me that in a time of dire necessity, with our Goddess's help, we could use all three treasures of Cuzamil to cast a blanket of protection over Her Island."

She tells us it has never been tried before, but perhaps the need was never as great as it is now. "Queen Cosmic Turtle said first we must meditate and pray," says Antler Skull. All the priestesses are listening closely now. "When the time is right we must focus our *chu'lel* into a single beam of light and pour it into the treasures of Cuzamil."

"Let us prepare the ritual," I say. How right it feels to be doing something to help protect our Island sanctuary!

"There is one more thing." She pauses and gives me a piercing look. "A Queen of Cuzamil must act as channel for the great force of *chu'lel*. She must be the one to transfer it into the treasures."

The others gasp. The risk is great. If the force of their *chu'lel* is too much for me to bear I will be destroyed. I hold my hand up for silence and nod to Antler Skull. "I will do it."

"May the Goddess protect you," my old teacher murmurs.

As the priestesses prepare the ritual space I center myself and send a wave of my heart *chu'lel* into my *pi*. I feel the sacred objects readily respond. I will need their great protection to survive this ritual. I open my heart again and send a prayer to the Great Mother to protect me and guide me. Then I am as ready as I can be for something that has never before been tried.

The priestesses form a circle around me and Antler Skull instructs me to hold Tun above my head. She deftly binds the Eye close to my heart with a white cloth and then positions the Rainbow Cenote on the ground between my spread legs.

"We come together to forge a shield of protection and peace over the Island of Women," I say somberly. "We ask for strength from Ix Chel, Mother of us all."

We each sink into meditation and when I am ready I give a nod and they stretch arms up to the heavens where She resides, and then down to the Earth, where She resides. Chanting, they begin to draw great rivers of pure light up from Mother Earth to fill their *chu'lels*. Even with my eyes closed I can See the intense brightness emanating from the treasures in the spirit world the sparkling rainbow light pulsing around each of us. It Is the life force Ix Chel gifted to all creation—a small piece of Her light shining in each of us at the moment we come into being.

I sink deeper into my *chu'lel* and open myself to the ancestral treasures. When I feel a strong connection to each sacred object, I open myself to the priestesses and draw their light together into a beam and send it into the treasures. The beam widens and brightens as I pull in more light from the well-trained women. The treasures buzz and hum with pleasure, receiving and filling and magnifying our united focus. I feel my capacity to channel this pure light expand like a bladder. I lose track of time. There is nothing but this current of power coming in, gathering, expanding Itself and me with it.

When I feel I can take even more, I give a wordless cry and each woman twists her right hand in a circle nine times and then pace nine steps to the east, nine to the west. In my inner Seeing it is like watching small ripples amass into a tidal wave. The flood of power the priestesses unleash crashes into the center of my receptive spirit, nearly knocking me over with its force. The obsidian slab absorbs the brunt of it and strengthens my heart. I feel it hot and humming against my breast. The crystal bowl receives it, yet somehow never fills. Tun is light as a feather in my arms and shines like a torch of rainbow light. I feel glorious, as if I am standing under a waterfall of Her pulsing presence. I have never before felt her aspect of Mother as strongly as I do now. My abdomen vibrates. I think I feel my uterus leap! I think I feel every uterus in the room leap! Great Mother, Creator, I feel Your power of creation in each of us!

I am liquid light, flowing like water sweet as honey; like molten rock grown strong and sure; like the cool minerals of the earth lively with elemental intelligence.

You feel our natures!

Who speaks to me?!

I feel Tun shaking with silent laughter in my hands. Of course! The ancestral treasures! I become aware of a deep, powerful voice praying and I realize the voice is mine, yet not mine. It has four tones. My voice is the voice of the Cuzamil's treasure. My heart is their heart. We are One in the light, called forth by our mutual love and faith.

Mother. Grandmother. Creator. Luminary of the Night.

Ix Chel, You who are in all three worlds.

Ix Chel, You, the Mother of Necessities.

Your divine power goes to the four extremes of the Earth

To the four extremes of the sea and beyond.

Spread Your mantle of protection over us all

Cover us with Your favor like a shield

Ix Chel, Great Mother, make us victorious over evil.

Kin, Father Sun, light our way to peace.

In my mind Tun tells me it is time. *Focus now, Dear One. Know where you would send this storm!*

I lock my mind onto the memory of Her double rainbows stretching from Pole to the far corners of Cuzamil.

"Ix Chel, Protector of Your Island sanctuary, Framer and Shaper, send forth Your rainbow light!" My voice is four voices shooting off in the four directions. "Let it cover and protect Your sacred Island and the homes of our allies in Pole and Tulumha! Strengthen our soldiers. Weaken, confuse and confound our enemies. Let their weapons fall from their hands and break in half. Let their hearts be opened to the sanctity of all life. Let Your waves stop their canoes from reaching our shores and let Your waters carry them far away from here. Gracious Mother, shelter Your creatures great and small and shield us with Your rainbow light!"

Ribbons of light stream through me. It is like nothing I have ever experienced. Magnificent! I feel like laughing and crying it is so beautiful. I start to get lost in the immensity and I feel my control slipping. It is so hard to focus. I want to ride the wave, this irresistible current of bliss.

Jade Skirt Chel Cocom, bring your mind back! warns Tun, showing me how to drag myself out of the seductive sensations and strengthen my will. I bring my attention back to the task, yet I am aware that I cannot make the storm of focused light go where I will it.

First contain it, like this, says the crystal bowl, allowing me to feel how to hold the force in and then channel it into a stream in any direction I choose. But where should I send it?

You must See what is far as if it is near, says the Eye, showing me the map of Cuzamil as if I am a bird looking down on the Island from above. The contours of Cuzamil match well the map Night Wind sketched on the dirt floor of the *polna*. Holding that in my mind now, I understand what I must do.

I cast the rainbow light out across Cuzamil. Countless rainbow *sacbes* unfurl and I will them to stretch over the whole Island and across the waters to Pole and Tulumha as well. I have never concentrated on anything this hard in my life. It takes everything I have to stay upright and not drop Tun or fall into the Rainbow Cenote between my legs.

Suddenly my arms ache and throb. I start to falter. I can't take anymore, but it's not enough! *Om bey!* If I fail now this flood will destroy what I seek to protect! Ix Chel, help me!

Antler Skull gives a wordless cry and the brave women redouble their chanting and bombard me with yet more elemental power drawn from earth and sky. The strength in my limbs is renewed. What a relief! I work quickly to take the rainbow light and shape it with my single-minded intention. I anchor it far and wide so it covers us like a shield. I lose track of time, but suddenly I know in my heart that it is done.

With a sigh, I lower my arms. The women sag with exhaustion, some lying right down on the floor and closing their eyes. Surprisingly, I don't feel the least bit tired. In fact, I feel refreshed! I place Tun gently on the floor, then unwrap the bindings holding the Eye to my heart and lay it beside the crystal skull. When I step away from the Rainbow Cenote I gasp. There are swirling rainbows trapped inside the crystal! I have never seen such a thing before. Then I see rainbows in the obsidian Eye and swirling around inside the crystal skull! They are beautiful!

I accept a cup of *chalche* tea from an awe-struck acolyte and inhale the complex fragrance, enjoying a moment to bask in the marvel we just wrought together. The others are falling asleep, but I am too restless with energy to sit. I check on Heart of Water. She sleeps peacefully. Blood Woman gives me a smile of wonder. I look to where she gestures and there are spirals of rainbow light dancing on the walls, ceiling and floor! I stop myself from laughing aloud so as not to wake my sister. I feel elated.

Blood Woman pulls me to the side to confer. "She is very strong of spirit, Lady, but her body is far gone. I fear she will not last much longer. She cannot eat and her pounding head keeps waking her. Her flesh is on fire. We tried to get her to eat, but her bowels gushed. All she can take are small sips of water. Before this day ends, we must give her the medicine that can purge the toxins, and even that is not a guarantee that she will recover."

I touch the Ancestral Stone in my sister's hands and feel my Grandmother's spirit wordlessly urging me to go now and collect the plants for the remedy. I grab a basket and march into the corridor. When a young warrior leaps up to follow me I surprise her by grapping her arm and pulling her in close.

"You will help me with a sacred task," I whisper to her. "Queen Heart of Water must be given a remedy before Father Sun is lost over the horizon or we will lose her." The soldier's eyes go wide. "You will take me in secret to the forest so I can gather what is needed. You will not argue with me. Do you understand?" She nods. Good. "*Cox!*" I say.

She takes the lead and I follow her down a maze of corridors and then she ducks into a narrow passageway where a door is concealed. Behind it are shallow steps that lead us into the bowels of the palace. I thought I knew every stone of this place, but I have never been here before.

"It is said your grandmother sometimes liked to leave the palace without her retinue," the soldier tells me. She is only a few *tuns* older than Nine Macaw. We exit through a tunnel cleverly hidden by boulders and a thick growth of trees. Once outside, I know these paths well and I take the lead. Spear at the ready, the young woman guards my back as we jog through the jungle. Are there Putun hiding in the trees? My heart flutters at the thought, but then I feel the rainbow light still buzzing in my body and I know that if the Putun are here I will be able to create a glamour to confuse and confound them. The Putun will do us no harm.

The plants that make up the antidote grow in many places on the island, but I seek them from a particular place of great power. They must be collected fresh and with prayers and used within an hour of harvest. My mother took me to the hidden cave I seek now on the day of my first moon. She bathed me in the waters of the stream and told me that this cave is the true dwelling place of the Goddess on earth. My mother made sure to show me the two vines and tree bark that are watered by the stream that flows from Her sacred cave.

"We see these plants in many places," I told my mother, confused. "Why are you showing them to me here?"

She explained, "Because the water they drink comes from Her sacred cave, she has made these plants more powerful." She described what I might someday need to use them for, and demonstrated how to gather and prepare the remedy. I remember how the vines wound around the base of a magnificent *ceiba* tree, whose branches were so tall they seemed to reach to heaven. My mother said Ix Chel dwells above it when she is with Her divine consort Itzámna.

The soldier and I make our way down a steep hill to the trickling stream, surprising a herd of deer and their young as they drink.

"Noble Jade Skirt, what is this place?" she whispers reverently. A peace radiates from the cave.

"This is the Goddess's sanctuary," I tell her, patting her on the arm. "No Putun will disturb us here. We are safer here than anywhere in the Known World. The Goddess will not allow any harm to come to us on Her doorstep."

I leave her sitting by the stream. Glancing back once, I think she almost looks like Nine Macaw. I feel a pang in my heart. I always imagined the day I would take my precious feather to this sacred place. Surprisingly, I also feel at peace with her absence. Perhaps it is the nature of this place, but I think it is more than that. I have come to understand and to accept that she should not be Queen of Cuzamil if she does not want the responsibility. I have only been acting queen for a day or two, and already I am chafing at the responsibility. How much more difficult it will be for a young girl who is just starting out on her path. It was wrong of me to believe only she can sit on the Rainbow Throne. This day I have met many gifted and devoted women who would make admirable rulers. Is it so important that the throne pass to one of our line? Is it not more important that it passes to one who wants to serve the Goddess with all her heart and gifts?

Thoughts of succession evaporate as I approach the cave entrance. I kneel down in front of the mighty *ceiba* that conceals the opening and bow my head to the soft earth.

"Great Mother of All, bless Your daughter Heart of Water. Bless Your servant Jade Skirt. Bless Your land, Cuzamil. Thank You for Your gifts."

The vines I seek are wrapped around the tree's trunk: the spindly *payche* and the slender *ya ax*. Growing beside it is the thorny-barked *zubin* tree. I say the herb collector's prayer for each of the plants I gather, whispering to the wind;

In the name of Ix Chel, Guardian of the Healing Plants, I give thanks to the spirit of this plant. I have faith with all my heart that it will heal Heart of Water. Rid her body, her mind and her soul of the poison and restore her strength and good health.

I slice off the parts I need, thanking the plants and wishing them quick healing from my cuts. When my basket is full, I fill a gourd with water from the sacred stream and cap it with a corn cob. I scoop up a handful of water and take a sip. I feel suddenly refreshed as never before. It tastes like fresh air.

We hurry back to the palace and I am out of breath when we arrive at the hearth room of the Rainbow Palace. I have met my sister's Hearth Mistress on several occasions and know she can be a bossy tapir with a serpent's tongue, but she is also loyal and much loved by Heart of Water.

"Precious Moon Beam," I greet her respectfully. "I require a small pot and a warm place at your hearth to cook my herbs."

"You!" she sniffs disdainfully. "And where were you when those pox-faced Cob women took over our palace? What took you so long?"

I remind myself that I don't have to explain myself to her, but confrontational people always make me nervous.

"Enough of that," I say dismissively, as if she is a temperamental child. "I do not answer to you. I must act quickly to brew this medicine for the Queen. Her life depends on it. Do not delay me."

Her manner changes in an instant, true concern written all over her wrinkled face. "Why did you not say so? Hurry! Over here is a pot. I will build up the fire."

I must make time later to get to know her better and win her trust. No doubt she knows every bit of palace gossip and intrigue. Our grandmother always advised us to be respectful of the Hearth Mistress because she has the power to nourish or poison the royal family. Precious Moon Beam is one I would much rather have as an ally than enemy.

She taps on a clay pot with her wooden spoon and two young girls about Nine Macaw's age appear from another room. The three assist me as I peel and grind the bark and vines to the correct pasty consistency. They do not disturb me as I whisper prayers and send my *chu'lel* of faith and gratitude into the plants to strengthen their healing properties. I carefully take the gourd of water I collected and pour it into the pot. When it just begins to boil I add the plants and cover the pot with a large leaf from a palm tree. I sing and hum a prayer and then another, and then one more while the assistants keep the fire burning. Finally, I sense that it is ready.

Precious Moon Beam is ready with a cloth to lift the pot off the fire. She hesitates before handing it to me. Inspired, I ask her if she would like to bring it to the Queen. A smile of gratitude lights her wrinkled face and she gives me a regal nod. I know she is deeply honored. She proudly marches in front, carefully carrying the medicine to her Queen.

There is no complicated protocol for administering the tea. Blood Woman pours it into a gourd and urges Heart of Water to take small sips. She makes a face at the bitter taste.

"Noble Lady, can we not sweeten it with honey?" asks Precious Moon Beam.

"I wish we could, but it will weaken the healing properties," I say. "Bitter cures; sweet does not." She grudgingly accepts this.

I brush my hand lovingly across my sister's cheek in a blessing and then leave her to the ministrations of these good women.

Now exhaustion hits me like a wave. The priestesses want to speak with me; Evening Star tries to get me to listen to reports about supplies. I wave them all away.

"I must rest," I confess. "I can do no more. I will return soon."

I leave the Queen's chambers and move down the corridor toward a small stone room that I noticed was empty. I'm thinking I can lay my head down in peace for a few minutes when a runner approaches and quickly touches her forehead and then the ground in front of me.

"Queen Jade Skirt," the novice says softly, "the Bird Oracle of the Great Temple of the Mother has just received messages that you must hear only from her lips, but she cannot leave the rooftop. Will you come?"

The thought of news about my beloveds puts energy in my step. We hurry across the plaza, with a contingent of eight guards following for my protection, and then we climb many steep steps to the rooftop ledge sheltered from wind and sun by a cleverly woven reed mat on poles. A wiry woman of the second age sits on a pelt holding a hawk on her arm. They are looking into each other's eyes, obviously deep in conversation. I wait patiently until the bird flies off. I start to approach, but then a bright macaw flies down and lands on the Bird Oracle's arm. Looking at the trees surrounding the temple I see they are full of birds waiting their turn. *Cuzams* and gulls, songbirds and raptors all sit peacefully in the branches. The Bird Oracle notices me and waves me over. Her eyes are bright with excitement. The multicolored feathers she wears in her hair make her look like a very exotic breed of bird.

"Noble Lady, I have much news, but I don't know what to make of it!"

"What is your name, Sister?"

"I am Green Feather, Lady."

"What is your news?"

"*Nacom* Jaguar Shield and the men from Tulumha stopped the Putun invasion on the western shore. A sudden storm at sea overturned and drowned many Putun canoes. Hundreds straggled ashore barely alive. There is now a garrison of prisoners in the Bolon *polna*, where your son, Spear Thrower, is in charge. On the eastern shore Putun soldiers turn and fight one another in mass confusion! They are frightened of the Goddess's power now and fear they will be punished for eternity for defiling Her sanctuary. They fear their women will be struck barren if they shed blood on the Goddess's holy sanctuary! Some fall on their own spears as an offering to the Goddess so She will spare their families." We both grimace.

"They still do not understand that Ix Chel holds all life to be precious," I say sadly. "She who created us does not want our deaths! She asks us to revere life and treat her gift with dignity and service to one another."

"The battle outside the Temple of the Maiden in the north was nearly lost," Green Feather continues, "but a sudden storm of lightning bolts fell from a clear sky and the Putun became afraid and abandoned the battle. They flee to their boats on the north shore. *Nacom* Night Wind is in pursuit and our soldiers are capturing the stragglers. And in the south, the Putun nearly overran the Temple of the Grandmother. They occupied the *polna* for pregnant women and took hostages. A flock of parrots descended on their guards and began attacking them with beaks and claws, making a fierce racket. The Putun *nacom* came out and the birds all turned as one and attacked him. He surrendered! He and his men begged leave to make offerings to Ix Chel. They believe their War God cannot defeat the Goddess."

I laugh in amazement. "Ix Chel protects us! Green Feather, your feathered messengers bring the best possible reports! Thank you, Daughter. Let us spread this good news far and wide!"

The guards with me cheer and clap one another on the back. In the Queen's chambers, the priestesses clap their hands and laugh with delight and relief. Evening Star gives me a hug and whispers, "There is nothing more powerful on this Earth than a circle of dedicated women!"

Before I can agree with her I fall asleep in her arms.

The worst part of war is waiting. I remember this well from all the *tuns* my Moon Eagle was a soldier. You must wait to hear if your loved one is dead. You must wait to hear if the enemy is marching through your corn fields. Even with the heartening news from Green Feather, I wake up the next morning with a sinking feeling. How fare my beloveds? I slept long and deeply. I feel vaguely guilty, as if a queen should not sleep while others do battle. But my body gave me no choice.

Once I am awake, I ask first about Heart of Water. Blood Woman reports that she is not yet out of danger. The medicine will either work or not, and until my sister gains strength there is nothing more the healers can do. She is too weak to tolerate massage; the *nulha* can interfere with the remedy we gave her, and likewise other strengthening herbs must wait until the medicine clears her blood of the poison. Only time will tell if she survives her cleansing.

Reports from Green Feather come in steadily now, and Evening Star (does she ever sleep?) screens them and repeats the most important as I eat a tamale and drink chocolate. I learn that this morning our soldiers captured three small groups of Putun trying to sneak into Tixchel. The birds alerted Green Feather, who told Tixchel's *guards*. Patrols are still looking for stragglers on the *sacbe* and jungle paths and watching for any Putun fleeing other battles who might travel this way. I receive reports from the *polna* in Tixchel that several women around the island gave birth early, no doubt from the stress and fear. One precious feather was lost, but the other newborns are doing well. I also hear reports from the administrators about alarmingly depleted stores of food and medical supplies. Most of the palace staff was dismissed three moons ago by Blue Monkey and replaced by Cob women, all of whom have been arrested. It is not clear where the supplies have gone, but I assign Evening Star to call back the women who served Heart of Water in those roles. Hopefully, they can make sense of our mismanaged storehouses.

I take a break from administrative tasks and wander over to my sister's alcove. Praise Ix Chel, she is awake!

"Ah, Sister Jade Skirt, you are here, at last," Heart of Water whispers. Her eyes are much less yellow, but her frail skin is still papery and sallow.

"My dearest, how I have missed you!" My eyes brim with tears.

"You must try to drink, my Queen," Blood Woman pleads, holding a gourd to Heart of Water's lips. I can see Blood Woman is frustrated and worried, as am I.

I help the healer lift my sister's head so she can sip from the gourd. Heart of Water falls back on the quilts and turns to look at me. For the first time I feel she really sees me. I smile and take her hand. "Goddess, help this one who served You so well," I pray aloud.

"He kicked me over and over again, from the inside," she whispers. "I fought and fought, but I could not defeat him!"

"I know, my love, I know. It was an evil spirit, but he is gone now. You must rest and sleep. You have also been poisoned by overdoses of the oracular formula. But now you have taken the antidote. I collected and prepared it myself just as our mother taught us."

She gives a tiny nod and squeezes my hand feebly. Then she closes her eyes and falls back to sleep. Despite her frailty, I feel heartened. She is a seed stronger than she was yesterday. Our Ancestral Stone is still with her, touching her arm. I place my hand on it and send my thanks to our ancestors. I feel a pulse of love come back to me.

Late in the afternoon, as Father Sun descends once again to the Underworld, Precious Moon Beam sends us a meal of turkey stew. A soldier interrupts me and requests my presence in the corridor. I follow her to a small room, and there is Night Wind! Perspiration glistens on her face and arms as she catches her breath. She touches the floor with one hand and her heart with the other.

"I bring astonishing news, Queen Jade Skirt!"

"Come and sit!" I say. "It was madness for you to run here instead of sending a messenger!"

"Amazing things have occurred that you must hear from my mouth so you can trust that they are true," she says, sinking onto a bench. As she stretches out her legs I see several wounds wrapped in bandages.

A soldier hurries in with food and water for her *nacom*. She serves it and then backs out, leaving us in private. I insist that Night Wind eat at least a few bites and drink before she starts her tale.

"I will tell you truthfully that the tides of war were not flowing in our favor, Sister. You know I have faith in our Goddess, but yesterday morning I wondered why she had forsaken us. The enemy outnumbered us and they were hungry for our blood. They fought like vicious animals, cutting out the hearts of the fallen and carving up limbs and heads with the most horrifying cries and screams. Our soldiers fought hard, but they were afraid of such brutality. Lady, I was afraid! When the sun was at its high point, twenty canoes of Putun reinforcements appeared on the horizon and I knew they would take the Temple of the Moon and all the western shore. We did not have enough fighters, and the Putun in the forest had us pinned down on the beach. I could see we would soon be trapped between the enemy, with no way to defeat them and no reinforcements coming to our aid.

"Even with defeat imminent, the women and men fought with courage to defend our holy Island home. Putun canoes reached the shore before Father Sun began his descent into the sea. Their soldiers poured out of the boats and swarmed up the beach. I called together our forces to make a last stand. And that's when She sent us a miracle! A cloud of butterflies and dragonflies descended on the Putun and covered them completely! There were so many of the creatures that the Putun could not breathe or see! The cloud of insects grew and grew until the sky buzzed and darkened with them, yet only the Putun were their focus. Not one of us or our allies was touched by the insects. Truly it was a Divine act!

"The Putun understood that this was a message from Her and they were terrified! They fought one another as they scrambled to get into their boats. I worried that they would simply paddle to the north shore and join forces with the Putun there, but they wanted nothing more to do with Her sacred Island. They aimed their prows for Pole and paddled away with frantic strokes!

"We gave a great cheer and thanked the Goddess for her help. That was when the Putun in the forest lost their will to fight. Snakes jumped up from under every rock where a Putun stood. More snakes fell on them from the trees. One of their men declared that it was a clear sign that the War God cannot stand against the Creator Goddess. Lady, when those words were spoken the Putuns' spears fell from their hands! It was chaos after that. We watched as some of the terrified enemy rushed into the sea and drowned themselves, while others burst into tears and lay down on the ground begging the Goddess to forgive them. Their *nacoms* were furious and tried to get their men to stand and fight, and then they began to slaughter their own troops with knives. But their obsidian blades all fell from their hands at the same moment! The sound was like lightning striking down a tree! A few fell on the shards of their blades and ended their own lives. The rest knelt down and surrendered to us. We took them into custody and they begged to be allowed to build an altar to Ix Chel and make sacrifices to Her. We explained that Ix Chel, the Gentle, does not require sacrifice. The only sacrifice our Goddess needs is an end to killing and that they open their hearts to the sanctity of all life.

"My soldiers report similar occurrences in every corner of Cuzamil! The Putun have all died or surrendered or fled across the waters. Lady Queen, the war is won!"

We embrace and tears of relief stream from my eyes. Truly, Ix Chel is magnificent! Not only did she defeat our enemies; she changed their hearts! Night Wind and I cry and laugh and dance around the room. When I finally collect myself, I place a hand over my heart and bow to Night Wind.

"*Nacom*, you saved our Island with your courage, foresight and bravery. You are a shining light! Heart of Water will be so proud! Your ancestors honor you."

"Does she ask for me?" she asks shyly.

"Of course! The very first thing she said when I saw her was, 'My love! Where is my love?' "

The strong commander breaks down and weeps with relief. I tell her how we faced Blue Monkey and Snake Tooth and drove out the demon.

"But tell me, what of Pus Master?" I ask. "And has my daughter, Water Lily, been found?" There is a lump in my throat. "And what news of my family?"

"Pus Master's canoe overturned and he became tangled in his blood-soaked robes and drowned before he could set foot on the holy Island," she says. I know I should not rejoice In the death of my enemy, but I feel so relieved that evil one is no more.

"Sister," she continues somberly, "your daughter also drowned." "You are sure about this?" I say more sharply than I intended. I mourned Water Lily once already, and then discovered she lived and was a pawn of my enemy.

"It was witnessed by your grandson, Jaguar Paw," she tells me sympathetically. "It was a near thing. The boy risked his life to save his mother. He dove into the sea and nearly reached her when a massive wave took them both under. He was unconscious when his body washed ashore during the chaos of battle. He is in the House of Healing on the western shore and he will make a full recovery. Your daughter's body has not yet been found."

Om bey! Water Lily is really gone! A wail rises up in my chest. Night Wind holds me as I shake. I feared that this would happen. Every day since we parted I knew in my heart that I would never see her again. I am overcome with regrets that we never reconciled. Will I ever know if she was being used or if she was Pus Master's partner in this treachery? Why could she not have allowed me to speak with her in Pole? It was our last opportunity. I would have explained, apologized.

Night Wind gives me a few minutes to compose myself. I pull myself back together as best I can. I know she has more to tell me, and there are bigger problems for the holy Island than the loss of my errant daughter.

"You should know that Jaguar Shield, Iguana Wind, Spear Thrower and the girls are all well," she continues. That comforts me greatly.

"Wait," I say, suddenly confused. "Jaguar Paw went to Pole to protect his sister. Why did he return to Cuzamil?"

Night Wind shrugs. "I do not know."

That is troubling. Is Nine Macaw safe? I start to panic and then tell myself I would Know if anything happened to her.

Wouldn't I?

• • •

Word spreads through the palace and all of Tixchel that the war is won. Night Wind is finally reunited with her love, and while she cradles Heart of Water in her arms and bathes her with glad tears, I tell the priestesses what the *nacom* recounted. I see pride and relief shining in every face as they sprinkle *copal* on the altar in Heart of Waters chamber to give thanks. A group of young women run off to lay offerings on every altar in the palace.

Evening Star sidles over to me and gives my shoulders a squeeze. "I am so sorry about your precious feather," she tells me sympathetically.

"Thank you," I say with a sigh. "I sorrow for her, but right now I must be a Queen. Let us go to the Great Temple of the Mother and lead the people in giving thanks for this victory."

The priestesses smooth their mantles and adjust their feathers. We retie our rainbow ribbons and form up in a line. I lead the way down the eighteen steps of the Rainbow Palace and across the plaza, which is filling with pilgrims, women and children, priestesses and administrators of the Island, all of whom have been anxiously hiding for the past two days. They mill about asking questions, hugging, laughing, gossiping. Conch shells blare from the round stone platform. Musicians parade out of the House of Dance playing a happy tune. Linking arms, women form spontaneous half circles to dance, and the children cavort around the edges of the plaza as if they have just been released from a long confinement. Pink and blue clouds of *chu'lel* suffuse the gleaming white plaza. For generations to come poems and songs will be written and sung about this day. Our victory will become a legend of Island of Women.

When we reach the Great Temple of the Mother we priestesses take up positions on the stairs in a U formation, symbol of the Moon Goddess. I signal the musicians to quiet and climb higher so I am standing at the top. Our five temples were designed so that whatever is spoken from the highest stair, even in a soft voice, resounds across the plaza. The crowd falls silent.

"Sisters. Mothers. Children. We are victorious!" A cheer goes up. "The Putun tried to poison our queen and steal Ix Chel's sacred Island, our sanctuary and Zone of Peace. Today, many of our enemies are imprisoned and on their way to Pole for punishment. Others are crossing the waters of the Underworld. Our enemies witnessed the power of Ix Chel and will not be returning." A great cheer goes up. Smiles light up every face.

"Some of our friends, allies and neighbors are also crossing the waters today," I say as the crowd quiets. "To them we send our prayers to Ix Chel to bless their journeys. May the spirits of our warriors return as butterflies to the sacred Island." I see many heads nod.

"Your queen was poisoned by the ones called Blue Monkey and Snake Tooth," I continue. There is surprised and angry murmuring. "I believe Queen Heart of Water will recover, but she will have to rest for a very long time. Until matters are settled, I, Jade Skirt Chel Cocom, sister of Queen

Heart of Water, rule with her blessing. She charges me to guard the Rainbow Throne for her heir. I dedicate my life, my soul and all that I am to serving you in the name of my mother, Nine Wind, and my Grandmother, Cosmic Turtle, founder of Her sanctuary, and in the name of Ix Chel, Goddess Protector of us all."

I expect a cheer, but instead the musicians strike up another happy tune and women in the plaza begin an intricate spiral dance. Stomp. Stomp. Stomp. The pounding echoes of their bare feet on the stone pavement are cheer enough for me. A strong wind from the north blows across the plaza and the conch shells atop the tower bellow as if the Wind God is cheering, too.

• • •

Jaguar Shield waits for me on the western shore. He sent word to me in the Rainbow Palace that he will leave Cuzamil on the morning of the festival of 1 Zip, which is tomorrow. Men cannot celebrate on Cuzamil, so he will return to Pole with the other men. Even though I have been busier than ever, I miss him every day (and dream of him every night!). The greatest festival of the entire *tun* is about to begin on Cuzamil. Everyone who is able-bodied scrambles to repair the damage done by the invaders and prepare the food, flowers and offerings for the festival. One of my first acts as Queen is to send traders to resupply the *polnas* along the *sacbe*. There will be many late-arriving pilgrims in the next few days who waited at Pole until travel to Her Island was allowed. *Om bey!* I had no idea being a queen entailed so many decisions and endless lists! I thank Ix Chel for Evening Star, who has proven to be a gifted administrator.

The Putun prisoners were removed from the Island yesterday. They are garrisoned at Pole and Tulumha and will be sold into slavery on the next market day. Ashes from the pyres of the Putun have been blessed and dedicated to the sea. Our brave soldiers' ashes now rest in clay pots in our burial shrines. Night Wind led the spirit-sending ceremony to welcome their return as butterflies.

Blue Monkey will be sentenced by the Women's Council of Pole to public stoning and exile for treason and evil magic. I sense she may not survive. Her daughter, Eighteen Rabbit, begged to be allowed to stay on the Island. I looked at her *chu'lel* and saw no malice so I consented. She is now an acolyte in the House of Weaving, one of Her divine professions. It will be hard for the young woman. The others shun her and spit when she walks by, but I admire her courage to stay and try to atone for the evil deeds of her mother by being of service to the Goddess. I pray that she finds comfort and purpose here. That is what the Island of Women is for.

Heart of Water, still weak as a newborn babe, is now able to sit up for a few moments a day. The remedy has returned her to her senses, which is a relief to all of us. Night Wind plans to move back into the royal apartments when her duties for 1 Zip are over. I sent word to the assistants who were dismissed—Sky Mirror and World Tree—to return to the palace at once. Heart of Water will be greatly cheered by the faces of her long-time companions.

A messenger from Tree Orchid let me know that Blue Stone is apprenticing at the Healing House of the Temple of the Moon. She has been attending to Jaguar Paw, who is slowly recovering from his near-drowning—brave boy!—and broken-hearted over the death of his mother. Tree Orchid did not explain why my grandson rushed back to defend the Island when I had tasked him to stay with his sister, nor how he is coping with his mother's drowning.

My poor daughter. May she cross the river and be greeted by Moon Eagle. Her battered body was found among the rocks and was burned by the priestesses. They assured me that many prayers were made, but I will make special offerings on this day, and tomorrow I will place her ashes in our family shrine in the Rainbow Palace. It will forever be a thorn in my heart that we never had the opportunity to reconcile. Perhaps when my time comes to cross the river she will be there to greet me.

Tree Orchid has gone to the Temple of the Oracle in the east, to start her studies at the *calmecac* for Bird Oracles. Already the women of Cuzamil are telling stories of her bravery during the battle. She and Kiki stayed close to Night Wind and conveyed vital messages to and from the other commanders across the Island.

Lady White Quetzal sent a politely phrased reminder that her precious feather is ready to come into the world and that she respectfully looks forward to being attended by me personally, as we discussed.

I set out at midday for the Temple of the Moon in the west. It is a very different journey than the one I made—was it three or four nights ago? I can hardly keep track, so much has happened. Now I walk with my nine priestesses who are the Queen's Retinue. Carrying aloft billowing banners and a paper snake, they accompany the Queen of Cuzamil everywhere and announce my presence to the people. The three maidens, three mothers and three elders nearly trip over one another—and me—in their eagerness to be of service to the Queen. When Blue Monkey took over she dismissed Heart of Water's loyal retinue and appointed her own. The former retinue was thrilled to be called back into service to the Rainbow Throne. It was Evening Star's idea. She is my chief advisor now. She said the people must not question my right to rule, and the retainers will remind them that I truly am Queen of Cuzamil. I did refuse to be carried in the Queen's palanquin. I still wear the blue mantle of an Island resident, but my white overdress is elaborately embroidered with snakes, rabbits and dragonflies. Evening Star, tears in her eyes, made my jade-and-pearl headband herself—I have no idea where she found the time—and suggested strongly that Heart of Water place it on my forehead herself in the presence of the retainers. Heart of Water did it with good cheer.

Everywhere along the *sacbe* villagers are getting ready to celebrate the festival of 1 Zip. Enveloped in *copal* smoke, I receive their greetings, smile and nod. I am trying to warm to my new role as a public symbol. Drums, flutes and horns blast out from every courtyard. Women and children in white, red and blue mantles dance with abandon. Great, shoulder-high clay pots of corn and plum beer are set up beside the road for tomorrow's celebration, when long lines of revelers with clay cups and gourds in hand will line up to receive the sacred libation to celebrate this most-favored day of the *tun*. Evening Star reports that the priestesses on the shore have already welcomed twenty-times-twenty women and children to Cuzamil since yesterday, and the same number is expected still to arrive.

There are many traditions I love about 1 Zip. A favorite is throwing gourds of lustral water infused with flowers and prayer at one another. I remember from my own childhood being drenched and deliriously happy. Shoulder-high pots brimming with Her sacred water and Her divine plants line the *sacbe* running through villages.

Wreaths and garlands of marigolds decorate every doorway, temple and each of the nine sacred arches. Every *tamale* made on the island for the next nine days will have a marigold flower pressed into it. All slave women who give birth across the realm will be freed and sent away with enough wealth to start a new life. Our carvers come out of seclusion tomorrow to present the wooden and clay images of Ix Chel they have been working on for the entire month, during which no one spoke with them so as not to disturb their meditations and prayers. Images of Ix Chel the Maiden, the Mother and the Grandmother made on Her Island for 1 Zip are revered everywhere and given as wedding and birthing gifts. On completion of her apprenticeship, each new midwife receives one from her mentor. On her wedding day, every new bride receives one from her mother.

I arrive at the Temple of the Moon in high spirits several hours later. Jaguar Shield is waiting for me outside the thatched hut where first we took counsel with Evening Star. I dismiss my retinue to refresh themselves so I can confer alone with my brother-in-law. He seems taller and stronger than ever.

"Battle suits you, my love," I say, admiring his graceful stance.

"And being Queen suits you," he says, touching his brow in a sign of respect, but adding a lustful grin that makes me tingle.

"We will always be grateful to you, *nacom*. You helped save the Goddess's sanctuary. May She look upon you with favor all the rest of your days."

"Jade Skirt, never before have I felt so empowered in battle! Her rainbow light washed over us and gave us strength and courage such as I have never felt before. Truly, She is magnificent!"

We sit together on a bench in the shade of palm trees and speak of the past days. The sound of the sea soothes me, but I feel melancholy. I wish we did not have to part. The taboo against a widow marrying her husband's brother is strong for our people. It would never be allowed.

"Now that you are Queen of Cuzamil, your duties will be more daunting than ever you faced as the Oracle of Chichen," he says, taking my hand. "I will make my new home in Pole. There is a small, abandoned hut with a very nice bed that I think will do well for me until I can build a stone house near your son." I smile at him. How I treasure the memory of that stormy afternoon of passion! "Do not leave me lonely and alone there," he says, his voice husky with emotion. "Come to me as often as you can."

"I will find a way," I promise.

"You have my undying love," he says simply. "Your dark eyes still make me weak in the knees. I do not want to sneak around, Jade Skirt. Let us tell Spear Thrower. Surely, in our old age, he will forgive us."

I am not sure how I feel about this. Shocked, delighted, nervous.

Daughter, I give you My blessing.

"Yes!" I suddenly say, and Jaguar Shield, who clearly expected me to argue and worry over this plan, looks startled. Then he gives me a slow, sexy smile. The jade inlays gleam in his teeth.

Evening Star interrupts with a list of tasks that need my attention. Before I am swept away, I whisper to Jaguar Shield to meet me here before he departs tomorrow. He smiles and presses my hand, then bows.

I stop by the birthing hut and explain to the head midwife what I require. She tries to tell me that now that I am Queen I should not be delivering precious feathers! My retainers chatter excitedly, agreeing with her. I cut them all off and inform them that the Goddess wills me to do this for a sister queen. Well, that stops their protests, and not just because I am their queen. Word of what the priestesses and I accomplished two days ago has traveled the length and breadth of the Island. They look at me with genuine respect, which does make my job easier. The good midwife supplies me with a jaguar-pelt shoulder bag packed with every powder and oil I will need to bring the infant prince down through his mother's serpent canal to meet Father Sun at dawn tomorrow. Only the secret ingredient to complete our royal conspiracy is safely tucked in my own pouch.

White Quetzal is housed with twenty of her retainers in a *polna* for visiting royalty. It is really a small palace with sumptuous gardens, fountains and birds in fruiting trees. I find her lying on a thick pile of quilts and animal pelts talking, as usual, to one of her women. She smiles with relief when she sees me. Her hair is pulled back in a simple knot of thick braids at her neck and she wears no face paint. One of her attendants massages her swollen feet and another cools her with an enormous fan of blue *cotinga* feathers. They all start to rise so they can bow to me, but I wave them to stay where they are.

"Leave me," I tell the nine women who accompany me.

"But, Lady Jade Skirt, we are bound to stay with you," they protest.

"The Lady White Quetzal needs her privacy," I explain patiently. "Please stay nearby if you prefer, but you can't all be in here while we bring her precious feather into the world. Surely you can understand that." They accept the truth of what I say and take their leave.

"My Lady Queen," says White Quetzal, "how kind of you to check on me in the midst of your royal duties."

With a wave of one hand I commands her servants, "Leave us. everyone. Go to the plaza and join the celebration. Dance. Drink. Someone add wood to the hearth fire. We need hot stones ready. Fill all the pots with water. Your Lady's battle to capture a warrior has begun. Do not return until I send for you."

In a flurry of chatter they run out, glad to be free to join the celebrations at the Temple of the Moon. From the hearth, I take glowing coals for the incense burner and throw several grains of white *copal* inside. I place our family's small, cedar-carved image of Ix Chel the Grandmother under the pregnant woman's bed and begin my prayers to the Great Mother of All, asking Her to bring this babe safely to the light of day by dawn. I move to the four corners of the room spreading the *copal* smoke and making prayers. I call on Her four sons, the *Bacab*, who hold up the corners of the Earth. Once that is done, I move to the center of the room and stand before White Quetzal. I sink into awareness of my *chu'lel* and feel the immense presence and power of the Great Mother. I ask for Her blessing and Her forgiveness.

The ritual complete, I examine the queen.

"How have you been feeling? The healers tell me you have been eating well and sleeping restlessly."

"Nothing to report, really, Jade Skirt," she says in a whisper. "There are no signs. This little one is too content to stay in his warm and cozy womb. Like all infant boys, he wants to stay as long as possible."

"Any signs of water?"

"No, none," she responds, shaking her head.

"Have you eaten raw *nopal* daily, as I instructed?"

In a loud voice, in case others are eavesdropping, she says, "Yes, of course. Just as you said, three small pads daily." Then she whispers, "Do you have what you will need?"

"Of course," I murmur. "You must leave everything to me now, White Quetzal. Forget that you are a queen. You will do as I say without question or complaint. You must make an effort to allow me to conduct the affairs of this day."

She raises her eyebrows and is about to protest then thinks better of it. "Very well, then," she says with a great sigh. "I surrender to your care."

First I take off my queenly garments and put on a plain, well-worn, blue mantle. It is likely I will get blood on it later. Midwifery is a messy business.

"We begin together with a prayer to the Great Mother of All to bless the world with a great and noble king for your people."

When the prayer is finished, I rearrange her on the cushions. "When I rub your belly this time, it will be more powerful than you have felt before.

If it hurts you must let me know."

Her eyes grow wide with anticipation. The birthing room of the royal *pol-na* is well supplied with quilts, cotton cloths, a steaming pot, a bowl of lustral water and a reed cradle. Overhead is a strong hemp rope tied to a roof beam. I remove two of the largest clay pots from a wooden hook, fill them with water from a shoulder-high jug in the corner and crush three large *cacaltun* plants into one to boil. On the grinding stones I crush the allspice berries and add them to the second pot. Their spicy aroma brings to mind many previous births I have attended. I place a few coals in the *copal* burner and add a generous sprinkle of white grains. Again enveloped in its aromatic smoke, I feel the sacred resin's powerful calming effect on both of us.

Every birth is a mystery and an uncertainty. One of the first lessons of my training as midwife was that one must be neither overly confident nor unsure of oneself. This is a dangerous game, to force a baby out before his destined calendar day. I hesitated to agree to this, but I do believe White Quetzal has had a true vision from the Goddess, so I promised I would help her. The baby is destined to be king of a great and powerful realm where politics will always be a part of his life, so perhaps it is fitting that his own life begins with a royal conspiracy by his mother!

I rub her belly vigorously with dolphin oil and the whites of turkey eggs—two reliable agents to start labor. I work her belly up, down and sideways for a very long time while she sips constantly from a gourd of hot basil tea. I lay my face against her moon belly and speak to the infant king telling him it is time to descend. Firmly, I press downward on the top of her womb and jiggle so that the infant's head will make contact with the doorway to the serpent canal. When that is finished, I give her more basil tea, as hot as she can bear it, and replenish her gourd again and again. I massage her back and pound several times on her low back and the bottoms of her feet, then roll her back and forth inside a long piece of cotton used for binding mothers after they give birth. If, after a reasonable time, the prince has not descended, I have a stronger remedy with which to prod him. I hope I do not have to use it. It is violent in action—but extremely reliable.

"Get up and walk," I tell her. "Walk vigorously around the birthing room with a slight hop in your step." I demonstrate. "At the same time, press down from the top of your womb."

Outside, the raucous shouts and whoops of revelers reach us. We can hear the conches blow and the drums beat from the great plaza in front

of the Moon Temple. Antler Skull has taken my place in the temple ceremonies for healers and midwives today in Tixchel. There will be long lines
waiting to have their medicine pouches, divining stones and tools blessed.

The drums make me think of the dancers and I wonder what Nine Macaw is doing to celebrate the festival. Dancing, no doubt, in the plaza of
Pole with her cousins and aunt, just as she wished. Does she miss me? Is
she relieved that I am far away and no longer pressuring her to follow the
path I hoped for her? How do my son and his wife grieve with her over
the loss of her mother? I picture Water Lily's funeral urn in our family
shrine and vow to commune with her soul often. These thoughts make
me sigh.

It is a long night. The hot teas cause the queen to perspire profusely, so
she must replenish fluids with water warmed over the hearth fire. Drinking
cool water now would be a setback. Spoiled girl that she is, she complains
about the taste of the tea, the hardness of the bed. If it were possible, she
would will the wind to change its direction for her. There are a few encouraging contractions, but they stop too soon.

"You must hold onto the rope and squat over these hot stones."

Her great belly rests on her thighs, and breasts as large as papayas with
dark purple nipples seem overly ready to suckle the new prince. I throw
water over the stones. Steam billows into her serpent canal. I wrap a braided cloth around her waist and pull down over her belly while she squats
lower and lower, still holding onto the rope overhead. She grunts with the
effort, but does not complain.

Finally, her water breaks, gushing onto the hot stones. Steam fills the
room. I see her swivel her head to check the night sky. How close is dawn?

"Let me worry about that, Daughter," I tell her. "The birth has started.
Goddess preserve you."

She gives me a nervous look. I wonder if she wishes her mother were
here. I take her hand and together we say the birthing prayer nine times.

Arise, come, be sent, arise. Come. Newborn child, arise. Come. Arise,
come, be sent, arise. Come. Jewel child, arise. Come!

Contractions come and go. Strong, then feeble. I can't afford to lose track of
time. I step into the courtyard to note the position of the Sky Wanderers. Dawn
is close. The queen is bearing the pain well, but she is weary and anxious.

I am sorry to do it, but I must use the powerful medicine. I had hoped
to avoid it, but it is guaranteed to bring down the babe quickly. If he is not

born the moment before dawn all will be lost. To save lives, I have used it on three occasions before this. Each time, the expulsion was rapid and sure, but when the placenta loosens there is a chance of hemorrhage. I remember a story my mother told of a midwife who gave just a pinch too much and the mother's uterus came out with the baby still inside. I feel confident enough about the dosage, and I am prepared to deal with the bleeding. I have a tea brewing now that will help. And I am counting on White Quetzal's youth and good health to see her through.

"Daughter," I tell her gently, "progress is slow and dawn approaches. The powder I will give you will cause the babe to come quickly. The danger is that his placenta will tear away with his birth. There may be a lot of blood, but do not worry. I am prepared to stop the bleeding."

"I…I trust you Jade Skirt. Do what you must. Much depends on it. The Goddess is with you."

Great Mother, You who knit us in our wombs, do not be angry with us. Forgive us. Save Your daughter and her precious feather. Bring him into our arms before the light of day.

In my medicine pouch is a small vial of powdered possum tail. We use it only in the most drastic, desperate cases to save the life of the mother or baby. I stir a mere pinch of the loathsome creature's roasted tail into a cup of allspice tea. I give it to the exhausted White Quetzal.

"Ugh! Bitter and foul!" she complains, gagging. "Why can medicine not taste sweet?"

"At least you will never have to drink it again. That I can promise. Now squat and pull hard on that rope over your head."

I can see her uterine contractions from the outside. Up and down her belly they roll. The great round belly hardens then spasms from side to side. The sky is beginning to lighten, the night is fading fast, but Father Sun is not over the horizon yet. We have only a few moments.

"Attend your Queen!" I call out, and my nine retainers and five of Queen White Quetzal's noble attendants rush into the room. They stand to the side and bear witness to the birth.

"Cough! Cough!" I command White Quetzal

She gives a deep groan and coughs once, twice.

There is the babe's head! Another pull on the rope overhead. I kneel before her on the pile of quilts to catch the prince. Gently, I push down to deliver the first shoulder, then raise the chest to deliver the second shoulder.

Pink and chubby, his little body squirms in my hands. Now is the moment I must use all my skills to save the lives of mother and child. I clear the mucous from his throat. He lets out a lusty wail. White Quetzal cries out triumphantly. She has done it!

"The prince is born!" cries one of the witnesses.

"The most auspicious birth for any child!" says another. "He arrived the moment before dawn on 1 Zip!"

"And see the sign of the serpent on his head!" Another says excitedly. I wipe the child's brow and indeed there is the birthmark I saw when Ix Chel showed me a vision of the child in the womb.

"The Goddess marks him as Her own!" I say with a smile.

The queen has her prince, born on Creation Day. There can be no greater honor. His reign as a spiritual son of the Divine Mother and Father is secured. White Quetzal's lineage will use this to its fullest advantage.

White Quetzal tries to get on her knees to hold him, but I stop her.

"Lie down. Lie down." I place the babe on her chest.

"My son, you will rule by Divine right!" she whispers into his perfect little ear.

She sighs with pleasure then cradles him to her dark purple nipple to suckle. He is a fine baby. Perfect in every way. I smile at the witnesses.

"The new mother and infant need their rest."

With smiles and nods of congratulations, they clear the room to spread the news. Once they are gone, I prop up White Quetzal's hips and massage both sides of her still-distended uterus, pushing inward and praying the placenta will pass without a hemorrhage. I remove a turkey feather from my *pi* and tickle the back of her throat while I place a firm hand against her lower abdomen. She gags. Out falls the placenta.

But it is broken! Some of it has stayed behind. I tuck the fallen placenta, still attached to the umbilical cord, on the baby's belly and wrap them both in a strip of cotton. Then I massage White Quetzal again to bring down the rest of the placenta. It must come out.

"Courage," I whisper in her ear. "The battle is nearly won. You have captured a warrior. Your lineage will honor you."

Bravely, she tries to smile. Beads of perspiration gather on her furrowed forehead. She looks as if she will pass out in a moment.

I recite the special prayer for just this moment.

Dear Mother who knits us together in our mother's womb, assist us! Bring down the remains of Your divine work within this womb, Your most sacred realm. Save this babe and his mother. They will serve You for the rest of their days.

I hold the new mother's wrists to let the prayers fill her *chu'lel* with floating blue clouds of calm. I whisper them nine times and I can feel the effects. I reach down and amidst clots of blood, the chunk of placenta plops into my hands. It perfectly matches the break on the other piece. Thank you, Ix Chel!

"Drink this tea!" I hand her a cup of already-cool plum bark and bird pepper tea. "Drink it all down. Now!"

She wants to sleep. She wants to rest with her infant. The bleeding is too much.

"Daughter, we are not done. We are victorious. You have taken a warrior in battle. But you must believe me, there is still work to be done."

She sighs as if irritated, but drinks the tea down in great gulps.

I say more prayers, sprinkle more *copal*, continue massaging and wait for the two powerful astringents in the tea to take effect.

The dawn has broken, the babe is suckling, but the mother bleeds. I wonder if I will regret this night. But then I check her and it seems…yes! The bleeding from her uterus has slowed. I sigh with relief. I must continue to watch her because the possum tail powder can turn again at any moment, but for now all is well.

"Lady, may we enter?" Three servants are at the door. "Does our Queen need us? May we see the new babe?"

"I will stay with her until the cord blood ceases to pulse," I tell her attendants, "but you can brew some chocolate and honey for me."

They coo and fuss over the beautiful baby boy, and the youngest takes the soiled quilts away to be washed and brings fresh ones. I sit next to the queen and sip my cup of chocolate while I hold her hand and tell her how strong and brave she was. Another wipes her brow.

By the time Father Sun's light touches the floor of the chamber, the cord stops pulsing. One of the queen's attendants produces a cob of blue corn. While we watch, she drips some of the cord blood onto the corn cob while we all pray out loud. The corn cob will be given to the prince's father, who will plant it again and again until the boy is old enough to harvest a field and plant his own, after his first coming-of-age ceremony. I feel a pang of sadness for Jaguar Paw, who did not have his cob at his coming-of-age ceremony. When the boy became an exile his father no doubt burned his cob.

I cut the cord and hand the precious feather to an attendant, who gently washes him in a stone basin then swaddles the prince in a fresh white cloth. Through the window I can see her lift up his little naked body to Father Sun four times. White Quetzal is sleeping peacefully. She is out of danger. Her flow of blood is normal.

With great relief, I wash myself thoroughly and change back into my fine robe. I leave White Quetzal in the competent care of her attendants and an island midwife. My nine retainers are sleeping on palettes outside the room. I don't wake them, but slip quietly away.

In the soft dawn light, I find Jaguar Shield waiting for me under the trees. Without a word, he takes me by the hand and leads me a few paces into the steaming jungle. His powerful arms enfold me. My head rests against his rock-hard chest. His hot, rough hands slide up and down my body, caressing me with his desire. This is Creation Day, when Father Sun and Mother Moon created the world and all its Beings through sacred sexual union. We both feel the Goddess's divine pulsations rising up from the sea, making our *chu'lels* more attuned to each other. How I wish I could disappear into the jungle with him, but his boat is waiting and my duties await me.

"Another day and in another place, we will be together," he whispers.

"My love, I will come to you in Pole as soon as I am able. But what life will you have there?"

"Spear Thrower says he can always use a seasoned *nacom* to help train soldiers." He tries to look indifferent, but I can tell how pleased he is with this invitation.

"Ah," I say. "You are very good at that."

He gives me a small smile and brushes his hand on my cheek.

"Also, I had a thought to go look for Sting Ray and ask him to be my assistant."

I remember the cave-dwelling dwarf we met in the jungle on our desperate journey to Na Balam, and how he helped us with his good cheer and generous spirit. A feeling of rightness washes through me.

"If any in Pole question you bringing an exile into your home, tell them the Rainbow Throne extends its protection to Sting Ray, who was a true friend to us when we were in need."

"Have I said recently how well-suited you are to being Queen?" he murmurs, kissing my brow.

I take a last deep breath of his scent of hearth smoke, tobacco and vanilla. The conch sounds, signaling the first departure. We walk down to the beach as the priestesses begin chanting the prayers for safe passage. The men are climbing into their canoes.

Jaguar Shield's eyes are full of words not spoken, of sadness and hope. He draws away and it feels like half of my own self goes with him. He turns without a word and, spear in hand, strides down to the shore. I allow myself to enjoy watching him. His fluid steps are like a dance. When small waves lap at his ankles, he turns to wave and then jumps gracefully into a canoe loaded with Bolon paddlers and soldiers from Tulumha.

There are other farewells being said on the beach. My grandson stands on the shore with Blue Stone. They rub noses and when they part their *chu'lel* pulls away from each other like *chicle*. I had no idea! But now that I do know, this new information pleases me greatly. So that is why he returned to Cuzamil! He whispers something in her ear and she blushes. How proud Moon Eagle would be of our grandson. Jaguar Paw jumps into the canoe beside his uncle. He catches a glimpse of me and waves.

I step in front of the priestesses when they finish their prayer and I hold up my hand. In a voice that carries over the sound of waves, I thank the men for their service to Cuzamil and the Rainbow Throne.

"You risked your lives for us. Know that the families of all those who fell or were wounded in battle will be taken care of. And to those of you who rushed to defend the Goddess's Island and risked your lives with no thought of reward, you have my thanks and now will be given a share of honey and salt, precious jade and cacao."

Evening Star has arranged this parting gift. Cuzamil's coffers are bursting, and we can well afford to reward our allies handsomely. As I speak, blue-robed priestesses distribute sacks to the headman of each canoe, who will distribute them fairly. The men cheer and stomp their feet. Many touch their foreheads and bow to me with respect. I see awe in their eyes. Like it or not, much of the credit for Her miracles are being attributed to me.

As I turn to leave the beach, someone calls my name. Iguana Wind rushes over with his wife and two nearly-grown daughters. He looks radiant with happiness. His poor wife looks old and worn down by life, but she holds her hand to her heart and then she and her daughters touch the ground twice with their foreheads.

"Lady Queen," she says in a hoarse whisper as she rises, "I wish to thank you for your kindness to my husband. We are united again as a family. He told us that you and your husband were always kind to him during his bondage. I am grateful to your husband's soul that he saved my husband's life. These many *tuns* without him were hard, Noble Lady, but now we are reunited, thanks to you!"

Iguana Wind proudly introduces his two look-alike daughters. I praise their beauty and graceful manners.

The last canoe is ready to launch. Iguana Wind leans over to press his forehead against mine in farewell. Then they hurry to their boat and I send him with prayers for his happiness and the happiness of his lovely family.

Before the canoes depart, priestesses from the Temple of the Moon, helped by my retinue, gently carry funeral urns filled with the ashes of male soldiers to place in their own boats. These same priestesses stood over their funeral fires for the past two days stirring their bones into ashes. I bear witness and make prayers to the Goddess to guide them across the rivers of the Underworld and let their souls rest in peace. I also welcome their souls to return to the Island of Women as butterflies.

I join the circle of priestesses to chant the farewell song. We spread *copal* smoke In the wind and then watch the canoes until they are only specks riding the great current. I turn from the sparkling, azure sea and walk up to the plaza to join the celebrations.

My heart is light. I should be falling down with fatigue, but instead I feel at peace, even with losing Water Lily. It has been a long journey in a short amount of time. So much happened, but through it all, Ix Chel guided me and protected us, as She promised She would. I feel deeply blessed, indeed.

I stop at a candy maker and select a sweet. I feel a pang of missing Nine Macaw as it is one of her favorites. Then I wander around the plaza and let it melt in my mouth. I linger over the wood carvings and stop to admire the dancers. I still have to make my way back to the Great Temple of the Mother in Tixchel for the evening celebration, but right now—despite my fatigue and having been up all night delivering a baby—all I want to do is dance! I head for the circle of dancers in the plaza, delighted to have escaped my retinue.

That is when I see a familiar lithe figure spinning and bending like a slender reed in the wind. She dances with such devotion that the others clear a space for her. She whirls and stamps faster and faster. The drummers cheer, hands flying to keep up, and then everyone is cheering this young whirlwind. She ends with a bow to the earth, and then she catches sight of me and her smile breaks my heart open with joy.

It is like a dream! Nine Macaw is in my arms and we are both crying and laughing.

"What—how—" I am not even sure what to ask.

"After you left, I thought I would be happy. You said I could be a dancer, and that was what I wanted most!" The words tumble out of her eagerly. "But then the priestesses told us there was war on Cuzamil, and Aunt Precious Tree and Jaguar Paw came to take me to a safe place. That was when I realized that I wanted to be with you and Tree Orchid and Blue Stone. By hiding, and by denying my heritage, I was letting Uncle Blood Gatherer and the Putun win! I have a duty to Ix Chel and our lineage. I accept it, Na. I want it." She gives a little shrug. "Once I realized that, I pretended to be a boy and convinced my brother to bring me here in secret. Lady Fire Bird told me to hide in the House of Maidens on Cuzamil until the war was over."

I am overwhelmed with emotion. I hold her to my heart. The drums throb and the dancers' feet continue to pound the earth around us.

"Na, before we landed on the shore, I saw Mother. She was with the Putun, and she looked awful. She was missing an eye! When she saw us she jumped out of her boat to swim to us, but a big wave suddenly rose up in the calm ocean and overturned the Putun canoe and brought it down on Mother's head. My brother jumped in to try to save her and then he nearly drowned!"

I embrace her and I feel her sigh in my arms. "I am sorry for everything you have been through, Nine Macaw. I am sorry for all the suffering of those we love—Red Earth, Water Lily, Tree Orchid. I am so sorry."

"Na, it is not your fault!" she says, patting me on the back as if I am the child who needs comforting. "Do you not always tell me that everything happens for a reason even if we can't know what that reason is?"

I hold her away so I can look at her dear face. "That is true, Nine Macaw. Thank you for reminding me. My feather, why did you not tell me you were here?"

She looks down shyly. "I was not sure you wanted to see me again." She looks away. "No, that is not true. I felt ashamed to face you after I had rejected everything you did for me."

"I understand, my precious jade. It is no easy task being Queen of Cuzamil. You don't have to do it if it is not in your heart to serve Her. Those who dance also worship Her."

She pushes back and looks at me earnestly. "I love to dance, Na. Why can a Queen of Cuzamil not also lead the dances? I want to be the *holpop* of Cuzamil just like Aunt Precious Tree in Pole! I can start a new tradition for the Rainbow Throne, can I not?"

"Indeed you can! You will worship Ix Chel with your words, your heart, your hands and your feet?"

The drums start up again and I pull her into the circle and together we dance. Rainbow sparks fly from our feet and we bend and circle and swoop like swallows in and out of the circle of women while the women chant: "Welcome home, Princess!"

Rainbow light wraps around us and I hear the Goddess laughing.

Welcome home, My children. Welcome home.

Glossary

of Mayan Terms, Maya Gods, Goddesses and Places

* All Mayan words are in Yucatec Mayan

Almehenob – nobles who claim noble parentage from both mother and father

Annatto – derived from the seeds of the achiote tree (*Bixa orellana*), often used to impart a yellow or orange color to foods, but sometimes also for its flavor and aroma

Aspergillum – implement used to sprinkle lustral water

Axcanan – *Hamelia patens* ("Forest Guardian" or "Forest Spirit."), a medium-size tree with red, tubular flowers used to bathe skin conditions

Bacab – four sons of Itzámna and Ix Chel. The four gods who hold up the corners of the sky, each associated with a color: red for the south; white for the north; black for the west; and yellow for the east

Balcheha – *Lonchocarpus yucatanensis*, a tree bark fermented with honey to make an alcoholic drink

Cacaltun – *Ocimum campechianum*, wild basil used as both a medicinal tea and condiment

Calmecac – school

Ceiba – Ceiba pentadora, kapok or silk cotton tree, also called Yaxche (Maya term for Tree of Life), "first," "sacred," "greenish-blue"; sacred tree of creation and center of the Maya cosmos.

Cenote – (*dzonot*) circular sink holes perennially filled with water formed by the collapse of underground caves.

Chac – rain god

Chacah – *Bursera simaruba*, a tree with red peeling bark that has many medicinal uses

Chachalacas – *Ortalis vetula*, a common, brown-colored bird first to call in the morning hours; makes a loud, squawking sound

Chalche – Pluchea odorata, a medium-sized shrub with aromatic leaves much prized as a women's remedy and a restorative

Chaya – *Cnidoscolus chayamansa*, cultivated plant like spinach whose leaves are high in iron and minerals

Chicle – *Manilkara zapota*, "chewing" or "move your mouth"; a jungle tree that exudes a milky latex that can be made into chewing gum when cooked

Chu'lel – inherent, sacred life force present in all things and called forth during Maya rituals and ceremonies. Chu'lel is thought to be especially strong in virgin water, rain, *copal* tree resin, wind, blood, plants, mountains, sun and sky

Chultun – underground storage cache of food and seeds

Coatimundi – *Nasua nasua*, ring-tailed coati; mammals of the raccoon family.

Coco kaba – nickname

Cocom – ancient lineage of rulers of the Yucatán until the time of the Spanish Conquest

Copal – *Protium copal*, tree whose resin is extracted and used as incense for rituals, prayers and ceremonies

C'ox – "Let's go!"

Cuzam – *Hirundinidae*, a species of the swallow (bird)

Cuzamil – "Place of the Swallows"; contemporary name is Cozumel

Cotinga – *Cotinga nattererii*, a species of bird found in lowland forests; plump, dove-like, with glossy blue plumage prized by the ancient Maya

First age – women of child-bearing age

Guanacaste – *Enterolobium cyclocarpum*, or elephant-ear tree, named for the shape of the seed pods; in the pea family native to Central and South America. Known for its large proportions, abundance, edible seed and pods from which soap can be made

H'men – "He or she who knows"; a shaman

Holpop – "He who sits on the mat"; a person of great authority

Huracan – god of wind and storm

Ik – god of wind and air

Itzámna – male creator god and consort to Ix Chel

Ix Chel – "Lady Rainbow," creatrix, Maya goddess of medicine, the moon, weaving, fertility and consort to Itzámna and the Sun god, the Vulture god, the Morning Star and the Rain god Chac.

Ix Tab – goddess of suicide

Katun – period of twenty years, or 7,200 days, in the Maya calendrical system.

K'nep – *Talisia oliviformis*, rainforest tree that bears delicious fruit encased in a juicy outer coating rich in Vitamin C.

Kawil – sacred snake-footed or double headed snake scepter of high office

Kin – Father Sun

Kulha – sacred waters

Middle world – the place of physical existence in between the Underworld and Upperworld

Mopan – an indigenous Maya people of Guatemala and Belize whose native language is also called Mopan

Nacom – military captain

Nanci – *Brysonima crassifolia*, a small, yellow fruit favored by children and often fermented into wine

Nopal (Nopales) – *Opuntia cochenillifera*, an edible and medicinal cactus with large, thorny pads and red fruits

Nulha – steam bath

Om bey – "Wow! Oh, dear! You don't say!"

Payche – *Chiococca alba*, skunk root, *zorillo* (Spanish), a medicinal forest vine with skunk-smelling roots; considered a shaman's ritual herb

Pi – bag belonging to a healer or shaman usually made from deerskin to hold an amulet or sacred items

Pixam – soul

Pixoy – *Guazuma ulmifolia*, a common tree of Yucatan whose bark is astringent and seeds are edible

Polna – public inn

Sacbe – raised roads built by the ancient Maya; also known as the "white way" because they were coated with limestone stucco; used as primary thoroughfares within cities and in some areas between cities.

Sastun – (*sas* meaning "light" or "mirror"; *tun* meaning "stone") a translucent divining stone of shamans

Second age – women age 35 to 55 years old

Sky Wanderers – stars, planets and constellations

Spondylus – a genus of bivalvemollusks, also known as thorny oysters, spiny oysters and spondylids

Third age – women older than 55

Tikul – two-toned wooden drum played with a rubber-tipped stick

Tun – 360 days, or a Maya year; also means "stone."

Tzitzimin – sky demons that can bring night terrors

Wasp star – Venus (also called "the Great Star")

Ya ax – *Securidaca diversifolia*, a highly prized medicinal vine of the Yucatan

Zubin – *Acacia cornijera*, a thorny, narrow-trunked tree inhabited by biting ants; bark and roots are used as a first-aid remedy for snakebite.

About the Author

Dr. Rosita Arvigo, DN, a native of Chicago, is a naprapathic physician, herbalist, international lecturer and author. She has lived in remote areas of Mexico and Belize for more than forty years, where she studied with many traditional healers, the most notable of whom were Don Elijio Panti, the renowned Maya shaman of Belize, and midwife/herbalist Hortence Robinson. Both were recipients of the coveted National Living Treasure Award.

Arvigo and her husband, Dr. Greg Shropshire, founded Ix Chel Tropical Research Centre in Belize, an organization dedicated to the preservation and study of medicinal plants of the rainforest. They founded the Belize Association of Traditional Healers; Bush Medicine Camp for children; The Rainforest Medicine Trail; and Rainforest Remedies, an herbal concentrate company. In 1987, they founded the Belize Ethnobotany project with Dr. Michael Balick of the New York Botanical Garden.

Rosita Arvigo is the founder of The Arvigo Institute, which trains practitioners in the Arvigo® Techniques of Maya Abdominal Therapy and Maya Spiritual Healing. Now retired from clinical practice, she divides her time between Belize, Mexico and Chicago. She is author of:

The Oracle of Ix Chel (Story Bridge Books, 2015)

Messages from the Gods: A Guide to the Useful Plants of Belize with Dr. Michael Balick (Oxford University Press, 2015)

Remedios de la Selva: Cien Plantas Medicinales de Belice with Dr. Michael Balick (Lotus Light Enterprises, 2013)

Plantas Medicinales en el Norte de Guanajuato; Medicinal Plants used in Northern Guanajuato (Arvigo Institute, 2013)

Food of the Gods: Vegetarian Cooking in Belize (Cubola Press, 2010)

Spiritual Bathing: Traditions from Around the World with Nadine Epstein (Celestial Arts Press, 2003)

Rainforest Home Remedies: The Maya Way to Heal Your Body and Replenish Your Soul with Nadine Epstein (Harper One, 2001)

Sastun: My Apprenticeship With a Maya Healer with Nadine Epstein (Harper One, 1994)

Rainforest Remedies: 100 Healing Herbs of Belize with Dr. Michael Balick (Lotus Light Enterprises, 1994)

For more information please visit www.RositaArvigo.com, or www.arvigotherapy.com.

CPSIA information can be obtained
at www.ICGtesting.com
Printed in the USA
FSHW022233100121
77566FS